"How did tha

Nash flashed a sex
mistletoe above Callie's head.

He knew he wasn't playing fair, using their attraction for each other to draw Callie all the way into the present. But there were times, like now, when it was the best way to make her see that the past was over. There was no use hiding behind it, not when they had a connection as fierce as the chemistry between them. Hooking the toe of his boot beneath the rung of a chair, he brought the chair all the way from the table and sank into it, dropping the mistletoe and pulling her onto his lap in the process.

"Nash..."

He drew back to see into her eyes, knowing he didn't need a cornball excuse to kiss her, touch her, hold her. "Kiss me, Callie..."

Wreathing her arms around his neck, she turned her head to his and smiled with a devastating mix of tenderness and mischief. "Is that your Christmas wish?"

He grinned. "One of them."

HOME ON THE RANCH:
TEXAS HOLIDAY DILEMMA

— ⚒ —

CATHY GILLEN THACKER

USA TODAY Bestselling Author
JUDY DUARTE

Previously published as *Lone Star Christmas* and
A Cowboy Family Christmas

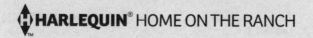

Recycling programs for this product may not exist in your area.

ISBN-13: 978-1-335-44566-7

Home on the Ranch: Texas Holiday Dilemma

Copyright © 2019 by Harlequin Books S.A.

Lone Star Christmas
First published in 2014. This edition published in 2019.
Copyright © 2014 by Cathy Gillen Thacker

A Cowboy Family Christmas
First published in 2017. This edition published in 2019.
Copyright © 2017 by Judy Duarte

Printed in U.S.A.

CONTENTS

Cathy Gillen Thacker is married and a mother of three. She and her husband spent eighteen years in Texas and now reside in North Carolina. Her mysteries, romantic comedies and heartwarming family stories have made numerous appearances on bestseller lists, but her best reward, she says, is knowing one of her books made someone's day a little brighter. A popular Harlequin author for many years, she loves telling passionate stories with happy endings and thinks nothing beats a good romance and a hot cup of tea! You can visit Cathy's website, cathygillenthacker.com, for more information on her upcoming and previously published books, recipes, and a list of her favorite things.

Books by Cathy Gillen Thacker

Harlequin Special Edition

Texas Legends: The McCabes

The Texas Cowboy's Quadruplets
His Baby Bargain

Harlequin Western Romance

Texas Legends: The McCabes

The Texas Cowboy's Triplets
The Texas Cowboy's Baby Rescue

Texas Legacies: The Lockharts

A Texas Soldier's Family
A Texas Cowboy's Christmas
The Texas Valentine Twins
Wanted: Texas Daddy
A Texas Soldier's Christmas

Visit the Author Profile page at Harlequin.com for more titles.

LONE STAR CHRISTMA

CATHY GILLEN THACKER

S

LONE STAR CHRISTMAS

CATHY GILLEN THACKER

Chapter 1

Nash Echols dropped a fresh-cut Christmas tree onto the bed of a flatbed truck. Watched, as a luxuriously outfitted red SUV tore through the late November gloom and slammed to an abrupt stop on the old logging trail.

"Well, here comes trouble," he murmured, when the driver door opened and two equally fancy peacock-blue boots hit the running board, then the ground.

His glance moved upward, taking in every elegant inch of the cowgirl marching toward him. He guessed the sassy spitfire to be in her early thirties, like him. She glared while she moved, her hands clapped over her ears to shut out the concurrent whine of a dozen power saws.

Nash lifted a leather-gloved hand.

One by one his crew stopped, until the Texas mountainside was eerily quiet, and only the smell of fresh-cut pine hung in the air. And still the determined woman advanced, chin-length dark brown curls framing her even lovelier face.

He eased off his hard hat and ear protectors.

Indignant color highlighting her delicately sculpted cheeks, she stopped just short of him and propped her hands on her slender denim-clad hips. "You're killing me, using all those chain saws at once!" Her aqua-blue eyes narrowed. "You know that, don't you?"

Actually, Nash hadn't. And given the fact his crew had only been at this a few hours…

Her chin lifted another notch. "*You have to stop!*"

At that, he couldn't help but laugh. It was one thing for this little lady to pay him an unannounced visit, another for her to try to shut him down. "Says who?" he challenged right back.

She angled her thumb at her sternum, unwittingly drawing his glance to her full, luscious breasts beneath the fitted red velvet western shirt, visible beneath her open wool coat. "Says me!"

He took in the hefty diamond engagement and wedding rings glinting on her left hand, squinted and asked in a way he knew would rankle, "Just out of curiosity, ma'am, does your *husband* know what you're up to?"

For a moment, his uninvited visitor seemed caught off guard. Perplexed, almost. Then she stiffened and squared her shoulders, even more militantly. "For your information, cowboy, I don't need 'permission' from anyone."

Amused, he looked her over slowly, head to toe. "Then your husband wouldn't *mind* you creating a ruckus?"

Another long, thoughtful pause. Followed by a glimmer of inscrutable emotion in her eyes. "No," she said finally. And without another word, left it at that.

Which meant what? he wondered. Her husband was used to her temperamental ways? Or was just so weak he had no say? Her cagey expression gave no clue. Nash knew one thing, however. If she were *his* woman he wouldn't want her out here, stirring up trouble with a group of cattle and horse wranglers temporarily turned lumberjacks. "And you are?"

"Callie McCabe-Grimes."

Of course she was from one of the most famous and powerful clans in the Lone Star State. He should have figured that out from the moment she'd barged onto his property.

Nash indicated the stacks of freshly cut Christmas trees around them, aware the last thing he needed in his life was another person not into celebrating the holidays. "Sure that's not Grinch?"

Her thick lashes narrowed. "Ha, ha." She blew out a frustrated breath. "I'm your neighbor, to the east."

Ah, yes. Nash nodded. "The owner of the Heart of Texas Ranch and Corporate Retreat."

He'd heard that the hot-shot marketing wiz had apparently decided to stop helping everyone else get rich and go into business for herself. And while Nash respected the latter, he detested dealing with the diva-offspring of famous Texas families. Especially those who felt that, by virtue of their name and connections, they should automatically rule whatever roost they found themselves inhabiting.

"Well, then," Callie huffed, "if you know that, then you also know that my business is located in the valley between Sanders Mountain and Echols Mountain."

Lifting a brow, Nash took in the pink color staining

her pretty face and the mutinous twist of her soft, voluptuous lips. "So?"

"So—" she waved at the dozen chain saw-wielding cowboys behind him, and the other six wrapping up recently shorn holiday trees "—all that racket you are making is carrying over onto my property!"

Nash squinted at the searing emotion in her eyes. This conversation was getting stranger all the time. "What did you expect when you set up shop next to a lumber operation?"

"There was no lumber operation when I purchased the property six months ago!"

Nash supposed that was true enough. He shrugged. "Well, there is now."

Panic warred with the fury on her face. "Since when?"

"Since I inherited the property from my great-great-uncle two months ago."

Callie sobered. "I'm sorry to hear about Mr. Echols's passing."

Nash studied her, pushing aside his own lingering grief. "You knew my uncle Ralph?"

"No," she admitted kindly. "I never had the pleasure."

"But if he was anything like me...?" Nash couldn't resist goading.

The stubborn look was back. Callie folded her arms in front of her in a way that delectably plumped up her breasts. "Let's hope he wasn't."

Nash tore his gaze from the inviting softness. Unable to resist teasing her a little more, however, he grinned. "Hasn't anyone ever told you it's the season to be jolly?"

Callie sighed in exasperation and shoved her hands through her chocolate-brown curls. "First of all, cowboy, it's not even Thanksgiving yet."

Yet, for him and his business, anyway, time was a wastin'. "It will be three days from now."

Callie threw up her palms in frustration. "Three days in which I will *lose my mind* if this racket keeps up."

No doubt about that. After all, from what he'd witnessed thus far, she did seem a little high-strung. He shifted his gaze to the pouting ripeness of her lips. Damned if he wasn't longing to kiss her, here and now, even though he knew as a married woman she was strictly off-limits.

Slowly, he let out a breath and returned his thoughts to the murky business at hand.

"And what would you have me do about it?" he asked grimly.

"I don't know." She paused to bite her lip, then asked, "Use one chain saw at a time?"

This time, Nash wasn't the only one who laughed.

When the ruckus from the men standing behind him quieted down, he winked at her and said glibly, "I'll think about it."

She stamped closer, not stopping until she was just inches away from him. "I want you to do a lot more than think about it, cowpoke!"

Nash took exception to her tone.

Her attitude.

Hell, just about everything about her.

His own temper rising, he schooled her quietly. "My name is Nash. Or Mr. Echols to you. And if that's all…"

Before he even had one ear covered up again, she planted her hand in the middle of his chest. Warmth spread instantly from beneath her delicate palm. Pooling in his chest, sliding ever downward, past his waist, to the place he least wanted to feel a rising pulse.

"Hold on there a minute, cowboy!" she declared. "I'm not done!"

Heart pounding, Nash plucked her hand from his chest like some odious piece of trash. "Too bad, little lady. Because I am."

She sniffed indignantly. "You can't just start up something like this without considering how it's going to affect everyone around you!"

Nash smiled. "Seems like—in your view anyway—I already have." He put the sound guards back on his head, then the hard hat, and gave his men the signal to resume.

She propped both hands on her hips. And this time she did stomp her pretty little foot as the whine of power saws echoed in the cool late November air.

Nash couldn't hear her muffled words of outrage, but he sure could see Callie McCabe-Grimes mouthing *something* as she glared at him, slapped her palms over her ears and spun on her heel. Her hips swaying provocatively, long luscious legs eating up the ground, she marched back to her truck and climbed into the cab. Then she extended her arm out the window, looked him right in the eye and offered him a surprisingly unladylike gesture before turning her pickup around and peeling away.

He stood there a moment, chuckling at her moxie. It was a good thing their personalities mixed about as well as oil and water, he thought, watching the dust fly in her wake. Otherwise a woman that beautiful and spirited could easily waylay him. And a distraction like that was something he did not need.

Especially at this time of year.

* * *

"There must be *something* I can do to stop that big buffoon!" Callie complained to her sister Lily over Skype, as soon as she got back to the ranch.

With the cool expertise of an accomplished attorney, Lily McCabe rocked back in her desk chair, at her Laramie, Texas, law office, and listened intently.

Doing her best to calm her racing pulse, Callie persisted. "Nash Echols has got to be violating some noise regulation—or something with all that racket!"

Lily shook her head. "First of all, there are no noise ordinances in rural areas."

Callie bit down on an oath. It was bad enough that her next-door neighbor was incredibly annoying, but at six foot two, with a lumberjack's powerful build, shaggy wavy black hair and slate-gray eyes, he was also handsome enough to grace an outdoor-living magazine cover. Not that his rugged good looks would help him where she was concerned...

"There are air rights," her sister continued practically. "But those belong to whoever is renting or residing on the property on which any noise is made. Which means any noise Nash Echols creates on his land is well within his rights."

Callie didn't care if Nash made himself deaf. It was her son—who luckily was still at nursery school—and the retreat clients set to start arriving the following week that she was worried about. Thankfully, though, at the moment she was the only one on her ranch, witnessing the ruckus.

"But his noise is coming over to my property! I mean, it's horrible." She opened up the window next to the phone, and just like before, the constant whine of multiple power saws reverberated in the brisk November air. She shut it again and turned back to the computer screen on her desk. "See what I mean?"

Lily nodded. "Just hearing it through the walls of your ranch house is enough to give me a headache— and I'm two hundred miles away! I can only imagine what it sounds like from your end."

"Exactly!"

Her sister picked up a pen and turned it end-over-end. "But you can't go to court on account of someone giving you a headache, Callie. Or the justice system would be jam-packed with nuisance cases."

Reluctantly, she supposed that was true.

Lily's demeanor gentled even more. "You want my honest advice, sis?"

Callie did her best to relax. Not easy, when she was still seeing—in her mind's eye, anyway—the smug expression on Nash Echols's blatantly handsome face. Still feeling the taut, warm muscles beneath the palm she had recklessly planted on his chest...

Callie swallowed, tamping down the whisper of long suppressed desire. She was romantically unattached now, and planned to stay that way.

"That is why I called you," she said quietly. Because, of all five of her sisters, Lily was always the quickest to cut to the chase with a solution.

"Go back. Apologize to the man. Tell him you temporarily lost your mind and want to work out an amicable solution, so that both your businesses can continue to operate."

The idea of groveling in front of the way-too-confident man next door rankled. Worse, just the thought of seeing him again made her pulse race.

Taking all that into account, Callie uttered a morose sigh and rubbed at the tense muscles in her forehead. "He's not going to go for it."

Frowning at her sister's defeatist attitude, Lily warned, "You better hope he does, because otherwise you're in a heap of trouble. In the holiday season, no less."

Nash had just gotten out of the shower when he heard a vehicle in the driveway. He pulled on a pair of jeans and, still rubbing a towel through his hair, walked barefoot to the front hall. The bell rang. Nash looped the towel around his neck, opened the heavy wood door and got his second surprise of the day.

On the other side of the portal was Callie McCabe-Grimes. She had a big wicker basket in one hand, and a handsome little toddler, clad in a tyke-size cowboy getup, in the other.

Although she was a married woman—with a kid, no less—and should be used to the sight of a partially disrobed man, she appeared taken aback by the sight of him. So much so that when she silently took in his bare chest and damp hair, she looked as if she wanted to bolt, but didn't.

Tightening her grip on the little boy's hand, and plastering a smile as big as Texas on her face, she said, "I'm here to apologize."

That *was* news.

Reluctantly, she lifted her eyes to his, and kept them there. "I'm afraid we got off on the wrong foot."

No joke.

"Hence, my son, Brian—" she indicated the curly-haired little boy beside her with a tilt of her head "—and I would like to make amends and start over."

If anyone had accompanied Callie for the mea culpa, Nash would have expected it to be her husband. But then, maybe Mr. Grimes didn't know what his little woman had been up to.

Nor did her son.

Unable to resist making things at least a little difficult for the Texas belle, Nash ran a hand across his jaw and pointed out, "*Brian* doesn't owe me an apology."

Callie flushed, obviously recalling her diva-like exit from his property. "Yes, well, as I said... I forgot my manners momentarily. And I do feel terrible about that."

She felt terrible about something—that was clear. Exactly what that was, he wasn't entirely sure.

Still, he had been raised with manners, too, and since his new neighbor had taken what had to be a difficult first step toward reconciliation, he felt obligated to be cordial, as well.

He stepped aside, suddenly concerned about the drop in temperature. It was just above freezing now. "Would you like to come in? It's pretty cold outside for your little one."

"Yes, thank you. That would be nice." Ushering his guests inside and shutting the door behind them, he realized that the foyer was a little chilly compared to the warmth of the rest of the rustically outfitted log-cabin-style ranch house. But that didn't seem to bother Callie or her son.

She glanced around, taking in the soaring cathedral ceiling and large fieldstone fireplace in the adjacent living room. Her eyes fell on the leather furniture and earth-toned Southwestern rugs.

While his great-uncle Ralph had been alive, the Echols Mountain Ranch house had definitely been a man's domain. Nash hadn't changed much since he had arrived.

Nor did he intend to do so in the future.

Aware the domain seemed all the more masculine with someone as feminine as Callie in it, he asked casually, "How old is your son?"

"Two and a half."

Nash had never been one to gush over kids, but there was something about this little guy—maybe it was his resemblance to his mama?—that drew him in. He smiled, inclining his head at the tyke. "Cute."

"Thanks," Callie murmured. And this time her smile appeared genuine.

Looking ready to make himself at home, Brian took off his Stetson and attempted to fit it over the newel on the staircase. It fell to the floor instead. He reached for it, tried again and missed by an even wider margin.

Nash leaned down. "Let me help you, little fella."

"No," Brian retorted with the stubbornness he evidently got from his gorgeous, dark-haired mama. "*I* do."

Nash lifted his hands and stepped back.

Seeming torn between correcting her son and getting on with it, Callie blew out a breath and handed Nash the basket. "Inside you'll find our welcome-to-the-neighborhood dinner. Homemade Texas chili and cornbread, fruit compote and chocolate cake."

Nash couldn't recall the last time he'd had a hot, home-cooked meal. Most of his meals were either from a restaurant or the freezer section of the local supermarket.

"Seriously?"

She shrugged. "Nothing I wouldn't do for anyone else moving in."

Nash figured that was probably true.

"The chili and cornbread are still hot."

She was killing him; she had to know that.

Aware he was attracted when he shouldn't be, he went on a fishing expedition. "I imagine your husband is expecting you home soon?"

Again, that pause. A definite evasion.

"Ah, no," she said finally.

Which meant what? Nash wondered. Was she separated? Getting a divorce? Just unattended and unhappy?

Not that it was any of his business. Except, they were neighbors and, in the Lone Star State, anyway, neighbors looked out for one another.

Furthermore, his gut told him that Callie McCabe-Grimes definitely was in need of some—if not TLC—then, at least, amiable concern.

Meanwhile, little Brian was still tossing his hat at the newel post. And missing. Again. And again.

To her credit, Callie stood back and let the little fella keep on trying.

Aware he wouldn't mind a chance to ease the rift between them and get to know a little more about his new neighbors, Nash turned back to Callie. She was right—there was no time like the present to start over. "Have you and your son eaten?" he asked impulsively.

Callie blinked, clearly taken aback by the question. "Well, no…not yet…but…"

Nash gazed deep into her aqua-blue eyes and took another leap of faith. Maybe there was a helluva lot more to her than had first appeared. "Want to join me?"

Chapter 2

Nash Echols was a man who was full of surprises, Callie acknowledged. The least of which was his current chivalry. Which seemed, at the moment anyway, to be as deeply ingrained as her own usual good manners.

Had she confronted him about the ruckus in any other way, she might have had a very different result. But she hadn't, and now she had to deal with the consequences of her earlier outburst. And what was, at best, a very awkward situation.

Nash's sexy smile widened as he continued in a silky smooth voice that ratcheted up the tension inside her even more, "I'm more than willing to share this delicious spread. I assume you brought enough?"

Glad she had one of the most effective chaperones ever put on this earth with her, as well as a reason to depart quickly once her mission was accomplished, Callie nodded. "Except… Brian doesn't eat chili. It's too spicy."

His gray eyes twinkled. "Will he eat cornbread and fruit, and—" Nash paused, clearly thinking how to phrase it " —the last course?"

Callie nodded, aware her son was listening intently now—and clearly a little enamored of Nash. Maybe this was a good time to work out a solution to their mutual problem. "Oh, yes. He loves c-a-k-e."

"Cake, Mommy!" Brian yelled.

"Some things, he can spell," Callie said dryly.

Nash chuckled. "Well, then, we're all set."

Callie studied him cautiously, trying—and failing—not to be turned on by the sleek, suntanned skin over his wide, inviting shoulders and nicely sculpted chest and abs. "You're sure it's not an imposition?"

A slow grin tugged at the corners of his sensual lips. "I wouldn't have asked if it was. Dishes are in the cabinets. Help yourself. I'm going to finish getting dressed then I'll be right back."

Yes, dressed was a good idea.

Standing there talking with him, when he was only half-clothed, had conjured up a wellspring of longing that was destined to go unmet.

"Right back, Mommy," Brian echoed, snapping her out of her reverie.

Callie knelt to help her son off with his coat.

Nash headed upstairs. By the time he came back down, Callie had set out the food, situated Brian on a stack of phone books and pulled his chair up to the table.

Nash extended his hand. "Let's start over," he said, every bit the Texas gentleman now. "I'm Nash Echols."

Warmth spiraled through her. "Callie McCabe-Grimes," she added with a smile. "And my son, Brian."

Nash helped her with her chair. For the next few minutes, they talked about where they both grew up. Dallas for him, Laramie, Texas, for her. The conversation then segued into where they'd gone to college, and the fact that, after graduation, she'd had her first business experience in Dallas, whereas he had spent ten years working in the Pacific Northwest, before coming back to his home state.

Nash helped himself to more chili. He topped it with pico de gallo, cheddar and sour cream. "How did you end up in this part of the state?"

Callie cut her son's cornbread into bite-size pieces. "My twin sister, Maggie, and I planned joint nuptials at the Double Knot Wedding Ranch on Sanders Mountain. She had second thoughts and bolted during the ceremony, so I was the only one to actually get married that day."

Nash grinned at Callie over the rim of his iced tea. "That sounds like quite a story."

Nodding, Callie returned his smile. "Maggie stayed on at the ranch after her failed wedding to work off her debt. Fell in love with their son, Hart Sanders, and his little boy, Henry. And then they eventually tied the knot." She paused. "Do you know Hart?"

Nash smiled fondly. "We go way back. I used to play with him when I was kid whenever I visited my uncle. Although, I haven't had a chance to see either Hart or his folks in the two weeks since I've been back."

Callie continued, "Hart's parents, Frank and Fiona Sanders, hired me to craft a new marketing campaign that involved utilizing social media for their wedding train business. I moved here to do that. Once I finished that, I decided to go into business for myself. Which is why I bought the one hundred acre ranch in the valley between Sanders Mountain and Echols Mountain last summer, and spent the past few months—" and almost all her savings "—turning it into a corporate retreat."

He regarded her with respect, one business person to another. His glance fell briefly to the rings on her left hand, before returning to her eyes. "How's that going?" he asked, seeming genuinely interested.

"My first event is a week from today."

A corner of his mouth twitched. "You're worried about the noise from the tree-cutting."

Callie forged ahead. "I advertise a peaceful setting for important meetings. If I don't deliver that right out of the gate…" She'd be out of business before she even got started.

Nash rubbed a hand across his jaw. He clearly hadn't shaved since morning, and the evening shadow gave him a sexy, rough-hewn allure. "How many bookings do you have?"

Seeing him push his empty plate and bowl away, Callie got up to cut them all a piece of cake. "I have four events planned from December first to December eleventh."

He thought a moment. "Are they day-only events?"

"Yes." Callie resumed her seat. "From eight in the morning till around ten in the evening, although if my clients' meetings are slow to wrap up, it could run slightly later than that."

Nash smiled, watching Brian dig into his cake. "I see where you are coming from." He leaned closer. "But here's my problem. I have been contracted to deliver four thousand fresh-cut Christmas trees by December seventh. I have a temporary crew of eighteen, coming in to help with the cutting and bundling and delivery, for the next two weeks." There was a long pause. "However, today, for a lot of reasons, we only managed to get two hundred trees ready to go. And that doesn't even include possible inclement weather because we can't cut down trees if it gets too wet. So for me to suspend operations for four whole days—"

"Would likely mean you wouldn't meet *your* business goals."

A quirk of his dark brow. "Unless…"

Trying not to think what his steady appraisal and deep voice did to her, Callie cleared her throat. "What?"

"I'm not sure it would work." His sensual lips thinned. "But…if I can get the guys to work through the weekends, including Thanksgiving Day, with the promise of equivalent days off during your events…" He paused to look her in the eye. "Would you be willing to bring in Thanksgiving dinner for everyone—if I order it and foot the bill?"

Callie was willing to do whatever necessary to facilitate peace. "I'll do better than that," she offered, beyond thrilled that they had found a solution at long last. "I'll cook. You-all can come to my ranch and have dinner there."

"I haven't seen you this excited since the first time you cooked dinner for Seth."

Callie turned to her twin sister. The six-months pregnant Maggie had come over with her husband, Hart, and their three-year-old son, Henry, to aid in the preparations. Currently, Hart had both Henry and her son,

Brian, out riding tricycles on the sidewalk that led from the converted bunkhouse, where the meal was being prepared, to the ranch house, where she and Brian lived.

Callie carved the first of two big roasted turkeys. "The first time I cooked for Seth, it was for just him and me. Tonight, we're having twenty-four people." Hardly an intimate setting, even if her meal with Nash three evenings before sort of had been. "So if I seem a little overwrought or whatever, it's because I'm using this evening as a trial run for my first hosted corporate retreat next week."

It had nothing to do with the ruggedly handsome man heading up the team of cowboys turned temporary lumberjacks. Or the cozy dinner they'd shared. Or that this somehow carried all the emotional impact of a date. Because she wasn't dating again for a good long time. If ever.

Maggie stirred the big kettle of gravy on the stove, clearly not buying it. "Hmm."

"Plus, you know how I like to stay busy during the holidays. It just helps, not having time to think." Because it was when she let herself ruminate on the events of the past that she felt her mood fall, and she couldn't let that happen now—not when she had a child depending on her to provide the best holiday ever.

"Furthermore, just because you're happily married and expecting another baby in the spring, doesn't mean I need to be doing the same." Callie finished slicing up the first turkey and started on the second.

Maggie brought out the cranberry relish and dinner rolls, and then carried them to the long plank tables. The scent of sage dressing and freshly mashed potatoes added to the delicious aromas in the air.

"I still think you're selling yourself short," Maggie told her. "You're still young enough to marry again and have another baby or two."

And Nash Echols was definitely sexy enough, Callie thought. *If* she were looking for a mate to father more children. Which she wasn't. "The only things that concern me right now are my son and my business—"

Callie stopped at the sight of the gorgeous man in the kitchen door.

He was dressed pretty much as she'd expected. In dark jeans and a slate-gray shirt that molded his sinewy shoulders and chest and brought out the mesmerizing dark silver of his eyes. His black hair was freshly shampooed and combed, and as he strolled nearer, she caught the tantalizing scent of his aftershave lotion.

"Sorry to interrupt." Nash Echols nodded at Maggie then turned back to Callie with a genial smile. "Hart said I should just come on in."

Callie set down the carving knife and fork. Trying not to feel too excited, she wiped her hands on her apron. He was a guest…that was all. "Are the rest of the men here, too?"

His glance moved over her lazily. "They will be momentarily—if you're ready for us."

Callie fought back a reaction to all that testosterone. She jerked in a bolstering breath and returned his smile. "We are."

The question was, was she ready to spend so much time with Nash Echols—even in a group? All he'd done was walk into the spacious bunkhouse and already her heart was going ballistic.

Fortunately, the crew was right behind him.

Clearly not one to simply stand around, Nash took

over the rest of the carving, while Callie pulled out big stainless-steel trays of buttermilk mashed potatoes, sweet potato casserole and green beans from the warming ovens. Maggie helped spoon hot food into serving dishes while her husband situated both little boys in booster seats. Their guests all pitched in to carry the food into the dining room.

One by one everyone found a seat. Callie took the head of the table. Nash, who had been busy filling water glasses, paused when it appeared there was only one chair left—at the other end of the long plank table. He lifted a quizzical brow her way. "Will your husband be joining us?" he asked.

It was a simple question, Nash thought.

One that should have been easy to answer.

Instead, Callie froze as if that were the last thing she had expected to hear. Her twin sister and her husband exchanged long, baffled looks. Then Maggie turned back to Callie, who wasn't really meeting anyone's gaze directly, and silently telegraphed something that her twin obviously decided to ignore.

Regaining her composure, Callie flashed an overly bright smile his way. "It's just us." She gestured graciously to the chair opposite her. "So if you'll have a seat, too…"

Which begged the question, Nash thought, where was the elusive Mr. Grimes? Not that anyone else but him seemed intrigued by the matter, as grace was said, the platters of abundant food were passed around and everyone dug in. During the meal—which was, by far, the most delicious Thanksgiving dinner he'd ever had— conversation revolved primarily around the sports teams playing and the results of the games thus far.

Maggie McCabe-Sanders and her husband worked to make sure everyone felt at home. While Callie seemed happy to concentrate on making sure her son got enough to eat, and the serving platters on the table were replenished as often as need be.

Not surprisingly, by the time dessert and coffee were served, the little ones were drooping with fatigue.

Callie looked at her sister. "Would you and Hart mind...?"

Maggie smiled. "Not at all. We'll take them over to the house and get them into their pajamas."

The lumberjacks lined up to help clear the table and thank Callie for the amazing dinner, and then they headed over to Nash's ranch house next door to play cards and watch football.

Finally, it was just Nash and Callie, alone in the bunkhouse kitchen. He surveyed the tall stacks of dirty dishes while Callie picked up her buzzing cell phone. She seemed to want to sink through the floor when she caught a glimpse of the caller ID screen.

Pivoting so her back was to Nash, she said hello. Listened. With a smile in her voice said, "Of course you can. Yes, absolutely. Right now is fine. I'm in the bunkhouse."

She hung up and immediately punched in another number. "Maggie? You heard...? Oh, good. Can you keep Brian awake? Thanks." She ended the call and swung back to Nash. Bright color highlighted her elegant cheekbones.

"Company coming?" Like maybe an estranged husband?

She nodded.

"Not to worry," he said. "I'll stay here and clean all this up."

To his surprise, she looked even more panicked. "Not a good idea."

The evening was getting stranger and stranger. "Why not?"

She bit her lip. "Because—"

The door opened and a couple in their early sixties walked in. Both were eclectically dressed. The woman in a violet cashmere wrap, multicolored flowing skirt and matching blouse. An abundance of costume jewelry, a hammered silver belt and elaborately crafted Western boots completed her free-spirited look. The man wore a tapestry vest shot through with silver and gold threads, band-collared shirt, jeans and boots. A Stetson covered his free-flowing shoulder-length silver hair.

"Darling!" The woman opened her arms. Callie went into them, returning a fiercely affectionate hug, then accepted an equally warm embrace from the man.

"The place looks wonderful!" the older gentleman said.

"This retreat will be the best in Texas within the year," the woman enthused. "In fact, I'm betting it will be featured in every magazine and newspaper in the state!"

The over-the-top prediction elicited a brief, pained look from Callie. "I'd settle for just a modest success," she murmured.

"You're going to do much, much better than that," the woman insisted. "And in the process, prove all the naysayers who thought you should stay in Laramie, wrapped in widow's weeds, wrong."

Widow. Had she said *widow*?

Nash's gaze fell to the diamond and engagement rings still sparkling on Callie's left hand.

Now, this was interesting.

The older woman turned to Nash. "I'm Doris Grimes, by the way. And this is my husband, Rock. We're Seth's parents."

Nash returned the smile and stepped forward to shake hands. "I'm Nash Echols, Callie's neighbor. My men and I joined Callie and her sister's family for Thanksgiving dinner."

Callie waited until the handshaking was concluded, then intervened, "Well, I know you're anxious to see your grandson," she told her in-laws, "so you-all go on ahead. I'll be up at the ranch house as soon as I get things squared away here."

After she ushered them toward the door, they left.

Nash didn't utter a single word until Callie turned back around and met his questioning glance. "Widow, hmm?"

Pursing her lips, she angled a thumb at her sternum. "Hey, it's not my duty to correct any wrong assumptions on your part. Or anyone else's for that matter."

"So this is a common ploy? Pretending you're still married?" To do what? Drag on the grief? Keep from doing what everyone had to do eventually, which was move on…?

Callie's jaw set stubbornly as she lifted her gaze to his. "I am still married. In my heart. And always will be."

The way she had inadvertently checked him out when he walked in, and apparently liked what she saw, said otherwise. She was still a woman, and still very much alive in *every* respect, whether she wanted to admit it or not.

Not about to let her get away with deliberately misleading him, he lifted a brow. "Bull."

She blinked. "Excuse me?"

He stepped closer, purposefully invading her personal space. "You wear those rings, and let people assume you're married, to keep guys from hitting on you."

Callie drew a deep breath and stepped back. Her blue eyes took on a cynical light. "So what if I do? In my situation you probably would, too."

"I don't go around misrepresenting myself."

"Oh, really?" she scoffed. "Because I'm pretty sure you wanted my in-laws to think you were an upstanding Texas gentleman just now."

"I *am* an upstanding Texas gentleman." Even if he had spent the past ten years in the Pacific Northwest.

"Really?" She pushed the words through gritted teeth. "Because I'm pretty sure a real Texas gentleman would not have brought up the fact that I'm a widow when it is *clearly* a subject I do not wish to discuss."

He answered her insult with a shrug, but did not disengage their locked gazes. "Fine with me," he said, just as carelessly. "I can do a search on Google on anything I want to know, anyway."

Briefly, Callie's shoulders slumped, but then she pulled herself together. Planted her hands on her slender hips. Stared at him long and hard. "Why are you so darn difficult, anyway?"

Did she really expect him to answer that? Well, turnabout was fair play, and he had a question of his own.

Why was she so damned pretty?

He'd thought she looked good the other day, when

she confronted him in the woods, and again when she had showed up at his place, bearing dinner and a sweet demeanor meant to turn him pliable.

Which it had.

But it was nothing compared to the way she looked this evening, in a trim black wool skirt, tights and pleated ivory blouse. The fact she was wearing comfortable leather flats, instead of her usual heeled boots, made the seven-inch height difference between them all the more apparent.

Aware she was still waiting for some explanation as to why he took her deliberate deception so personally, he replied, "I don't like being lied to."

And he didn't like people who hung on to their grief in ways that hurt everyone else around them, either.

Callie stepped closer and leveled a withering glare on his face. "I wasn't lying." He challenged her with a raised brow.

Averting her pretty blue gaze, she mumbled, "I just didn't tell you everything you wanted to know."

Which, in turn, made him wonder. "And that is...?" he prodded casually.

She whirled away from him in a drift of perfume. "Probably that my husband died a little over three years ago in a car accident. I'd just been married a few months. I was pregnant at the time."

Nash felt for her. Losing a loved one was always hard. Especially so unexpectedly.

"And then what?" The edge was still in his voice, for a different reason now.

She walked back into the kitchen and, rolling up her sleeves, began loading dishes into the large stainless-steel dishwasher. "My family—my parents mostly—

convinced me that I needed to leave Dallas and move back to Laramie, Texas, where I grew up, and be near them."

He took a stack, as well, and began loading dishes, too.

"And that's where I was," Callie continued, with a matter-of-factness that did nothing to disguise the aching loneliness in her eyes. "Until a year and a half ago when I moved here. First as marketing director with the Double Knot Ranch, and then as owner of my own ranch and business. See? Nothing all that exciting about that. "

Finished with the plates, she began working on glasses, while he began loading the silverware.

Frustrated by her sudden silence, Nash drawled, "Which brings us to yet another problem."

Callie looked up, the pulse working in her slender throat. She rinsed her hands beneath the faucet. "Really. And what might that be?"

Nash stepped in beside her to do the same. "You're young. You're single. You're gorgeous." He leaned close enough to draw in a whiff of her hair, which was as enticing as the rest of her. "There damn sure should be something exciting going on in your life."

Callie straightened slowly.

"Let me guess." She reached for a paper towel to dry her hands. "You're just the man to give it to me."

Nash shut off the water, and once again did the same.

"Well," he said lazily, wadding up the towel and tossing it into the trash. "Since you asked so nicely." He smiled broadly. "I just might be."

Chapter 3

Callie stared up at Nash in dismay. "You wouldn't dare."

His gaze roved her face, lingering on her lips, before returning ever so slowly to her eyes. He flashed her a sexy grin, chiding, "Another thing you should never do…"

Callie caught her breath, aware she had never been around such an impossible, arrogant man. Never mind in such close quarters! "What?"

He wrapped one hand around the nape of her neck, the other flattened on her spine. Then his slate-gray eyes shuttered to half-mast as his head slowly dipped toward her. "Challenge me."

Callie shivered as his lips ghosted lightly across hers. "I'm not…" But already her eyes were closing, too. Already, she was losing herself in the feel of his hard, strong body pressed against her, the brisk wintry smell of him, the implacable masculine taste of his mouth and the resolute possession of his lips.

She thought she'd been kissed before.

She hadn't been.

Not like this.

Like he wanted to savor every iota of her heart and soul.

Yearning swept through her, fierce and undeniable. It had been so long since she had been kissed, touched, held. So long since anyone had wanted her like this. Her whole body radiated heat and he responded by kissing her even more deeply. Unable to help herself, unable to resist the probing pressure of his lips, she surged against him. And still he kissed her, over and over again. Hard, fast. Slow, easy. Tenderly. Erotically.

Dazed, she heard a low groan wrenched from his throat, as if he wanted her beyond reason, too. It was answered by the hardening of her nipples, and lower still, the beginning of an ache that nearly rendered her senseless.

And that was, of course, when he groaned again, jerked in a breath and called a halt to their steamy foreplay.

Frustration mingled with her desire, adding to the tumultuous emotion of her day. She glared at him. "I can't believe you just did that."

He met her gaze evenly, his eyes dark, warmly assessing. "I can't, either." The corners of his mouth lifted ruefully. "I'm usually a lot more sensible. But then—" gently, he tucked a strand of hair behind her ear "—you seem to bring out the recklessness in me."

Callie let loose a rather unladylike phrase, then stepped back. "Your ego knows no bounds."

He laughed, the desire in his eyes every bit as hot and enticing as his embrace had been. He leaned close enough to press a fleeting kiss across her brow. "You could say that with some impunity if you hadn't kissed me back, Callie. Unfortunately, for *your* ego, you did."

"I don't see what the problem is," Maggie told Callie later that same evening, when everyone but the two of them had gone on to bed. Together, they carried their cups of hot apple cider into the family room and settled before the fire.

Maggie sized her sister up. "You said you were tired of being viewed as this poor tragic young widow who's constantly being handled with kid gloves."

Which was true, Callie thought, kicking off her flats and tucking her legs beneath her.

"And Nash didn't feel sorry for you," Maggie continued.

Callie sipped her cider and pointed out ruefully, "He kissed me instead."

"And that's a problem because…?" Maggie asked, grinning.

Callie closed her eyes against the sultry memory and the new flood of desire it conjured up. "I didn't want him to."

"Really?" Her sister's eyes twinkled all the more. "'Cause I think you doth protest a little too much. I mean—" she shrugged "—it's not as if he's the first guy who made a pass at you since Seth died. You handled those missteps, barely blinking an eye."

All too true. Callie rubbed at an imaginary spot on her wool skirt. "That's because…"

Maggie ventured wryly, "You didn't kiss any of them back?"

Callie paused. "How do you know that?"

"Because I'm your twin. And I know the way you think. Always have, always will, remember? Plus, I saw the way you looked at him when he came into the bunkhouse today." She waggled her brows. "Like you wanted to gobble him right up."

Callie blushed despite herself. "Okay. I admit there's a definite physical attraction there. But that's all it is."

Maggie chuckled. "You keep telling yourself that."

And Callie did.

All through the rest of her late-evening gabfest with her twin, all that night as she tossed and turned in her bed, and into the next morning. Fortunately, she had a lot to keep her busy. Breakfast to prepare for the family still gathered there, a holiday to-do list a mile long and a whole lot of distant whining chain saws in the distance to ignore.

First on the list was the purchase of two Christmas trees. As they lingered at the breakfast table, her brother-in-law listened to her plan. "Of course I don't mind driving into San Antonio to pick them up for you," Hart said. "But don't you think it's a little silly to go all that distance and drive all that way back with two trees lashed to the pickup truck when there is a perfectly reputable business selling them—likely at wholesale no less—on the ranch right next door?"

Callie had been afraid he would bring that up. Especially since she now knew that Hart and Nash were childhood friends. "Nash is not in the retail business," Callie argued.

Her former mother-in-law shrugged. "He seemed like a reasonable guy. Why don't you just ask him?"

"Or better yet, text him and see," Maggie said, still keeping an eagle eye on the two preschoolers playing in the next room.

Noticing the two little boys were beginning to get a little too rowdy, Hart went on in to supervise directly. "You have his cell phone number, don't you?" he said over his shoulder.

Callie nodded, as Hart settled onto the floor and began building a wooden block tower. Two-and-a-half-year-old Brian and three-year-old Henry immediately joined in.

"He gave it to me when we were setting up the Thanksgiving dinner," Callie admitted.

"Then...?" Maggie persisted.

Everyone stared at her, wondering why she was so reluctant to make the holiday decorating as easy as she possibly could.

Because, Callie thought, *I don't want to end up kissing him again.*

But knowing there was little chance of that, with the group of four adult chaperones at her side, she shrugged off her lingering desire and went to get her cell phone.

All eyes were upon her as she texted Nash. I need two trees. One for the house and one for the bunkhouse retreat. Can I buy them from you?

She hit Send.

Thirty seconds later, her phone chimed. No problem, Nash texted back. What size?

Twelve foot for the bunkhouse, and six foot for the ranch house, Callie typed in return.

Again, the reply coming in was nearly instantaneous. I'll get them to you this morning, Nash wrote, with the symbol for a wink. Last night was great, by the way. Especially before you kicked me out.

Reading it, Callie had to stifle a laugh but could do nothing to contain the telltale heat climbing to her cheeks.

"What?" Maggie asked, drawing nearer.

Callie shook her head and slid her phone into her pocket. "He was talking about the dinner, how much everyone enjoyed it," she fibbed. "That's all."

Maggie lifted a speculative brow.

But before anyone had another chance to say anything, a ruckus broke out in the adjacent family room. "My daddy!" Henry shouted.

"No," Brian disagreed, climbing onto Hart's lap and wrapping his arms around Hart's neck. "He's *mine*!"

Henry attempted to push his cousin aside. "No," Henry shouted back emotionally. "He is your uncle Hart. He's *my daddy*!"

Hart wrapped both boys in his arms. "Hey now," he soothed, holding them both close—to no avail. "I'm here for both of you…"

Brian let out another outraged howl, and Henry followed suit. Her heart breaking, Callie rushed to the rescue.

But Brian did not want to go with her. Or his grandparents. Or his aunt Maggie. So Callie did the only thing she could do, the thing she always did, and she went to get Brian's picture of Seth.

Nash could hear the ruckus inside, the moment he pulled up to the Heart of Texas ranch house in his pickup truck.

Inside, Nash found, it was little better. Callie was in tears. So were both preschoolers. Hart and Maggie were doing their best to separate—and soothe—the two quarreling little boys, but emotions were at an all-time high. Only Callie's in-laws were calm.

"This is exactly why you've got to think about re-marrying," Doris was telling Callie.

Rock agreed. "We loved our son dearly, honey, and we will always miss him, but we know, like it or not, that life goes on. It has for us. And it must for you and our grandson, too."

Callie shook her head, understanding—if not agree-ing. She wiped the moisture from her face and, picture in hand, went to her son. She hunkered down beside him. "Brian, honey, we have to talk."

The tyke turned to Callie with a heartfelt glare. "No, Mommy," he said. "No talk. No picture!" He pushed the framed photo in her hand away.

Deciding to do what he could to break the tension, Nash stepped forward and interjected brightly. "Who wants to see how many Christmas trees I have in the back of my pickup truck?" He squinted at the two boys. "I'll bet you anything you can't count them."

Henry straightened. "I can, too!" he said with im-portance.

Brian scrambled off Hart's lap and headed for Nash, doing his best to push his cousin out of the way in the process. "I want to see!" Brian declared.

"Well, okay then." Nash put out a hand to each child. "Let's go see. You think you fellas are old enough to see into the bed of my pickup truck, if I lift you up?"

"Yes," Henry and Brian shouted in unison.

Out the door they went. When they reached the tail-gate, Nash bent down to take a boy in each arm and lifted them high. Their quarrel forgotten, they leaned over to look into the bed of his truck, where four unwrapped, fresh-cut pines, of varying sizes, lay.

"Wow," the cousins said in unison.

Nash let them study the trees. "Think we should get them out, to see just how tall they are?"

The boys nodded.

Nash handed off Brian to Callie, and Henry to Hart. "Okay then," he said with comically exaggerated importance. "Everyone stand back…"

The next few minutes were spent admiring the trees from all angles and selecting which one would go into the bunkhouse retreat and which would go to the ranch house.

By the time they secured each in the stands Callie had already purchased, the boys were filled with wonder.

"You're a lifesaver," Callie said, as she walked him back to his truck, while the others all returned to the ranch house.

Nash tipped his head at her. "Happy to be of service," he drawled.

Callie's eyes drifted to his mouth. Flushing, she sucked in a breath and returned her gaze to his. "What do I owe you for the trees?"

That was easy. "Dinner—tonight."

Her slender shoulders stiffened. "I don't think that's a good idea."

He studied the mutinous expression on her pretty face. "Why not?" he prodded, enjoying the display of temper.

Aqua-blue eyes narrowed. "Because."

He stepped close enough to inhale the flowery scent of her hair and skin. "We might end up kissing again?"

Scoffing, Callie folded her arms in front of her, tightening the cashmere fabric of her sweater over the rounded softness of her breasts. "That's not going to happen."

He moved even closer. "Mmm-hmm," he said huskily. It took everything he had not to touch her again. Haul her into his arms. And...

"And what if I promise not to kiss you again?" he asked. "At least tonight?"

A pulse throbbed in her throat. "Meaning?"

"I only like to think about things like that short term."

"Well, I don't like to think about them at all!"

He'd been able to tell that it had been a while. A long while. "So noted," he said dryly. Besides it wasn't a vow which would necessarily be hard to keep if she continued to have as many chaperones as she had inside her home at that moment.

"Seems like your son could use the distraction," he persuaded.

He had her there...and she knew it.

Callie blew out a gusty sigh. "Fine," she conceded. "But don't expect anything other than leftovers."

Leftovers sounded a heck of a lot better than she knew.

"What time?" he asked, before she could change her mind.

Another breath, so deep it lifted—then lowered—the soft swell of her breasts.

Not that he was noticing, he told himself firmly.

She bit her lip, as she considered. "Seven-thirty?"

Nash shrugged. "Sounds good to me."

And then, before he was tempted to forgo all reason and kiss her again, he turned and walked away.

Chapter 4

Nash was surprised to see only Callie's SUV parked in front of her ranch house when he arrived Friday evening. And even more surprised to see the way she was outfitted when she opened the door to him.

"Ah," he couldn't resist teasing, "you dressed up just for me."

Callie flushed. Clearly she had meant her attire to send a message that this evening meant nothing to her. And he had to admit, on that score, she had done a fine job.

She was definitely dressed to un-impress—in old jeans and a loose-fitting blue chambray shirt, washed so many times it was soft and thin as silk, socks and moccasins, all her makeup scrubbed off.

Looking around the foyer, he realized that everyone else appeared to be gone. She had massive to-do lists spread out on the coffee table, as well as photos of her late husband and wedding pictures prominently displayed on the mantel.

Which was even more amusing, Nash noted, since none of that had been there earlier in the day.

He shrugged out of his shearling jacket and hung it on the coatrack, then followed her into the kitchen. The scent of sage dressing, turkey and cranberries wafted through the air.

"Brian asleep?"

Callie nodded, clearly disappointed about that, too. "I had hoped he would be up, but he is so overtired, it's probably for the best."

"And your in-laws?"

Another tight officious smile. "They're off to spend the weekend at the holiday craft show in San Antonio." She gestured for him to have a seat at a table set for two.

She went to the oven and pulled out casserole dishes. Turkey smothered in gravy. Potatoes and stuffing. Some sort of vegetable medley that hadn't been on the table the evening before. Warm cranberry and apple compote. A loaf of what appeared to be homemade bread. And butter.

When she had everything at the table, she sat down, too. "Rock and Doris have a wholesale Texana souvenir business. Basically they sell or make anything and everything that has to do with the history and culture of Texas. They trade with businesses all over the state, so even though they are based in my hometown, they are on the road a lot."

Nash heaped food on his plate, then dug in. "I gather they supported your decision to start your own business and move away from Laramie?"

"They did."

Her food was every bit as good the second time around. "Are your parents as understanding?"

"No," Callie admitted. "They wanted me to stay closer to home. But I still see them a fair amount, since they're both doctors, and attend a lot of medical education seminars in San Antonio."

"How do they feel about the prospect of you getting married again?"

She kept her eyes on his a disconcertingly long time, then lifted her chin. "We haven't really talked about it."

"And yet your in-laws want you to take another leap of faith, as soon as possible it would seem."

"What can I say?" Her silver Christmas star earrings jangled as she tilted her head slightly to one side. "They're hopelessly romantic. My late husband was the same."

"And you…?"

"Used to be a romantic fool," she said. The enticing curves of her breasts pressed against her blouse as she inhaled sharply. "No more."

Wishing he could give in to his desire, haul her onto his lap and lock lips with her again, Nash recalled his promise not to kiss her again tonight. "So you're not interested in getting married again?"

The mutinous light was back in her blue eyes. "Nope. Not at all. Been there, done that. See no reason to ever do it again. Or even, really, date."

Message sent, Nash thought, but not necessarily received.

He grinned, the man in him rising to the womanly challenge in her. He leaned back in his chair, his shoulders flexing against the rungs. "You're going to live your whole life without sex?"

"I didn't say that, exactly."

Now they were getting somewhere! "Then...?"

Her flush deepened, as if she knew how ludicrous she sounded. "Why are you asking me this?"

Lazily, he looked her up and down, amazed at how gorgeous she was, under any circumstances. Aware she was waiting for an answer, he said, "I'm curious."

She studied him coolly in return. "Okay, if you must know," she said, clearly not understanding why this was so, "I could see myself having an affair—at least in theory—if I could keep it strictly as a bed-buddy, casual-sex type of thing."

This was news. "Bed-buddy," he repeated in shock.

She leveled another long, droll look. "You know. Someone you have sex with when the mood strikes, but don't have any kind of romantic attachment to."

Her matter-of-fact assertion sounded even more ludicrous the second time around.

"Or you could 'hire' a companion," he quipped. "Someone like...say, me...who would 'work for food' under those circumstances."

She shook her head at the merriment twinkling in his eyes. Knowing even without him saying so that he was already half-serious. "You're so funny."

He chuckled. "So are you."

Again it took everything he had to resist touching her.

They locked eyes, drawing out the sensually charged moment.

"You don't believe I could have a casual affair, do

you?" Callie challenged. He stood and carried his dishes to the sink. "Not for one second. No."

She rose, too, her motions as graceful as they were deliberate. "Why not?"

He watched her slide the plates into the dishwasher, then ease the door back into place with more than necessary gusto. "Because you might say you've let go of your romantic ideals, but those to-do lists you had out for me to see, of everything you want to do to celebrate Christmas, say otherwise."

Callie swung toward him, her body nudging his in the process. "Those lists have nothing to do with how I feel. And everything to do with how I want *my son* to feel."

He studied the conflicted expression on her face. "I don't understand."

"The truth is… I haven't felt like celebrating Christmas since my husband died. But," she added the all important caveat, "I have a child who needs to experience all the wonder and hope and joy that the holiday can bring, so I go through the motions. For him."

"You don't think he knows that's what you're doing?"

Callie released an exasperated breath. "He's two and a half."

"So?"

Another silence fell, this one fraught with tension. "So…he can't even figure out what a daddy is. *Yet*." Nash lounged against the counter, legs crossed at the ankle, his hands braced on either side of him. "Except that he knows he wants one and doesn't have one."

Her jaw took on the determined tilt he was beginning to know so well. "Brian will get over it."

"And if he doesn't?"

"He is going to have to," Callie insisted, looking Nash right in the eye, "because I am not going to marry again without love. And I'm not going to marry for purely romantic reasons, either."

Her words were true. Nevertheless, Callie still wished with all her heart that she hadn't said them. Hadn't revealed nearly so much about herself to the man standing opposite her.

Nash looked shocked. "So you won't marry again, period."

His low, masculine voice sent a thrill through her. "Nope." Determined to keep him at arm's length, she continued, "Once you've had the best, anything that follows is bound to be second-rate, and who wants that, right?"

His chuckle was warm and seductive. Gazing down at her, as if she had just given him the opening he needed, he turned to face her, trapping her between the counter and his big hard body. "Not even for companionship and sex?" he taunted softly.

Pretending she couldn't feel the sizzle of awareness sifting between them, she backed up as much as she could, which turned out to be about half an inch. "Why do you keep bringing the subject back around to sex?"

He remained close. Still not touching her, he shrugged. "Not sure." His gaze traced the shape of her lips before returning evocatively to her eyes. "Just seems to be on my mind whenever I'm around you."

Hers, too. She flattened her hand across his chest. "Well, stop thinking about it." Her attempt to shove him aside failed.

He remained as unmovable as a two-ton boulder.

Dipping his head, he kissed the back of her forearm. "Easier said than done."

Her entire body leaped into flame. And he hadn't so much as actually touched her yet. She lifted her hand away from the hard musculature of his broad chest and the slow, steady beat of his heart. "Listen to me, Nash Echols, I am not the woman for you."

He flashed another thoughtful half smile, then lowered his head and slanted it across hers. "Actually, Callie," he said, pausing to deliver a gentle, persuasive kiss, "you might be just what I need." Hands still braced on the counter on either side of her, he kissed her again, even more provocatively this time. "And I might be just what you need," Nash persisted, trailing kisses over the nape of her neck, across her collarbone. "Since you're in the market for sex-with-no-strings-attached..."

Callie's eyes shuttered closed, but she forced them open. Forced herself to look him in the eye. "I never actually said that." Although she had been thinking it, at least whenever he was around.

His chuckle remained confident. "Speaking hypothetically is one step away from actually doing something. You know that."

Fine. So maybe the idea of going without making love again—ever—was not only depressing, it was a tad unrealistic, too, given the signals her body had been transmitting the past few days.

But not about to give him the satisfaction of being right, she squared her shoulders. "I didn't say I wanted the sex to be with you."

He looked down at her old, loose chambray shirt—seeming to visually strip her naked, to see what was beneath. "Not verbally. Physically," he looked again, as if he could tell her nipples had peaked, "you seem to be hinting at just that."

She moaned as his hands slid under her blouse, moved upward to cup her breasts. "I knew you were trouble the first day we met."

He bent to kiss her again. Slowly, tantalizingly. "But it's the kind of trouble you want to be in. Would be in, if you weren't so set on living the life of a nun."

One button was undone, then the next, and the next. "And it's a damn shame to see you so alone."

She willed herself to move, but found her legs would not cooperate. Nor would her knees. She swayed back against the counter, holding on to the edge on either side of her. "Why?"

The side of his hand moved across her collarbone, lower still, to the valley between her slowly rising and falling breasts. "Because you're young and vital and beautiful." His fingers grazed across her skin. "And, judging from your display of temper the other day, have way too much passion locked away inside."

Passion that welled up, unchecked, whenever she saw him. Passion that—like now—made her helpless to fight the desire roiling inside her. She moved her hands up to his shoulders, intending to push him away and failing. "You don't know anything about me," she whispered, looking deep into his dark silver eyes. "Not really."

He reached around behind her, unfastening her bra, caressing and claiming her beneath the sheer lace cloth. "I know," he rasped, "that widow or not, you miss being kissed. Touched. Loved."

"I do. Not—" Her words were smothered by the feel of his lips on hers.

She meant to resist him, she really did, but the heat

and pressure of his mouth sent a thrill spiraling through her. For too long she'd been treated with kid gloves by everyone around her. For too long, she'd felt only half alive. Yet now, with his hands on her skin, his mouth on hers, that was no longer true. She was more alive than she had been in her entire life.

"See?" he whispered, stepping back. "That wasn't so bad, now was it?"

She exhaled slowly, wishing there were some way to discretely refasten her bra. As embarrassment and anger surged within her, she scowled at him and turned away. "I should have known you wouldn't be a gentleman for long."

He stepped behind her, fastened her up again. Then, coming around to face her, reached for the buttons on her blouse, declaring proudly, "I thought my kiss was very…gentlemanly."

She shoved his hand away and put her shirt together herself. "Erotic, yes." She looked down to make sure the buttons were in the right holes.

He chuckled. "I can go with that."

Finally, Callie was dressed again, but her breasts were still tingling. Lower still, a wildfire of need raged.

She drew a deep, bolstering breath, determined to put him in his place. "But let's be clear here. A gentleman wouldn't have kissed me at all. Especially after promising me that he wouldn't!"

Mischief danced in Nash's eyes. "You're right. It is all a little too soon. This being our third date, after all."

"*Third!*" Callie sputtered. Now she knew why she

had never dated a bad boy before. They were definitely too much trouble.

"The first was the night you brought me dinner. The second, Thanksgiving."

"There were twenty-six people here, if you count my in-laws!"

"I admit it was kind of a group thing. Till after…" He waggled his brows suggestively. "Then, it was just you and me. And then of course, there's tonight. I really enjoyed tonight."

The hell of it was, so had she. From the moment he had stepped through her front door, she had felt incredibly excited and alive. But that was neither here nor there. "You may annoy the heck out of me."

He grinned.

"But this isn't seventh grade."

"You're right." He rubbed the flat of his hand beneath the underside of his smoothly shaven jaw. "I never went to second base in seventh grade…and I suspect you didn't, either."

Ignoring that last comment, she plunged ahead. "Furthermore, I don't get involved with sexy upstarts. Never have. Never will."

His expression sobered, all but his eyes, which were still gleaming merrily. "Good to know."

Feeling like a schoolmarm in front of an unruly class, Callie lifted a lecturing hand. "From this point forward, there is not going to be anything going on between us— except cooperation of a business nature."

Nash went back to the table to claim the serving dishes. "Speaking of which…did Frank and Fiona Sanders tell you that they have invited me and my crew to join the Old-Fashioned Christmas Celebration at Sanders Mountain on December twenty-first?"

Callie stared at him in shock. "The Sanders did what?"

"Asked me to participate. They said you are organizing it."

Telling herself she had not just stumbled into a lion's den of temptation, Callie kept her eyes locked with his. "Although I no longer work full-time at the Double Knot, I still advise them part-time and help out with all the marketing."

"Is this an annual event?" he asked.

Glad to be moving back to a conversation that was strictly business, she got the last of the serving dishes and slid them into the dishwasher. "It's the first, although we're expecting it to become a beloved yearly tradition."

Nash stepped back, giving her room to work. "How did it come about?"

Callie added soap to the dishwasher and turned it on. "They don't book a lot of outdoor weddings for Nature's Cathedral in December and January—the weather is too cold for most. So I suggested that Frank and Fiona use the lag time to put on an old-fashioned Christmas Celebration for their clients, suppliers and referral partners and their families, both as a way of saying thank you and to drum up future business."

She switched off the light and he followed her into the hall. "For you, as well?"

Callie nodded. "We could do the same for your Christmas tree business."

"As well as the xeriscape plants and trees I am hoping to sell to local garden centers."

She paused next to the coatrack in the foyer. "In the meantime, you could do what I am going to do, and raffle off free trees and/or evergreen wreaths to whatever number of lucky guests you decide upon."

"How many people are you hoping to host?"

"Five hundred or so. Although invitations are going out for close to one thousand guests."

He smiled. "Impressive."

She reached for his hat and coat, and handed them to him. "We're setting up the party barn at the Double Knot as a Santa's Village. Hart is going to play Santa. We'll also have photographers, train rides up the mountain and a choir and a brass quintet at Nature's Cathedral to get people in the holiday mood."

"Sounds great."

She arched a brow. "So you're in?"

"Absolutely."

"It means you'll have to help the day of the event, as well as the week or so leading up to it," she warned. "Sure you're up to that?"

"No problem. As soon as I fill the orders for the Christmas trees I already have, my schedule will free up considerably."

They looked at each other.

Callie knew if he stayed they would only end up kissing again. She made a show of stifling a yawn.

He grinned, as if knowing however tired she might be, sleep was going to be a long time coming. Especially if she started thinking about the way he had kissed her, and touched her, again...

Which, she told herself firmly, she would not.

His grin widened all the more. "I can take a hint." He shrugged on his coat and ambled toward the front door. "If you need anything before Monday…" he said over his shoulder.

"I'm good, but thanks." She reached for the knob and opened the door for him.

"Seriously." He paused, looking down at her, tenderness pushing aside the mischief in his eyes. "I'm here for you."

Callie nodded, a lump in her throat. It had been a long time since she had been looked after by any man.

He settled his Stetson square on his head. "This is where you tell me you're here for me, too."

She continued looking at him, poker-faced.

He winked. "Us being neighbors and all…"

He really knew how to put a gal on the spot. Lucky for him, she'd been brought up to be a Texas lady. "I'm here for you—as a neighbor—too," she said finally.

He looked like he'd won the lottery. "Just what I wanted to hear."

To her surprise, she felt like she had won it, too.

"In the meantime," he went on, stepping over the threshold, "it's supposed to rain tomorrow. So we probably won't be working."

Callie lounged in the doorway, arms crossed, aware he had planned for weather delays.

"So if you and Brian are up for it," Nash continued genially, "I was going to see—"

Callie held up a hand, cutting him off. "Actually, we already have a get-together planned for tomorrow. But maybe some other time?" For a moment, Nash looked like he wanted to say something else. Then he stopped himself, nodded. "Some other time, then," he said.

And, looking more cheerful than ever, left.

Chapter 5

"Bad day?" Maggie asked, when Callie and Brian showed up at her home the following afternoon.

"Unbelievably bad so far." She carefully hung up their rain-spattered coats on the tree in the hall. Then watched her son stomp off to join his cousin in the family room, where Hart was busy setting up a child-size table and chairs.

It had been one temper tantrum after another since the moment Brian had gotten up that morning. And, as it turned out, the steady, pouring rain and ever-present gloom hadn't helped either of their moods.

Maggie hugged Callie as tightly as her pregnant-form would allow. "Well, this, too, shall pass," she promised cheerfully. "At least that's what Hart and I tell ourselves whenever Henry is overtired and out of sorts."

Appreciating the support, Callie smiled, then took

a moment to admire the decorations her sister and her husband had put up. A beautiful wreath hung on the front door, and a big tree in front of the bay window dominated the formal living room. Garlands laced the staircase, stockings the mantel. Colored lights and a Santa sleigh and reindeer set adorned the exterior of the house. Clearly, they had gone all out. Which only reminded her of the work she had yet to do.

The trees Hart had previously delivered for the bunkhouse and her home remained undecorated. As did the rest of the interior of her home. Callie bit her lip, wondering when she was going to find the time to get everything done.

Drawing a deep breath, she moved farther into the house. "Anyone else here yet?"

Maggie shook her head. "You're the first. Although the cookie dough I made is ready to roll out."

Callie carried the two containers of spritz dough, baking sheets and the cookie press she'd brought with her into the kitchen. "Mine is ready to go, too."

Before they could talk further, the doorbell rang, again and then again. The other two couples came in out of the rain, their preschoolers in tow. Callie was still saying hello to the other four adults when the doorbell rang a third time.

Hart went to get it.

"Hey, buddy," her brother-in-law said cheerfully. Callie turned, and her heart did a little somersault in her chest as she came face-to-face with Nash Echols. What in the world was he doing here? At a gathering of preschool kids and their parents, no less?

"Glad you could make it," Hart told Nash, slapping him on the back.

Recognition dawned. Suddenly, she had to know. "Was this what you were talking about last night?" Callie asked Nash, moving closer. When he had off-handedly tried to make plans with her for today, then backed off without ever saying what it was he had been wanting to do?

Nash took off his jacket and hung it up. He was wearing jeans and a gray-and-black-plaid flannel shirt that brought out the dark silver of his eyes Beads of water clung to his face and shone in his hair. Once again, he had shaved closely.

"Yeah. I was going to offer you and Brian a ride, but I could see you wanted to drive yourself." His glance moved over her lazily, appreciatively taking in her cowl-necked sweater and jeans. "And if it hadn't rained, as predicted, I wouldn't be here."

He would have been working on the mountain cutting down trees with the rest of his crew, Callie knew.

He regarded her affably. "So, I figured we'd just each do our own thing."

Which, for Callie, now included feeling warm and tingly all over...

Oblivious to her overtly sensual reaction to their guest, her brother-in-law urged Nash forward. "The Texas game's on. Come on in, let me introduce you to everyone," Hart said. The two men headed off to the family room.

Callie sighed with relief and made a beeline for the kitchen. Taking advantage of the momentary privacy, Callie whispered to Maggie, "Is this a fix-up?"

Her twin scoffed and adjusted the racks in the double convection ovens so three pans of cookies could be baked in each simultaneously. "No."

"Really?" Callie countered. "Because everyone else here is married, except Nash and me, and everyone has a child in the Country Day Montessori Preschool, except Nash. So…"

Maggie pulled an apron out of a drawer and handed it to Callie. "It's just the holidays can be a hard time to be alone," she explained.

Callie knew that better than anyone. Still… Starting any kind of romantic dalliance, no matter how causal, this time of year wasn't wise, either. And if Nash were equally at loose ends—because he had just moved to the area—then it was a doubly bad idea.

"Surely he has family somewhere," she protested, wishing she weren't so attracted to him. Because it would have made things a whole lot easier if she hadn't wanted to kiss him again.

Maggie got a funny look on her face as her glance drifted to a point behind Callie. "Actually—" she stammered.

"My parents live in Japan these days," Nash said, joining them at the kitchen island. He helped himself to a can of soda, then lounged against the counter, making himself at home.

Callie luxuriated in the warmth radiating from his tall, strong body. "They don't come back for the holidays?"

Setting the can down, he folded his brawny arms across his powerful chest and kept his glance trained on hers. "Nope."

She waited. To her frustration, no other information was forthcoming. "I'm sorry," she said finally.

His gaze remained steady.

She couldn't help but notice the smile on his mouth did not reach his eyes.

"No reason to be," he continued matter-of-factly. "My folks don't really like Christmas anyway so it's not like I'm missing much by not being with them."

"How could anyone not like Christmas?" Polly, one of the other mothers, asked as she came in to join the conversation.

"Long story," Nash said, taking a long swig of soda.

And definitely not one he planned to elaborate on, Callie noted.

After quenching his thirst, Nash rubbed his hands together and grinned. "So, ladies, what can I do to help?"

The last thing Callie needed was Nash underfoot. Especially when he was looking and smelling so good. Like the middle of a forest after a hard winter rain.

Luckily, her twin jumped in to help Callie get the space she needed.

Maggie took Nash's elbow and steered him toward the adjacent family room, where cheers and sports commentating could be heard. "We're still trying to get set up in the kitchen, so if you want to help the other guys watch the kids…"

"And catch the second half of the football game?" he teased.

"Well—" Maggie smiled, like the gracious hostess she was "—there is that."

Nash ambled off.

And for a while, all was good. Callie and Maggie filled cookie sheets with dough and slid them into the oven to bake, while the two other mothers set up a decorating station with various frostings and sprinkles for the kids.

They were just ready to call the kids in to do their thing, when a ruckus broke out in the other room. "I sit on *my* daddy's lap," Petey announced loudly. He climbed up on Phil.

"I sit on mine!" Henry clamored up to give Hart a hug.

"This is my daddy," Bobby stated proudly, climbing onto Ted's lap.

Once again, Callie noted, her son, Brian, was the odd man out.

And once again, her next-door neighbor injected himself into the calamity that was her life.

Nash hunkered down beside Brian. "Hey," he said to the little boy in mock indignation. He thrust out his lower lip in a parody of a toddler tantrum and angled his thumb at the center of his broad chest. "I don't have anyone to sit on my lap!"

Brian immediately sympathized. He laced his arms about Nash's strong shoulders, volunteering importantly, "I do it!"

"Well, thanks, buddy." Nash scooped Brian into his arms, stood and carried him over to an armchair.

Before Callie could do so much as send Nash a grateful glance, her son looked into Nash's eyes and asked loudly enough for everyone in the room to hear, "Are *you* my daddy?"

No, Nash thought, feeling the weight of the adorable little boy in his arms, *but at this moment I'd sure like to be.*

Before he could respond, Callie rushed forward, a stricken expression on her face. She handed her son a pocket-size version of the same photo she had shown him the day before. "Seth is your daddy," she reminded gently.

Brian scowled and shoved the photo away. "Don't want heaven!"

Nash couldn't blame the little boy. Knowing a loved one was in an unreachable place far away was no comfort at all. Although he didn't blame Callie. She had to tell her son the truth about Seth from the get-go. Especially now that Brian was old enough to start noticing other kids had dads around to love them, when he did not.

"Want *this daddy*," Brian continued, wrapping his arms around Nash's neck and snuggling close.

Callie flushed all the more. "Honey, Nash is not your daddy."

"I'm your friend," Nash added.

"Friend *and* daddy," Brian bartered with perfect two-and-a-half-year-old logic. He squinted up at Nash, persisting, "Like story…?"

Nash had no clue what Brian was talking about. Nor did anyone else. Except Callie, whose cheeks went from hot pink to sheer red. "I think he's talking about one of his favorite storybooks. It's about a baby bird, who is looking for his mom, and asks all the other animals if they are his mother before he finally finds her…" Her voice trailed off.

Suddenly, all the other parents seemed to know what she was talking about, Nash noted, as they nodded their heads in unison.

"Yeah, that's a great one," Polly said.

Appearing happy someone understood where his question came from, Brian turned back to Nash.

"Are you my daddy?" the little boy asked again, even more determinedly.

Really seeming to mean, Nash thought, *will you* be *my daddy?*

And he had absolutely no idea what to say to that.

Luckily, the team they had been rooting for scored. A cheer went up on the TV, along with excited chatter from the sports announcers and lots of on-field celebration by the players. Everyone, including the children, were momentarily distracted by the on-screen commotion.

Callie wasted no time clapping her hands together. "Okay, boys! Is everyone ready to decorate the cookies for the firemen and the policemen?"

When enthusiastic shouts filled the air, Maggie and the other moms shepherded the kids toward the kitchen. Callie paused to shoot Nash a grateful look, then went to join the others.

The rest of the afternoon went smoothly.

And, to Nash's relief, Brian seemed to forget all about wanting a daddy who was not in heaven.

He decorated the cookies with cheerful zeal, and then played well with the other kids and the adults present. By dinner time, though, the little boy was sagging with exhaustion and looking on the verge of another meltdown.

And though Maggie and Hart invited them all to stay for dinner, to Nash's disappointment, Callie declined the invitation and coaxed Brian into his coat with the promise of his favorite music on the drive home.

Dutifully, the two said goodbye to everyone, then Brian came back to give Nash an extra hug. His heart swelling, he crouched down to accept it. Damn, the little fella sure was cute.

"Friend *and* daddy," Brian declared stalwartly, looking Nash right in the eye while patting his arm.

Nash wished.

Callie had just settled Brian into his toddler bed when the doorbell rang. Pausing to adjust the covers over his contentedly sleeping form, she went downstairs. A look through the viewer confirmed her suspicion.

She swung open the door. Nash stood on the portal, looking handsome as ever in a sheepskin coat and Stetson. He had a large take-out bag from a popular Tex-Mex restaurant in his hand, a hopeful grin on his ruggedly chiseled face, the rain still pouring down in sheets behind him.

This made it the third evening in a row he had shown up at dinnertime.

And though she knew she shouldn't be happy to see him, she secretly was.

"I took a chance you hadn't had dinner yet," he drawled.

Deciding not to make things too easy for him, Callie lounged in the portal and folded her arms in front of her. "Depends on whether you count a bite of my son's macaroni and cheese."

He mimed horror. "Definitely not."

Because the aromas coming from the bag smelled too good to resist, she stepped back to usher him inside. "Come on in."

He took off his hat and flashed her a sexy grin. "Don't mind if I do."

"So you didn't stay for dinner at Maggie and Hart's, either, I guess?"

His hand brushed hers as he handed her the bag. "A little awkward, don't you think? Me being the only single adult left?"

She sighed, knowing all too well what it was like to be included out of duty or pity…or both—especially at this time of year. "People mean well."

He took the bag from her, their fingers brushing again, and followed her into the kitchen. "I know. And I do appreciate the sentiment behind the gesture."

"So why did you really show up there today? And don't tell me that it was the football, because you didn't seem all that interested in the on-field action to me."

"Hey, I went to Texas A&M, so to root for the Texas Longhorns…"

"Would be blasphemy, I know. But you didn't answer my question. Why did you show up there today?"

He flashed her another smile. "You."

She studied his handsome face and tall, muscular frame. He was who he was, take it or leave it. She tried not to think how much they had in common that way. "You felt sorry for me?"

"I wouldn't say pity entered into it. At all."

Oh, dear. Telling herself she needed to be driven more by practicality than emotion, she said, "So if not pity, then…?"

His gaze turned tender. "I want to get to know you," he said softly. "And Brian, too."

Now she was *really* in trouble.

Callie cleared her throat. "Speaking of which… I do owe you for coming to our rescue before."

He lent a hand as she began to set the table for two. "No problem."

"So what's this?" He pointed to the to-do list labelled For Brian's Christmas that she had left on the kitchen table.

"A compilation of all the activities I have planned for him in December."

Nash picked up the list and read, "Go to see Santa. Take a tour of the lights. Help decorate the gingerbread house. Figure out a way to see snow. Bake cookies. Go caroling. Decorate the tree. Make presents—"

"I thought it would be more meaningful than buying something."

"Wrap presents."

"He can help."

Nash handed it back to her, clearly not as impressed as she would have hoped. "That's a pretty ambitious list."

Callie nodded, sober now. "I figure if I can keep Brian busy enough he won't have time to think about not having a daddy." At least that was the plan.

"And what will staying this busy do for you?" Nash asked.

Good question, Callie thought. "It will help me get through the holidays." With my heart intact.

He studied her through narrowed eyes. "Is that all you want? Just to *get through* the holidays? Not really enjoy them?"

Callie gave him a droll look, not surprised he was back to challenging her again. "Of course I want to enjoy them." With a beleaguered sigh, she pulled several tinfoil trays with cardboard lids and heating instructions from the bag, as well as a bag of chips and containers of queso and salsa. "What I don't know is, what I am going to do about Brian's desire for a daddy."

Solemn now, too, Nash asked, "What do you mean?"

Glad she had someone who could be objective to talk with this about, Callie reached into the fridge and pulled out two long-necked bottles of Texas-brewed beer and a single lime. While she quartered the lime, Nash twisted off the caps. Finished, she traded a beer for a lime wedge. "I've tried and tried to explain to him that Seth is in heaven, but he just doesn't get it." With a frown, Callie pushed the lime down into the beverage and watched as Nash did the same.

They clinked bottles in a wordless toast and took a sip.

Because Nash was so understanding, she went on, "I put a photo of Seth next to Brian's bed. And I carry a laminated one in my purse for him to look at whenever the subject comes up. Which recently has been a lot. I've even read him this storybook about it."

Callie slid the dinners into the oven to warm, then went off, returning with the aforementioned picture book. "I've read this book to him and told him what a wonderful place heaven is…that he will see his daddy there one day, when it's time." Her throat suddenly began to ache, and she took another small swallow of beer. "But he doesn't want to hear it."

Nash opened up the fresh bag of tortilla chips, then the dips. "He is pretty young."

"I know that." Callie scooped some warm, savory melted cheese with tomato, jalapeno and onion onto a crispy tortilla chip. "I don't expect him to understand the finality of death. The fact is that children don't really begin to comprehend that until they are at least eight years old. But I do know that Brian can hear a story, get the gist of it and recall it later. Even apply the facts of it to something else."

Nash sat opposite her, his knees nudging hers beneath the table. "Like the search for a mommy morphs into the search for the daddy."

Callie sighed and rested her chin on her hand. "Right."

Nash reached over and tucked a strand of hair behind her ear. "He's pretty smart for a two-and-a-half-year-old."

"As well as determined." Callie sighed and sat back. She pulled the edge of the paper label from the bottle, then gave up when it refused to budge more than a quarter inch.

Once again, she leveled her gaze on Nash. "I just don't know how to give my son what he needs."

He reached across the table and took her hand in his. "I think you already are. You love him. You care for him." He made an inclusive gesture at the cozy environment. "And provide for him." Then he pointed to her holiday to-do list for her son. "And he's certainly not short on new experiences."

Callie bit her lip. "But I still can't give him a daddy."

And Brian was unwilling to settle for less.

"Yet." Their gazes met, held. "One day you will," Nash promised.

Callie smiled, despite herself. "You seem awfully sure of that," she noted wryly.

He regarded her with utter certainty. "A woman as beautiful and talented as you are is not going to stay single for long, wedding rings still on her finger or not."

"Somehow I knew you'd get around to bringing that

up," she shot back. Then paused to let her next words sink in. "And no, I'm not going to stop wearing them." Blushing, she got up to check on dinner, even though she knew it wasn't quite heated through yet.

Nash tilted his head to one side. "I figured as much."

But it didn't seem to deter him, Callie noted.

Not at all.

Chapter 6

"So, not so much as a good-night kiss?" Maggie asked when she and Callie chatted on the phone the next day. In the distance, the whine of power saws continued unabated. Nash Echols and crew had been working since shortly after dawn.

Imagining they would go until dark, Callie replied, "No. We just ate and talked, and then he told me to call him if I needed anything and headed out."

"At least tell me you enjoyed yourself."

Enjoyed herself hadn't been the half of it, Callie thought. She had loved every second she spent with him. Even when he was challenging her on the fact she still wore her wedding rings.

Speaking of which… Callie looked down at her left hand. It had been itchy and uncomfortable since she had gotten up that morning. The irritation seemed the worst on the third finger of her left hand.

"Have you ever had a rash around your rings?" she asked her twin.

"Only that one time, when the guy I was dating in high school gave me a fake-silver-finish friendship ring. Remember? It turned my finger green?"

Callie laughed, thinking back to their relatively stress-free childhood. "I do, actually."

"Why? Do you have a problem?"

"Not really." Callie brushed it off. "I think my hands are just dry from the winter weather. I'll put some extra hand cream on. That should take care of it."

"So…are you ready for your first event tomorrow?" her twin asked.

Callie smiled. At least one thing in her life was going exactly the way she had planned. "Yes, I am." The bunkhouse was already set up for the eight executives and their staff.

"I'll pick up Brian at preschool and keep him overnight, the way we agreed."

"Okay. But let me know if there are any problems," Callie told her. "The meeting will break up around 9:00 p.m., so if Brian can't settle down to sleep, I can come and get him then."

"Will do," Maggie promised. "And, Callie? Good luck!"

As it turned out, luck was not needed. The group arrived on time, was relatively undemanding and left shortly before eight that evening.

Nash had kept his word, too. There hadn't been a single inkling of any tree-cutting the entire day.

Happy everything was proceeding smoothly once

again, Callie called her sister to see how things were going with the boys. She was relieved to learn they had gone to bed at seven and fallen asleep right away. Maggie urged Callie to enjoy the night off. Callie promised to do so, thanked her sister and hung up the phone. She looked around another long moment.

The evening stretched ahead of her.

Without Brian there, without Nash just dropping by, the house was suddenly oddly quiet.

In that instant, Callie realized she had never felt lonelier in her life.

Which meant there was only one thing to do. She released a determined sigh. *Get back to work.*

A half mile down the road, Nash was just stepping out of the shower when he heard the email notification on his laptop ring. Wrapping a towel around his waist, he padded into the bedroom and saw the message from Callie. Instead of writing her back, he picked up the phone instead. She answered on the second ring, her voice every bit as soft and alluring as he recalled.

More enamored of her than ever, he said, "You wanted to talk to me about the Christmas Festival?"

"I know it's another three weeks away, but I really need to get information about your business, so I can put together a brochure showcasing everything Echols Mountain has to offer. Is there some time in the next day or two you can meet with me in person?"

His spirits rose. "How about right now?" he asked, opening his bureau drawer.

"Sure, why not. You want to come here?"

He grabbed his boxer briefs and socks. "Be there in ten."

It was more like seven. Three of which were spent driving from his ranch to hers.

Callie opened the door wide. Her hair was a silky cloud of dark curls that ended just above the nape of her neck. Smiling appreciatively, wishing he could haul her into his arms right then and there, his eyes drifted down over her delectable curves. She was clad in a red sweater dress that covered her from neck to knee, and sheer panty hose adorned her spectacular legs. A pair of big fluffy reindeer slippers covered her small, dainty feet.

He grinned. "Like your shoes."

She facetiously modeled her footwear. "Brian and Henry picked them out for me last Christmas. They were so comfy I've made them my official holiday slippers."

For someone who claimed not to be able to really celebrate Christmas, she sure looked happy now. Nash shrugged out of his coat and hung it on the rack. He ran his fingers through his still-damp hair. "Speaking of Christmas, what's that incredible smell?"

"Gingerbread." She grinned and walked him into the kitchen. "I'm trying to get the underlying cardboard house assembled tonight, too."

He knew nothing about either baking or constructing the traditional confection. However, it didn't mean he wasn't willing to lend a hand. "How's it going?" he asked casually.

She looked at the collapsed cardboard walls of the chalet-style building. "Not all that well, as you can see. Any ideas how we could stabilize it?"

Nash moved nearer. In the process he got a whiff of the flowery shampoo she used in her hair. Turning his attention back to the matter at hand, he studied the flaws for a moment. "I think I would double or triple up on the cardboard frame, and use a stronger tape to hold it all together."

"Okay, I'll gather up what we need from my office. In the meantime, how about you have a seat and go through some of these marketing brochures." She handed him a clear plastic storage box, her delicate fingers briefly brushing his in the process. "Pick out a few that appeal to you."

There was an impressive selection. All sizes, colors, fonts. Even the presentation seemed different in all. To the point if she displayed them all, side by side on a rack, each one would still stand out as unique. "Did you do all of these?" he asked.

"Mmm-hmm." She disappeared, and then came back with tape, scissors and extra cardboard. She disassembled the house, then began tracing the individual pieces she'd already made onto other pieces of cardboard with a pencil. "I'm putting together brochures for the local businesses participating in the festival. They'll be tucked into the gift baskets the guests take home with them."

Finished, she cut out the identical cardboard components along the previously traced lines.

He slid his glance to her once again. "What kind of information do you want?"

Another small, inviting smile. "Whatever you'd like to include. How you came to own Echols Mountain, for instance."

"My great-uncle Ralph Echols was like a grandparent to me. As a young kid, my family visited him every summer. When I got older, I spent longer periods at the ranch, even worked there from time to time."

"Did you always want to be in the tree business?" she asked curiously.

"I started thinking about it when I was about eighteen. My uncle said if I was serious, I needed to get a degree in forestry—which I did—and then spent ten years working in the industry in forest management." He paused. "I saved every penny I could while I was working in the Pacific Northwest. I was just getting ready to come back to Texas for good when my uncle died and left the place to me."

"Do you have any plans for the mountain besides selling Christmas trees and landscape plants?"

"I want to selectively harvest some of the pine for furniture and flooring companies, while keeping conservation in mind."

"In other words, you can't cut down too much."

"Or too little." As his uncle had, toward the end.

"Do you think you could write a few paragraphs explaining that in layman's terms? Because honestly, I think that is a pretty major selling point for your business."

"Sure."

Nash picked out a couple of small brochures with color photos. All the while, he thought long and hard about what the ranch meant to him, how it had only been known for providing Christmas trees in the past—and for the past five years, not even that.

"Maybe I could take some pictures of the mountain, too? Show how the forest has evolved during the time it lay fallow? How, as a business, we can take advantage of that to make the woods even more productive while remaining environmentally sound?"

"That's *exactly* the kind of information I need to have

to devise a solid marketing brochure for you," Callie enthused, just as the kitchen timer went off. After removing the gingerbread pans from the oven, she returned to the table, where the eight triple-cardboard pieces sat, ready to assemble. Her lips twisted ruefully. "Now, if I could just get the house walls to remain upright, instead of collapsing in on their sides..."

Glad to have something to do rather than just sit there while she worked, he grinned. "Let me help you."

Finding it easier to work standing up, they carried the pieces to the kitchen counter. Nash held them in place while Callie cut and pressed the tape. When the last piece of roof went on, Nash let go. So did Callie.

She grinned as she realized it really was standing. "I don't know if it will withstand hurricane force winds... or even the weight of the gingerbread cake slabs, but..."

"Well, there's one way to find out," he drawled. Winking mischievously, he bent down and pretended to see if he could blow it over.

"No!" Callie cried. Laughing, she tugged at his arm and pulled him upright so quickly and carelessly their bodies collided. The softness of her breasts pressed into the wall of his chest. Lower still, she was just as malleable and feminine.

Just that swiftly, the playful contact turned into something else. She looked into his eyes. He looked into hers. And then did what he had been wanting to do ever since the last time he'd held her in his arms.

Callie knew Nash was going to kiss her. Knew all the reasons why she shouldn't let him. However, her will to resist faded when his mouth covered hers. Throwing caution to the wind, she rose on tiptoe and pressed her lips to his. They were hot and supple, wickedly sensual and possessive. His body tautening, he drew her closer yet. His hands slid down her spine, flattening her against him and guiding her deep into his embrace. And still his tongue explored her mouth, laying claim to her inner recesses, again and again, until passion swept through her and she released a small moan. Of pleasure. Of need. Of the wish to be closer.

She had never given much thought to her own needs. Her own desires. But being with Nash made her want to change all that. He made her want to do something for herself, instead of just everyone else. He made her want to give in to the moment, just for a little while. Explore the proof of his desire. She arched against him, wanting and needing so much. To be held. Touched. Kissed. Loved. And though love, per se, wasn't exactly in the equation, a feeling of femininity swept through her, intensifying the yearning she felt deep inside. She wrapped her arms around him, holding him so close they were almost one, her pulse pounding, her breasts rising and falling with each breath she took.

"Callie," he whispered against her mouth.

Reluctantly, she drew back and opened her eyes. Said what was on her mind. What she refused to let encompass her heart. "Let's go upstairs."

Nash knew he was going to make love to her. He just hadn't figured it would be tonight. He was pretty sure from the stunned, yet somehow dreamy, expression on her face, she hadn't bargained on it, either. And that, more than anything, gave him pause.

"Callie," he said again. Not wanting this, or anything

about them, to be something she might later come to regret.

She lifted his hand to her lips, kissed the back of it. "I'm not going to pretend I don't want you. When I do." Releasing a tremulous breath, she continued, "And since the times I have without my son are few and far between…"

She didn't have to say more.

He swung her up into his arms. "Which way?"

"Upstairs… First bedroom on the right."

It was, as he would have half expected, a feminine haven. With a four poster bed, pale blue silk bed-linens, romantic chaise. Soothing neutral walls. Plush carpet.

He set her down next to the bed. Still thinking she might have changed her mind.

Instead, her hands went to the hem of her sweater dress. Swept it up over her head. It hit the floor. The panty hose followed. Then the red lace-edged slip. Clad in bikini panties and matching bra, she turned back the covers and sat on the edge of the bed.

She regarded him boldly. "You next."

He knew her striptease had been part of a statement. She was an adult. She wanted sex-with-no-strings. She wanted it now. And she wanted it with him.

So he gave her an equally matter-of-fact show in return. Stripping off his boots, socks, shirt, jeans. And then, for good measure, removed his boxer briefs.

Her eyes widened. "Oh. My…"

Oh my was right. He sat down beside her, unclasped her bra and let that fall to the floor. The instant he lay her back on the sheets, her hands went to the elastic of her panties. He caught her fingers in his. "That can wait."

He stretched out beside her, lowered his head and

kissed her again. Slowly. Reverently. Until her lips were wet and swollen from his kisses. Her hair tousled, her cheeks pink. He shifted her back against the pillows, gathered her breasts in both hands and lifted the lush flesh to his mouth. She sighed in pleasure as he laved the tight buds with his tongue. Knowing this was the surest way to make her feel the connection between them, he kissed his way down her body, across her abdomen, to the apex of her thighs, her navel and back again. Needing her accessible, he swept off her panties, and then found the sweetest, silkiest part of her.

She arched and caught his head in her hands. Perspiration beaded her body, lower still moisture lined the insides of her thighs. She whimpered low in her throat and gave him full rein. He suckled the silky nub and stroked inside her, fluttering his tongue. Her back arched and her thighs fell even farther apart. She quivered as he cupped her bottom with both hands, rose and penetrated her slowly. She closed around him, like a wet hot sheath.

"Nash," she whispered, wreathing her arms around him, her entire body shivering with need. He kissed her hard, still thrusting, claiming, feeling a little like a conqueror who had just captured the fair maiden of his dreams. She arched up to meet him, her response as true and unashamed as he had hoped it would be. He plunged and withdrew, aware of every soft, warm inch of her, every moan, every whimper, every clear declaration of need.

Until there was no more waiting, no more delaying, only the pleasure, only each other. And he went free-falling into the sweet and sexy oblivion right along with her.

* * *

Afterward, Nash felt her pull away. In less than a minute, Callie sat on the edge of the bed, released a sigh and buried her face in her hands. "It's not in me to be reckless."

And yet she'd climaxed nevertheless. As had he...

"But I guess I shouldn't be surprised." Her chin set with customary determination, she got up and wrapped herself in a thick, luxurious, pale blue robe.

Although it covered her from neck to ankle, she only managed to look sexier. Maybe because he knew she was still naked—and quivering slightly—beneath.

She found a brush and restored order to her short, chin-length curls. And continued her litany of excuses, "It's Christmas. I was on a high from having successfully hosted my first executive retreat. And—" she sighed again, even more loudly this time "—I'm lonely. At least in the sense of—"

"Having someone to make love with," he guessed.

She nodded briefly, but did not meet his gaze.

He continued, a tad more cynically, "Hence you ended up in bed with me."

"Right." Callie paused, the edge of her teeth raking across her plump lower lip. She swung back to face him, her troubled gaze searching his face. "I imagine you're a little lonely, too, having just moved to the area."

Nash would have been insulted, had he not just made love with her, and known—firsthand—how completely she had given herself to him. How completely he had made love to her in return.

He rose lazily. Picked up his clothing. Began to dress. "Or in other words, your kicking me out now is nothing personal," he said, his tone as suddenly matter-of-fact as hers.

She drew a deep, bracing breath and flashed a weak smile. "Of course not."

He shrugged on his shirt and, still holding her flushed face firmly in his sights, began to button. "It's the holiday season."

"And why we shouldn't be alone," she swallowed, "with each other."

The slight catch in her voice revealed more than she knew. He sat down on the edge of the mussed covers of her bed and tugged on his boots.

She came closer, her fingers working the ends of her snugly tied belt. She looked guilty, upset, contrite and unapologetic, all at once. "This wouldn't have happened with anyone else."

Nash was not sure why he was so irked. He had known from the outset, when he'd allowed himself to follow her up here, that it would end this way. He stood. "Good to know."

She caught his arm before he could brush past her. "Nash."

At the imploring nature of her touch, his whole body tensed. He looked down at her, jaw set. "I get it. You'd rather we not do this again."

She dropped her hold. Stepped back. Gave him a beseeching glance. "We live next door to each other. We have to work together. I don't want things to be… awkward."

He snorted. "A little too late for that, don't you think?"

Silence fell as their gazes met again.

Callie leaned back against the bureau, arms folded at her waist. "Can't you just accept that I'm confused?"

He shook his head in silent admonition. "You're not the only one."

"I want to go back to being friends."

Was that what they were? He'd felt they were on the verge of a lot more than that. "Of the strictly platonic variety," she added hastily.

The practical side of Nash knew he should say yes to whatever she wanted and get the heck out of there, now. Before the situation got any more complicated. Instead, he followed his instincts once again. Slowly but surely closed the distance between them, drew her close and kissed her slowly, lingeringly, until she melted against him. As he enfolded her tighter in his arms, her right hand encircled his neck, her left hand—the one with the rings still on it—splayed helplessly across his chest.

Once again, he reluctantly lifted his head. "If that doesn't show you we're way past platonic," he told her gruffly, "I'm just going to have to try harder. In the meantime…" He looked pointedly down at the red skin glowing, bright as Rudolph's nose, beneath her wedding and engagement rings. "If I were you, I'd really see what I could do about that."

Chapter 7

The next morning, Callie held her hand up to the camera on her computer screen. "Do you have any idea what this is?" she asked her mom.

Lacey McCabe responded to Callie with the same care and concern she showed her pediatric patients. "It's contact dermatitis."

Glad they could Skype, since her mom was a hundred miles away, Callie countered practically, "But my rings have never bothered me before. What's changed?"

Lacey's glance narrowed, as she continued studying the picture of Callie's hand on her computer screen. "Is it possible you got some soap or some other substance stuck on the inside of the bands?"

"I don't know. Maybe. All I know is it itches like crazy and it seems to be getting worse."

"Do you have the rash anywhere else?"

"No."

Her mom paused. "It could be stress-related, too."

"But only on my ring finger, beneath my rings?" Callie said skeptically.

Lacey's dad appeared beside her mom. He, too, was getting ready to go to the hospital for morning rounds. "Looks like contact dermatitis to me," he concurred.

"What should I do for it?" Callie asked.

"First, take off your rings and take them to the jewelers to be professionally cleaned to make sure there is nothing on the inside of the bands or stuck anywhere in the setting," her mom said. "Then leave the rings off until the rash goes away."

"And in the meantime?" Callie pressed, aware her finger had started to itch like the devil again.

Her dad volunteered, "You might try putting a little petroleum jelly or fragrance-free moisture cream on it to form a protective barrier over the irritated skin. And then wrap the area with a couple of bandages, or some gauze and waterproof tape, so nothing else can rub up against it."

"And be sure you don't get any soap on the area until the rash has cleared." Her mom added earrings and a necklace to her ensemble. "So if you need to wash it, do so only with plain water."

"It should be better in a day or so," her dad assured her.

"But if it's stress-related, it could take a little longer than that," her mom cautioned as she pulled a cardigan over her blouse and paused to adjust the collar. "I wouldn't worry about it unless it spreads past the irritated area. Or gets a lot worse."

"If it does, call us." Her dad knotted his necktie then

slipped on his suit jacket. "We'll hook you up with a dermatologist in San Antonio."

"Thanks, Mom, Dad," Callie said.

"Is everything else okay?" Her mom paused, intuitive as ever. "Anything else we should know about?"

They certainly didn't need to know she'd lost all judgment and had slept with Nash Echols the night before! "Not a thing," Callie said merrily, doing her best to affect a Christmas cheer she still didn't really feel.

Her mom squinted into the Skype camera. "Like a new boyfriend?"

Callie drew a deep breath, as her depression turned to sheer nerves. "I don't know where you got that idea."

Her parents exchanged glances, then her dad said, "Maggie said something about a friend of Hart's last time we talked. Nash Heckles?"

"Echols," Callie corrected, pretty sure Dad had confused the last name on purpose. "And there's nothing there." *That I'm going to call home about anyway.*

Her mother's expression gentled. "Well, just be careful, honey. This can be a hard time of year, you know."

Her dad nodded. "It can be easy to mistake loneliness for something else."

Like lust? Or the possibility of falling in love? Callie told herself she had a handle on the first, and nothing to worry about regarding the second issue. "I know," she said, in a hurry to cut the conversation short before her folks could scout out anything else. "Listen, I've got to go and pick up Brian. He spent the night with Maggie last night—because the event here ran late—and I'm chaperoning his class field trip this morning."

And thankfully, Callie thought, if the sound of mul-

tiple chain saws echoing in the distance was any indication, Nash Echols was very busy, too.

Nash hadn't figured Callie could look any lovelier
than she had the previous night. But when she opened
the door this evening, she proved him wrong yet again.
In a white sweater set and black plaid skirt, her hair
falling loosely around her face, she was a picture of
maternal beauty.

Callie also didn't seem all that surprised to see him,
though he had given her no warning for fear she'd tell
him not to drop by.

He held up the reason for his visit. "Here's the info
you wanted."

"Mommy!" Brian shouted from inside the house.
"Mommy! Need you!"

Without warning, her son came dashing around the
corner and into the hall that ran the length of the stairs,
and into the foyer. "My friend!" Brian said, in surprise.
Hands spread wide and high in the air, he ran toward
Nash and catapulted into his arms.

Nash caught him and lifted him high in the air. 'Well,
what do you know—" he winked and was rewarded
with a burst of giggles "—it is *my* friend, Hortense!"

"Brian," Callie's son corrected.

Nash made a face. "Jimmy-Bob?" He tried again
with comic intent.

More giggles. "No." Brian held up his arms. "*Brian!*"

"Oh." Nash reacted as if he'd had an epiphany. "Brian!"

"Yes."

"Well, how are you, friend?" Nash asked.

"Make candy. House," Brian said, squirming in his
arms. When Nash gently set him down so the little

boy could run off again, Brian tugged at Nash's hand. "Come see."

Nash looked at Callie, a question mark in his eyes.

"Sure," she said, after a small pause. She flashed a faint welcoming smile that was probably more good manners than any sincere wish to spend time with him.

It was better than the greeting he'd expected, however. So Nash grinned back and let her assume he thought she was as genuinely happy to see him as he was to see her.

"Wow," he remarked when they rounded the corner into the kitchen. Thick white frosting and layers of gingerbread covered the cardboard bungalow he and Callie had built the night before. On top of that was more frosting and a smattering of gumdrops and assorted other candy that had clearly been placed by a child.

Nash pulled up a chair and sank into it backward. He rested his hands along the rungs and took a moment to admire the colorful decoration. "Did you do all this?"

"Mommy help," Brian said proudly.

"We've been 'done' for a while now, at least for this evening," Callie interjected, "but I've been unable to convince my culinary assistant that it is time to hang up our aprons and call it a night."

Nash grinned at the way she was talking in code to ward off a temper tantrum.

"Perhaps you could do the honors?" She looked at him.

"Hey, bud, isn't it time you got in your pajamas."

"No." Brian said stubbornly. He picked up a green gumdrop and pressed it onto the top of a red one, already glued to the roofline. With no frosting there, it fell off.

The lower lip went out.

Uh-oh, Nash thought.

Callie picked up the spoon with icing on the back of it. "Here," she said to her son. "Let's put a little frosting on the back of it and…"

"No," Brian pouted. He held the green gumdrop out of Callie's reach, moved around and tried to stick it on a purple gumdrop. Without frosting, it fell to the table again.

Callie reached for it. Brian got to it first. "*Me do it!*" he yelled in frustration.

"Honey, it won't…"

Glowering, Brian let out a rebel yell and pressed the gumdrop as hard as he could into the middle of the roof.

A dent appeared where none had been, and the gingerbread began to crumble.

Brian stomped his foot and began to sob.

Nash picked the little boy up into his arms and carried him across to the not yet decorated tree. "Hey now, buddy," he said. "That happens to all of us and it's nothing that can't be fixed."

Brian cried all the harder.

Callie disappeared for several long moments, but Nash kept talking, soothing as best he could. When she returned, she had a baby blanket and a stuffed pink pig in her arms. She held her arms out to a still sobbing Brian. This time he went willingly.

Before Nash knew it, they were moving upstairs, and he was alone again. Not about to leave until he was sure she didn't need his help putting Brian to bed, he ambled back over to the table and sat down in front of it.

In the distance, the squalling waned, then stopped

entirely. Five minutes later, she was back. "You fixed the roof!" she said, looking both exhausted and relieved.

He put down the spoon he'd been using to smooth the edges. "Didn't I tell you? I was a pastry chef in a former life?"

Looking more frazzled than ever, Callie blinked. "Really?"

"Nah. But this frosting is sort of like glue, as I'm sure you know, and if you slather enough of it on, you can apparently fix just about anything."

Callie drew up a chair and sank into it. "Sorry about his behavior."

Nash shrugged, glad to have things going back to semi-normal. "He's two and a half. I think that's how they're supposed to act." He teased her with a wink. "Especially when it gets close to their bedtime."

A delicate flush crept across her cheeks. "Or past it, in Brian's case." She looked at Nash and sighed. "He was pretty wound up from his field trip today."

Nash nodded, knowing he should go. Wanting to stay. So he lingered as she got up again and went to the stove, put the teakettle on. "Yeah, I heard about that."

Callie tensed. For a moment, she didn't move. "From whom?"

"Hart." Nash waited until she turned to face him again, before he continued, "He stopped by to pick up a few trees for some people in his office. I guess Maggie had filled him in." Unable to resist, Nash grinned and asked, "So how many guys did he identify as his potential daddy?"

Callie should have known a cutup like Nash would bring this up. She covered her face with her hands, still reeling with remembered humiliation. "Three firemen and two policemen. He got a laugh every time, so you can imagine how eager he was to try it again."

Nash stood and hovered closer. "Pretty eager, I'm guessing."

Callie got out two packets of instant spiced apple cider. "Very eager, as it happens."

She ripped both open and shook them into mugs. Looked like he was staying on, at least for a little bit. He watched her as she walked past him to throw the empty packets in the trash. Damn, she smelled good, too. Like gingerbread and sugar, and the special fragrance that was just... Callie.

She peered at him again, this time beneath a fringe of thick dark lashes. As if thinking about throwing him out—before they could even think about flirting or kissing again...

He sobered. "Do you know you have frosting in your hair?"

"Noooooo." Her eyes glittered as if she weren't sure if he was joking or not.

He wasn't.

She lifted a hand to the left. He pointed to the right. She ran her palm over her curls and still missed it. So he stepped forward and ever so gently removed the sticky substance clumped in the strand. Then he opened his palm so she could see what her decorating had wrought. "Hmm."

"What? No thanks?"

"Okay," she said drolly. "Thanks."

"You're welcome. And by the way," he continued, as the teakettle began to whistle, "how come you have no rings on your left hand?"

Maggie switched off the burner and grabbed the kettle. Once again, she managed not to look at him as she filled the mugs. "It's because I'm having an allergic reaction." She stirred the contents of each mug briskly, then handed him his.

"An allergic reaction," he repeated, being careful to hold the stoneware by the handle.

She remained lounging against the counter, some distance away. "Yes. An allergic reaction."

"To me?" He studied her over the rim of the mug. "Or to continuing to pretend to be married?"

"Verrrry funny."

Nash had thought so.

Callie paused. "Turns out there might be something on the rings or in the setting that is causing said allergic reaction."

"Really?"

"Yes." She released a breath. "So when I asked my parents for their medical advice, they told me to take my rings to the jeweler's to be professionally cleaned, and to also have the setting checked."

"And?"

"The jewelry store is pretty busy this time of year, so the rings won't be ready to be picked up for another week or so."

Nash tried not to feel relieved about that. Although he was pretty sure everyone who cared about Callie knew that the longer she was away from those rings, and the now defunct marriage they represented, the better. "So how is your hand today?"

"I don't know." Callie set down her mug and held out her hand. "I haven't looked at it since I put the moisture-proof bandages on this morning. But now that you mention it, it is feeling a little itchy."

He set his mug down, too. "I could unwrap it for you."

A lift of her chin. "Is that the only thing you want to unwrap?"

He moved his brows playfully. "What do *you* think?"

She held up both hands in a gesture that seemed both warning—and surrender. Then slayed him with a look that invited him to do what no one had been able to accomplish thus far—to try to tear down the barriers around her heart, to find the emotionally vulnerable woman underneath. "Nash…" Her tone was soft. Wary. Enticing.

He caught her palm and held it over his thudding heart. "Just a kiss, Callie. To hold us over."

She caught her breath at the sensual intent in his gaze, and went very still. Her delicate brows arched inquisitively. "Until what?"

Nash lowered his head, tilting it slightly to one side, so his lips were just above hers. He threaded his hands through her silky ringlets. "The next time we make love."

Her lips fell apart in surprise. He moved in to kiss her, intending only to curb their frustration and restore humor to a situation that was fast getting out of control. She swayed against him for a millisecond. Satisfaction roared through him. Then her hand came up, pushed on the center of his chest.

She squared her shoulders and drew back, with customary resolve—and maybe a bit of sass, too. "I've got a better idea."

Sounded good. Especially if it meant they were about to head upstairs again…

Aqua-blue eyes sparkling with a light he couldn't quite decipher but was enamored of anyhow, she took his hand and led him toward the hallway that ran from the front of the house to the back. "Come with me…"

Anytime.

Only instead of heading upstairs—to her bedroom—she stopped at the door tucked under the stairs. "Since you're so tall…"

He did have a good seven inches on her…

"And such a manly man…"

Okay, he wasn't sure if she was serious about that accolade or not.

She let go of his hand, opened the door and reached for a red-and-green plastic storage container. "How about you do us both a favor?" The corners of her lips curved mischievously. "And help me finish something that absolutely must be done?"

Chapter 8

Nash stared at Callie, as if unable to comprehend the task. Which, given what he had clearly expected her to ask him to do, was understandable. "You want me to carry storage boxes for you?" he repeated.

"For starters," Callie admitted, pulling out three for him and keeping three for herself. Pretending he wasn't her greatest male fantasy come to life, she shut the closet door with her hip. "All of them need to be taken into the family room. Then I'm hoping you'll volunteer to help string lights on the tree."

He fell into line behind her. "I think it's pretty clear by now I'll follow you anywhere."

Trying not to think of the view she had just inadvertently given him, she turned and arched a brow. "Really, Echols. Still flirting?"

He grinned at her deadpan tone, then responded in kind. "Let's just say you bring out the 'manly man' in me."

Callie couldn't help it—she laughed. If there was ever a guy with too much testosterone...

As if on cue, he set the boxes down and folded his arms across his brawny chest.

Callie swallowed hard. She told herself not to stare, to keep things light and carefree, but it was difficult with him showcasing all those magnificently sculpted muscles right in front of her.

"So is your tree decorated?" she asked, forcing her attention back to the conversation.

Broad shoulders flexed.

"Tell me you even *have* a tree."

Another somewhat evasive smile. "The guys got me one already."

She trod closer. Studying him, she inclined her head. "Why do I feel there's a catch to that?"

His sexy grin widened while he contemplated that. He rubbed the flat of his hand across the bottom of his jaw. "Let's just say it has a lot of personality."

Uh-huh. "Where is it?" she asked.

"Currently?" His expression was one of total innocence. "Standing in a bucket of water on my back porch."

He was kidding. Wait...he *wasn't* kidding. "Echols!" she chided, upset. Even she, with her problem celebrating Christmas in her heart, knew that was no way to treat a holiday tree.

He ambled closer, too, not stopping until there were mere inches between them. "You know I like it when you call me by last name. It's sort of a turn-on."

Figuring the best way to avoid making out with him

again was to get busy again, Callie lifted the lid off a box and pulled out a long strand of white Christmas lights. "Now that I know that," she said dryly, "I'll be sure and go back to Nash."

Callie unraveled one end and handed it to him. He held on to it while she kept right on unraveling. "Back to your tree," she continued. "Why is it on your back porch?"

Another mysterious shrug. "I haven't had a chance to bring it in."

"And if I buy that, I'm sure you have some mountain air you'd like to sell me..."

Now that they'd completely unwound the strand, he strolled over to plug it in. The test worked. The lights all came on.

"Nor do I actually have any decorations." He wandered back to the tree and, accepting her wordless direction, began threading the lights through the top of the pine.

"What about your uncle?" Once again, Callie tried not to notice how his soft flannel shirt stretched across the taut muscles of his chest.

Nash paused, treading more carefully now. "If he had any, I can't figure out where he would have put them, except the attic, which is a pretty jumbled mess. For all I know, he never even bothered putting up a tree himself."

Like uncle, like nephew.

Sensing there was something behind that sudden faint glimmer of sadness and outward cool, Callie asked, even more casually, "You never visited your uncle at Christmastime?" From what she had come to understand, Nash and his folks were all the relatives Ralph Echols had.

Nash moved around behind the tree, focused on his task. "No. Just summers mostly. When we—I," he corrected with a shake of his head, "was out of school and had the time to come and stay awhile." So his parents hadn't visited then, either, Callie deduced, following Nash around the tree.

Silence fell between them as he bent to thread the lights through the branches at midtree.

"What did you do in the summers?" he asked finally.

Callie reflected with a smile and a small shrug. "Survived the chaos, mostly."

He lifted a speculative brow. "Care to elaborate…"

Trying not to think what his low, masculine voice did to rev up her insides, Callie took a trip down memory lane. "Well… My oldest sister, Poppy, was always painting and rearranging and redecorating stuff. My twin, Maggie—whom you now know—and I both babysat a lot. The *triplets* loved spending time at the pool. Lily was on the swim team. Rose worked in the snack bar. And Violet lifeguarded."

Nash blinked. "Your parents had *triplets*—in addition to *twins*?" Briefly, he looked terrified by the notion of all those children and all that estrogen. Which was, Callie admitted wryly, the usual reaction to the knowledge she had five sisters. Five of whom were multiples!

Callie lifted a hand, reminding, "And don't forget Poppy—the only single birth. She gets ticked off whenever she's discounted." Boy, did she get ticked off.

Which made sense. Callie knew it couldn't have been fun to be the regular-birthed kid amidst all that chaos and excitement.

"I guess Poppy would at that." He paused, recollecting. "They all had flower names…?"

"Including me, since my given name is Calla. I just like going by Callie."

He remained flabbergasted. "Wow."

Finished with one strand of lights, Callie went to get the other. "So does this mean you now want to meet all my sisters?"

Nash took the end and they began the same unraveling process. "Depends." He slanted her a wicked look. "Are they all as gorgeous and funny and sexy as you?"

"Subtle," she replied with a grin. "And not at all."

They laughed together, then kept working. The second strand went faster. Once they were finally done, Callie plugged the end into a power strip, then handed Nash a tree-topper in the shape of a star. He plugged that into the existing strands. And suddenly it was all lit up. Ready for her son to help her decorate the next day.

Callie stepped back to admire their handiwork, acutely aware just how much she enjoyed spending time with Nash—no matter what they were doing. She propped her hands on her hips, conscious of the fact that her attempt at staying busy had failed. She still wanted to pull him close and make out with him. More than he would ever know.

She forced her attention away from her fantasies and back to the task at hand. "Hey, that really looks nice. Thanks for helping me out with it."

He winked. "Anytime you need a manly man, you just call. I'll come running, promise."

Callie knew Nash would, which was precisely the problem. She had to get some boundaries erected between them, and fast. And the best way she knew to do that was to forget the personal, yet again, and concentrate strictly on the business.

She squared her shoulders and went to get her work calendar. "Before I forget, there are a few things I should mention."

Clearly intrigued, he met her gaze. "Okay."

"My in-laws are going to be here on Thursday evening."

His brow furrowed. "Meaning what? You want me to make myself scarce?"

"Of course you can come over on a purely professional basis."

"But," he concluded, smile fading, "you'd just rather I not drop in."

His sardonic tone stung. Callie pressed her lips together, tried again. "Doris and Rock tend to…overreact…to things." Which was putting it mildly.

"Like when they said you were going to have the best corporate retreat in all of Texas, right out of the gate."

"They mean well. But…it's a lot of pressure to put on a person, if you know what I mean."

He nodded, beginning to understand. "You think they'd disapprove of our friendship," he said quietly.

Callie walked Nash into the hall and handed him his coat. "I'm not really sure how they would feel." She paused to look into his eyes. "And given how much I have on my plate, I'd rather not find out just now."

His expression gentled. "Understood."

"Thanks."

Nash pulled on his coat and headed toward the door. "How long are they staying?"

"Through Saturday afternoon. They're going to help out with Brian while I host my second executive retreat on Friday, and then attend the organizational meeting for the Old-Fashioned Christmas Celebration at the Double Knot Ranch."

"The Grimes are participating in that, too?" he asked in surprise.

"Doris and Rock won't be working the actual event—they have a conflict on that date. But their company is going to be supplying some of the Texana memorabilia we're going to be putting in the gift baskets. So they will be there Saturday, taking orders and nailing down the details of the giveaways. As a participant, you should be at the organizational meeting, too." She paused, aware this should have been mentioned sooner. "Will that be a problem?"

He shook his head. "My last day to cut down trees is on Thursday. The trucking company will pick them all up on Friday."

She walked with him onto the front porch. The night was clear and cold and filled with the smell of wood smoke and pine. "And then what?" she asked, suddenly reluctant to see her time with him end.

Oblivious to the romantic nature of her thoughts, he said, "I begin cataloging trees and making a list of the native shrubs I'll excavate and the big pines I plan to cut down next spring. But that's a ways off."

Callie nodded, as if she hadn't just been thinking of kissing him again. "So you'll have plenty of time to help out with the preparations for the holiday celebration?" she said in her most businesslike tone.

Nash turned his collar up against the chill and headed briskly down the steps. "Anything you want," he called over his shoulder. "You just let me know…"

Since he had been warned to steer clear of Doris and Rock Grimes, Nash was more than a little surprised to see Doris drive up to his ranch Friday afternoon. He handed out the last of the paychecks to the departing horse and cattle wranglers turned temporary lumberjacks, then walked over to greet Callie's former mother-in-law. She was dressed as eclectically as ever and had an unusually serious expression on her face.

Aware Callie had an event going on next door, Nash asked, "Everything okay?"

Doris nodded. "Mind if I talk to you for a few minutes?"

"Would you like to go inside?"

Doris looked around at the blue sky and unseasonably warm December afternoon, taking in the abrupt but not unusual change in the Texas weather. "It's so beautiful here on the mountain. How about we sit on the porch?"

Nash escorted her to an Adirondack chair. "So what's on your mind?"

Doris wrapped her lightweight shawl around her. "Callie, obviously. And Brian. Rock and I are worried about them."

"In what sense?"

"The holidays have always been hard for Callie since my son died," she explained. "And now with Brian becoming a handful at times as well, Rock and I would feel better if we knew her closest neighbor was keeping an eye on her."

Nash heard the caution in her tone, and felt it, too. "What about Fiona and Frank Sanders—on her other side?" Wouldn't they have been the logical first choice?

"Her sister, Maggie's, in-laws? They're already watching out for Callie and Brian, but they are also awfully busy at the Double Knot Wedding Ranch. And since you're obviously spending a lot of time over at her place now, at least according to Brian…"

"He's mentioned me?"

Another nod. "He seems to think you are the leading candidate for becoming his new daddy." Doris surveyed him carefully, waiting for Nash's reaction.

Doing his best to maintain a poker face, he lifted a hand. "I understand Brian's confused about that story-book of his…and how it might apply to his own life."

Another long, steady look. "He also likes you very much."

"I like him, too," Nash said sincerely. But that did not mean he and Callie were getting married. Especially since she had said more than once that she was dead set against ever tying the knot again. Past romantic experience told him if he were wise, he would take her word on that. Not push for more.

Doris handed him a business card. "Because you're nearby and might be the first to notice if there is anything amiss, Rock and I would appreciate it if you would let us know if Callie and or Brian need anything. We travel constantly for our business, but all our contact information is on the card."

Nash paused. "You're that worried about her?"

Doris hesitated, then finally said, "Really, it's just a precaution."

Then why, Nash wondered, did he get the feeling that it was a helluva lot more than that?

"Got a minute to talk privately?" Nash asked Hart later the same day.

"Sure." His friend led him into his office at Sanders

Security Services. He shut the door behind them and gestured for Nash to have a seat. "What's up?"

"I had a visit from Callie's former mother-in-law this afternoon." Briefly, Nash recounted the conversation. "Do you have any idea what's behind her request?"

Abruptly, Hart looked as if he were about to walk over hot coals. "Callie can't know I told you any of this."

"Okay."

He settled behind his desk. "She came here to have a fresh start."

Nash sat down, too. "What happened?"

Hart picked up a pen and turned it end-over-end. "You know her husband died right before the holidays a few months after she was married, right?"

"Yeah…but I don't really know much more than that."

"Callie was a couple of months pregnant at the time," Hart began. "At first, she seemed to take it remarkably well. According to Maggie, she cried and stuff, but she seemed to soldier on. Stayed in Dallas. Kept working her job. Had as normal a life as possible."

This was beginning to sound ominous. "And then what happened?"

His friend grimaced. "She was at a big Christmas party for her job at some swanky downtown Dallas hotel. And she just lost it. Started crying. Couldn't stop. They had to hospitalize her for exhaustion. Her parents had to come and take her back to Laramie. They got her into counseling. She joined a grief group. Had the baby."

Nash paused to take all that in. Although he knew she was a passionate woman at heart, it was hard to imagine Callie as anything but strong and resolute.

"And was okay after that?" Nash guessed, still feeling a little rattled by the revelation.

"Till the next Christmas. Then the same thing happened. Not as bad. I mean, she wasn't out in public or anything, but again—according to Maggie—she had a pretty bad couple of days."

"How old was Brian then?"

"Six months, I think. Anyway, Callie recovered pretty quickly from that relapse, and she went on with her life, but the word was out she was still struggling to cope with the loss of her husband and she got a lot of sympathy, which she interpreted as pity. You know the drill from your own experiences."

Nash's gut tightened. "Yeah. Grief sucks. And it's even worse when everyone is watching you, ready to rush in at the smallest sign you might not be as 'over it' at that moment as everyone wants you to be."

Hart sympathized, too.

Nash rested his arms on the sides of his chair. "How was she the second year after her husband's death?"

"There was a day or two before the holidays when she had an anniversary reaction, but she talked to her counselor and seemed to come even more to terms with her loss." He cleared his throat. "Especially when she made the decision to start fresh and create a whole new life for herself, first by taking a position with my parents in their business, and then by using Seth's life insurance money to buy her own ranch and start her own company."

"And the third year?"

"Nothing of note this year, thus far," Hart said inconsequentially. "Unless you've noticed something…?"

Aside from a rash on her ring finger and an apparently uncharacteristic desire to have a fling with him? "I wouldn't know what to look for."

"You understand grief."

Better than anyone. How it hit when you least expected it, and that the only thing that really helped was time. And a willingness to recover.

Aware his old friend was still sizing him up, Nash shrugged. "Yeah, but I don't have a good handle on Callie." One minute he thought he understood her, and the next...

Nash thought about the fact he might be dealing with a ticking emotional time bomb. He exhaled roughly. "What do you think all this means? How do you think your sister-in-law is doing?"

Hart lifted a hand. "She's either far enough along in her grief process to be able to accept the death of her husband and not suffer the way she did in past holiday seasons..."

"Or the worst is yet to come," Nash surmised unhappily.

Hart lowered his brow. "For the record, I think she's ready to move on. She's certainly been happier the past few weeks than I recall seeing her in a very long time."

Nash hoped her willingness to get involved with him—even on a strictly physical level thus far—proved that was indeed the case. That if her mind and body were moving on, soon her heart would be, too. Because if there was anything he knew for certain, it was that a woman as spirited and beautiful as Callie was not destined to end up alone.

Curious, he asked, "Is that why her parents didn't want her to leave Laramie and move here?"

Hart nodded. "Jackson and Lacey McCabe worry

Callie might be too isolated at the ranch. Seth's parents feel the same way."

"And yet," Nash noted, "Doris and Rock Grimes apparently support Callie's decision to strike out on her own, away from Laramie."

"Probably because they worry if Callie were to stay in Laramie, she would always be viewed as Seth's widow. And they really want her to marry again. They want their grandson to grow up with a mother and a father in his life." Hart studied Nash. "Is this going to be hard for you?"

Of course his old friend would ask. And of course he would dodge the question in return. "Why would it be?" he challenged mildly.

Another long, telling look. "The similarities."

"Callie is nothing like my parents," Nash declared flatly.

Because if she were, he could not be involved with her. It was as simple—and heartbreakingly difficult—as that.

To Nash's relief, though, Callie seemed more together than ever when he saw her the next day at the Double Knot Ranch party barn. "You're in a chipper mood," he observed as she stepped up to take his measurements for the costumes that everyone working the event would be wearing.

"With good reason." Callie ran the measuring tape from his shoulder to wrist. "Seven hundred and fifty-two people of the one thousand we invited have RSVP'd that they will be attending the first annual Old-Fashioned Christmas Celebration. Plus…" Callie paused to scribble down a number, then moved in to wrap the tape around his waist "...the event at my ranch on Friday was a wild success, with the group so pleased they have already booked three more events. One each quarter, for the next year. With the possibility of an even bigger Christmas bash next year."

"That is good news."

"Plus, Brian and I have had a nice visit with my in-laws."

Nash looked over to see her little boy walking around with his grandfather, hand in hand. "And as you can clearly see, my son has calmed down somewhat from where he was earlier in the week." Callie wrote down a second number, stepped back. "Why are you looking at me funny?"

Nash pushed aside his earlier worry and shrugged. "No reason. Nice to see you so happy, is all."

Callie laughed. "'Tis the spirit of the season," she said lightly. "But you're right." She paused reflectively, her blue eyes sparkling. "I haven't felt this genuinely festive in a long time."

He leaned forward to whisper conspiratorially, "Like you almost have the real Christmas spirit?"

Tensing only slightly, she whispered back, "I wouldn't go that far. But—" she looked around again to make sure no one was listening "—I was going to take Brian to get some pizza and see the light displays in San Antonio this evening." She knelt to get his inseam, the sight of her before him like that almost enough to make him groan.

Clearly having no idea at all what was on his mind, she asked, "Interested in tagging along with us?"

With effort, Nash ignored the feel of her hands brushing against his inseam. "You bet."

* * *

To Callie's delight, her son remained the perfect little angel even after he said goodbye to his grandparents. His exemplary behavior continued throughout dinner with Nash, and then the drive to see the lights.

Nash was on his best behavior, too.

Actually, he appeared a little on the cautious side. Studying her kindly one minute, treating her with reverent tenderness the next.

And that irritated—and confused—her.

She liked the way he challenged her. Made her defend her actions as well as her feelings and come out of her self-imposed safety zone to deal with him head-on. Now, suddenly, instead of going toe-to-toe with her, the way he had from the first moment they had crossed paths, he was starting to treat her with kid gloves.

Why, she didn't know.

Unless it was guilt. Because he thought he had seduced her unfairly. When really it was the other way around...

She figured she would find out later. Or be forever distracted by the shift in his attitude from sexy devilry to the perfect Texas gentleman.

In the meantime, she knew, there was still much to revel in.

So she sat back in the luxurious leather passenger seat of Nash's pickup truck and focused on enjoying the festive sights along with her son and the handsome man beside her.

"Look, Mommy! Santa! Reindeer! Angel, Mommy. Snowman!"

And so it went.

Brian identified everything he saw with shouts of joy.

By the time they got back home, carrying their boxed-up leftover pizza, he was fast asleep in his car seat.

Still fretting a little over Nash's quiet mood, Callie unlocked the door while he carried her little boy inside and right up to his bed. Brian didn't wake while she put him in his pajamas. A good sign he was out for the night.

Callie went back downstairs. Nash was standing in front of the fireplace, hands shoved in the back pockets of his jeans, his jacket still on. He turned to her, every bit the gentleman she had wanted him to be from the outset.

Only tonight, Callie realized, it wasn't his good manners she was interested in. She walked toward him, suddenly not wanting him to leave. On impulse, she kissed his cheek, found her way to his mouth. "Thank you for tonight." She hugged him fiercely. "You were great."

He turned toward her so they had full-body contact. "So were you." Threading his hands through her hair, he bent his head and kissed her again. Slowly and deliberately. Until her mind was rife with all the possibilities she'd been forcing herself not to consider. She wanted a relationship again.

With him.

How crazy was that?

His eyes opened, smoldering and intense. He studied her as if he found her as endlessly fascinating as she found him. Lower still, his hardness pressed against her. And yet, to her mounting frustration, he was still treating her like some fragile flower. Which was the last thing she wanted. *Especially* from him.

"Something on your mind?" she asked finally, easing him out of his coat. Which wasn't easy, since he half resisted her on that, too.

"Yeah." The word was rough, impatient, in the way his touch was still not. "What is this?"

When she tried to evade his dark, penetrating look, he eased her back against the wall. Her heart pounded as he framed her face with his hands. And something unfurled deep inside her.

"Um…sex?" The beginning of what she hoped would be *more sex*?

Nash scowled at her lame attempt at a joke. "You know what I mean," he said impatiently, giving her another long, indeterminable look. "Is this something fun and easy?"

Or in other words, the kind of thing that could end up breaking her heart—if she ever let her heart get involved?

"An actual date?" He continued his litany of choices with a certain unexpected weariness of soul. "The beginning of another one-night stand?"

Which, clearly, Callie noted by his deepening frown, wasn't good with him.

He prodded her with a lift of his dark brow. "Something more?" he asked, the weariness sliding into hope. "Like the beginning of a long-term affair?"

Unable to bear the way he was searching her face, never mind the long-suppressed emotions he was conjuring up, Callie made a frustrated sound. Sighed.

He brought her close and kissed her again, even more persuasively. Until her breasts pearled and her knees weakened. Then he made his way down her throat.

Still a force of masculinity and stubborn resolve, he continued to persist.

"Or something a lot less…?"

It sure felt like a *lot*.

Except not less…more.

So much so, it felt like she was on the brink of falling in love.

But not wanting to say that out loud for fear of exposing herself to heartbreak again, she shook her head, looked deep into his eyes and coaxed a smile from him instead.

For reasons she told herself she was just going to have to accept, Nash seemed to be wanting reassurance that she would be okay no matter how this attraction of theirs turned out.

And now that she finally knew how strong she was, that was something, Callie realized, she could actually give him.

"I don't know what this is, Nash." Her back still against the wall, she reached up and kissed him in return. Reveling in the hot, male taste of him, she admitted, "I'm doing my best to try to figure it out. In the meantime, I'm not about to confuse sex and love. And…" Callie flattened herself against him, ready to let herself need —to feel—just a little bit. "Neither should you."

His body relaxed in relief. "Sure?"

"Positive." Determined to prove she spoke the truth, Callie molded her mouth to his, savoring his heat and strength, the fact he was so big and tall and male. So upfront about his desire for her. Yet so willing, when he let his guard down, too, to let her call the shots and set the pace, if that was what she wanted.

She sighed, inhaling the brisk, wintry scent of his cologne, the unique masculine fragrance of his skin. Then set about to show him how truly unfragile she was. And got his deep, steady pursuit, his ability to make her practically burst into flames with just a kiss, instead.

She didn't know why she was so surprised he had taken what she started and commandeered this for his own. When Nash put his mind to something, he persevered with single-minded concentration. And when he wanted to tease her to distraction, and maybe start to seduce her in the process, well, he did that, too.

Excited to have him finally reacting the way she wanted him to, she fisted her hands in his shirt and rose on tiptoe, aware that once again she was incredibly, amazingly alive.

As was he…

Dear Lord, so was he.

His mouth continued working little miracles, first on her lips, then her jaw, down her throat, to the *U* of her collarbone. She shuddered against him, wanting him desperately, trembling with need. Then he kissed her again, until he was breathing as raggedly as she was.

He slipped a hand beneath the hem of her sweater, past her bra, to the top curve of her breast. Her body melted into the possessive caress.

He drew back to look at her. Smiling now. Definitely reassured. "Figured it out yet?"

She grinned at the return of his playful side. "Figured what out?"

He found her nipple, caressing it so gently she moaned.

"What this is."

"Still working on it," she promised, kissing him again, and jumping back into life.

"Me, too," he murmured back, sounding every bit as intent on finding intense satisfaction as she was.

Callie laughed. "That and more," she said coyly.

Bodies on fire from the inside out, still making out, they slow-danced their way through the living room, up the stairs, down the hall, to her bedroom. Behind the locked door, in the soft lamplight of her bedroom, they faced each other yet again.

And Callie knew.

None of this was simple, not at all. But at least she had one thing.

Somewhere in the past fifteen minutes, Nash had stopped treating her with kid gloves.

Nash let her tug her sweater over her head just because it was so exciting to watch her begin a deliberate striptease. He took over when it came to her bra. Her breasts were round and luscious, the nipples a deep impertinent rose. He bent his head, resolved to cherish and care for her the way she deserved. She tasted every bit as good as he recalled, and he moaned, taking her all the way into his mouth. She quivered against him, holding him close, urging him on.

Heart racing, he found the zipper to her jeans. When they were both naked yet again, he backed her toward the bed. He kissed her long and hard and deep, until she made that helpless sound, low and soft, in the back of her throat, the sound that said she knew how much he wanted her and always would, and his own blood began to boil.

Determined to make her his, he knelt before her, positioning himself between her legs, stroking the silken insides of her thighs and the satiny petals until dampness flowed. Over and over, his fingers made lazy circles, moved up, in, his lips hotly, rapaciously tracing the sensual trail. She arched, bucked, suddenly right where he wanted her, shuddering with release, pleading, murmuring his name.

Eager to please her even more, he drew her down onto the bed.

"My turn," she rasped, moving over him. Giving him everything he wanted, her fingers, hands, lips roving over him, laying claim to every sensitive ridge and plane.

Taking his time, making it last, he lifted her over the top of him. Straddling him, she gave him full rein, her back arching as he slowly, deliberately penetrated her, her thighs falling even farther apart.

Until he was aware of every soft, warm inch of her, inside and out. Every sigh of surrender and pulsation of need. Until there was no more reason, no more holding back, nothing but pleasure for both of them. Only a sweet, swirling oblivion that led to the most magnificent peace Nash had ever known.

For long moments, they held each other tightly, still shuddering, breathing hard.

This time, when she collapsed against him, her face pressed against his neck, she didn't pull away. Loving the warmth and softness of her, he stroked one hand through her hair, cuddled her closer still.

Finally he lifted his head and, unable to resist, said, "Just out of curiosity…*is this* a date?"

She laughed, as he meant her to. And continued looking at him as if she, too, felt connected in a very fundamental way.

"Not sure about that, either," she drawled, looking

every bit as strong and resolute as he had estimated her to be.

Gently, she rubbed her palm across his chest. "What do *you* think?" Her hand came to rest in the region of his heart. Her gaze grew as tender as her voice. She waited for his response.

"It's definitely something," he proclaimed tenderly. And to prove it, he rolled so she was beneath him, and made love to her all over again, even more slowly and thoroughly this time.

Although Callie was tempted to stay wrapped in Nash's arms and fall asleep, she knew it would be too confusing for her son to find *his friend Nash* there in the morning.

And maybe, despite the depth and breadth of her attraction to Nash, too unsettling for her, too. Because although she knew she was ripe for "just an affair"— and a possibly short-lived one at that, given how confused things still were—she wasn't sure Nash was. So as soon as her aftershocks faded, she extricated herself from his arms, rose, slipped on a robe and went to check on her son.

To her relief, Brian was sleeping soundly.

Restless, she went back downstairs, where the lights were still blazing. Realizing she was starving, she found her way into the kitchen.

Seconds later, Nash joined her. Barefoot, jeans on and unsnapped, unbuttoned shirt hanging loosely across his broad shoulders, he looked sexy, disheveled and tender as could be.

Her heart took a telltale leap, then constricted with

the equally potent fear that she was getting in too fast, too deep.

"Missed you."

"Couldn't sleep," she fibbed.

He ambled closer, wrapped a possessive arm about her waist and pressed a kiss on the top of her head. "Without you, neither could I." He looked around and saw she was already preheating the oven. "So. What's going on?"

"I'm hungry. How about you?"

He nodded. Waited. As if knowing there was a lot on her mind.

Callie sighed. "I thought I would feel guilty when I finally made love with someone again." She layered the leftover pizza on a baking sheet and slid it in the oven. Going to the fridge, she brought out a couple of Texas beers and two slices of lime. Maybe it was time to relax.

He accepted the drink with a wordless look of thanks. "And did you?"

"A little." Callie paused to work the citrus wedge into the neck of the bottle. "The first time." She'd also been pretty confused.

He untwisted the cap on his and took a sip of the golden brew. "And now?"

Callie drew a breath and said honestly, "To my surprise, I'm not at all conflicted." She felt, as odd as it might sound, that the two of them were fated to be together.

"And that bothers you?"

Callie took another sip of the simultaneously tart and mellow beverage. "A little. I never thought I was the type of person to have a casual affair, or to make love without being in love, but…"

Setting his beer aside, he hooked his foot beneath the rung of the chair, sank down into it and pulled her onto his lap. His hands moved soothingly up and down her spine. "Keep talking."

Callie settled cozily on his thighs and wreathed her arms around his strong, warm shoulders. "I really like being with you." She smiled affectionately. "And Brian enjoys your company, as well."

He lifted the curtain of her hair, brushing against her chin, and kissed the shell of her ear. "I really like being with you and your son, too."

Callie swallowed, as she began to feel nervous all over again. She arched her brow. "Sensing a pattern here?"

His gaze narrowed. "If so, it's definitely one I like." He hugged her close before drawing back again to lock gazes with her. "We don't have to put a label on this, Callie." Gently, he tucked her hair behind her ear. "We don't have to think about what it all means, at least not right now."

Her anxiety beginning to subside, Callie studied him in return. "You're okay with that?" she asked. "Taking it one day, one moment, at a time?"

Nash nodded. He tilted his head and kissed her again, even more tenderly and evocatively. "I am."

Chapter 9

Nash opened the door Sunday afternoon to a very welcome sight. Brian stood next to his mother, a yellow kiddie construction hat tilting precariously on his dark head. A tool belt was slung around his waist. He held a toy wrench in one hand, a play screwdriver in the other.

"Ho, ho, ho, and Merry Christmas!" Callie exclaimed, a bag of goodies in each hand. "We're here to help you put up your tree!"

"Me fix." Brian held up a screwdriver and wrench. He could not have been more serious.

"Long story." Callie shook her head, her chocolate-brown curls bouncing around her face. "Involving a very convoluted misunderstanding that doesn't bear going into. Suffice it to say, this little elf got the idea that your tree needed fixing, and fixing usually involves tools of some sort. And, well, you can see the rest for yourself."

"Actually, little Brian here is not far off the mark," Nash admitted, happily ushering them in.

She blinked. "What do you mean?"

With a wink, he walked them through the house and out the back door, to the bucket on the back porch. "I'll let you decide for yourself."

Callie stopped at what she saw. "That's…"

Aware how pretty she looked, standing there in the afternoon light, Nash couldn't help but chuckle. "The saddest little tree you've ever seen in your life?"

She whirled to face him in a drift of hyacinth perfume. "Well, it does give new meaning to the phrase a Charlie Brown Christmas Tree."

"Beginning to see why I didn't rush to put it up?"

"Um…yeah…actually…" With a slant of her head, she conceded him the point.

Oblivious to their disdain, Brian pointed to the tree, then the top of his own head. "Look, Mommy. Me."

Callie interpreted for Nash. "I think he's trying to say it's his height."

"It is indeed," he observed. "At least on the one side that has branches."

Callie moved around to see what he meant. "Oh! It is a little lopsided, isn't it?"

Exactly why it had made such a good prank.

She sauntered back to his side, standing comfortably close. "How come you haven't gotten rid of it?"

He shrugged. "I felt a little sorry for it, to tell the truth."

"I see…" Callie wavered, as if not sure what to do next.

Nash figured, however, that it was not too soon for Brian to learn how to get into the spirit of the season. He bent down to the tyke's level. "You ready to help me get this tree up?"

Nodding solemnly, Brian held out his toys. "Tools." Then he pointed to his head. "Hat."

"Tell you what," Nash said, adapting the same ultraserious look as his little helper. "I'll get mine, too."

Nash returned with a real hard hat, small hand saw and tarp. "If everyone will step back, just a bit…"

Callie kept her son safely to the side. Then the two of them watched as Nash pruned. Short minutes later, they had the tree in a stand, a fact that delighted the little boy to no end.

His little chest puffed out proudly, Brian "helped" Nash carry the Christmas tree inside and set it in the living room. Afterward, Callie wrapped a red velour skirt around the base, got out the lights, the star and some unbreakable ornaments in red, green and white. Together, they all worked to decorate the tree. It was the most Christmas Nash'd had in years.

"Pretty." Brian beamed.

"Very Christmassy," Callie decreed.

"It looks great. Thank you." On impulse, Nash enfolded them all in a group hug. "This means a lot to me," he confessed in a low, gruff tone.

To his satisfaction, though she refrained from saying as much, it seemed to mean a lot to Callie, too. Nash relaxed. Maybe this was exactly what the three of them needed. Maybe they were all on their way to having their best Christmas in a very long time.

"Hey there, sweetheart," Callie's mom said Tuesday morning, when they caught up with each other via phone. "How are things going?"

Callie switched the call to speaker. Aware it was almost time to leave to take Brian to school, she continued loading the breakfast dishes into the dishwasher. "Good." She thought about the last time she'd made love with Nash, and knew it had been so very good.

"Did you have a nice weekend?" Lacey continued.

Callie smiled, reflecting. "Very." Since most of it had been spent with Nash.

"How did your retreat go yesterday?"

"Really well." Callie told her mom the details while she made her son's lunch.

"And the rash on your finger? How is that doing?" Lacey asked with maternal concern.

"It took a few days to fade completely." But after the second time that she and Nash had made love, it had disappeared.

"So no more itching or redness?" her mom prodded.

Callie held out her hand. Her ring finger was smooth as silk. "Nope," she confirmed.

There was the hiss and steam of the coffeemaker in the background. "Have you been able to go back to wearing your rings?"

Callie listened to the distant clatter and knew her mother was filling her thermal work mug and getting ready to leave, too. "They're still at the jeweler's in San Antonio. I haven't had time to pick them up yet."

"Okay. Well, pay attention when you do start wearing them again."

If I start wearing them again, Callie thought.

"Or if the rash comes back before then," her mom warned, sounding more like a physician now than a parent.

Callie and her mom talked a little more. Her mom reiterated how much she was looking forward to seeing them at Christmas.

"Me, too, Mom," Callie said.

Even though it meant leaving Nash behind.

And that, she wasn't so happy about. But, Callie reassured herself, it was only for a couple of days. He'd still be waiting for her when she got back. At least she hoped he would. They hadn't exactly figured out what they had going—except friendship and a blossoming affair.

Time would tell if it turned into anything more. In the meantime, Callie knew, she had to get her son to school.

Callie had never been one to eavesdrop, but there was something about hearing her name that always stopped her in her tracks. And that morning was no exception.

"Look," Molly Franklin, the head chef of the Double Knot Ranch bakery and catering service said, from inside the party barn, "if Nash Echols were okay with being alone during the holidays, he wouldn't have invited himself to Callie's for Thanksgiving dinner."

Callie's twin, Maggie, spoke up, her voice loud and clear. "It wasn't just him. He asked to bring all the men working for him, too."

"Still," Fiona Sanders said, with maternal wisdom, "it doesn't hurt to welcome Nash back to the community, now that he's here for good."

"And introduce him to all the available women in the area, to boot," Ginny Walker, the new assistant manager, chimed in.

"Well, luckily that doesn't include me," Callie said casually, figuring enough had been said on the subject, and walking in.

"Yes—" her twin sister winked "—since you already know him."

Callie put down her briefcase.

She felt obliged to defend the handsome man they were all conversing about. "I know you-all mean well, but I'm not sure Nash is going to appreciate this."

"Sure he will," Molly Franklin disagreed. "And you know why? Because single men are always up for a good, hot, home-cooked meal. And that's all everyone who is going to ask him into their domains is going to be offering him."

Fiona Sanders held up her hand. "There's still a lot to be done for the Old-Fashioned Christmas Celebration. So let's get down to business, shall we?"

For the next few hours, Callie concentrated on the tons of details yet to be ironed out.

By the time she left the Double Knot Ranch, it was nearly noon.

She wasn't due to pick Brian up from the Country Day Montessori Preschool until three that afternoon, which gave her plenty of time to stop by her ranch, grab a few things and head for Echols Mountain.

Nash was right where she thought he would be. Halfway up the mountain, in a staked-off area he planned to work in next.

He had sunglasses on to protect against the glare of a partially cloudy winter day. A knit cap covered his shaggy black hair. Black thermal underwear, a pine-green flannel shirt and a khaki field vest covered his massive chest. Worn jeans and brown leather hiking boots cloaked his legs. He had a leather apron stuffed with rolls of scissors, markers, pruning shears and varied colored plastic ribbon slung around his waist. He was unshaven, sexy as all get-out and so very male.

Her heart leaped as she returned his wave and

trooped out to join him. It was easy to see what he had been doing. He had been marking trees and other native plants and shrubs for harvest, then recording the results. As she neared, he let the clipboard fall to midthigh. "Hey." He hooked an arm about her shoulder and brought her close enough for a quick, casual kiss to her temple. "Didn't expect to see you today."

She knew it was a little corny, but still… She lifted the wicker basket in her hand. "Thought I would bring you a picnic lunch."

"Thanks, I'm starved."

He put down the gate of his pickup truck and spread a tarp, lifted her up into the bed, removed all his gear—including his hat—and joined her. "You going to stay and eat with me?"

"Why, Nash Echols—" she batted her lashes at him "—I thought you'd never ask."

"So what's up?"

Stalling, Callie handed him an overstuffed turkey, bacon, lettuce and tomato sandwich on sourdough bread. She had hoped to work her way into this.

He watched her pour steaming coffee from a thermos. "You have that look on your face. Like you want to tell me something."

Callie spread a napkin across her lap. "That obvious, hmm?"

"Yup."

While they ate, she relayed the conversation she had overheard. "I saw what they've been doing. They've got a whole social calendar planned for you during the month of December."

Finished with his sandwich, he opened a bag of

chips. "Yeah, I know. The invitations have already started coming in."

"So you don't mind?" She found she wasn't nearly as hungry.

Looking more interested in her reaction than what had gone on behind his back, he leaned against the metal side, legs stretched out in front of him. "That people want to socialize with me? Or that I'm considered a catch in these parts?"

Ah, humor. Was there ever a time when he did not use it to his advantage? "I imagine you're a catch in whatever part of the country you end up in." She tried not to sound as jealous as she actually felt.

His brow lifted. Then his gaze roved her languorously, head-to-toe, before returning to settle on her eyes. "To you, too?"

Callie tried unsuccessfully to fight a blush. "You know I'm attracted to you," she said, doing her best to keep her voice calm and steady. "I think I've made that clear."

He nodded, his expression maddeningly indecipherable. "And I to you."

She sipped her coffee, the heat of the beverage a nice panacea to the lingering chill of the wintry afternoon. "What I can't figure out," she continued, as the sun went all the way behind a cloud, "is why anyone would think you would have trouble finding 'available' women to date all on your own."

Nash drained his cup, crumpled up his napkin and put it in the paper sack she'd provided for trash. "Probably has something to do with Lydia," he said.

An awkward silence fell.

Funny, she hadn't allowed herself to imagine him

with another woman. But of course there had been other women.

Was there now, too? Finally, Callie worked up enough courage to ask, "Who is Lydia?"

Nash had known they would have to talk about this sooner or later. Unable to sit still a moment longer, he sighed restlessly and climbed down from the bed of the truck. He paused long enough to give Callie a hand down, too, then walked back out to resume his work. Aware this wasn't an inquiry likely to go away, he said over his shoulder, "Lydia was a woman I dated for five years."

Callie meandered after him, tramping through the undergrowth. "Was she from around here?"

"No." Nash picked up a roll of orange tape and measured off another section of virgin woods. "We met when we were both working in the Pacific Northwest. I brought her home to Texas to propose to her."

Callie ducked beneath the tape to lean up against a particularly sturdy fifty-year-old live oak. "I'm sensing it didn't go well."

"That's putting it mildly."

She shoved her hands in the pockets of her jeans, looking as wary as she had the first time they'd met. He hated seeing her that way.

"And it caught you off guard?" she gathered.

Nash fought the urge to take Callie in his arms and kiss away all her distrust. He also knew it wasn't going to happen unless he gave her the information she was looking for.

Wearily, he shoved a hand through his hair, recounted, "I made it clear from the time Lydia and I first met that I was looking to get married and have a family. She said it was what she wanted, too, once she had established herself in a career."

Callie looked around, found his hat and tossed it to him. "And you believed her."

Inside, Nash's annoyance built. "Yeah, Callie, like a damn fool, I believed her. Right up until the time I got down on my knee, popped the question and she told me that not only did she not want to have kids, but she did not want to actually be married, either."

Callie blinked, for a second looking as confused as he'd felt at the time. "Then why did she ever indicate otherwise?"

Nash sighed. Dropped the roll of tape. Strode nearer. "Because Lydia assumed I was just doing what she had been doing—just saying what people wanted and expected to hear."

Nash paused a moment to let his words sink in.

He looked into Callie's eyes, then matter-of-factly went on, "Lydia was willing to get engaged as long as it never went any further than that. We never got around to actually setting a date or planning a wedding."

Callie rubbed her temples as if she felt a headache coming on. "A lot of people seem to be doing that these days."

He nodded but said nothing.

She trod closer, her eyes soft, serious now. "You must have been really hurt by Lydia's deception."

Nash didn't want her pity. Aware he still felt like a damned fool, he rubbed a hand beneath the stubble on his jaw. He wished he had taken the time to shave that morning. Would have, had he known he would be having lunch with Callie.

He strolled closer. "What made it worse was that I'd told Hart and a few others what I was planning. So when it all went bust, and Lydia went back to Oregon without me, everyone knew what had happened."

Callie wrinkled her nose. "I'm guessing you got a lot of sympathy."

Gazing down at her, he took her hands in his. They were as soft and silky as his were rough and calloused. "Plus well-meaning advice on how to pick 'em next time."

She winced.

Nash let go of her hands. "And that's probably why they all think I need a little 'help' in the romance department." He threaded his fingers through her hair, lifted her face to his. "There is one way to put a halt to all this not-so-subtle matchmaking on my behalf."

"Really?" Color heightened the delicate bone structure of her face. "And what's that?"

Nash took her all the way into his arms. "We could tell everyone I'm already romantically involved. With you."

Another long awkward silence stretched between them.

His pulse accelerating, Nash watched Callie's reaction to his proposal.

Knowing that this was where—if things were really going his way—Callie would leap at the chance to tell everyone they were, if not in love with each other, at least pretty damned smitten.

But if the expression on her face was any indication, he realized with ever-deepening disappointment, she did not want that. Not at all.

Nash pushed aside a sinking feeling of déjà vu. The fact he never seemed able to anticipate when his heart was about to be stomped on. Warning himself not to jump to conclusions, however, he played devil's advocate instead. "Not interested?"

"I'm very interested in you. You know that." Wringing her hands together, she spun around and paced a distance away. Stared down the mountain, to the valley where her ranch sat.

Finally, she turned back to meet his gaze with a level one of her own. "I just like to keep my private life private, that's all. Especially now that I have a son. Plus—" her lower lip quavered "—we haven't...even said...we'd be exclusive. So—"

Nash regarded her in dismay. Was that what was bothering her? She thought what they had was too casual—too inconsequential—to be mentioned?

"You're right." Deciding if it was a fishing expedition she was on, she was going to catch more than she bargained for, he strolled toward her lazily. "We haven't nailed down anything." He caught her around the waist and moved her up against the same broad oak she'd been leaning against earlier.

She caught her breath, and he quantified further, "Yet."

And that, he thought, was mostly because she hadn't seemed to want to do so.

Knowing actions always spoke louder than words, he undid his tool belt and dropped his clipboard. Then, ignoring the look of indignation on her pretty face, he leaned in even closer.

"What are you doing?"

If he didn't know better, he would think it was Callie's heart that was hurting, not her pride. His own body humming with aching, overpowering need, he planted his arms on either side of her so she was pinned between his body and the broad unyielding surface of the oak.

"Making my intentions clear," he told her brazenly, not afraid to put all his cards on the table.

She released an unsteady breath but kept her eyes defiantly on his. "And that is…?"

"To make you my woman." Caught up in something too primal to fight, he kissed her. Once, then again. Until her body softened and she surrendered against him. "I don't care if it's in public or in secret as long as I know that you're the woman for me, and I'm the man for you."

She sighed with pleasure. "I think I could live with that."

It was a start. "Good." He unbuttoned her shirt, unfastened her jeans.

Eyes huge, she whispered, "Here?"

He claimed her supple, hot flesh with the palms of his hands and the pads of his fingertips. "Unless you want to wait?"

His answer came in the speed with which she found his lips, kissed him back. Found the zipper to his jeans.

They kissed again.

And then there was nothing between them but the cold of the outdoors and the heat of their bodies, the swift, searing pleasure that catapulted them to new heights. For once, his control seemed as absent as hers. He didn't hold back, and neither did she. They came, quick and hard. And even after they stopped shuddering, they lingered. Clinging together. Kissing. Prolonging this fierce, intimate experience for as long as possible.

And Nash knew whoever thought Callie was fragile was wrong. She was, in fact, one of the strongest, most resolute women he had ever met.

"Just so you know, I'm going to Frank and Fiona's for dinner this evening," Nash told Callie later, as she was getting ready to leave the woods. "I already said yes. So, if you and Brian want to join me…"

Callie thought about what fun that would be, then the inevitable gossip that would cause, and shook her head. "I meant what I said about keeping this just between the two of us for now. I don't mind everyone knowing we're friends, Nash. That we enjoy hanging out. Or that my son adores you. But beyond that…"

She had a business to run. A past to put all the way behind her. A future to build. She didn't want a hot, sexy love affair detracting from any of that. She didn't want to worry she was jumping headfirst into something else that could leave her emotionally devastated and ripped apart if it ended.

Knowing she would be disappointing him, she cleared her throat and pushed on honestly anyway, "I still want my private life kept private."

He showed no reaction to her decision. "Can I drop by and see you later, then?"

"Sure." Callie nodded, looking down to make sure her buttons were all done up right.

"Although," she added practically, "I can't promise much…" in the way of time or sex "…given how much I have to do."

He walked her to her SUV, lingering long enough

to give her a kiss that was so potent, she could barely catch her breath.

"I promise I'll find a way to make myself useful."

"I'm sure you will," she returned dryly. Looping her arms around his neck, Callie kissed him back, knowing she would be counting the minutes until they were together again.

And honestly, if that wasn't proof she was getting in too fast, too deep, yet again, what was?

Chapter 10

"You look all stressed out," Nash observed the following afternoon when Callie opened the door. Beautiful, but stressed out. When he'd left her the night before—late—after making love again, she had been glowing with happiness. He'd been pretty darned happy, too. But something had obviously changed between then and now.

"What's going on?" he asked in concern.

She let out a beleaguered sigh and reached for his hat and coat. "I took a look at my to-do lists for Christmas a while ago. My work one is reducing nicely, but my personal one is still chock-full of stuff I have yet to tackle."

Nash knew she had scheduled one mother-son activity for every day during the yuletide season. At least it was quiet in the house now—except for the Christmas music playing softly in the background. "What's on the agenda for Brian this evening?"

Callie hooked her arm in his. "He is supposed to be finger painting pictures for both of his grandparents."

Leaning down to kiss her, Nash inhaled a whiff of her perfume. "Let me guess. He's not cooperating?"

Briefly, Callie laid her head on his shoulder. "Actually, the little rascal is overly enthusiastic—*when* I can get him to follow directions—which hasn't been all that often."

She led the way into the playroom adjacent to the kitchen. Brian was standing in front of a child-size easel, a pout of fierce concentration on his face. He was wearing an old adult-size shirt, buttoned up the back. The hem came down past his knees, covering his clothes, and the sleeves were rolled up to just beneath his elbows. A rainbow of colors was splashed all over the paper canvas.

When they walked in, he was focused on the work of art in front of him. The moment he spied Nash, he let out a whoop of pure joy and ran toward him, yelling, "My friend! Here!" at the top of his lungs. Before Callie could intercept him, his hands wrapped around Nash's knees.

Callie gasped as the paint on her son's hands transferred to Nash's pants.

"It's fine," he reassured her good-naturedly, his eyes still on her son. It wasn't often he got such a warm welcome. Was this how dads felt when they came home from work?

Grinning broadly, Nash hefted Brian up into his arms. "How are you, buddy?"

"Good!" Brian transferred even more paint to Nash's

shirt and freshly-shaven jaw before smearing more across the collar.

Nash grinned. "Me, too."

Callie groaned at the mess. She rushed to pull a clean cloth from a drawer. "I'm so sorry, Nash."

He wasn't worried about it.

She dampened the cloth beneath the faucet, then came close enough to wipe her resisting son's hands. "The paint is washable. So if you bring your clothes to me tomorrow, I'll launder them for you."

"Nah. I can do it." Reluctantly, Nash set the energetic little boy back on the floor. Brian promptly ran back to his easel. "Look!" He grinned, proud as could be of the abstract art. "For you!"

Callie refolded the damp cloth so only a clean square was visible, then went to intercept her son. "Actually, honey, that's for Grandma Doris and Grandpa Rock."

"No." Brian ripped off the picture before anyone could stop him. "My friend!" He carried it hurriedly to Nash. "Present! You!"

Nash knelt down to receive it in the spirit it was given. "Well, thank you, buddy." He held the still-damp painting to one side and hugged Brian.

"Want to do some more?" Callie asked.

Brian took Nash's hand. "You help."

The next half hour was spent making more paintings. Nash pulled up a chair and worked on one side of the easel while Brian stood on the other. By the time Callie had her son's dinner fixed, Brian had made more paintings for both sets of grandparents. And a third for Nash.

Nash had made some, too.

A colorfully decorated Christmas tree, with presents beneath.

A snowman.

And a ranch house that resembled her own, covered with snow.

And it was only when they were cleaning up that Nash noticed the unexpected addition to the kitchen trash can.

"Brian, did you do this?" Callie asked, lifting Seth's photo out of the trash.

Her son walked over, took the plexiglass-framed photo that usually resided next to his bed and promptly pushed it through the swinging top on the kitchen waste can yet again. "All gone," Brian announced, dusting off his hands.

"Honey, that's your daddy's picture." Callie fished it out of the trash yet again.

"No. Away," Brian said, even more emphatically. And that, it seemed, was that.

So while Nash sat with Brian and supervised his dinner, Callie did what she always did when confronted with questions on how to care for her son; she consulted with the resident pediatrician and parenting expert in the family—her mom.

Briefly, she recounted the events to her mother over Skype.

"Was he crying when this happened?" Lacey asked. Home from work, too, she was clad in a casual blouse, jeans and sneakers. She had her bifocals on a chain around her neck. Her short silvery-blond hair was mussed from her long and busy day.

"No. Just frustrated. And determined, as usual."

Her mother's expression gentled. "Maybe you should

give any discussions of Brian's daddy a rest for a little bit then. Unless he brings it up specifically."

"Easier said than done when Brian's going around asking every man he sees if he is his daddy. And..."

"What?" On the other end of the connection, her mom continued making a salad for dinner.

Callie swallowed and forced herself to continue, aware she needed advice on this matter, too. "He's starting to get really attached to Nash Echols." *To the point I'm beginning to wish that Nash were Brian's daddy, too. And where would that lead? To more foolish romantic notions? The kind that had pushed her over the edge in the first place?*

"Nash Echols, your nothing-but-trouble next-door neighbor?" her mom asked, her delicate brow furrowed in surprise.

"And friend." And lover. And potential soul mate—if she were ever going to fall in love again.

As loath as she was to lose herself completely in romance ever again, Callie wasn't sure that she even had it in her to fall all the way in love.

Still, there was no denying that Nash was pretty much the exception to every rule she had made for herself upon becoming a widow.

She hadn't needed to make love with him to know that. With effort, Callie forced herself to get back on track. "So, is Brian's behavior cause for concern, Mom?"

"No. Not as long as you respond to what he's telling you and give him the break he needs, while still providing him with a strong and positive male influence in his life..."

Callie breathed a sigh of relief, glad they were still

able to talk like this. Video-conferencing made up for being in different parts of the state. "Okay. Thanks, Mom." She smiled her gratitude.

"And, Callie?"

She hesitated, her finger over the disconnect button. "Yes?"

"I know it's an emotional time of year for you. So please proceed with caution when it comes to matters of the heart."

She should have known her mom would see beyond what Callie wanted to reveal; her parents always had been extraordinarily keyed-in to all six of their daughters.

Callie bit her lip, figuring they might as well discuss this, too. "You're afraid I'll get hurt?"

"I'm just saying you're vulnerable, and you have been since Seth died." She hesitated for a long moment, then continued softly, "Therefore, having Brian act out the way he has been just makes you more susceptible."

Although she was outwardly cheerful, Nash's gut told him that Callie's chat with her mom had upset her on some level. So he asked her about it as soon as Brian had gone to sleep.

Callie settled next to him on the sofa. "She thinks throwing Seth's picture in the trash can is all part of the same phase he's already been going through, and that if I try not to overreact, Brian will relax about not having a daddy, too. At least for the time being."

He draped his arm about her shoulders. Able to feel the residual tension in her body, which hadn't been there when he arrived, hours earlier, he guessed, "You disagree."

Callie turned toward him. "I think the loss is always going to hurt him on some level. I also think it will be easier on Brian if I can figure out a way to give him some sense of his father. Even at this young age. Clearly, a photograph isn't doing it."

Brian savored the warmth of her thigh pressed against his, but tried to keep his libido in check. "Have you tried telling him stories about his dad?"

Frowning, Callie shook her head. "Anything on that level is too abstract for him to grasp. Even if I'm showing him a photo at the same time."

"What about a video?"

She snuggled closer, apparently needing the intimate physical contact as much as he did. "All I have of him as an adult is our wedding video. And Brian was not the least bit interested in that. He barely made it through the frames of me walking down the aisle on my dad's arm."

Nash chuckled. "That would be a hard sell—for any boy."

"Tell me about it."

He rubbed a silky dark curl between his fingertips. "Would Doris and Rock Grimes have anything?"

Another sigh. "Just film taken when he was much younger. Seth is so young he doesn't look like a daddy to Brian. But—" Callie flashed a wan smile "—I'm sure I'll figure it out eventually."

Nash moved her onto his lap and ran a hand down her spine. "What are you supposed to do in the meantime?"

Callie turned halfway to face him. "Make sure he has positive male influences in his life whom he can interact with. Like Rock, my dad, his uncle Hart…"

He volunteered with a smile. "I'm here, too."

Callie's expression fell. "Which is yet another problem," she admitted, "since Brian clearly ranks you way above every other man in his life thus far."

He studied the turbulent emotion in her blue eyes. "That worries you?"

"What if he gets too attached and then we…" She broke off, unable to finish.

Sensing she was feeling vulnerable again, he wrapped his arms around her. "I'm not going anywhere, Callie."

She bit her lip. "You know what I mean."

He lifted her hand to his lips. "I can see you're scared."

Her expression grew all the sadder. "I let myself view the world far too romantically once, and ended up devastated when everything didn't turn out as optimally as I expected."

"I'm not going to die on you, Callie."

She moved off his lap and wandered over to the Christmas tree. The lights were sparkling every bit as much as the star on top. She paused to adjust a small Snoopy ornament. "You don't know that," she said thickly. Nash rose and crossed to her side. He wrapped his arms around her and tenderly kissed the nape of her neck. "So life is a mystery," he told her, drawing back to look into her eyes. "That doesn't mean we can't have a little faith," he said softly. "And hope. And joy…"

She let out a shuddering breath. "Nash…"

He knew she was fearful of loss. So was he. More than she knew. Forcing himself to find the courage deep within, he kissed her again. "Focus on the present, Callie," he whispered against her mouth. "Focus on this. And how we make each other feel…"

The rest would come.

He was sure of it.

* * *

"Well, don't you look gorgeous today," Maggie gushed the following morning when Callie walked into the work party at the Double Knot Ranch. Stations had been set up at some of the banquet tables. Wreath-making at one, assembling yuletide centerpieces at another, gift-wrapping door prizes at a third.

"In fact, you're positively glowing!"

That's what she got for making love all evening long with Nash Echols.

Callie shrugged out of her coat. Comically, she pressed her hand against her cheek and went into a half swoon. "Maybe I'm coming down with a fever."

"Don't joke about that." Fiona Sanders threaded fragrant pine boughs through a metal frame. "The flu epidemic is really starting to take hold in south-central Texas."

"Don't remind me," Maggie moaned. "We've all had our flu shots, except for Hart, who is still putting his off because he's so busy at work."

Fiona scowled. "That son of mine! Do you want me to call him?"

Maggie shook her head. "Hart promised me he would get it sometime in the next week or so."

And Hart always kept his promises, Callie knew.

Just like Nash.

Fiona turned back to Callie. "How are the brochures coming along?"

Callie took a seat at the wreath-making station. She told herself it was because it was a skill she needed to learn, but it was actually because she had come to really love the scent of fresh-cut pine. Maybe because it reminded her of the man in her life.

Forcing her attention back to the business at hand, Callie said, "I've got everyone's done and ready to go to the printers but Nash's."

"What's the hold-up?" Maggie asked.

He's been "distracted," Callie thought silently. *We both have.* "He hasn't given me the old-fashioned photos of the ranch."

"The printer is clamoring for them," Fiona warned.

"I'll get them later today," Callie promised.

"Speaking of Mr. Elusive," Polly said with a lift of her brow. "I hear he's been turning down dinner invitations right and left. Aside from the dinner at your place, Fiona, I don't think he's accepted a single other invitation." She cut off a strand of red Scotch-plaid ribbon and fashioned it into a decorative bow. "You don't think he's depressed, do you?"

Callie kept her head down while she threaded the fresh cut pine boughs through the round metal wreath frame. "Why would he be depressed? He and Lydia broke up several years ago."

Plus, even though he had just taken over the ranch he inherited, his business seemed to be going great.

All eyes turned to Callie. "What do you know about Lydia?" Polly asked.

Me and my big mouth. Callie shrugged as if it were no big deal that he had bared his soul to her. "He mentioned he was almost engaged once."

Another silence fell.

Maggie averted her gaze. A big sign that had Callie wondering if her twin was hiding something, too. She put down her wreath. "What are you-all talking about?"

Abruptly, everyone exchanged glances and clammed up. Like they were afraid to tell her.

Callie waited, not about to let them treat her with kid gloves.

"Because of his family," Fiona said finally.

"The fact they're so far away?" Callie guessed. And promptly realized to her frustration that she had still missed the mark.

"What's going on?" she asked her twin when they were alone. And still got nothing. "What don't I know about Nash?"

Chapter 11

Nash opened the door to Callie at four that afternoon, feeling incredibly happy to see her. Unfortunately, it appeared the emotion was not shared.

He inclined his head at the empty space beside her, aware she had a certain cool fire in her eyes that had not been there the day before. Wondering what had happened since they'd seen each other, he moved to let her pass. "I thought you were bringing Brian over."

"I sent him to Maggie's for a playdate instead so we could get right down to business."

Wow. She certainly did not have lovemaking on her mind.

Callie walked into the great room that encompassed half of the first floor. She slipped off her coat and scarf, and draped them over the back of a living room chair. Opened up her briefcase and withdrew a mock-up for a pamphlet, then turned to him with an officious smile. "The promotional brochures we're handing out at the Christmas celebration need to be at the printer tomorrow." She ran her slender fingers over the print. "Here's what I've done for you so far."

He admired the work she had done. "Looks nice."

Callie kept her eyes on the brochure. "Is all the information accurate?"

Curious as to what burr had gotten under her saddle, he read through the history of the Echols Mountain Ranch Christmas tree operation as well as a brief summary of his plans for the future.

It was as perfect as he had expected, and he told her so, adding, "I like what you've done with the color photos I provided of the mountainside. And the close-up of an actual tree, grown here." He tapped the blank space. "But what's supposed to go here?"

"Two photos from back in the day."

Nash swore inwardly. He'd been so caught up in his budding relationship with Callie, he'd forgotten all about that.

Callie squared her slender shoulders. "I know we talked about you getting a couple for me."

The last thing he wanted to do, when the present was going so well, was go digging through his family's past.

"Do we really need them?"

"If we're to keep with the 1880s theme and the look of every other brochure we're producing for the celebratory event, yes, we do. Unless…" Callie paused, her expression suddenly cagey. "There's some reason you don't want to touch on the past?" Nash sighed. So her brusque attitude was founded in something else. "Who have you been talking to?"

A glimmer of hurt flashed in her eyes. "That's just it." Callie exhaled slowly. "No one will tell me anything. At least not outright. But it's clear something happened here that has everyone worried about you during the holiday season." She held up a hand before he could interrupt. "And it's not anything to do with your breakup with Lydia, either. So don't pretend that it is."

"I'd really rather not go there," Nash said, setting the pamphlet aside. *Not during the holiday season.* He caught her around the waist and pulled her close.

Callie splayed her hands across his chest. "So you'd prefer to keep things purely superficial between us?"

Emotion rose. "There's nothing superficial about the way I view you or our relationship," he told her softly, threading a hand through her hair.

Disbelief tightened the corners of her mouth. She extricated herself, her resentment clear. "If that's true, then prove it. Here and Now. Tell me the truth."

Callie'd had one relationship that was built on fantasy, whimsy and her and Seth's mutual vision of romantic perfection. And while it had been fun while it lasted, such careful idealism hadn't served her well when she was left on her own to pick up the pieces.

If there was tragedy or hurt in Nash's past, powerful enough to make him shut down emotionally, she had to know about it. Otherwise, things would never work out between them.

He gave her a look that told her a wall was already going up around her heart. "We all have our sad stories to tell, Callie. It doesn't mean we have to ruin Christmas by dwelling on the past pain."

There was a time in her life when she had believed

that if something wasn't wonderful, it didn't warrant her time or attention. Living that way, however, had left her woefully unprepared to deal with the harder facets of life.

"So in other words," she said, so disappointed she could barely look him in the eye, "you're shutting me out, too?"

"We can talk about it later."

She knew an evasion when she saw one. "When? January?"

He shrugged, but said nothing more. Clearly, at least in his view, they were done with this conversation.

Outside, the wind picked up. In the few minutes she had been inside his home, the sky had grown dark and gray.

Aware she could not—would not—live this way again, Callie shut her briefcase. Then picked up her coat. "Like I said… I need those photos, Nash." She ignored him as he moved to help her with her wrap. "So if you want to get them for me now."

He did not move.

Which figured. When Nash did not want to do something, he was as unmovable as a two-ton boulder.

Fighting the insane urge to pull him into her arms and hold him close, until everything real—and potentially upsetting—went away, Callie swallowed. "Or if you could scan them into your computer and email them to me by tomorrow morning, at the latest, I'd appreciate it."

Something flickered in his eyes. Disappearing before she could even begin to identify it.

Aware there was nothing more to be said, Callie looped her scarf around her neck and walked out the door. She left, still upset Nash had refused to confide in her. Not sure where to go from there.

And she was still wondering whether she should try to get closer to him or take a big step back when he appeared at her doorstep at nine-thirty that evening. His hair was mussed, as if he'd been running his hands through it. His lips set, strong jaw stubbled with shadow. But it was his turbulent dark silver eyes and stark expression that sent an arrow into her heart.

"Brian asleep?" he asked.

The need to comfort him as fierce as her yearning to see him, Callie nodded. She ushered him in, aware he looked like he'd been through hell in the hours that had ensued. "For hours now."

He handed her a manila envelope. "You'll find everything you want to see inside."

She opened it while he hung his coat, walked over and stoked up the fire in the grate.

There were fading color photographs of a fifty-year-old man standing in front of the Echols Mountain ranch house he currently occupied—albeit a much smaller version of the same log-cabin-style dwelling. "Is this your great-uncle?"

Nash nodded fondly. "Ralph Echols."

The next photo was of Nash, at the beginning of his teen years. Beside him was a kid several inches shorter, with the same thick black hair, rugged broad-shouldered physique and handsome facial features. "Is this your cousin?"

"My younger brother, Rob. He died a few months after that was taken. He was twelve. I was fourteen."

"Oh, Nash." In that moment, he looked so battle-weary, she wanted to cry.

He shoved his hands in his pockets, his body posture indicating he wanted to keep a physical distance between them. "We always went to Colorado over the Christmas holidays," he recounted in a flat, expressionless voice. "My brother and I would head for the slopes while our parents relaxed by the fire."

His jaw tightened. Regret came into his eyes.

Nash swallowed and pushed on. "Because I was older I was supposed to watch out for my kid brother, but Rob was so reckless, and it was impossible to get him to listen to me."

Callie listened with mounting unease.

Nash shook his head, began to pace. "Anyway, we had just gotten snowboards, and we weren't very good with them yet, but Rob insisted we tackle one of the tougher trails anyway."

He paused, mouth flattening, shoulders hunching, as if to protect against the pain. "I should have just said no, but I knew if I did, Rob'd probably just take off and go it alone. So I went with him."

As a good brother should.

Another silence fell.

Nash's gaze grew distant. "A quarter way down the mountain, Rob spun out of control. Went head over heels and landed hard on the edge of his board. His windpipe was crushed and he died instantly."

Oh, my God. "Nash."

"My parents never got over it. And of course they blamed me for not being able to prevent it."

"It wasn't your fault.

"Anyway, after that, my folks never wanted to celebrate Christmas again. So for the rest of the time I was in high school, we always went somewhere else—like the Caribbean—and pretended it didn't exist." He exhaled, regret mixing with sorrow and hurt. "I figured my mom and dad would get over it, come to realize that they still had one son left, but their mourning only got worse as time went on."

He turned to her, the hurt in his eyes so fathomless she felt her own heart turn inside out.

He came toward her. "I couldn't live in a perpetual state of grief. And I sure didn't want to be in the shadow of my brother's ghost for the rest of my days. So they moved to Japan and I stayed here and we talk once, maybe twice, a year. And that's it."

Callie took his hand in hers. "And your great-uncle?"

Nash took her other hand, too. "Was family to me— the only family I had left. And now he's gone, too." He let his gaze fall briefly to their intimately entwined fingers before meeting her eyes again. "Which is why I guess the locals are so worried about me. Because they all know what happened."

Callie wrapped her arms around his waist. Still holding him close, she tilted her head back and searched his face. "But you don't think they need to be?"

He drew her closer without hesitation. "I'm not going to tell you my brother's death doesn't still hurt," he told her quietly. "It does. And it probably always will."

He threaded one hand through her hair. The other remained clasped tightly around her waist.

Acceptance radiated in his expression. "But I'm not going to let that one tragedy dominate the rest of my life. And I'm sure as hell not going to let it ruin every holiday I have from here on out."

He paused to look deep into her eyes. "Christmas is an affirmation of everything positive in this life. I intend to celebrate it every year with every fiber of my being."

The warmth of his body seeped into hers.

"Which is why I don't like to talk about or dwell on what happened in the past. But," he added, with raw apology, "me not telling you created a wedge between us." He shook his head. "I don't want that, either," he said gruffly. "Not when things are starting to go so well."

"I don't, either." Callie moved closer. She caught his face in her hands and their lips fused together in a fiercely emotional kiss. "Nash..." Tears blurred her eyes for all he had been through.

"Let's live in the moment, Callie. Let's celebrate the joy of the season and have faith that everything will work out."

She knew he had not come here to make love to her this evening, and that made the culmination of everything they needed, everything they felt, all the sweeter.

And when at last they came back to earth, she felt closer to Nash than ever. And for now, she realized contentedly, that was gift enough.

"Are you sure you want to do all this?" Nash asked several days later. He strolled into her kitchen, looking tall and indomitable.

Aware that once again, all his raw male power was focused on her, wreaking havoc with her senses, Callie rushed around, trying to simultaneously pack a picnic supper and get their Christmas cards ready to mail.

She handed Nash a stack of envelopes to finish sealing. "I am very sure."

"Because?"

Aware his laissez-faire attitude and rakishly sexy presence could easily sidetrack her into doing something naughty, she worked on trying to find enough postage stamps to keep him busy and her mind where it should be—on the upcoming holiday.

"I've been so busy this week, I've gotten way behind on my list of the Christmas events and activities that I want Brian to experience," she explained. "So this is the only way I can think of to work it all in."

Nash stood at the counter next to her, casually sealing and stamping.

"Besides—" she brought out the wicker hamper, too "—Brian doesn't have school today. My in-laws are coming tomorrow, and they have offered to babysit while they're in town so I can get my own shopping or whatever I need to do done."

Finished, he lounged next to her, arms folded in front of him. Even in a sweater and jeans, he looked impossibly sexy.

"That look tells me you have something specific in mind."

Aware they had managed to make love every day they had been together, Callie basked in the warm familiarity of his gaze. Which was, she admitted, yet another reason why she was so behind this year. She wrinkled her nose at him. "Let's just say 'the elves' may need some assistance putting things together."

His eyes drifted over her. "Looking for volunteers?"

Callie grinned. "Always."

Nash caught her hand and reeled her in. Despite herself, she found herself melting against him when he bent down and kissed her tenderly.

Small shoes clattered in the hall. Nash lifted his head and let Callie go just before Brian came dashing in.

"My friend!"

Nash responded by scooping Brian up into his arms. "What do you know," he teased, "it's *my* friend, Brian!"

Brian beamed, looped his arms around Nash's neck and gave him a big hug. "Go. With?" he asked.

Callie grabbed her son's jacket and knit cap. "Yes. Nash is going with us to see the Christmas All Over the World exhibit at the children's museum. After that we're going to have a picnic dinner in the park, and hear the outdoor concert put on by the all-city children's choir. And then on the way home we'll take the drive-through Christmas lights display at Santa's Ranch."

"Santa Claus," Brian repeated, smiling.

"Which reminds me," Callie said, "we still have to write a letter to him, too."

As it turned out, though, to her disappointment, not everything went according to plan.

The museum was so crowded Brian had a hard time seeing anything, even when Nash lifted him up in his arms.

He wanted his dinner way before the outdoor concert was due to start, and then was so excited and restless he barely ate a thing.

He shouted so loudly during the performance they had to leave. And fell asleep long before they ever reached the last destination.

Nash caught a glimpse of her slumbering child in the rearview mirror as they fell into line behind a huge string of cars waiting to get into Santa's Ranch. "What do you want to do?" he asked.

Callie sighed, aware she had never been so exhausted. Or frustrated. "Head home, if that's okay with you."

"Sounds good."

Unfortunately, Brian woke up when they were getting him out of the car. Cranky and overtired, he burst into tears that Callie could not soothe. A feeling of failure overwhelming her, tears flooded her eyes, too. Nash caught her glance, then held out his arms to her son, creating enough of a diversion for Callie to pull herself together. A sobbing Brian went into Nash's embrace, and together they went into his room and got him ready for bed.

Although Callie had regained her usual composure by then, Brian still wanted Nash to rock him. So he sat down in the glider and cuddled the little boy close. Sighing contentedly, Brian wreathed his arms around Nash's shoulders and rested his head in the crook of Nash's neck.

Tearing up all over again at the unbearably tender sight, Callie slipped from the room.

Eventually, Nash joined her.

He was so calm and reassuring. It was no wonder her son adored him and wanted Nash for a daddy.

In Brian's place, Callie would have wanted Nash, too.

Aware the void in her little boy's life was only going to get bigger as years passed, Callie asked, "He asleep?"

Nash nodded. Understanding only part of the reason behind her dejected mood, he sank down on the sofa beside her and sent her a sympathetic glance. "Parenting is hard work."

Callie absorbed the heat of his body pressed up against hers. *You got that right.* "Some days, like today, are harder than others. And for the record," she forced herself to voice the mea culpa, "you were right in your estimation of my plans. It was too much."

Nash draped his arm around her shoulders. Pressed a kiss in her hair. "He's two and a half, Callie. I think he had a good time."

"I just don't want him to feel shortchanged because it's Christmas and he doesn't have a dad."

He gave her a reassuring squeeze. "You do more than most two parents combined that I've ever seen." He paused. "Want some advice?"

Callie winced. "I have a feeling you're going to give it to me whether I want it or not."

He slid a finger beneath her chin and turned her to face him. "Ease up a little. Let Brian enjoy the small things."

She smiled wistfully. There was so much comfort to be gained just from being here with Nash, like this. It made her long to be married again. "Like cookie baking and decorating?"

"Or just cookie eating."

Callie rolled her eyes. She let her head drop to the back of the sofa then threw her forearm across her brow. "You're such a man."

He chuckled at her comical "Oscar-worthy" performance. "You're such a mom."

She straightened. Turned serious. "For the record, Nash Echols. I'm glad you're here."

"Want to know something?" he returned softly, kissing her yet again. "So am I. This is the best holiday season I've had in a very long time."

Chapter 12

"We still on for tonight?" Nash asked the next morning when he stopped by to have breakfast with the two of them. Being here was a great way to start off his day. Especially when Callie looked so darned beautiful and welcoming.

He could tell that, like him, she wasn't long out of the shower. Her dark curls were still slightly damp, and smelled of the flowery shampoo she used. Her ivory skin was smooth and flawless, her cheeks tinged with pink. But it was the lively light in her deep blue eyes—the one that indicated she was considering kissing him again—that really drew him in.

His spirits soaring, Nash lounged against the counter, watching as Callie stood at the stove and poured pancake batter onto the griddle.

She met his glance and nodded in answer to his question. "Yes. My in-laws will be here at three. I want to spend a little time with them, too, but should be free to leave here around six this evening."

Sounded good to Nash. "How about I come pick you up then?" he asked, as Brian ran over to him and held out his arms, indicating he wanted to be picked up.

Callie smiled as Nash hoisted her son in his arms.

"Wouldn't it be easier for me to drive to your ranch, since all the things that need assembling—" she continued talking in a code only the "grownups" could comprehend "—are going over there this morning?"

"Whatever you think is best." Noting that Callie had her son's breakfast ready, Nash carried him over to the booster seat and set him down. When Brian was centered in the cushioned insert, he slid the big chair closer to the table. "Do you have a curfew this evening?"

"Um, no." Callie poured a little syrup on her son's plate and handed him a fork. "Not really." With Brian eating, she returned to the stove. She looked at Nash, speaking in code once again. "Doris and Rock already know it's going to take however long it takes to do that stuff."

And anything *else* we might get around to, Nash thought mischievously.

Callie continued, "They're going to go on to bed at their usual time, which is around ten."

Nash accepted the mug she handed him and poured himself a cup of coffee. "Well, then, since you have an actual babysitter, how about you and I make it a date?"

Which was something, up to this point, they hadn't actually had.

Callie paused then squinted at him uncertainly. "To put together stuff?"

"To have a grown-up dinner first, just the two of

us—in San Antonio. And then put together stuff. Or I can do the assembling this afternoon at my place. Then you and I can just have the grown-up dinner on the River Walk." Which was, he admitted, what he really wanted. Uninterrupted time alone with Callie.

She handed him a plate with a piping hot stack of buttermilk pancakes. "You really wouldn't mind all that direction reading and so on?"

He shrugged. "I love that stuff." Sitting down at the kitchen table, he spread some whipped butter over the stack, drizzled some maple syrup on top and then dug in. "Seriously, anything I can do to make your holiday a joyous one is great with me."

"Well…" Callie regarded him happily. "I really do suck at that kind of stuff. I'm always putting things on upside down and backward."

He chuckled, glad he had won her over. "Then it's a date?"

"Yes." Callie brought her own plate to the table and sat opposite him. She wrinkled her nose. "As long as we don't refer to it as that to anyone else."

Somehow, Nash wasn't surprised she remained cautious. Lifting a shoulder, he watched her over the rim of his coffee mug. "So it will be a secret date."

His teasing brought a flush to her cheeks. "Do you mind keeping our private life private?" She searched his eyes.

"Not at all."

It was enough she had officially agreed to go out with him.

Because that was one step closer to where he wanted to be. Nash grinned. Who said Christmas didn't come early?

* * *

Nash completed the tasks for Callie, as promised, then dressed as they had agreed he would. Happy to be spending the evening with her, he headed for the ranch next door.

"Well, hello, Nash!" Doris Grimes opened the door. "Come on in. Callie's running a little late this evening."

Rock Grimes came forward to shake Nash's hand, too. "Good to see you, son. You're quite the hero around here."

Hero? Nash kept his expression inscrutable. He strolled into the living room. "Callie said that?"

"Didn't have to." Rock beamed. "We could see it in her eyes. And of course little Brian can't stop talking about you, either. It's 'my friend Nash this,' and 'my friend Nash that.'"

That wasn't such a big surprise. Nash couldn't stop talking about Brian, either. He was such a cute kid. As for Callie, well, was there a moment in the day when she wasn't on his mind…?

Aware Callie's in-laws were waiting for his reaction, Nash returned pleasantly, "It's nice to have such great neighbors. And nice to see the two of you again."

Weary of the grown-up conversation, Brian ran up to his grandfather. "Are you my daddy?" he asked Rock.

Giving Rock no chance to reply, Brian hammed it up and shook his head dramatically, as if enacting a scene from his favorite storybook. "No. *You're* not my daddy."

Brian ran up to Doris and comically repeated the same thing.

The coatrack was next. Then the grandfather clock. Finally, Brian turned to Nash and, arms spread wide, said with complete and utter confidence, "*You're* my daddy!"

Silence fell.

Talk about an uncomfortable moment, Nash thought, given the fact that Rock and Doris were Seth's parents. To their credit, though, they seemed to accept their grandson's clowning around as the mischievousness that it was meant to be.

Figuring the best way to put an end to it was to react in kind, Nash scooped Brian up into his arms. "No," he declared, pointing his finger at the center of the little boy's chest. "*You* are *my* daddy!"

Brian burst into gales of laughter that soon had everyone chuckling, too. "No!" he proclaimed, flushing and shaking his head. "I not your daddy! I little boy."

"Yes, you are, and a cute little dickens at that." Nash gave Brian another hug, silently beseeching him to let the search for an acceptable daddy go——at least for the evening——then attempted to transfer him to his grandfather.

Brian reacted by holding on to Nash a little tighter.

Again, neither of Seth's parents seemed to mind. "Why don't you come in and sit down," Doris invited. "We can get to know each other better while you're waiting for Callie to come downstairs."

Nash sat on the sofa. "Sure." Although it suddenly felt as awkward as his teen years when he had arrived to pick up a date.

"I gather you're not married," Rock said.

Brian slid onto the floor, picked up two toy construction trucks and brought them back to the sofa. He kept one and gave the other to Nash.

"No, I'm not married," he replied genially, resurrecting his best poker face. What had Callie told them about their plans for the evening anyway?

"Would you like to be?" Doris asked.

Bored, Brian settled on Nash's lap and worked at undoing the knot of his tie. "Married? Yes, I would," Nash said. *Especially if the bride in question were Callie.*

"What about kids?" Rock persisted. "Any plans there?"

Another easy question. "I love them. I'd like to have some."

"Any particular number?" Doris smiled.

"Definitely more than one," Nash said.

Brian yawned and snuggled close to Nash. He cuddled the little boy close in return.

Abruptly, Callie appeared in the door.

She was dressed in a cranberry-red suit and heels, her cloud of dark-chocolate curls beautifully encircling her face. She had a briefcase in hand. "Ready?" she asked in a brisk, professional tone.

Nash kissed the top of Brian's head before setting him down. Stood.

"I go?" Brian asked plaintively, clinging to Nash's leg.

"No, honey, this is a business meeting." Callie picked up her son and danced him around the room. "But you are going to have fun with Grandma Doris and Grandpa Rock tonight. I promise…"

A smiling Doris and Rock distracted Brian so Nash and Callie could take their leave. When they were completely out of earshot, he echoed, *"Business meeting?"* He had assumed she would say they were going out either as friends or to meet friends. Not this.

He held the door for her, aware all over again just how beautiful she was.

"Trust me," she said, her manner as formal as her

words. Looking past his shoulder, she waved at the threesome standing in the window, then climbed gracefully into the cab of his pickup truck. "This is for the best."

"This is actually a great time for me to go over the suggestions I have compiled to help advertise the expansion of your business," Callie told Nash once they were en route to the city.

While he drove, she talked. By the time they reached downtown San Antonio, she had talked about each option in depth. "Of course, I've written it all down for you," she said. "So you'll be able to take it home later and review it at your leisure."

"Great job," he said.

"So what was the interrogation from my in-laws about?" she asked, once they were strolling along the River Walk. It had been beautifully decorated for the holidays. Thousands of twinkling lights formed a glittering canopy overhead. Long rows of glowing luminaries lined the walkways. On the river that cut through the heart of the city, boatloads of carolers and bands serenaded them.

Looking resplendent in a dark suit, striped shirt and tie, Nash took her hand in his. He had shaved closely. Maybe gotten a haircut, too. "I think they were trying to figure out how marriageable a guy I am."

Callie moved in closer, to avoid a group coming their way on the sidewalk. Nash responded by curving an arm about her waist and pressing a kiss to the top of her head.

"And the result was…?" Callie asked, trying not to get too caught up in the brisk masculine scent of him.

Aware they were still a little early for their dinner reservation, he took her up to one of the stone arches that overlooked the river below. He lounged against the side of the walking bridge and looked down at her. "They seemed to approve. They sure didn't appear to mind when Brian was facetiously claiming me as his daddy. I have to tell you…" He paused, shook his head. "I wasn't sure how that was going to go over. Their late son actually being Brian's father, and all."

Callie had been nervous about it, too—unnecessarily it had turned out. "They know how hard I've worked to give Brian some sense of his dad. They also know I may have come up with a solution."

He lifted a brow, listening intently.

Callie drew a breath and pushed on. "I'm going to make a video like the ones they show about the bride and groom at rehearsal dinners, and have it set to music. It will only run a couple of minutes, but I think it will be more engaging to Brian than a simple photo."

He kept his eyes locked with hers. "That's a good idea."

Bolstered by his support, she continued, "Doris, Rock and I were working on it this afternoon, going through some old photos. And I think I have the ones I'm going to use."

"That should help."

"I hope so." Callie sighed, then pushed on to the more difficult part of the conversation. Once again, she lifted her gaze to his, and kept it there. "In the meantime, Doris and Rock really want me to get married again."

A wealth of feeling was in his eyes. "To anyone in particular?"

"Yes. You."

He stared at her a long silent moment. Then leaned closer once again, inundating her with the tantalizing, masculine scent of his cologne. "You're kidding."

Suddenly, she was having trouble catching her breath. "I wish I was."

His voice dropped a seductive notch. "They barely know me."

She gazed into his eyes, adding even more softly, "They feel they know enough about the important things."

Incredulity mixed with the concern on his face.

"You have a good reputation within the community and the business world," Callie continued, figuring for all their sakes she should tell him everything she had learned. "Yes, they are pragmatic enough to have had you checked out by their attorney."

"Wow."

She had never seen so many expressions cross his face in one minute. Shock. Disbelief. Wariness. Joy. "They're impressed by how attached Brian is to you already."

"I care about him, too, you know that," he interjected gruffly, squeezing her hand.

"And—" she drew a quavering breath, ignoring the warmth spiraling through her "—they can see there is a basic attraction between you and me. Enough of one to build a relationship on, in their view."

He closed the distance between them and gazed at her as if she were the sexiest, most desirable woman on earth. "What about love?"

Callie's heart thundered in her chest. "They don't expect me to duplicate what I had with Seth with anyone else. But they do think both Brian and I would be a lot happier if we had a man in our lives, and to them, at least, you are the perfect candidate."

His eyes crinkled at the corners and his lips took on a mischievous tilt. "How so?"

Callie shrugged, aware they were headed into dangerous territory here.

"You already live next door." She did her best to maintain her pragmatic attitude. Not easy, when all she could think about at the moment was kissing him again.

"You're committed to the land and the business you inherited, just as I am committed to my new venture." She paused to wet her suddenly dry lips and saw his eyes track the movement in return.

"Brian loves you. And you adore him in return. And like I said, they have noticed there is a physical chemistry, as well as a budding friendship." And like her, had difficulty figuring out a reason why she shouldn't get closer to this big strapping man. Maybe even come to depend on him…in the same way she had once depended on their son.

Nash put his hands on her shoulders and gently ran them down the length of her arms, to her hands. He peered down at her. "What do your parents think of all this?"

"The exact opposite. They urged me to be cautious and not leap into anything, given the enormity of my loss and the fact that I'm still in a 'vulnerable' state."

He searched her face, then asked huskily, "What do you think?"

I don't want to make the same mistakes I made when I was married to Seth and overly romanticize things to the point I lose sight of myself and my ability to stand on my own.

But, not wanting to get into a discussion about her late husband, she simply said, "I don't want to think. I just want to spend time with you."

And make love with you. And not worry about the future and all the things that could go wrong if I tie myself to you the way I tied myself to Seth.

All of a sudden, the grin was back on his handsome face. He lifted her hands to his lips and kissed the back of her knuckles, in turn. "Sounds good to me."

On impulse, she wound her arms around his neck, went up on tiptoe and kissed him tenderly. "Then how about this?" she proposed softly. Nearby a mariachi band broke into the cheerful melody of "Feliz Navidad." "Why don't you and I be each other's Christmas present—to each other?"

Nash kissed her back gently, lovingly. "You've got yourself a deal..."

"Santa's workshop is coming along nicely," Maggie observed from the corner of the Double Knot party barn on Thursday afternoon, where the setup for the Christmas celebration was taking shape.

Callie grinned, admiring the sight of Nash in rugged work clothes and a tool belt jangling around his waist as he helped fasten the various parts of the North Pole into shape.

"Good thing we have so many big strapping Texas men to help."

"Speaking of the one in your life, how are things with Nash?" Maggie asked.

Callie went back to draping cranberry-red tablecloths over the tables. He had become so much a part of her life in the past four weeks, it was astounding. "Fine."

Maggie added the centerpieces—tall hurricane glasses with thick white candles, surrounded by pretty red-and-green wreaths. "I mean, really."

No use pretending; her twin knew her thoughts and feelings almost before she did. "So good it scares me," Callie admitted quietly.

With her last event for the month over, and his schedule relatively freed up, the two of them had had plenty of time to spend together. To the point they found a reason to be together at least once every day.

"I hear you're helping him devise ways to market the extension of his business into xeriscape plants and lumber."

After the tablecloth was situated, Callie replaced the chairs. "Yes. I think he's going to be enormously successful."

Maggie moved on to the next table along with Callie. "So, why haven't you told everyone you're dating?"

Callie focused on her task, rather than her twin's assessing look. "Because we're not dating exactly," she protested. "We're just hanging out a lot as friends." *And lovers*.

Maggie regarded her with sisterly affection. "Well, just don't wait too long to let him know how you really feel. Otherwise, he's likely to think you aren't as serious about him as *I know* you are."

To Callie's relief, the rest of the day passed quickly. It pleased her to no end that preparations for the celebration were coming together so well.

Finally, right before they all headed home, costumes for everyone working the event were passed out. Maggie's husband, Hart, got two.

The first, the same "Texas gambler" all the men were wearing. The second, a complete Santa ensemble.

"Now be sure you keep this under wraps," Fiona Sanders told her son. "We don't want Henry to guess his daddy is going to be Old St. Nick when the time comes."

Hart grinned. "Mum's the word, Mom."

Callie turned to Nash. Garment bags looped over their arms, they walked out to their vehicles, which were parked side by side. "You don't think Brian will recognize his uncle, do you?"

Nash held her costume for her while she unlocked her SUV. "If anyone can pull it off, Hart can." He leaned past her to put it in the cargo area.

Callie followed him over to his truck. She watched as he opened up the rear passenger door. "That's not really an answer."

Nash leaned across the seat to lay his bag flat. "You want me to be blunt?"

She tore her eyes from his firmly muscled thigh. "I'm not sure…"

He removed his tool belt, set it on the floor in front of the seat and then straightened to his full six foot two inches. "Your son is one of the brightest little kids ever put on this earth. Under normal circumstances, not much gets by him."

True, Callie knew.

Nash flashed an inviting grin. "On the other hand, he can be as starstruck as everyone else. And once he gets a load of all that fake snow, the glittering trees, the elves from the high school drama department and the big guy in the white beard and glasses and red suit, it will probably be all he can do to tell Santa what he wants for Christmas."

Callie relaxed at the reassuring words. "You're right. That will be okay. What might not be is Brian's preschool party tomorrow."

Accurately sensing she had something important to say, Nash waited.

Drawing a deep breath, Callie pushed on, "Most of the other kids are going to have a mom and a dad there for them. Unfortunately, neither of Brian's grandfathers are available. Hart will be there—for Henry—and could sort of step in for Brian as his uncle, at least part of the time, but…"

"You're worried Brian is going to pick up on the fact that he doesn't have a daddy again. And be upset about it."

Callie nodded. Tears pressed at the back of her eyes. "This is the first Christmas he's ever had where he's really aware of what's going on. I really want it to be a good one for him." Nash's expression gentled. Because there were others around them, heading to their vehicles, he didn't touch her, but he might as well have. She felt his tender concern that intensely. "You want me to go—as his friend?"

And mine, Callie thought.

But aware they were still in a place where they could be overheard, Callie only smiled and responded as casually as possible, "I know it would mean the world to him—" and to me "—if you could."

Chapter 13

"What's wrong with Hart?" Callie asked her sister during the preschool party Friday afternoon.

Maggie refilled the punch bowl. "He's had a throbbing headache all day."

Callie set out a platter of vanilla cupcakes, decorated with green and red frosting holly berries. "He's not getting the flu, is he?" It had been going around.

"He thinks it's just dehydration and lack of sleep. He worked at the Double Knot all day yesterday, then headed up security for a rock star doing a concert in San Antonio last night."

"What time did he get home?"

"Four o'clock in the morning."

"Ouch."

"Yeah. He wasn't supposed to work last night but one of his employees had a sick child, so Hart took his place."

Callie recalled, "And he hasn't had his shot, has he?"

"Actually, he did get it. The problem is it takes two weeks to be fully effective, and he was just vaccinated a couple of days ago."

"Well, hopefully, lack of sleep is all it is."

"From your lips…" Maggie grinned, watching her husband help Henry polish off the last of their pizza. Nash did the same for Brian. Finished, the four joined the Clean Plate Club and headed over to the table to claim their dessert.

Unable to resist, Callie called out as they passed, "Having fun?"

Nash nodded.

Brian patted Nash's hand. "My friend here, Mommy."

"I can see that, honey," Callie said with a satisfied smile.

When Brian's teacher headed their way, the little boy grabbed Nash's hand. "Go me." Proudly, Brian led Nash over to converse with Mrs. O'Reilly.

And so it went. Brian took Nash to meet all his friends and their dads.

And Callie knew she had been right to invite Nash to be here for Brian. It seemed to mean a lot to both of them. It was certainly doing a lot to fill her with the Christmas spirit…

Beside her, Maggie asked, "What's Nash doing for the holiday?"

"I'm not sure," Callie murmured. She'd been wondering the same thing herself. "He mentioned he has a lot of invitations—he always does this time of year."

"If I were you…" Maggie suggested meaningfully.

Callie lifted her palm. "I know what you'd do," she told her twin.

However, that didn't mean *she* was ready to put *her* heart on the line that way. It was way too risky. Still, she did enjoy spending time with Nash. So very much...

By the time they left the school, dark blue clouds were visible on the horizon.

Callie studied the sky with a sigh. "There's the Blue Norther coming in." A chill was already in the air. She turned to Nash. "I hope it doesn't rain tomorrow. A winter storm would ruin a lot of what we have planned for the Old-Fashioned Christmas Celebration. Especially the train rides up Sanders Mountain to Nature's Cathedral, where the caroling and sing-alongs are supposed to take place."

Nash helped Brian get situated in his car seat, then held the driver door open for Callie. "The party starts at ten and concludes at 4:00 p.m.—an hour and a half before dark. Precipitation isn't expected until six tomorrow evening, at the earliest. And with the temperature still in the midthirties, all it's going to be is rain."

Impressed, Callie climbed behind the wheel of her SUV. "You've been checking the weather report, too?"

"Hey," he teased, settling into the passenger seat beside her, his big body filling the compartment with laudable ease. "We have to have Mother Nature on our side." He angled a thumb at the center of his broad chest and regarded her with a devilish glint in his eye. "And I think she will be, it being Christmas and all."

Callie smiled, aware how much like "family" they already felt at this moment. What would it be like, she wondered wistfully, if they ever became one? For real?

"See Santa?" Brian piped up from his car seat, interrupting her thoughts.

"Yes." When they reached a stop sign, Callie turned

briefly to look at her son. "Santa—" or in other words, Uncle Hart "—is coming to the party tomorrow."

"Sit lap," Brian said.

Callie nodded and resumed her driving. "Yes, you and all the other children are going to have a chance to sit on Santa's lap and tell him what you want him to bring you for Christmas."

Nash shifted as much as his seat belt would allow and looked at her son. "What are you going to ask Santa for, buddy?" he asked curiously.

Tensing, Callie braced herself for him to say, "A daddy."

Instead, her son offered a toothy grin. "Tractor!" he said. "Sit on."

"What are we going to do?" Callie said several hours later, after they had finished dinner and put her exhausted son to bed. Still in the black wool skirt, tights and red cashmere sweater she had worn to the preschool party, she ambled into the living room with Hart at her side. "I had no idea Brian wanted a play tractor to ride on. I thought all he wanted was the play-construction stuff."

Nash had shed his sport coat and tie when they got to her place. While helping her with dinner, dishes and the bedtime routine, he'd undone the first two buttons of the pale blue oxford shirt and rolled up the sleeves to just below the elbows. With the hint of evening shadow lining his jaw, he looked rumpled and sexy in the way of all devoted dads. Except he wasn't Brian's daddy. Or even a permanent fixture in her life. She just wished he was.

Oblivious to the increasingly possessive nature of her thoughts, Nash pulled up a chair and sat down at her desktop computer in the living room. "It's still six days to Christmas. We've got plenty of time to make sure all of Brian's wishes come true." Ready to make that happen, he hit the on button on Callie's desktop.

Her computer had been in sleep mode. The screen lit up with what she had last been working on.

The montage of Seth through the years. There were forty pictures, thumbnail size. Some of them featured Seth as an adult, but most of them were of Seth and Callie.

Callie had to hand it to Nash. She drew in a quick rueful breath, because it felt as if she had just seen a ghost, but he didn't so much as blink.

"Sorry," he said, voice neutral as his low-key expression. Avoiding her eyes, he started to rise. "I should have asked first."

She put her hand on the swell of his biceps before he could move away and guided him back to her desk. "It's all right." She slipped onto the seat, casually indicating the photos on-screen. "This is all for the video I'm putting together for Brian. It's already saved, so all we have to do is get out of this window, bring up the internet browser and then we can go shopping." Twenty minutes later, she and Nash had narrowed their search down to two possible items.

A green toy farm tractor Brian could sit on and pedal with his feet. It was sturdy and safe and just the right size. Or a yellow construction-style digger, with a dual action lever that could scoop up objects and move them elsewhere. It, too, was sturdy, and had a seat Brian could sit on. Instead of pedals, he would power it with his feet.

"I don't know." Callie bit her lip uncertainly, really needing a guy's opinion. Really needing Nash... She turned to him for help. "I can't decide. I think he would like both."

Straddling a ladder-back chair, Nash lifted his shoulders in a lazy shrug. "Why don't you get him one, and I'll get him the other?"

She studied his expression. "You really want to do that?"

His smile widened. "I was planning to get him a gift anyway, and this way, whenever Henry visits, both boys will have a 'tractor' to ride."

It did sound like the perfect solution.

Callie leaned across the expanse between them and kissed him on the cheek. "Thank you."

He caught her by the shoulders, returning the sweet caress. Finally, knowing as well as she that if they kept this up, they'd completely lose track of what they were supposed to be doing, he drew back. "Now, let's get these gifts ordered so they can be here by Monday at the latest."

Nodding, Callie turned back to the computer and began filling in the online form.

When she moved from billing information to shipping, Nash asked, "Would you like to have them delivered to my place—instead of yours?"

That would be so great. "Would you mind?"

"Not at all," he told her. "I'm glad to help out, as always."

Once the orders were confirmed, they went into the kitchen. Feeling genuinely festive, Callie turned on a Christmas CD. She was about to ask Nash if he wanted a dish of peppermint ice cream when he held a sprig of mistletoe above her head. Using his other arm to pull her close against him, he drawled, "Well, look here." He flashed a sexy grin. "How did that get in my pocket?"

Nash knew he wasn't playing fair. Using their attraction for each other to draw Callie all the way into the present, but there were times, like now, when it was the best way to make her see that the past was over. There was no use hiding behind it, not when they had an emotional connection just as fierce as the chemistry between them. Not when he craved contact with her, craved…love.

Hooking the toe of his boot beneath the rung of a chair, he brought it all the way from the table and sank into it, dropping the mistletoe and pulling her onto his lap in the process. Gasping, she laughed in surprise as her bottom hit his thighs, and then all amusement faded as he kissed his way from temple to cheek, to the lobe of her ear, the hollow of her throat. "Nash…"

He drew back to see into her eyes, knowing he didn't need a cornball excuse to kiss her, touch her, hold her. "Kiss me, Callie…"

Wreathing her arms around his neck, she turned her head to his. Smiled with a devastating mix of tenderness and mischief. "Is that your Christmas wish?"

He grinned. "One of them."

Her answering laugh was soft, feminine, enticing. Rising slightly, she tugged the hem of her skirt to the top of her thighs, giving him quite the view and giving her maximum mobility. Blue eyes glittering, she swung one leg gracefully over his, then settled on his lap again, this time facing him.

His body roared to life.

"Like this?" she purred, all innocence, shifting her

body over his in a way that let him know she was already every bit as turned on as he was.

"Exactly like this." Excitement rumbling through him, he waited to see what she was going to do.

She took his head in her hands, sifted her fingers through his hair and slowly, effortlessly lowered her mouth to his.

The first contact of her lips on his sent another jolt to his system. Lower still, where she pressed against him, she was soft, hot…and damp.

Not at all sure he could control himself, he closed his eyes. Five minutes into the kiss, he was drowning in pleasure, kissing her back, devouring her mouth. Learning everything about her anew.

Needing more, he slid his hands beneath her cashmere sweater, found the front clasp of her bra. Her breasts came tumbling out. Wanting to watch her, to push her over the edge, he drew back, brought his hands to the outside of her sweater, then fit the cashmere fabric across her breasts, molding it to her soft curves. Her nipples poked against the fabric and she moaned. Smiling, he caressed her through the cloth, watching with pure delight as she began to tremble.

"Two can play at this game." She shifted again, rising slightly. She found the buckle on his belt, then his fly.

He caught her hand. "If mine come down, your tights and panties come *off*."

She laughed again. Kept going until his pants and shorts were at midthigh. Then, her soft, delicate hands found and claimed him.

"Callie…" He throbbed beneath the tender, knowing ministrations of her hands.

"Eventually," she promised. "First, I want to…" She

stroked her thumb from tip to base, over the rim, back down again, finding every sweet pleasurable inch. Kissing him all the while. The insides of her thighs moving back and forth over the outside of his, the friction of cloth to skin slowly but surely driving him insane.

His palms left her breasts. He tightened his grip on her hips. Making his own demands now, he moved his palms over her hips, pushing her skirt up around her waist, tugging the tights, then the panties down.

She broke off the kiss. Moved to let him peel them all the way off.

Then, skirt still on, she climbed astride his lap once again, making his every fantasy come true.

She lowered her head, and they kissed again, hotly, wantonly, lost in the moment. He stroked the inside of her thighs, the rounded curves of her buttocks, the taut silk of her lower abdomen, then tilted her in a way that pleased him. She moaned, shifting, writhing with pleasure. Knowing she was close, he touched her again, from the inside and out, as their breathing grew hot and heavy. She trembled, tried to hold back, as surely as he had. But it was too late. She could no longer deny him than he could deny her. He entered her as she came, pushing into her, filling her to the brim.

She whimpered in response and whispered his name.

Nothing had ever sounded so good or so right.

He brought her in closer still, feeling as if his heart was going to pound right out of his chest. Kissed her all the more deeply, the sensation of being locked inside her, rocking his world.

Hers, too, he thought in satisfaction, if her erratic breathing and wild, abandoned kisses were any indication. He slowed and erotically shifted his angle, aware that making love with her was the most amazing thing he had ever experienced. And then there was no more thinking, only feeling. No more holding back. Only letting go. And together they soared into the sweetest, hottest pleasure either of them had ever known.

Callie collapsed against Nash, every single cell in her body tingling. Sated. She was still throbbing with the force of her orgasm and yet she wanted him again. Wanted him so bad her toes curled. How wild was that?

No wilder than the feelings she was beginning to have for him.

No wilder than the thought that she might—just might—be on the verge of falling—

No, she couldn't think that way. Wouldn't let herself think that way. What they had now was good enough to get them through the holidays and more. Once the sentimental time had passed, life would go back to normal. And with that, would come the normalization of her feelings, too. She'd stop feeling like her life wasn't right without him in it. She wouldn't feel so restless. So in need of a man. Of marriage and a complete family. So in need of Nash…

As if reading her thoughts, Nash ran a hand up and down her back in a way that felt so good she nearly moaned. "Want to go upstairs?" He brushed a kiss against her ear.

She did. More than he would ever know. She also knew relying on someone else to that degree again was not wise. She'd barely survived her first loss, and she hadn't felt anywhere near as passionately about Seth as she did about Nash.

Tamping down the need welling inside her heart, she returned his tender smile with a playful one of her own. "You know if we do, we won't get any sleep at all tonight." She stroked her hand through his thick black hair. "And with the big celebration tomorrow…"

Once again, he understood her with the patience of a saint. "We both need to be on our A game."

"Plus—" Callie drew a deep breath. Knowing this had to be said so the possibility wouldn't come up again, she sat up straight. "You see how much Brian talks. If my son were to find you here in the morning, and realize you'd spent the night…" *In my bed.* He'd know how real and right this all was.

He'd want and expect it to happen more.

And so would I.

Nash kissed the inside of her wrist, finishing her thought. "Everyone would know."

Callie trembled at his evocative touch. Lower still, where she straddled him, she could feel the resurgence of his desire. And hers. Doing her best to keep her mind on the topic at hand, she said, "Preschool pals. Teachers. Friends. Family…"

Nash looked deep into her eyes. He traced her lower lip with the pad of his thumb, his touch on her calming. "Which is not what you want."

Callie luxuriated in his warmth and understanding. Was there anything she did not love about this man? "If I ever have a man stay the night, I want it to be because we're married. And I'm not sure I want to be married again." She studied his reaction. "Does that sound hopelessly old-fashioned?"

Nash brought her close and kissed her tenderly. "It sounds," he murmured huskily, "exactly like you."

"Trouble?" Nash asked the next morning when he arrived to pick up Callie and Brian. He'd left the night before—reluctantly—but the good night's sleep was worth it today.

Callie was looking absolutely gorgeous in a red-and-black taffeta striped gown. The high-collared, long-sleeved dress clung to her breasts and waist before flaring out at her hips and swirling elegantly to the floor. It rustled when she walked.

Unfortunately, despite her well-rested appearance, her day appeared not to be starting off as smoothly as she had hoped.

Callie sighed with frustration. "Brian doesn't like his vintage clothing. I'm hoping you can help."

Nash hoped so, too, since they were due at the Double Knot Ranch in fifteen minutes. He walked into the family room and carefully scoped out the situation. Brian was lying prone on the floor, his expression mulish. Nash knelt down to greet the tantrum-throwing little boy. "What's the problem, buddy?" he inquired matter-of-factly. As if this were something he dealt with every day.

Brian plucked at his charcoal tweed knickers and kicked his legs like a bucking donkey. Callie had managed to get a white T-shirt on him, too, but that was all. The black knee socks he was supposed to wear had been hurled off to the side. Ditto the lace-up black shoes, tweed newsboy cap, matching jacket, red bow tie and white shirt.

"Don't. Like." Each word was accompanied by another donkey-like kick of the legs.

Nash arrowed a hand at his chest, demonstrating. "Hey, I'm dressed up, too."

Brian turned his head. He surveyed Nash's dark Western suit, finely pressed shirt, red-and-gold brocade vest, matching tie and black Stetson.

"Everybody has to get dressed up to see Santa Claus today," Nash explained.

At the mention of Old St. Nick, Brian's eyes lit up.

Nash continued using the carrot-and-stick approach. "I know you want to see the North Pole and sit on Santa's lap so you can tell him what you want for Christmas." While he talked, Nash gathered up the clothes.

"And besides," he pointed out gently, easing Brian to a sitting position, "our shirts match. See? Mine is white, and it has buttons up the front. And yours is white and has buttons up the front, too. It's a big-boy shirt."

Mollified, Brian held out his arms so Nash could ease them into the sleeves.

"You—Santa—too?" Brian asked.

Nash grinned as he helped Brian put on his socks and shoes. "I think I'm too big to sit on Santa's lap." He made a comical face, eliciting a giggle from the child. "I might *squish* him. And then what would we do? If Santa was all *squished*?"

Brian giggled some more.

On went the jacket. The snap on tie. The cap.

Callie hovered nearby, chuckling, too.

"There," Nash said, arms waving with dramatic flourish. "You're looking good, buddy. And just like me." He turned to Callie, "Okay, Mommy, I believe we're good to go. What do you say we take our picture before hitting the road?"

Callie got out her phone, aiming at Nash and Brian. Nash motioned her closer. "I meant all three of us."

Grinning, Callie rustled closer. Nash picked Brian up, clasped him against his chest, then put his other arm around Callie. She held out the phone. And the first selfie of their relationship was taken.

Chapter 14

Although the Old-Fashioned Christmas Celebration would not begin for another hour, the 1880s Western-garbed waitstaff was already busy setting up a sumptuous holiday buffet when Callie, Brian and Nash walked in to the party barn. Admiring the festive decor, she smiled with relief that all their hard work and planning had truly paid off.

In one corner, children's arts and crafts tables were situated. Santa's village occupied another corner. Musicians were tuning up on stage. Beautifully adorned gift baskets for the guests were being laid out. Gifts for the door prizes—handmade candles, quilts, cakes, Christmas trees and wreaths—were also on display. Along with the brochures that Callie had made for the local businesses sponsoring the event.

She settled her son with the other kids being supervised by local art students, then went to work setting up, too, while Nash assisted with some of the heavy lifting. "You look happy," Maggie said, when she caught up with her.

Callie returned her twin's hug. "And you don't." She paused. "What's wrong?"

Maggie frowned. "It's Hart. He's got the flu."

Callie sympathized. "Oh, no."

"He went to the urgent care clinic first thing this morning, and got started on antiviral medicine, which should limit it, but he's not going to be able to be—" Maggie paused as a couple of children passed by "—You Know Who today. And we got the, um, You Know What to fit him. So…" Maggie waved Nash over then paused to size him up with a critical eye. "You're about the same size. Six foot four, give or take, two hundred and twenty pounds…"

Of pure solid muscle, Callie added silently. *A very sexual being. Kind, loving, funny, charming. Intelligent. And so much more…*

Oblivious to her adoring thoughts, Nash asked, "Need a volunteer?"

Maggie shot him a grateful glance. "Pronto. So, if you wouldn't mind… Callie can you help him? The costume is in the main house, in one of the upstairs bedrooms. You can't miss it. When you're ready, let us know, and we'll set up for your 'big entrance.'"

"And here I was just getting used to your Texas Maverick look," Callie quipped, picking up her skirts and leading the way as she and Nash slipped out of the party barn and headed across the lawn.

On the other side of the parking lot, the steam engine warmed up beside the train station, preparing for the run up to the mountaintop and Nature's Cathedral, where an outdoor concert would be held every hour on the hour. Overhead, the skies were still a wintry gray, but perhaps that wasn't such a bad thing given it was a Christmas celebration. Had it been sunny and seventy degrees, it would have been a lot harder to get in the mood.

Playful as ever, Nash winked. "I can put it all back on later, if you like. In fact, I'm going to have to—unless you want me to go home au naturel."

Callie snickered. "Cute. And no, G-rated is fine." They moved inside the house, out of sight of others. "This is a family event. Remember?"

As soon as the words were out, she regretted them. "Oh, Nash, I'm sorry," she breathed, embarrassed.

"Don't be," Nash returned gruffly. He leaned in and kissed her cheek. "I've got lots of friends."

"But—"

He tightened his grip on her. "Right now you and Brian are the only family I need."

To her surprise, as she luxuriated in the feel of his strong arms around her, Callie felt the same.

It was easy to tell which room was designated as Santa's dressing room. There was a cutout sleigh taped to the shut door. Callie knocked, just to be on the safe side. When there was no answer, they slipped on in. "You may need a little help adjusting the padding."

Nash flashed her a sly grin. "No volunteer I'd rather have." He shucked the gambler clothing in no time flat.

Doing her best to keep her mind on the business at hand, which wasn't easy given his mouthwateringly fit physique, she handed him the red fleece pants then went to retrieve the black knee high boots.

"Have you ever done this before?" she felt compelled to ask.

Nash deliberately misinterpreted her question. "Taken off my clothes in front of you? Why, yes, ma'am." He tipped an imaginary hat and strolled closer still, crisp white T-shirt clinging magnificently to his bare chest and broad shoulders. "I have." His glance roved her up and down, lingering on each and every sensitive spot. "I have to admit I enjoyed it, too."

She batted his mischievously roaming hands away and fought back the desire to kiss him. "I meant played Santa."

"No." He pulled her closer still, his hands sliding down her waist to her hips. He fitted her against him—at least as much as her full skirt and his loose-fitting trousers would allow. "Can't say that I have."

A thrill swept through her as she felt his hardness and the answering tingle within her body. Extricating herself, she went to get the padding that would give him the girth he needed to play Old St. Nick. With him watching her closely, she adjusted the elastic straps over his shoulders and around his waist, situating the pillow where his belly should be.

"I could get used to this," he drawled.

So could she. Whoever would have thought playing dress-up with the man she lo—lusted after—could be so much fun? Doing her best to keep her feelings in check, she batted her lashes at him flirtatiously. "Ho, ho, Santa."

His low laugh filled the room as she tugged the suspenders holding his pants up over his broad shoulders. The red coat with the white fur trim followed. He sat down on the edge of the bed so she could properly situate the curly white wig, mustache and beard. Still standing between his spread thighs, she planted the hat on his head and then stepped back slightly to admire her handiwork.

"Sexy Texas maverick to old man in three minutes. Not bad."

Nash vaulted to his feet, unabashed desire in his eyes. He wrapped his hands around her waist and guided her close. When she was snug against him, he tugged down the beard, lowered his head and delivered a long, hot, scintillating kiss that rocked her world.

When he finally released her, she was trembling all over. Wanting him so much it hurt.

He winked. "Consider that a down payment for later."

"If I didn't know better," Maggie remarked after Callie had returned to the party barn alone, "I'd think you'd been making out." She paused, cookie tray in hand, and looked closer. "You *have* been making out!"

Callie struggled not to blush and busied herself filling bowls with individually wrapped chocolate peppermint candies. "Shush."

"Hmm. Well, at least one of us is getting a little yuletide action," Maggie teased dryly, looking genuinely happy for her sister.

Then she sighed abruptly, her expression becoming fretful once again.

Callie sympathized, "Worried about Hart?"

Maggie set a row of snowball cookies next to the gingersnaps. "It is so hard to keep that man in bed," she lamented.

Callie snorted.

Maggie suppressed a laugh at the accidental double entendre. "*Resting*, I mean. You know these big tough guys. They hate being sick."

"And hate following doctor's orders even more?" Callie guessed.

"Exactly."

And getting extra sleep was the fastest way to recovery from any illness, they both knew. "So rest with him," Callie suggested, as they headed back to the kitchen, empty trays in hand. "I mean it. You've kept Brian for me several times recently. Why not let me reciprocate this evening with Henry?"

Her twin offered a faint smile. "Only one problem with that. Frank and Fiona have already called dibs on him." And grandparents ruled, that Callie knew. "But," her twin continued, hopefully, "if you wanted to have Henry over to play with Brian tomorrow…"

"Consider it done," Callie vowed with a hug.

No sooner had they deposited their trays and returned to the party, than the music struck up. "Jingle Bells! Jingle Bells! Jingle all the way…"

All eyes turned, as Santa strode into the party barn, a big sack of toys slung over one brawny shoulder. "Ho, Ho, Ho! Merry Christmas!" Nash said in a deep and rumbling voice that sounded nothing like his usual Texas drawl.

"And here we go." Maggie beamed.

Together, she and Callie rounded up the children congregated in the arts and crafts area of the party barn, and took them over to see Santa, one by one.

Henry did great. As did all the other children. Finally, it was Brian's turn.

Callie led him over to the North Pole. His normal

bashfulness in such situations absent—maybe because so many kids had already gone ahead of him—Brian climbed importantly up onto Santa's lap, an inquisitive look in his baby-blue eyes.

Oh, no, Callie thought. *Please tell me he's not going to ask Santa if he is his daddy?* And for a second, that was exactly what she thought her son was going to say.

Instead, Brian stared at Santa long and hard. Putting both his hands on Santa's bearded cheeks, Brian stared deep into his eyes.

Santa looked back, kindly, lovingly.

Callie could not tell whether or not her son recognized Nash, but he definitely sensed some sort of connection.

"Well, hello there, young man," Nash said in an impressively well-disguised baritone. "Have you been a good boy this year? Helped your mommy out? Picked up your toys and gone to bed on time?"

Brian had to think about that. Finally, he nodded soberly. "That's good to hear," Santa said, quietly and authoritatively. "What would you like me to bring you for Christmas?"

Again, Callie held her breath.

And Brian said, "My friend Nash."

Nash had prepared himself for many things. The request for a daddy, for instance. Or being recognized, his identity blown.

But never this.

Sensing Nash just wasn't getting what he meant, Brian added, "Stay—me."

"You want Nash to stay with you?" he asked.

Brian nodded soberly. "Stay—Mommy, too."

"Oh. Well..." Nash worked to stay in character "... that's not the kind of thing Santa and his elves can bring you." But it was the sort of thing *he* could work on. "Santa can bring you toys, though." He stroked his beard thoughtfully. "So, young man, what would you like Santa to bring you that you can play with?"

Again, Brian had to think. He settled back down again, leaning against the curve of "Santa's" big, strong arm as he gave the question careful consideration.

"A puppy," he said at last.

Beside them, Callie nearly fell through the floor.

Figuring he should quit while he was ahead, Nash said, "All right then, Brian. Let's get your picture taken with Santa. Mommy, you can be in the photo, too, if you like, and then you'll be good to go..."

Just that quickly, the visit was concluded, and Brian scrambled off Nash's lap. After one long last thoughtful look back at him, the two-and-a-half-year-old went off to ride the steam engine with his mother and a whole host of other parents and children.

Nash continued to be Santa for several more hours.

He left with the same flourish he'd entered the party barn with, then slipped off to change back into his Western garb to hand out the free Christmas trees and wreaths—on behalf of his business—to departing guests. Meanwhile, Callie was in charge of presenting the gift baskets to all the adults, and Maggie had the goodie bags for the kids.

The incredibly successful day ended with a private celebratory dinner for everyone who had worked the event. It was a lively affair, and by the time Callie and Nash returned to her ranch, still in costume, Brian was already sound asleep.

Callie tucked her son into bed, then returned with a bottle of champagne and two glasses. The cold winter rain that had been predicted began to fall, and they settled before the fire and began discussing the day.

"It could have been worse," Nash told Callie, when talk turned to Brian's visit with Santa. "He could have asked for a sibling. In fact, he probably will once Maggie has her baby and his cousin Henry has a little brother or sister."

Callie groaned and then buried her face in her hands. "Let's not jump ahead of ourselves. Let's focus instead on what we're going to do about the puppy situation."

Nash liked the way she was including him in the decision-making process—as if he were truly part of her immediate family now. He also liked the way she looked in that vintage red-and-black-striped taffeta gown—*and* the fact that she hadn't taken it off yet. Because he had been fantasizing about doing just that, all day long...

Callie handed him the bottle. He loosened the wire cage holding the cork in place and then, holding the bottle forty-five degrees away from them, opened it carefully. "Are you ready for a little four-legged critter?" He poured while she held the glasses.

Callie hesitated. "When Brian is older, yes. Not now."

Nash toasted her with a smile, then clinked his glass against hers.

"I might be."

She studied him. "Seriously?"

Nash shrugged, admitting, "It gets a little lonely at the ranch. I wouldn't mind some company." *I wouldn't mind having you and Brian there.* But he knew that was the kind of overly romantic declaration she didn't want to hear. Not yet, anyway. "But we digress," he said, taking her free hand in his.

"Yes." Sighing softly, Callie shifted around so she was nestled in the curve of his body, her head resting on his shoulder. "We do."

Enjoying their closeness, he leaned down to breathe in the fragrant flowery scent of her hair. "How about I pick up a stuffed toy puppy for him?" He pressed a kiss against her temple. "I have to go into San Antonio tomorrow anyway." *To get a present for you.* "I could get one for Santa to bring him then."

She shifted again, her thigh bumping against his, causing his body to harden. "You wouldn't mind?"

Nash took another sip of the chilled champagne. "Not at all." He set his glass aside, relieved her of hers, too. Standing, he took her by the hand, drew her to her feet. "Of course," he teased, retrieving both glasses and bottle of bubbly before leading her mischievously toward the stairs, "I am going to need payment for my trouble."

She accompanied him down the hall, stopping to kiss him every five or six steps. Eventually, they ended up in her bedroom. She locked the door behind them, pausing to turn on the bedside lamp, then sashayed toward him. Her blue eyes as mischievous as her voice, she watched him put the champagne aside for later, then asked, "What kind of payment?"

What kind indeed? "Hmm…" Nash pretended to think as she came to a halt in front of him. He bent and kissed the side of her neck, felt her arch pliantly against him. "I have been wanting to try to get you out of this dress all day—or see what was required to get you out of this dress."

She batted her lashes in all innocence. "And leave my virtue intact?'

He laughed, loving the playful, womanly side of her. "No one said anything about virtue…" he teased, unbuttoning one fitted sleeve from wrist to forearm. Then the other.

She trembled when he reached for the row of buttons that stretched from the high-banded collar to just below her waist.

One by one, he undid them, opening up the cloth at her throat, past the ridges of her breasts, her ribs, all the way to her waist. Finished, he parted the cloth. "No modern-day garment this," he breathed.

It was sexy as hell. Made of some sort of soft, delicate, nearly transparent linen. Laced snugly up the front. Her breasts spilling over the lace-edged décolletage…

He hardened just looking at the imprint of her rose-colored nipples pressing against the cloth.

A tug and the top of her dress slithered to her waist. Another shift and the skirt pushed past her hips, fell to a circle on the floor.

However, to his chagrin, the sexy-as-hell chemise disappeared into another floor-length slip-style thing. "What's this?" he asked.

"Petticoat."

"How do I get it off?"

She turned, offering him her back. "Untie it."

He did, but upon pushing it off, found the chemise only went to midthigh. "Anything beneath *this*?" he asked huskily.

She wreathed her arms about his neck. Looked him in the eye. Smiled coyly. "Find out."

He slipped his hands over her thighs, slid them upward, encountered…the one modern-day garment she had on. Tiny red silk bikini panties. "These I am familiar with."

Another smile. "No way was I wearing pantaloons."

"Can't blame you. Although—" he went back to unlacing the front of her chemise "—I do like this."

"I thought you might."

He opened up the edges. Her breasts spilled out. The curves round and silky and pale. The nipples jutting proudly. He covered them with his hands, felt them press into his palms. He lowered his head to hers. She shuddered in response as he kissed her. Her eyes drifted closed, even as her hand slid between them and went to the buttons on his vest. Then his shirt. He shrugged out of both, still kissing her, then spread the edges of her chemise so her breasts were crushed against his bare chest.

She moaned, her body responding to the friction of their skin. Lower still, she was damp, trembling. He eased his hand beneath the elastic of her panties, touching, caressing, tempting, teasing. She reached for the belt of his pants. He caught her hands and held them behind her. Turned her so her back was to his front, then let his free hand slide lower to find the softness.

She whimpered as he slid his palm over her mound, tracing the flowering petals with his fingertips, easing his way inside. Again, and then again. And again. "Nash…"

"Open for me, Callie. All the way. Show me how much you want me…"

She sagged against him, knees weakening, trembling, coming apart in his hands. And again he touched her. Finding. Soothing. Stroking. Until there was no more waiting. Only wanting.

He turned her so she was facing him. Eased her back against the wall. Swiftly disrobed. Loving the sight of her, clad in nothing but the filmy chemise, body aching with the need to claim her, he stepped between her spread thighs.

Breathing raggedly, he lifted her until she was at just the right height. Feeling her full voluptuous breasts tautening, her whole body quivering, his pleasure intensified threefold as her naked thighs brushed against his. Welcoming him home into her silky softness, she tangled her hands in his hair, forcing his mouth back to hers, kissing him until he felt his soul stripped bare. His head got a little lighter, his body got harder. And still they claimed each other. Kissing again and again and again. Moving together. Ever higher. Loving each other with everything they had. Until at last, there was no more holding back, no more waiting, nothing but the most incredible pleasure. And the exaltation of their hearts.

And Nash knew the Christmas he had been longing for, the meaning he had coveted, was finally here.

Chapter 15

Nash was headed out the door of his ranch house the following morning, when his phone rang. "Hey, Nash, it's Fiona Sanders. I was just checking to see if you had made a decision about our open house on Christmas Day."

Nash checked his pocket to make sure he had his wallet. "When did you need to know?"

"Got a better invitation?" she teased, clearly in matchmaker mode.

No, but he was hoping for one. "Actually," Nash said honestly, "this year I've had a half-dozen invitations for both Christmas Day and Christmas Eve." Seemed as if now that he was back for good, everyone was trying to fix him up.

"So you haven't made up your mind, in other words," the older woman guessed.

"I'm not sure if I want to try to hit every gathering—at least for a little while—or just spend the time at home, chilling out." And missing Callie and Brian, who were both due to be in her hometown of Laramie, Texas, on December twenty-fourth and twenty-fifth.

Fiona paused, understanding as always. "Just know you are always welcome in our home. You always have been."

Gratitude welled in his throat. In many ways, Hart's mom had taken the place of his own, in his life, since his parents had moved to Japan. Looking out for him, always making sure he was doing okay, the way any mom of an adult son would. "Thanks, Fiona."

"So what's on your agenda today?" Fiona asked cheerfully.

"Every man's favorite thing—shopping." He had a lot of gift buying to do, and given it was now December twenty-first, not a lot of time left to do it.

The rain was still coming down in droves when Maggie arrived at Callie's home at midmorning, little Henry in tow. After hearing that Hart was definitely on the mend and would be well in time to celebrate the holiday, Callie asked, "Mind looking at something for me?"

"Sure." Maggie left the boys playing with blocks and followed Callie into the living room.

"This morning, the video-guy sent me the finished compilation of the DVD I made for Brian about Seth. Want to tell me what you think?"

Maggie sat down in front of the computer and hit Play. The volume was adjusted to low, but an orchestral version of an upbeat Disney tune could be heard in the background of the five-minute video that tracked Seth from early adulthood to his courtship with Callie to their wedding day and subsequent move into their first place. Sadly, there was nothing after that to showcase.

"Looks good," Maggie said approvingly. "But clearly something is bothering you."

Callie swallowed, trying to get ahold of herself. "I put a rush on this because I wanted to have it ready in time for Christmas, in case there were any issues with not having a male parent around."

"And now?" her twin asked gently.

"Brian's been so happy lately."

"Because of Nash?"

Callie nodded, feeling happy that this was the case—and, at the same time, a little worried it wouldn't last. That something unforeseen would happen to her and Nash, too...

Maggie stepped away from the computer. Fondly, she recollected, "That was something yesterday, what Brian asked Santa to bring him—and you—for Christmas."

Callie blushed, aware how much she wanted the same thing. Nash—for Christmas. "I know." She walked into the kitchen and set the teakettle on to boil.

"My only question is, what are you going to do about it?" Maggie lounged against the counter. "Have you even bought him a gift?"

Sort of. "You know how I had Brian make everyone a gift this year?"

Maggie nodded.

Callie got out the tea and all the fixin's. "I was thinking about doing something along those lines for Nash, too."

"Sounds good," her twin encouraged.

The question was, Callie thought, would Nash think so, too?

* * *

She found out when he stopped by later that evening. Brian, tired from a whole day of playing with his cousin Henry, was already upstairs, fast asleep. Nash was dressed casually like her—in jeans and a sweater. With raindrops glinting in his thick dark hair, his cheeks ruddy with cold, he was sexy as all get-out. Their gazes met and held, and deep inside her, desire built.

"How did the shopping go?" Callie asked, ushering him inside.

He hung up his coat, and taking her hand in his, gave it a squeeze. "Good. Finally. I think… I hope."

Deciding she wanted more, she turned around to give him a full-body hug. He returned it in spades and followed it with a long, leisurely kiss that kicked up her pulse even more.

"I guess we'll find out soon," Nash added humorously.

"You sound like you have my talent when it comes to gift giving," Callie teased. She wrinkled her nose at him.

"A whole lot of thought without necessarily reaping a whole lot of result?" Nash paraphrased.

She laughed and drew him into the living room to sit before the fire. "And the more pressure there is to come up with the perfect gift, the more unpredictable the result."

"Pretty much, yeah. Although," he boasted as he settled next to her on the sofa, "I think I may have nailed it with you."

Which made it even more important that he like what she wanted to give to him. Sobering, Callie cleared her throat and took both of his hands in hers. "Speaking of presents, I want to talk to you about the one I am proposing that Brian and I give you."

"Okay."

She struggled with a myriad of emotions. "You know that I'm supposed to drive Brian home to Laramie on December 24 and spend Christmas Eve with my in-laws, and Christmas Day with my family. It's tradition. And I'm really looking forward to it." She tightened her fingers on his. "But I really wanted to spend Christmas with you, too."

He gazed into her eyes and returned softly, "I've been thinking about that, too. Because I really want to enjoy the holiday with you and Brian."

"So here's what I propose. What if tomorrow night, you and I create our own Christmas Eve celebration here, and then have our own Christmas Day celebration together early on December 24? Before I head to Laramie with Brian."

He lifted a shoulder. "Or I could go with the two of you to your hometown and enjoy Christmas with you there." He paused. "Seems like it might be easier for you and less confusing for Brian. Although I would also like to be with you on the twenty-third. So we could still do our own private celebration before we left."

Callie bit her lip, wondering how everything could go awry so quickly. "You want to meet my parents?" she asked in shock, not sure she was anywhere near ready for that.

"And all your sisters." Nash flashed another easy half smile. "I've already met Doris and Rock."

Her emotions in turmoil, Callie withdrew her hands, stood. Outside the rain continued to fall, harder now.

Unable to look into his eyes, she paced away from Nash. "That's not a good idea."

He followed her to the hearth. "Why not?"

She whirled to face him. "Because if I were to take you home it would be a whole different holiday than the one I have planned."

His face took on a brooding expression. "In what way?"

"You know how wildly enthusiastic Doris and Rock are, under the best of circumstances. They already have us practically married off. So if I were to just show up with you on my arm, they would take it to mean we were as serious about each other as they had hoped." She winced. "And then they'd be shouting it from the rooftops to everyone in town."

Tension knotted her gut as she forced herself to continue as pragmatically as possible. "And, on the other end of the spectrum, we'd have my parents jumping to the same conclusion as Rock and Doris." She paused to look Nash in the eye, and her throat ached with the tears she suppressed.

"Only my folks wouldn't approve, Nash." She moved closer. "Because the last thing they want to see is me diving into something heart-first, when I've already made that mistake once before."

He regarded her soberly, still listening.

"And then there's my son to consider. You've heard him, Nash! He already wants you to come and live with us. If I take you home to Laramie, and everyone reacts the way I predict, Brian will be elated when he's around Doris and Rock, and even more confused and upset when he's around my parents." She sighed wearily. "It would just be a bad situation, all around."

He folded his arms across his chest. "And of course that's not what you want."

His accusation stung. Again, she tried to make him understand. "I just want things to stay simple, and easy, and uncomplicated." Even though that didn't really seem possible, especially when her feelings for Nash were so complicated. And getting more so every day. "At least whenever I'm in Laramie," Callie added lamely.

"Where you are still known as the tragic young widow." He lifted a hand before she could protest. "Those are your words, Callie, not mine."

She lifted her chin. "I don't like being referred to that way!" It was a miserable way to live. And he knew it, too—since he had suffered a similar fate due to his own family tragedy.

He continued to study her calmly. "Then why not do something to change it?"

Irked by his refusal to understand, Callie threw up her hands. "I have. I moved away. I struck out on my own." All of that had helped her cast off the stigma of being a young widow. "And that's where I would like to keep things for now."

"Meaning what?" he countered. "You don't want any man in your life—at least publicly? It's okay if we have an affair in the shadows, as long as no one else knows about it? Is that what the deal is?"

Pretty much. "For now. However, in the future," Callie promised sincerely, when she felt she could handle it, "things will be different."

Cynicism darkened his slate-gray eyes. "Okay. Give me a timetable. If not now, when will you let people know that you and I are seeing each other? *Seriously* seeing each other?"

"I—"

He stood his ground. "January? February? March? Six months from now? A year?"

"I don't know. Whenever it feels right!"

He exhaled roughly, looking as ticked off as she felt. "Or maybe never."

An ugly silence fell. To the point Callie wondered if she had ever really known him at all.

"Why are you putting all this pressure on me?" she asked, upset.

His jaw clenching, he braced himself as if for battle. "Because you aren't the only one who doesn't want to make the same mistakes you made before," he said in a low, accusing tone. "Because I spent the last half of my childhood pinning my hopes on my parents' promise that one day they would get over my brother's death, that one day things would be normal again, that one day we'd be able to celebrate Christmas and treasure all that we still had, instead of dwelling on what we had lost."

He moved closer, pain radiating in his eyes and voice. She could swear she saw the glimmer of tears. "Only it never happened, Callie. Those were empty promises given by two people who had either forgotten— or maybe were just unwilling—to ever fill their lives with love again."

Now she was crying, too. "I'm not like that."

His glance raked over her sadly. "You just don't want to ever marry again."

Feeling as if her whole world was crashing down upon her once again, she moved closer, locking her eyes with his. "I was honest with you about that from the very first," she reminded him quietly. Before he had come into her life, she hadn't thought she could ever risk it. She still wasn't sure she could.

Nash's shoulders sagged in defeat. "You're right—you were up front about that," he admitted. "I just didn't listen." He gave her one long, last look, then said quietly, "Merry Christmas, Callie. Tell Brian I wish him the same."

He grabbed his coat, and without a backward glance, walked out into the icy December rain.

Chapter 16

"Well, there you are!" the jeweler said. "We didn't think you were ever going to come in to pick up your rings."

Callie forced a smile she couldn't begin to feel as she handed over her credit card for payment. "I'm sorry it's taken me so long."

"Busy time?" The kind older man gave her the slip to sign, then went to retrieve her jewelry.

"Very," Callie told him when he returned. At least it had been. Now, with Nash out of her life, things seemed lonely. Quiet. Too quiet.

The jeweler put the engagement and wedding rings out for Callie to inspect. "How do they look?"

"Beautiful," Callie said softly. The platinum bands gleamed and the diamond sparkled radiantly—yet seemed like a lifetime ago, too.

"Would you like to wear them out?" the jeweler asked.

Callie knew her days of wearing her rings and pretending she was still married—even if it was just to discourage men from approaching her—were over. "I'll carry them, thanks."

The jeweler tucked her rings into the satin folds of a small velvet box. He closed it and slid it into a bag. "Have a merry Christmas!" he said.

"You, too," Callie replied. Although inwardly, it was hard to imagine how she was going to be very merry without Nash in her life. But like it or not, she had to move on.

So Callie went to the bank. She placed her rings in her safety deposit box, along with all the other important papers relating to her marriage to Seth. Then headed to her sister's to pick up Brian, who was happily playing "Reindeer and Santa Claus" with his cousin Henry in the family room while Maggie wrapped presents for the extended family nearby.

Callie made herself a cup of peppermint tea and sat down. "Where's Hart?"

"Out doing stuff for Christmas."

Glad to turn the spotlight on someone else, she said playfully, "Don't tell me he's a last-minute shopper."

"Are you kidding?" Maggie fit a blender on the wrapping paper, then began to cut it to the appropriate size. "He took care of all that weeks ago. He's on a more personal mission today, and don't ask me anything more, because that's all I know. And speaking of being kept in the dark…" She taped the paper into place. "You want to tell me what's going on with you and Nash? Brian told Henry that you were sad last night."

Callie tensed. "He wasn't supposed to know that." In fact, still determined to give her son the best Christmas ever, she had done her best to put on a merry front for her little boy's behalf.

Maggie affixed a big bow to the package. "Well, obviously, he picked up on your mood anyway." She paused to give her twin a pointed look. "So what's going on?"

Briefly, Callie brought her sister up to speed. When she'd finished, silence fell between them. Maggie reached for another gift. "Do you still think you made the right decision?" she asked quietly.

Callie helped her sister center the present on the paper, then handed her the scissors. "I can't take Nash home to Laramie with me, Maggie. Not at this point, anyway. It's hard enough for me to get through the holidays, as is."

Her sister folded the ends into neat triangular shapes and taped them against the seam. "You don't think Nash would make it all easier for you?"

Callie swallowed her tea with a grimace. "Here at the ranch with just me and Brian? Yes. Back in Laramie, with Seth's parents trying to get me to marry again as soon as possible, and Mom and Dad trying to keep me from rushing into anything heart-first? No."

"Come on, Callie. You can handle parental meddling. You always have."

She shrugged. "So?"

Maggie gave her another look that saw way too much. "There's more to your not wanting to take Nash home with you than what you've said thus far. And don't tell me it's gossip from the locals, either, because even if you don't like it, you can handle that, too."

Knowing it would be cathartic to unburden herself to her twin, Callie sighed. "I'm in a good place now, Maggie. At least I have been, up until yesterday." She traced the handle on the tea mug, then took another sip. "And you know why I've been feeling so strong and to-gether?" Deciding the tea tasted way too bitter, she got up and rummaged around for some sugar. "Because I've maintained my independence and kept everything in perspective."

Maggie finished another present and set it aside. She got up to make herself a cup of tea, too. Suddenly they heard whoops came from the family room, then the jingle of bells and more hearty ho-ho-hos. Mugs in hand, Maggie and Callie peeked around the corner. The boys were seated side by side on the sofa, pretending to drive the sleigh.

Grinning, the twins returned to the gift-wrapping and their unresolved conversation. "Look, I'm the first to admit you've been doing great, Callie. And yet, there's been something vital missing from your life. Even Brian—as young as he is—feels it."

"Hey, I do a great job as a single mom."

"No one said you didn't," Maggie returned gently. "But there's more to life than putting a moat around your heart. More to teach your son, too." She paused to let her words sink in. "Especially at this time of year."

Guilt flooded her. She knew Christmas was about giving, and that Nash had been giving a lot more than he had been taking, and she had been taking a lot more than she had been giving. She had hoped to rectify that by giving him the happy family Christmas he'd been longing for—a day early—but he'd rejected that as too little. Not realizing what it had cost her to stop protecting herself and her son to even offer that. And now the two of them were at a stalemate. Feeling like more of a failure than ever, Callie sighed again. "Look, Maggie, I know your life is more wonderful than you ever dreamed it could be. And it's all because of the joy Hart brought to your life."

"He taught me to lower my guard and put myself out there." Maggie hesitated. "It seems to me that Nash is doing the same for you. Or trying."

"I know that." Callie felt on the verge of crying once again. She was never as happy as she was with him. The same went for her son.

"But?"

She blinked back her tears. "Everything was moving too fast."

"Sometimes life does."

Fear gripped her heart. "I can't go back to living in a cloud of romance."

Her twin shook her head at her in exasperation. "As opposed to a cloud of despair?"

Callie dug in stubbornly. "I have Brian to think of now. I can't afford to fall apart again, the way I did after Seth died."

"You're talking about your bout of exhaustion," Maggie guessed.

Callie nodded miserably. "If I hadn't allowed myself to wrap my whole life around Seth, if I had maintained at least some emotional independence, then I would have fared a whole lot better after his death."

"Oh, Callie." Maggie's own eyes filled with tears as she took her sister in her arms and hugged her fiercely, understanding as only an identical twin could. "It wasn't that you felt too much, it was what you refused to allow yourself to feel that sent you reeling."

Was her sister right? Callie wondered in shock. Was that really the case?

She wondered about it all the way home. By the time they reached the ranch, her son had taken on her low, dispirited mood. Thinking maybe this was the time to show him the comforting video montage of his father she had made, she popped the DVD in and sat down with him on the sofa.

He watched the five-minute video of Seth, which had been set to some of his favorite upbeat music, with quiet fascination. Heartened by his positive response, Maggie turned to him and said, "Again?"

Brian nodded.

He watched it again, still thoughtful. Then, when it had ended, turned to her and asked, "Where my friend, Mommy?" Brian's lower lip quavered and his blue eyes were so sad they broke her heart. "Where Nash?"

Late on the afternoon of December 22, Nash opened the front door. He took one look at Hart's face and knew the word had spread. "You heard."

Hart stepped inside the ranch house, his expression grim but determined. "Maggie told me. And for the record, I think you're making a terrible mistake letting Callie push you away."

Nash shrugged. "It's not like I have much choice."

"There's always a choice," his friend said.

"I'm looking for someone who's in it for the long haul. She doesn't want to get married, any more than my ex did."

Hart slid him a sly look. "You're that bad of a catch?"

Nash poked at the fire in the hearth. "It doesn't have anything to do with me."

"Sure about that?"

He shifted the logs until the flames leaped once again. "It has to do with the fact she's still mourning the loss of Seth and may never be ready or able to move on."

Hart lounged against the mantel and folded his arms across his chest. "She seemed over him to me. To Maggie, too."

Nash released a short, mirthless laugh. "She was still wearing her wedding rings a month ago."

"She's not wearing them now."

Nash replaced the screen, stood. "Because she had a rash on her hand."

"The rash on her ring finger went away as soon as she started spending quality time with you. Maggie and I both noticed that."

So had Nash, but he was through deluding himself into thinking that Callie cared about him the way he needed her to. Aware the roaring fire had done nothing to dispel the chill in his home, he walked over to the bar and poured them each a neat shot of whiskey.

"She has all these pictures of Seth on her computer." And who could compete with a ghost who, according to everything Nash had heard, had been the most perfect, romantic guy in the entire world?

Hart sipped his drink. "She's making that DVD for Brian. So he'll have something of his dad."

The whiskey burned as it hit Nash's throat, but did nothing to allay the emptiness in his soul. "And one day, when he's older, I am sure that Brian will deeply appreciate everything he discovers about the dad he never got to meet. But right now, he is just a little kid, and he needs more than photos in his life."

Hart took off his jacket then sat down. "Finally, something we can agree upon."

Nash continued to pace. "He needs a man in his life who can give him the love and attention he needs."

"And guess who Brian would like to fill that role?"

Nash looked down at his drink, admitting in weary resignation, "I'd like him to be my son, too. But that's hardly the point."

Hart's eyes were sharp and penetrating. "What *is* the point?"

"Callie is refusing to let us take things any further. Hell, she doesn't even want anyone to know we've been seeing each other." And though he hadn't minded keeping what was happening just between them in the beginning, as time went on, he had started to resent skulking around in the shadows.

"So you're saying she's serious about protecting her reputation?"

Nash finished the rest of his drink and set the glass aside. "I'm saying she's serious about making sure we never get to the point where we actually make a lasting, lifelong commitment to each other."

Hart settled more comfortably on the sofa. "She just wants to see you when it's convenient for her to do so."

"And when it's not, I can damn well find somewhere else to be."

His friend rubbed his jaw. "I can see why you'd be ticked off. No guy ever wants to be treated as a sex object."

Nash rolled his eyes. "It was more than that," he returned impatiently.

"Sure about that?" Hart challenged mildly in return.

Nash thought about the way she had kissed and touched and held him. The way she had looked at him when she thought he wasn't aware. Emotion roiled in his chest. Tightened his throat. "Yes." He moved to the window and focused on the bleak winter weather outside. "She was…"

A heavy silence fell. "What?"

Nash resumed his pacing. "Starting to fall for me, the way I was starting to fall for her."

"And yet—here you are. And there she is."

He pivoted, hurt warring with the anger in his gut. "What are you saying?"

Hart stood and looked him square in the eye. "Just that if you were as giving and patient and understanding as she needs you to be, given what she's been through—and what *you've* been through—you'd probably be spending the Christmas holiday in a whole different way."

Callie was still trying to figure out the best way to make things right when she received a text from Nash at eight that evening. Need to get Brian's presents to you. If he's asleep, can I drop them off now?

Her pulse racing, she texted back, Yes. Now is fine. I'll leave the bunkhouse door open for you. See you soon.

Ten minutes later, his pickup truck cruised down the lane. She was waiting on the front porch of her ranch house, wrapped in her coat and hat, the path to what she hoped would be reconciliation resting in her pocket. Because it was raining again and colder than ever, he parked his pickup so the passenger side aligned with the covered bunkhouse porch. He hopped out and,

Stetson slanted rakishly across his brow, opened up the rear passenger door.

Her heart hammering in her chest, she watched as he carried in the toy workshop and two riding tractors he had painstakingly assembled.

Finished, he set the lock and pulled the door shut.

Callie waved him over. He closed up his truck and strode toward her, looking tough and sexy in the evening light. He smelled good, too, like pine and winter and Nash. She tilted her head back, gaze roving his handsome face. Then her throat went tight. "If you have a minute..." she said softly.

The corner of his mouth tipped up beneath the masculine reserve. "I do."

"Good, because I'd really like you to come in."

He followed her into the hall. Waited, more patiently than he ever had.

Callie swallowed hard. "May I take your coat and hat?"

His eyes never leaving hers, he handed them over.

She hung the damp garments on the tree rack. Tried not to throw herself into his arms and beg forgiveness right off the bat. First, she knew, they had a few things to work out.

"Can I offer you some coffee?"

His gaze remained serious, but his smile broadened. "Sounds good," he said huskily.

Nervous now that the moment was upon them, she gestured inanely at the platter of vanilla and chocolate spritz cookies. "There are cookies, too."

He nodded and, ignoring everything else, took her into his arms. His body was warm and strong against hers. He threaded his hands through her hair and gazed down at her. Repentant. Somber. And most of all, gentle. "I'm sorry about the way things ended between us."

She splayed her hands over the steady thrumming of his heart. "So am I. And, just for the record, I don't want what's been between us to end."

"I don't either."

She paused and moved away from him. "But there are some things I have to say before we continue."

He went still. "I'm listening."

"Up until the time my husband died, I led a charmed life. Nothing really bad had ever happened to me, and I had convinced myself it never would. So when I lost Seth so unexpectedly, it turned my whole world upside down. Everything I thought I knew about what the future held was suddenly wrong. And yet I was pregnant, so I knew I had to carry on…"

She released a deep shuddering breath, forced herself to look him in the eye. "So I ignored all the grief and the fear, the pain and the confusion, and I pretended to everyone that I was stronger than anyone had ever expected. Only I wasn't. And I crashed and crashed hard."

He reached over and took her hand, squeezed it encouragingly. With effort, Callie continued, "The medical explanation was a combination of electrolyte imbalance, fatigue and dehydration. A few days of rest and IV fluids, a referral to a grief specialist and a return to my hometown and family, and I was fine again. Or so I thought. Only I wasn't okay, Nash. I haven't been for a long time." She hitched in a breath. "Not until you came along and helped me see that my fear of loss, my refusal to let myself really feel much of anything, was the real enemy."

He took her other hand, too. Studied her kindly. "And you're not afraid anymore?"

She relished the warmth and tenderness of his grip. "I wish I could say I wasn't. I wish I could say that I know I wouldn't crash harder than ever if I lost you, but I can't. What's different now is that I'm willing to forget about holding back. I'm willing to take the risk."

Nash sensed what it was costing Callie to open up her heart to him like this. But she wasn't the only one who had a confession to make. Hooking his foot beneath a chair, he pulled it away from the table, sank down in it and lowered her onto his lap. Wrapping both arms around her waist, he admitted in a low, rusty-sounding voice, "It's not just you who's been stuck. The truth is—" and it was a truth she had helped him see "—I've had my guard up for years. Since my brother died, really. Until you and Brian came along, that was. Suddenly, I couldn't turn away."

She offered a tremulous smile.

"Part of it was my attraction to you," he confessed.

She settled more intimately against him, curling one hand around his shoulders, resting the other over his heart. "Our chemistry *is* pretty strong."

He nodded, continuing honestly, "Another part was the way I feel about your son. Because he's not just a cute, engaging, precocious little boy with the biggest heart I've ever seen—" Nash grinned "— he's also so much like you in so many ways it's uncanny."

Callie laughed, admitting, "He does have the McCabe stubbornness and determination."

"Yet another thing I love about him," Nash declared.

Callie sighed contentedly, apparently ready to lighten the mood. "He loves you, too."

But Nash couldn't shift to play until they had worked out their future. In a way that would last this time. More than ready to meet her halfway, he said quietly, "The question is, what do you want from me? Is it friendship? A friends-with-benefits arrangement? A secret love affair? Because whatever it is, Callie," he vowed huskily, "I'm prepared to give it to you." *Because giving is what Christmas is all about.*

She smiled impishly and he felt his mouth curve in return. "How about all of the above, minus the secret component? Plus—" she pulled him closer still, till their lips were just an inch apart "—how about we throw in all the love I have for you—for the rest of my life?"

Love. She'd said she loved him? He kissed her fiercely. "You mean that?"

Nodding, she took his face between her hands. "I do." She kissed him until they were both breathless and then rested her forehead against his. "I love you, Nash."

The softness of her surrender was all he had ever dreamed. "I love you, too." He shifted her off his lap, then stood, as well. "And I'm willing to give you all the time you need. Which is why—" he reached into the pocket of his jeans "—I got you this." He handed her a small velvet box.

Callie opened it up. Inside was the most beautiful garnet he'd been able to find. Judging by the look on her face, it suited her perfectly. "My birthstone," she breathed in delight.

Glad she liked what he'd picked out for her, he said, "To symbolize new beginnings." He took it out of the case, then took her hand in his. "I had the stone mounted on a ring, because the circle—like my love for you— is never ending. And, as you can see," he noted as he carefully slid it over her knuckle, "it goes on your right hand, not your left."

Humor sparkled in her pretty blue eyes as she held out her hand to admire his gift. "Because you're afraid I'll get another rash?"

"No." Shaking his head, he lifted her wrist to his lips. "Because I don't want you wearing a ring on that hand until you're ready."

Color swept into her cheeks. "You do understand."

"I'm sorry I rushed you."

She cuddled against him. "I'm sorry I didn't tell you sooner how I felt." He kissed her again, lingeringly this time.

Finally, she pressed her hand to his chest, drew back reluctantly. With a smile, she admitted, "I got you a present, too."

First was a framed photo of their selfie. "I love it," he said.

"Good, because it's only a hint of all the good times to come."

Second was a card.

"Open it," Callie urged in excitement.

Nash read, "You are cordially invited to spend December 24 and 25 with Callie and Brian at the Heart of Texas Ranch, a place where all your yuletide dreams can come true." He paused to look at her. "You're not going home to Laramie?"

"Not until after Christmas, on the 26th. And when we do, I'd very much like you to accompany us, so I can introduce you properly to my parents and the rest of my sisters."

Nash regarded her solemnly. "You're sure?"

"I am." Callie beamed up at him. "This way we can have the best of both worlds. The new life we're creating, and then the introduction of the rest of the family and friends you'll be joining when you hook up with me."

He flashed her a wicked smile. "Hooking up sounds good," he teased.

"Mommy." A small voice called before he could kiss her again. Familiar footsteps pounded down the stairs. "Santa here?" Brian asked.

"Even better," Callie informed with a smile.

Getting a glimpse of their company, the pajama-clad little boy opened his arms wide. He scampered across the floor. "My friend! Nash!"

"Merry Christmas to you, too, buddy!" Nash said. Even though the holiday was officially another twenty-eight hours away, it felt as if it was starting now.

"Mer' Chris—" Brian said right back. He hugged Nash and then his mom fiercely before inclining his head toward the exit. "Outside! See, Mommy!"

Perplexed, they headed for the door.

"Well, what do you know!" Callie and Nash stared in disbelief. "Snow?" she breathed.

On December 23! Aware they now had everything they ever wanted and needed, Nash took both Callie and Brian into his arms. "Seems like dreams do come true."

Epilogue

Callie and Nash were in the ranch house kitchen, assembling a gingerbread house, when the voices drifted out to them from the adjacent playroom.

"I got a daddy," Brian said to his cousin Henry, while the two of them worked on constructing their version of the North Pole with wooden building blocks. "Do you have a daddy?"

"Of course I got a daddy." Henry moved around to put on the roof before adding importantly, "And I got a baby brother, too."

"I'm going to have a baby brother," Brian boasted.

Callie and Nash looked at each other. They had been at this for a month now.

Grinning, Nash rose with gentlemanly leisure. "My turn?"

Contentment flowing through her, Callie smiled back. "Have at it." Because if there was anything she and her new husband had learned, it was that when Brian did not *want* to understand something, he did not *ever* understand something.

"Actually, fellas, Brian might have a baby brother, and he might have a baby sister," Nash hunkered down to explain to three-and-a-half-year-old Brian and four-year-old Henry. "His mommy and I don't know what kind of baby is in her tummy right now. We're just very happy that she is going to have a baby next summer. It won't matter if it's a girl or a boy."

"I know what it is, Daddy." Disregarding Nash's careful explanation, Brian stood and moved carefully around the beautifully decorated Christmas tree from Echols Mountain to work on the other side of his budding creation. *"It's a boy."*

"Yeah," cousin Henry chimed in, "I think so, too."

Nash stood as well and eyed the gloomy winter weather outside.

Callie knew what her husband was thinking. Rain, not snow, was predicted, but you never knew…especially when they were in the midst of record cold.

Her husband braced his hands on his hips. "Well, like I said, it could be either one, fellas. We'll find out for sure when the baby is born in six months."

"Daddy! We already know," Brian countered in exasperation. "It's a boy. And when he gets here, then we'll have four boys to play with. Me and Henry and his brother and my brother."

Callie strolled in to join them—and rescue Nash. "Seems like you boys have it all figured out."

Brian and Henry scowled. "'Course we do," they said in unison.

Callie took Nash's hand in hers. He squeezed her hand in return. They exchanged smiles and retreated to the adjacent kitchen. It was hard to believe how much her life had changed in just one year, Callie reflected happily, but there was no denying that all was good.

After a six-month courtship that was at once low-key and highly romantic, she and Nash had married at the top of Echols Mountain, with just a few family and friends present. Nash had moved into Callie and Brian's home. And he was using his ranch house as an office to accommodate his growing business.

Once married, they'd gotten busy at expanding their family. And now they were enjoying their second holiday season together. With, she hoped, a very special surprise for them all still to come.

"So what do *you* think?" Nash asked, as Callie spread the creamy white icing over the roof and down the sides of the gingerbread house. "Since you're the one with the miracle growing inside you. Girl or boy?"

"You never know," Callie teased. She dipped an extra piece of gingerbread into the buttercream and lovingly fed it to him. "It could be twins. Possibly even one of each. Multiples do run in my family…"

"Can't say I'd mind that." Nash brought her close and kissed her tenderly on the lips. He tasted of sugar, spice and man. "Although it *would* upset the logistics of Brian and Henry's plans."

Callie shrugged and fed him another piece of icing-dipped cake. "Well, then," she reckoned, "Hart and Maggie would just have to get busy again."

Nash sobered comically and fed her cake, too. "You're right." He dabbed a little bit of icing from the corner of her lip. "Why should we have all the fun?" He threaded his hands through her hair and kissed her again, even more thoroughly this time.

Youthful footsteps pounded on the wood floor behind them. "Ugh! Kissing!" Brian and Henry said in unison.

Reluctantly, Callie and Nash moved apart.

Brian squinted. "Why do grown-ups do that?"

"I don't know," Henry declared, "but my parents are always kissing, too. 'Specially under the mistletoe."

Tired of discussing something he found so disdainful, Brian stepped closer to the kitchen table. "Mommy, is the house ready to decorate?"

Callie brought out the bowls of colorful candy she'd already prepared. "It sure is."

Nash pulled up two chairs. The boys climbed on and got busy. And for a while all was lost in the magic of placing gumdrops and other assorted candies on the yuletide creation.

When they were done, they all stepped back to admire their handiwork Nash looked out the window once again. "Well, what do you know," he said in wonder, shaking his head.

Everyone turned in the direction of his gaze. An older couple was coming up the walk. They looked a little jet-lagged. Their arms were laden with gifts.

Nash turned to Callie, a question in his eyes. "I asked your parents to come," she said softly. "I pointed out that healing the rift would be the best gift of all."

"And they agreed?" he asked hoarsely.

Callie's eyes filled with tears of joy, as she nodded. "They love you, Nash. They always have. They just..." Her voice caught, too. "They had a hard time showing it."

He hugged her close. "This couldn't have been easy," he said in a low, choked voice.

It hadn't been. But there were some things worth fighting for. Family, paramount among them.

She hugged him back, just as ferociously. "They know, with the new baby on the way, it's time we put the heartbreak of the past behind us and start celebrating all that we have now, in this moment. So what do you say?" Callie took Nash's hand and then turned to Brian and his cousin Henry. "Are you fellas ready to greet Nash's mommy and daddy and have them spend Christmas here, too?"

The "fellas" in her life grinned.

"You bet!" they said in unison.

Nash opened the door.

Once again, Callie noted with a smile, they were going to have the Christmas of their dreams.

* * * * *

Since 2002, *USA TODAY* bestselling author **Judy Duarte** has written over forty books for Harlequin Special Edition, earned two RITA® Award nominations, won two Maggie Awards and received a National Readers' Choice Award. When she's not cooped up in her writing cave, she enjoys traveling with her husband and spending quality time with her grandchildren. You can learn more about Judy and her books on her website, judyduarte.com, or at Facebook.com/judyduartenovelist.

Books by Judy Duarte

Harlequin Special Edition

Rocking Chair Rodeo

Roping in the Cowgirl
The Bronc Rider's Baby
A Cowboy Family Christmas
The Soldier's Twin Surprise
The Lawman's Convenient Family

The Fortunes of Texas: All Fortune's Children

Wed by Fortune

The Fortunes of Texas: The Secret Fortunes

From Fortune to Family Man

The Fortunes of Texas: The Rulebreakers

No Ordinary Fortune

Brighton Valley Cowboys

The Boss, the Bride & the Baby
Having the Cowboy's Baby
The Cowboy's Double Trouble

Return to Brighton Valley

The Daddy Secret
The Bachelor's Brighton Valley Bride
The Soldier's Holiday Homecoming

Visit the Author Profile page at
Harlequin.com for more titles.

A COWBOY FAMILY CHRISTMAS

JUDY DUARTE

To my aunties: Dorothy Johnston Eggleston and Loraine Shaw.

Thank you for your incredible love and support over the years. I love you both!

Chapter 1

Dear Debbie,
I'm desperate and need your help.

Elena Montoya studied the first of several letters she'd been handed during her job interview at *The Brighton Valley Gazette*. She'd come here today, hoping to get her foot in the door at the small-town newspaper, but as a reporter. Not someone offering advice to the lovelorn in a weekly column.

Mr. Carlton, the balding, middle-aged editor, leaned forward, resting clasped hands on his desk. "So what do you think?"

Seriously? Elena would be hard-pressed to offer advice to anyone, especially someone with romantic trouble. But she didn't want to reveal her inexperience or doubt. "I'd hoped to land a different assignment—or another type of column."

"Let's see what you can do with this first." Mr. Carlton leaned back in his desk chair, the springs creaking under his weight, the buttons of his cotton shirt straining to contain his middle-age spread.

Elena knew better than to turn down work, even though this job wasn't a good fit. Worse yet, the pay he'd offered her wasn't enough to cover a pauper's monthly expenses. And since she was new in town, she needed a way to support herself.

But as an advice columnist? The irony was laughable.

"You look a bit…uneasy," the editor said.

She *was*. Either Mr. Carlton had neglected to read her resume or he'd confused her with another applicant.

"It's just that…" She cleared her throat and chose her words carefully. "Well, don't get me wrong. I'm happy to have this position, but I only took two psych courses in college. And since I majored in journalism, I'm more qualified to work as a reporter."

"Don't worry. It shouldn't be too difficult for a young woman like you, Elena."

She cringed at his use of her given name. The last thing she needed was for her new co-workers at the newspaper—or any rodeo fans in the small Texas community—to connect the dots and realize who she was. And why she looked familiar—in spite of her efforts to change her appearance.

"By the way," she said, "I go by Lainie." At least, that's the childhood nickname her twin sister had given her.

"All right," Mr. Carlton said. "Then *Lainie* it is. But

keep in mind you'll be known as 'Dear Debbie' around here. We like her true identity to be a secret."

A temporary secret identity was just what Lainie needed. After that embarrassing evening, when rodeo star Craig Baxter's wife had caught him and Elena together at a hotel restaurant in Houston and assumed the worst, Elena had done her best to lay low. The next day, she'd relocated to a ranch outside of Brighton Valley, where she could hide out until she could rise above those awful rumors—all of which were either untrue or blown way out of proportion.

Elena had tried to explain how she'd come to be there that night—how she had no idea that Craig was a rodeo star, let alone married—to no avail. Kara Baxter had been so angry at her husband, she'd thrown a margarita in Elena's face and read him the riot act. As if that hadn't been bad enough, someone at another table had caught it all on video, and the whole, ugly scene had gone viral. And now Kara's friends and Craig's fans blamed her for splitting up a marriage that wouldn't have lasted anyway.

"Do you have any other questions?" Mr. Carlton asked.

As a matter of fact, she had a ton of them, but she didn't want to show any sign of insecurity.

"I do have one question," she admitted. "Some of the people writing these letters could be dealing with serious issues. And if that's the case, I'm not qualified to offer them any advice." Nor should she counsel anyone, for that matter.

Mr. Carlton shook his head and waved off her concern. "Our last Debbie used to have a stock answer for the bigger problems. She told them to seek professional help."

Lainie nodded. "Okay. Then I'll use that response." A *lot*.

"Just focus on the interesting letters or on those that trigger a clever response," Mr. Carlton said. "It's really just entertainment for most people. But keep in mind, if the readership of the Dear Debbie column increases, I'll give you a bigger assignment in the future."

At least, he'd given her a chance to prove herself, something she'd had to do time and again since the third grade, when she'd gone from a foster home to a pediatric intensive care unit and lost track of her sister. "I'll give it my best shot, Mr. Carlton."

"Okay, kid. What's the best number if I need to get a hold of you?"

"I listed my cell on my resume, although that's not the best way to reach me. I'm temporarily staying at the Rocking Chair Ranch. Since the reception isn't very good there, and the Wi-Fi is worse, you'd better call me on the landline." She pointed to her resume, which he'd set aside on his desk. "I included that number, too, and marked it with an asterisk."

"If you don't mind me asking, why are you staying at a retirement home for old cowboys?"

"Because I'm filling in for the ranch cook, who'll be gone for the next three weeks." When Lainie first heard about the temporary position, she'd declined. But after that awful run-in with Kara Baxter, she'd changed her mind and accepted it out of desperation, realizing it would provide her with a place to stay until she could find something better and more permanent in town.

Oddly enough, she actually felt a lot more comfortable staying at the Rocking C than she'd thought she would. And she liked the old men who lived there. Most of them were sweet, and even the crotchety few were entertaining.

Mr. Carlton pushed back his chair and got to his feet, signaling the interview was over.

Lainie stood, too. Still hoping for something more respectable and better paying, she said, "I minored in photography, so if you need a photojournalist, that's another option."

"I'll keep that in mind. Consider this your trial run, kid."

Lainie nodded and reached for her purse.

Mr. Carlton headed for the door of his office and opened it for her. "I'll send you a copy of the letters electronically, and even if you're somewhere with terrible web access, your column is due by email before midnight on Wednesday. I can't wait to see it."

"You won't be disappointed. I'll channel my inner Debbie." Lainie tamped down her doubt, offered him a smile and lifted the letters in her hand. "You'll love what I do with these."

Mr. Carlton beamed, clearly convinced that she'd work a miracle of some kind, but Lainie knew better. And she feared that by Friday morning, when her first column came out, her inadequacy would come to light.

Rodeo promoter Drew Madison drove his pickup down the county highway on his way to the Rocking C Ranch, listening to a Brad Paisley hit on the radio and sporting a confident grin. His plans for the Rocking Chair Rodeo were finally coming together, and a date had finally been set. The county-wide event would be held at the Brighton Valley Fairgrounds in April.

Drew's boss at Esteban Enterprises had granted him free rein on the project, although he'd insisted that Drew move in to the Rocking Chair Ranch for a few weeks, interview the old cowboys who lived there and write a few blog posts sharing their stories.

While Drew had graduated from college and certainly knew how to put a sentence together, he'd never considered himself a writer. But his promotion to VP of the company was on the line, so he'd brushed away his doubt and agreed to do it.

Besides, how hard could writing a few stories be?

His cell phone rang, the Bluetooth automatically shutting out the Brad Paisley tune. He assumed it was another business call, but when he looked at the dashboard and spotted his sister's name on the display, his heart clenched.

Kara Lee had been going through a lot lately, so he'd made it a point to check up on her each morning and evening. To have her contact him in the middle of the day was a little unsettling.

He answered quickly and tried to keep his tone upbeat. "Hey, sis. What's up?"

"Not much. I'm just bored, I guess. I called your office, and they said you were traveling. Not that it really matters, but I thought you would've mentioned something about it to me."

He hadn't meant to keep it a secret, but neither had he wanted her to worry about him being gone and unable to get to the hospital in time if she went into labor. She'd nearly lost her baby last week and was on complete bed rest now.

"Actually," he said, "it's a new assignment. I meant to tell you about it, but I had to cut our morning call short."

"How long will you be gone this time?"

Longer than he wanted to admit, although he was looking forward to meeting the retired cowboys. "I'll be gone for a few weeks, but I'm not far from Houston. If you need me, all you have to do is call. I can get there within a couple of hours."

"I'm sure that won't be necessary," she said, but the tone of her voice betrayed her words. "I'll be fine."

He certainly hoped so. Kara Lee had wanted to be a mother for as long as she could cuddle a dolly. And after three miscarriages, she'd made it to the fifth month this time around. For each day the little boy remained in the womb, the better chance he had.

"So where's this assignment?" she asked.

"The Rocking Chair Ranch. The rodeo will be sponsoring them in the spring, so I'm working on the promotion."

"Is that the retirement home for cowboys?"

"And ranchers." He'd been reluctant to mention anything about rodeos or cowboys since the night she found out her husband, rodeo star Craig Baxter, was having another affair. The stress from the confrontation with him and his lover had caused her to go into premature labor.

When Drew got word of the public blowup and learned that Kara Lee had been hospitalized, he'd wanted to beat the tar out of his brother-in-law. But Kara Lee had begged him not to, and he'd been reluctant to do anything to upset his kid sister, especially when the survival of her son was precarious. But that didn't mean he wouldn't be tempted to knock Craig's lights out the next time he saw him.

Kara Lee had told Craig to pack his crap and to get out of the house, which he did. But she hadn't yet filed for divorce, mostly because she wasn't able to deal with the legal proceedings when she was lying flat on her back. But once the baby came, Drew would do whatever he could to facilitate a fair and amicable split. One of his friends was a divorce attorney in Houston, and he'd already mentioned the case to him. He just hoped his sister didn't soften and take Craig back.

"You sure you're okay?" he asked her again.

"Yeah, especially since I've made it to the twenty-sixth week. At least the baby now has a chance to survive."

"That's good to know."

As silence filled the line, he decided to change the subject. "So what are you doing?" The moment the question rolled off his tongue, he wanted to reel it back in. Hell, what could a bedridden pregnant woman possibly do, other than read or watch TV?

She let out a sigh. "I wish I could work on the nursery, but I'll have to wait until after little Robby gets here."

"I'll tell you what," Drew said. "As soon as I finish this project at the Rocking C, I'll spend a few days at your place. Make a Pinterest board of stuff you like. When I get back, I'll be your hands and feet. We'll have it done before you know it."

"I love you, Drew."

"Aw, for Pete's sake. Don't get all sappy on me, Kara Lee." She'd been a tomboy when growing up—and a barrel racer in high school. So he wasn't used to seeing her softer side. It must be her hormones.

"You're the best, Drew."

"No. I'm not." He'd taken on a demanding job that required him to travel, so he hadn't been there for her recently, like he'd always been in the past.

He kicked himself for that now. If he'd been around more, he might have talked her out of marrying Craig. But that was all muddy water under the bridge now. From here on out, Drew was going to be the brother she deserved.

If Kara Lee suffered yet another miscarriage, losing the baby she'd already named and loved, there was no telling what it would do to her.

"By the way," he said. "I called an agency that provides home health services and asked them to send someone out to your house for a few hours each day. She'll do some light cleaning and run errands for you while I'm gone."

"You didn't need to do that."

"I know, but I wanted to. It makes me feel better to know someone is with you or at least just a phone call away." He thought she might object, more out of pride than anything else. But she surprised him by accepting his effort to help.

"You know what, Drew? You're going to make some woman a wonderful husband."

He laughed. "My last two relationships didn't fare very well, thanks to all my travel." Well, that and the fact that he was beginning to enjoy being a tumbleweed, rolling through life on the whim of the wind.

Just like your old man? He winced, then discarded

the thought as quickly as it came. He wasn't at all like his father.

"Besides," he added, "I'm not cut out for marriage, family or a home in the suburbs. If I was, I wouldn't enjoy being on the road so often."

"A woman who really loves you wouldn't complain about you being gone."

"I don't know about that. You'd be surprised."

"At least, you'd never cheat on her." She paused for a beat. "You wouldn't *cheat*, would you?"

"*Me?* No, I've always been honest with the women I date. From the very first time we go out, I make it clear that I'm not the domestic type."

"I'm not buying that," Kara Lee said.

Drew wasn't about to let his little sister psychoanalyze him. Who knew what assumptions she'd come to, right or wrong.

When he spotted the big yellow sign that indicated he'd reached the Rocking C, he said, "Listen, I have to hang up now. But I'll give you a call this evening."

"You don't have to. I know how busy you are."

"I'm never too busy for you."

And that was the truth. Kara Lee was the only family Drew had left, and after all they'd been through, especially *her*, she deserved to be happy—and to finally be a mom.

"I'm curious," she said. "Where will you be staying while on the ranch?"

"They're putting me up in one of the cabins so I can get a feel for the daily routine. It's not just a retirement home, it's a working ranch. So the whole enterprise is new and innovative. I'd like to check it out."

"Good luck."

"Thanks. I'm actually looking forward to having a change of pace—and to being in the same place for longer than a few days."

"So says the family rover. Maybe you're more cut out for home and hearth than you think, especially if you meet the right woman."

"Oh, yeah? We'll see about that." Drew turned onto the long, graveled drive that led to the Rocking Chair Ranch. "I'll talk to you later."

When the line disconnected, he slowly shook his head. If there was one thing he'd learned over his thirty-one years, it was easier to be a rover than to deal with the countless people who weren't what they seemed and were bound to disappoint you.

Thank goodness he wasn't likely to meet any of that type on the Rocking C.

It had been two days since Mr. Carlton had hired Lainie to write the Dear Debbie column, but she still hadn't made any headway in answering a single letter.

She'd been busy settling into her temporary job. But that wasn't the whole story. In fact, none of the problems of people seeking Debbie's advice had triggered a clever or witty response, and Lainie was stumped.

She sat at the kitchen table, reading through the letters, trying to choose an interesting one or two to include in her first Dear Debbie column. While she pondered, her fingers tapped softly on the keyboard without typing out a single word. She glanced at the clock on the microwave, noting how much time had passed since she'd done the breakfast dishes, and blew out a sigh. Her midnight deadline loomed.

"You can do this," she whispered aloud. Then she reread the letter on top of the stack.

> *Last year, I met John, the most handsome, amazing man in the world, and I knew I'd finally met Mr. Right.*

Last month, Lainie had met Craig…

Darn it. She had to stop projecting that jerk into each of these stupid letters written by someone who'd either been jilted or disappointed by various people in their lives.

> *All I've ever wanted was to fall in love and get married, but now my heart is broken, and my life is a wreck.*

"Tell me about it," Lainie muttered. Well, not the broken heart. She'd gone out with Craig only three times, but the rest of it sounded pretty darned familiar.

> *Then, a few weeks ago, a woman who works at John's office started hitting on him and lured him away from me.*

Lainie leaned back in the chair and shook her head. From the comments left on the YouTube video of her that night at the Houston hotel, it seemed everyone in the rodeo world thought she'd targeted a married man and tried to lure him away.

During the blowup, his wife had told him off, implying that he was a serial cheater, a secret he apparently kept from his legion of fans.

"Aw, come on," Lainie scolded herself. "Focus on *this* woman, *this* letter, *this* problem."

Yet how could she? She was the last person in the world who should offer romantic advice to anyone, let alone a stranger who hoped for an easy fix.

Darn it. No matter how badly she'd wanted a job at the *Gazette*—and she *needed* one if she wanted to support herself—she'd been crazy to agree to taking over for Dear Debbie.

Footsteps sounded in the doorway, drawing her from her reading. She glanced up to see Otis "Sully" Sullivan enter the kitchen. The sweet, kindhearted old man had a jolly way about him. Each time she laid eyes on the retired cowboy, she couldn't help but smile. With a head of thick white hair and a full beard, he reminded her of Santa Claus, especially today when he wore a solid red flannel shirt.

"Hey, Sully."

"I'm sorry to bother you, but is there any more coffee?"

Lainie set aside the letter she'd been reading, pushed back her chair and got to her feet. "It's no bother at all. And you're in luck. There's still at least a cup left."

She poured the last of the carafe into a white mug. "I could make a fresh pot."

"No need for you to go to any extra trouble." Sully took the mug she gave him, gripping it with gnarled hands, and thanked her. "That was a nice breakfast you fixed us today. I haven't had good chilaquiles in a long time. My late wife used to make them for me every Sunday morning, but she usually overcooked them."

Lainie laughed. "Did she? How were mine?"

"Best I've ever had. Nice, crispy tortillas. Perfectly scrambled eggs. Mmm, mmm, mmm."

Lainie beamed at the compliment. She wasn't used to getting many. "Thanks, I'm glad you liked them. When I was a little girl, my grandmother used to make them for me and my sister."

"You got a sister?"

"Yes, a twin."

Sully brightened. "Where is she?"

Lainie had no idea. The two of them had been separated years ago, when Lainie had been taken from the group home and sent to the hospital to be treated for an undetected congenital heart defect. It had taken a while for the doctors to decide upon a treatment plan, and by the time Lainie recovered from her lifesaving surgery, a couple arrived at the children's home, adopted the healthy girl and left the sickly one behind. From what Lainie had gathered, her sister's new parents had been afraid to assume financial responsibility of a child with such serious medical issues.

As a result, she hadn't seen her twin since, but she offered Sully the happy outcome she'd imagined for Erica. "She's happily married to her high school sweetheart and has a two-year-old daughter."

Before Sully could press further, Lainie turned the conversation back to the chilaquiles. "Anyway, my grandmother passed away before she could pass on her recipe. But when I got older, I did some research and a little experimenting until I came up with a batch that tasted nearly as good as hers. I hope they weren't too spicy."

"No," he said, "not at all. The salsa was perfect. In fact, that was one of the tastiest meals I've had since I moved in here. Not that Joy, our regular cook, isn't a good one, but she's more of a down-home, meat-and-potatoes gal. And I like good Mexican food once in a while."

"That's a relief. I knew I'd have some big shoes to fill, taking Joy's place in the kitchen while she's on her honeymoon."

"I haven't heard any complaints yet. And that's saying a lot, considering some of the old geezers who live here. They rarely keep their opinions to themselves." Sully glanced at the letters on the table. "I didn't mean to bother you. I'll just take my coffee into the living room and let you get back to whatever it was you were doing."

"Actually, I don't mind the interruption." Although she really should. With each tick and tock of the kitchen clock, her midnight deadline drew closer. And who knew if the ranch internet would work? She might have to drive into town and find Wi-Fi somewhere. *Darn it.*

"You look fretful, which doesn't do your pretty face any good. What's bothering you?" Sully nodded toward the stack of letters. "I hope it isn't bad news."

"It's just…a friend with a problem." Lainie chewed her fingernail and stared at the pile of unanswered letters. "I'm trying to come up with some wise advice, but I'm not feeling very wise."

Sully's smile softened the lines in his craggy face. "Wisdom comes with age and experience. Back when I was in my twenties, heck, thirties, too, I was under the false notion that I was as smart as I'd ever get."

Lainie had thought the same thing after her college graduation, which wasn't very long ago. Then Craig had taken her for a ride, leaving her with an unearned bad reputation and distrustful of sweet-talking men who couldn't tell the truth to save their souls. She'd learned a big lesson the hard way, but that hadn't made her an expert at facing romantic dilemmas.

"Want me to give it a shot?" Sully asked.

Was he offering his advice? Lainie wasn't sure what the dear old man might have to say, but at this point, she'd take all the help she could get. "Sure, if you don't mind."

Sully pulled out a chair, took a seat and rested his steaming hot mug on the table. "What's the problem?"

Lainie scanned the opening of the letter and caught him up to speed, revealing that her "friend" was twenty-four years old, relatively nice-looking with a decent job and a good sense of humor. Then she read the rest of it out loud.

"Three weeks ago, I found out the guy I was living with, the man of my dreams, was seeing another woman. We had a big fight, and he moved out. I've been crying every day, and I'm desperate to win him back."

Sully clucked his tongue. "A man who cheats on his partner, romantic or otherwise, isn't a prize worth winning back. That's what I'd tell her."

Lainie had once thought Craig was a prize, and boy, had she been wrong about that. It's a shame she hadn't had Sully nearby when she'd been taken in by that liar's soft Southern drawl. But Sully was here now. And providing the wisdom this letter writer needed.

"That's a good point," Lainie said. It was clever, too, and a good response for the column. "I'll mention that to...my friend."

Male voices sounded outside, growing louder until

the mudroom door squeaked open. A second later, Nate Gallagher, the acting foreman, entered the kitchen.

Sully acknowledged Nate with a nod, but Lainie focused on the man walking behind him. She guessed him to be a rancher or horseman, since his stylish Western wear suggested he could afford to hire someone to do the dirty work. He was in his early to midthirties, tall and nice looking, with broad shoulders and a rugged build.

He removed his black Stetson, revealing sandy-blond hair, which he wore longer than most of the rodeo cowboys she'd met. Not that she'd ever been a buckle bunny or even attracted to that kind of guy before she'd met Craig.

And after that awful night, she'd sworn off men indefinitely. Yet she found herself stirred by this one's presence. He also looked familiar. Had she met him before?

"Meet Drew Madison," Nate said. "He's handling the Rocking Chair Rodeo promotion."

Just the word *rodeo* sent Lainie's heart slamming into her chest. Had she seen him while on one of the few dates she'd had with Craig?

No, she'd never forget a man like him.

But if he and Craig ran in the same circles, he might recognize *her*. For that reason, she'd better get out of here. She didn't mind being around the older cowboys, some of whom had ridden in the rodeo back in the days before cable television and social media. But a recent connection spelled trouble—and further humiliation.

Nevertheless, she wouldn't be rude to a ranch visitor. So she placed the letter she'd been holding upside down on the rest of the stack on the table. Then she got to her feet and said, "It's nice to meet you. I'll put on a pot of coffee."

Then she did just that. If there was one thing she'd learned in her short time at the Rocking C, it was that the cowboys, young and old, loved a fresh brew.

As the coffee began to perk, Lainie studied the pot as if it might bounce off the countertop if she didn't stand guard.

She fingered the side of her head, checking to see if any strands had come loose. She used to wear it long, the curls tumbling along her shoulders and down her back. But after that video had gone viral, she'd pulled it up into a prim topknot—just one of several alterations she'd made to her appearance so she could fade into the background until that ugly incident was forgotten.

When the coffeemaker let out a last steamy gurgle, she poured two cups, then turned to face the younger men. They continued to stand in the middle of the kitchen, speaking to Sully, who was still seated at the table. She was about to excuse herself and leave them to chat among themselves, but her curiosity betrayed her and she took one last glace at Drew, who'd zeroed in on her.

"For some reason," he said, his gaze intense enough to see right through her, "it seems as if I've met you before."

"That's not likely," she said. "I'm not from around here."

"Where are you from?"

She wanted to ask, *What's up with the third degree?* Instead, she said, "I'm from up north—originally. But I'm sure we've never met. I just have that kind of face. I get comments like that all the time. Sugar? Cream?"

"I like it black."

His gaze continued to roam over her, as if removing her façade one piece at a time. But she pushed through the discomfort and handed him a mug.

He thanked her but didn't take a drink. Instead, those baby blues continued to study her as if trying to pinpoint where they'd met. But wouldn't she remember if they had? A woman wouldn't forget a man like him.

No, he was mistaken. She glanced down at the loose blouse and baggy jeans she wore today. She hadn't used any makeup. Her curls had been pulled into a bun.

But when she again looked at him, when their gazes locked, her heart soared and her hormones flared. For a moment she wished she'd been wearing that red dress Craig had given her for her birthday and insisted that she wear to the hotel that night, their first significant date, where they were to celebrate by having dinner. But she suspected someone who frequented thrift shops had already snatched it up, pleased with their find.

"If you'll excuse me," Lainie said, "I have work to do."

Then she left the kitchen and headed for her room.

After that awful night in Houston, she'd made up her mind to steer clear of handsome cowboys. And Drew Madison was as handsome as any cowboy she'd ever seen.

Chapter 2

Drew leaned back in his chair and watched the housekeeper stride toward the kitchen doorway. She wasn't the kind of woman he usually found attractive, but for some reason he did, and he hadn't been able to keep his eyes off her.

She had a wholesome, clean-cut way about her. Maybe it was the lack of makeup, which she really didn't need. She looked cute in those baggy overalls and plain white T-shirt, but there seemed to be real beauty underneath.

Her dark hair had been pulled up in a simple topknot, but he imagined it'd be lush and glossy if she wore it loose. And those brown, soulful eyes? A man could get lost in them.

She'd said they'd never met, and she was probably

right. Her name didn't ring a bell. Laney? It wasn't one you heard every day.

Even though she'd already stepped out of the kitchen, he continued to watch the open doorway until Nate mentioned Drew's sister.

"How's Kara Lee doing?" he said. "It must have been devastating for her to lose another baby."

"She's still pregnant, thank goodness."

"Really?" Nate said. "That's good news. I'd heard otherwise, which would have been a real shame."

"There're a lot of rumors going around." Hell, Drew had heard most of them.

"Speaking of babies," Drew said. "How's little Jessica?"

Nate, who'd recently assumed custody of his newborn daughter, a preemie, broke into a proud papa grin. "She's doing great—and growing like a weed."

"And Anna?"

Nate's smile deepened. "She's the best thing that ever happened to me. I love being married."

"Better you than me," Drew said.

Nate chuckled. "Anyway, I'm glad Kara Lee's doing all right."

"Part of what you heard was true," Nate said. "She did go into labor the night she caught Craig cheating. Thankfully, her obstetrician managed to stop the contractions, but she's on bed rest for the time being."

"That's got to be tough," Nate said. "Especially for an active woman like her."

"You got that right, she's determined to have this baby. And she'll do whatever it takes."

"Well, give her my best," Nate said. "I know how badly she wants a kid."

"This one's a boy. And she plans to name him Robert. Bobby for short."

"I hate to even bring up his name, but how's Craig fit into the picture? I heard he's been begging her to forgive him."

Drew's back stiffened. "Where did you hear that?"

"Just around. There's been a lot of talk."

Drew wished that was one rumor he could debunk, but it was true. Craig had been calling her, promising her the moon. "I can't see her taking him back. Hell, I wouldn't be surprised if he was still seeing that sexy brunette who was with him in that hotel restaurant."

"Knowing Craig like I do, you're probably right." Nate crossed his arms. "I didn't see the video, but a couple of the other guys working here did. They say that woman looked like a pop-star wannabe. Did you see it?"

"Yeah." Way too many times. "I didn't get a clear look at her face, but she was certainly dressed the part in that curve-hugging red dress and high heels."

Other than that, Drew didn't know much about the woman, other than what he'd either heard through the rodeo grapevine or gathered from social media. Rumor had it her name was Elena, that she knew how to get what she wanted and that she'd set her sights on landing a champion bull rider, even if he was married to someone else.

Now there was another person he'd like to confront—if he ever crossed paths with her.

Kara Lee had told him that the brunette had claimed it was all a mistake, that Kara Lee had it all wrong. But there were plenty of nearby bars and restaurants where that woman and Craig could have met. So there was only one reason for them to be at a hotel.

Nate clucked his tongue and shook his head. "Craig never did deserve a woman like Kara Lee. And she sure as hell didn't deserve the way he treated her."

"You got that right."

As they both pondered the truth of that fact, the room grew silent for a couple of beats. Then Sully spoke up and snagged Drew's attention.

"Where did you two fellas meet?" Sully asked.

Drew glanced first at the retired cowboy, then at his buddy. "Nate and I competed in the junior rodeo as kids, and we went to the same high school. But when I left for college, I quit the circuit."

"I never could figure out why," Nate said. "Drew was always the guy to beat. He might not look it now, in those fancy duds and shiny new boots, but he's a damn good cowboy."

Drew shrugged off his friend's compliment, as well as the good-humored ribbing about his success in the business world. "Yep, don't mess with my hair."

They all laughed, but Drew suspected all the rodeo talk struck a tender spot in Nate, who'd suffered a career-ending injury and hadn't had an option when it came to hanging up his spurs.

"Do you guys miss the rodeo?" Sully asked. "I sure did when I had to give it up. But we all have to do that at some point. Our bones don't stay young forever."

Nate shrugged. "Sure, I miss it. I loved the thrill of competition. But now I've got a beautiful wife and baby, and they're more important to me than anything. I actually enjoy being at home these days." He winked at Drew. "Maybe you should consider finding a nice woman and settling down."

"You sound like Kara Lee, but I don't see that lifestyle in my future." He hadn't seen it in his past, either. He and his sister had grown up on their mother's run-down spread outside of Brighton Valley, and the only real memories they'd had consisted of hard work and sparse meals.

"Well, fellas," Sully said, "if you'll excuse me, I think I'll go check the football spreads. A couple of the guys have a Last Man Standing pool, and I'm still in contention."

"Not me," Nate said. "I had to drop out during the second week."

As Sully left the room, chuckling at his good fortune, Nate turned to Drew and pushed away from the table. "I've got to get back to work. I'll let you get started on that interview process. It'll be lunchtime before we know it."

Speaking of lunch, Drew wondered when the cook would be back to start the food prep. He'd like to see her again. Maybe he'd ask again where they might have crossed paths.

It really didn't matter, he supposed. Yet for some weird reason, it did.

Lainie had barely gotten to her room when she realized she'd left those darn Dear Debbie letters on the table. Sure, she'd turned them face-side down, but what if…?

Darn it. The last thing in the world she wanted was for someone on the ranch to see them. So, in spite of her plan to avoid Drew Madison while he was visiting, she hurried back to the kitchen.

She'd no more than entered the room when Drew pulled out a chair and took a seat at the table, right in front of those blasted letters. He placed his hand on them, pushing them aside, and her breath caught.

She'd better move quickly. All she needed was for him—or *anyone*—to learn that she was the new lovelorn columnist, especially since Mr. Carlton wanted Dear Debbie's identity to remain secret. Besides, Lainie wasn't looking forward to adding any failed journalism jobs to her resume.

So she scooped them up, clutching them to her chest. "Let me get rid of this mess for you."

She was about to dash out of the kitchen again when Nate said, "Lainie, you'll need to set out an extra plate for meals for the next few weeks."

"Sure, I can do that. But who…?" She paused, afraid to pose the question when she was already connecting the dots.

"Drew will be staying with us for a little while," Nate said. "He wants to interview the men who live here. Get to know them. Learn their daily routines. I think there's at least one empty cabin that's decent. I'm not sure what's available, but I know Joy gave you a tour of the ranch before she and Sam left on their honeymoon."

If you could call it a tour. Joy had taken Lainie on a quick walk and pointed out a few buildings, none of which she thought would be her concern for the short time she'd be here. But if Drew was going to stay on the Rocking C, she'd take him out to the cabin that was the farthest from the kitchen.

"Of course," she said. "I'll make sure it's aired out and ready for him."

"I hate to inconvenience you," Drew said, his gaze unwavering and kicking her pulse up another notch.

"It's not a problem." She feigned a lighthearted grin

and tamped down whatever nervous energy he provoked, either through guilt or fear...or downright sexual attraction. "I'll take care of that cabin right away."

When Nate nodded, Lainie took her chance to escape.

"If you men will excuse me," she said, "I have chores to do." Then she headed toward the living area, clutching the letters to her chest.

As she reached the doorway, she overheard Nate say, "I've gotta get back to work. Next time you talk to Kara Lee, give her my best."

Kara?

Lainie nearly stumbled at the mention of a name that sounded similar to that of Craig's wife. Then she shook it off.

Boy, she was jumpy today. Nate had said Carolee. Or possibly Carrie Leigh. Either way, they surely weren't the same woman.

Thank goodness for that. If Kara Baxter was Drew Madison's friend, and if he realized who Lainie was and believed what people said about her, then having him on the ranch would be a lot more than an inconvenience.

It would be a humiliating disaster.

Lainie had no more than returned from Caroline's Diner, where she'd accessed the free Wi-Fi and emailed her first column to the editor, when she spotted Drew and Nate leaving the barn and heading for the house.

Her pride and enthusiasm waned, and her steps, once light and quick, slowed to a near stop. Her first impulse was to slip into the kitchen before they spotted her, but she couldn't very well do that, even if she did have the dinner meal to prepare.

The men waved to her, and she made her way toward them as if it was the most natural thing in the world to do and greeted them with a forced smile.

"There's the lady we've been looking for," Nate said. "Have you had a chance to get one of the cabins ready for Drew?"

Oops. Her first priority had been to make her deadline—well before the midnight cutoff. She lifted her hand to her throat and fingered the ribbed neckline on her T-shirt, as well as the bib of her overalls, both of which covered the long, thick scar that ran the length of her sternum. "I haven't made up the bed yet, but the cabin on the knoll behind the barn will work best. It's empty, and I'm pretty sure it's clean."

"Do you have time to check on it now?" Nate asked. "I'm sure Drew would like to get settled in before dinner, if possible."

Lainie was already behind schedule, but she couldn't shirk her responsibilities, especially when this job paid her a lot more than the newspaper did. "Of course. Just give me a minute to get fresh linens and a set of towels from the house."

"Thanks," Nate said. "I'd do it myself, but I'm going to be tied up for a while."

Lainie shot a quick glance at Drew, who was perusing her every bit as intently as he'd done before. Why did he keep doing that?

Her hand began to reach for her chest again, but she let it drop, her fingers trailing along the denim and brushing away imaginary dust. The scar wasn't visible, and she had to stop reverting back to the old habit she'd once kicked.

"I'll see you at dinner," Nate told Drew. "I need to

have a chat with a couple of hands who are at odds with each other. It seems they're both dating the same cocktail waitress at the Stagecoach Inn. I couldn't care less what they do with their time off, but it's begun to affect their work."

"The woes of being a supervisor," Drew said.

Nate rolled his eyes. "That's *acting* supervisor. And you're right. It's not an easy job, especially with a young and inexperienced crew. Once Sam gets back from his honeymoon, I'm going to turn over my keys to the ranch and hightail it out of here."

"We're looking forward to having you join us at Esteban Enterprises," Drew said.

"I'm glad to hear that, because I can't wait." The guys did some elaborate hand shake and fist pump ritual.

Lainie planned to move on once the honeymooners returned, too. Only problem was, she didn't have another job lined up, like Nate did.

Nate would undoubtedly be successful at Esteban Enterprises, but Lainie'd hate to work for a company that had anything to do with rodeos. Cowboys weren't her thing—except maybe for Sully and the other oldsters. But she'd prefer to never cross paths with the younger ones again.

She glanced at the handsome promoter. Drew might be dressed like a fancy Texas businessman, but his more casual demeanor shouted urban cowboy. So the sooner she could escort him to his temporary quarters and be done with it, the better off she'd be.

"I'll go inside for the linens," she told him. "Do you have your bags?"

"Just a suitcase and my briefcase. They're in the back of my pickup. It'll only take me a minute."

"Then I'll meet you back here."

Moments later, with her arms laden with freshly laundered sheets, pillowcases and towels, Lainie returned to the yard and found Drew waiting for her. He held a suitcase in one hand and a leather briefcase in the other.

"There it is." She pointed about fifty yards away from the barn, where a lone structure sat. The outside needed a coat or two of paint, but the inside was probably just fine. It looked sturdy enough and should keep him dry and cozy. "It doesn't look like much, but I think you'll be comfortable there."

"I don't require much."

No? She found that hard to believe. She glanced across the driveway at his spanking new Dodge Ram truck, then at his fancy denim jacket, his silver belt buckle and his shiny leather inlaid boots. No, this guy clearly liked the finer things in life.

"This way." She began walking along the graveled path toward the knoll, and he fell into step beside her.

"There's something you should know," she said. "The cell and internet access on the ranch isn't very good. There are some random spots here and there where you might get a bar or two, but it's sketchy at best."

"I won't need to get online right away."

"Okay, but when you do, it might be easier and faster to drive to town. Caroline's Diner offers free Wi-Fi now. And they also have the best desserts you've ever tasted."

"Thanks for the suggestion. I'll keep that in mind."

They turned to the right, following the incline to the cabin. A cool winter breeze kicked up a bit, sending the scent of his cologne her way. It was a clean woodsy fragrance—no doubt expensive—that suited him.

For a moment, her femininity rebelled, scolding her for not applying makeup earlier this morning, for choosing a plain white T-shirt and baggy overalls. But her days of enhancing her curves—whether they could be considered a blessing or a curse—were behind her now.

Yet despite her resolve to remain low-key and unaffected by Drew's presence, she stole a peek at him, hoping he wouldn't notice. But he caught her in the act. Her cheeks warmed, and she quickly looked away, placing her focus on the pathway.

"Have you ever been to Houston?" he asked.

The first image that flashed in her mind was the swanky hotel restaurant, where Craig had invited her for a birthday dinner. But she shook off the memory the best she could. "I went to college in Houston, but I'm originally from Amarillo."

He nodded, as if storing that tidbit of information away to use against her someday. *No, come on. That kind of thinking is crazy.* But she couldn't help being a wee bit suspicious. For some reason, he seemed to have locked onto the idea that they'd met before, and they hadn't. She was sure of it.

Still, there seemed to be something familiar about him. Probably his lanky, cowboy swagger.

She cut a sideways glance his way. "Why do you ask?"

"Just curious about everyone here."

She reminded herself that she'd have to stay on her toes around him.

They approached the small front porch, which appeared to have a rickety railing. Maybe the cabin wasn't so sturdy after all, but it would have to do.

"This is it," she said, hoping the inside was more

appealing than the outside. "I probably should have checked things out before bringing you here."

"All I need is a place to sleep."

Lainie climbed the three steps ahead of him, when a crack and crunch sounded behind her.

"Dammit." Drew lurched forward and, apparently to steady himself, grabbed her hip, sending a spiral of heat to the bone and unbalancing her, too.

She didn't have to turn around to know what had just happened, but she couldn't help herself. Sure enough, he was removing his foot from a big crack in the wood, scratching his fancy boots in the process and banging his fancy leather suitcase against the steps.

He grumbled something she couldn't comprehend, then removed his hand from her denim-clad hip. Yet her skin sizzled from his touch, tingled from his grip.

"I'm sorry," she said. "I didn't realize that step was loose."

"The wood's completely rotten."

"I can see that. I know the owners plan to refurbish the cabins before the rodeo comes to town, but I don't think there's a lot of extra cash right now. Are you okay?"

Their gazes locked, and her pulse struck a wacky beat. His features softened, and his annoyance disappeared.

"Yeah, I'm fine. But this porch needs to be fixed pronto."

"I agree, but I think a repair like that'll have to wait."

"Seriously?" He straightened and slowly stepped onto the porch, testing the wood before placing his full weight on it. "Fixing that step can't wait. I might break my leg next time."

She clutched the linens to her chest. "Good point. But…like I said, Nate can't spare the extra cash right now."

He shrugged a single shoulder. "I'll fix it myself. I'm not too bad with a hammer and nails. Tomorrow morning, I'll go to the hardware store and get supplies I'll need to rebuild the broken step." He glanced around. "And the porch. It's just a matter of time before it falls apart, too."

"You're taking it upon yourself to do that?"

"I may as well pay for my keep."

"That'd be nice of you. And appreciated." For some reason, she hadn't expected him to actually do any physical labor. He didn't look like the kind of man who'd risk getting blisters or building up a sweat.

Lainie turned back to face the entrance and shuffled the linen to one arm. She reached for the knob and opened the door. As she crossed the threshold, into the tidy and modestly furnished interior, she caught a whiff of must and dust. "I guess we'd better open some windows and air it out."

"That's not a problem." Drew followed her inside. He set his suitcase on the hardwood floor near the small green-plaid sofa and his briefcase on the oak coffee table.

Lainie carried the linens to the bed and placed them on the bare mattress. Then she took the towels and washcloths to the bathroom. When she returned to the bedroom, she found Drew opening the window. He looked especially nice from the backside—broad shoulders, narrow hips…

Enough of that. Drew Madison was a cowboy—fancy duds or not. And what was worse, Lainie hadn't lucked out when it came to assessing the characters of men she found attractive.

"The pillows, blanket and spread must be in the closet," she said.

"I can take care of that. I'm sure you have other things to do."

She had a ton to do before her day ended. When she'd checked her email at Caroline's, Mr. Carlton had forwarded the next batch of Dear Debbie letters. But Nate had asked her to help their guest get settled. It wouldn't be right to take off and leave him on his own.

"No, I—" She'd just slid open the small closet door, when a brown furry streak jumped from the top shelf, landing on her head. She screamed and swiped at her hair to no avail. The damned creature dropped to her chest and scampered under the bib of her overalls. She shrieked again, and Drew was at her side in an instant.

"What's wrong?" he asked. "Are you okay?"

"No!" She continued to scream and shudder. She hopped up and down in an attempt to dislodge it, but it scurried around her waist and into her pant leg. She grabbed Drew's arm as if he could save her.

His brow furrowed, his expression one of concern. "What? What is it?"

"It's a mouse. And it ran down my…" *Oh, my God.* It was still in there, trying to find a hiding place.

A childhood memory replayed in her mind—the abandoned warehouse in their run-down neighborhood, the innocent game of hide-and-seek, the rat's nest that turned into a little girl's worst nightmare…

Lainie let go of Drew, who wasn't any help, unhooked the overall buckles and shimmied out of the baggy britches until they bagged at her ankles. She struggled to kick off her laced shoes.

"How can I help?" he asked.

If she wasn't in the midst of a mind-boggling crisis, she might have offered a suggestion. But all she could think to do was to scream yet again.

The nasty little creature was burrowing into the folds of the fabric, squirming to escape almost as frantically as she was. When she finally tugged off her second shoe and stepped out of the overalls, she turned to Drew and pointed at the pile of denim. "Get it. Take it *outside*."

Drew bent to do as she'd instructed, but not before the mangy little beast took the opportunity to zip under the bed.

Lainie shuddered and straightened, then she turned to him.

He stood there stoically, his gaze on her. Apparently, he didn't give a fig about the mouse that could easily burrow into his bed tonight.

He studied her for a couple of beats, then he looked away.

It took her those same beats and another to realize she was standing before him in her stocking feet, wearing only a baggy T-shirt and a pair of pink panties. And skimpy ones at that.

Her cheeks heated and her lips parted. Oh, no. Now what?

Drew snatched a folded sheet from the mattress and held it out to her.

She grabbed it and rushed to the bathroom, but it wasn't the blasted mouse she hoped to escape this time. It was the dashing cowboy who'd seen more of her than she'd wanted to reveal.

Chapter 3

Now that the crisis was over, some men might have found Lainie's reaction to a panicked field mouse a bit comical, but Drew had been too focused on her shapely, bare legs and those pink lacy panties. He hadn't realized what she'd been hiding behind all that denim, but certainly not curves that were that sexy.

Most women would flaunt them, but apparently Lainie didn't.

When the bathroom door creaked open, she came out with the sheet wrapped around her waist. Her cheeks were flushed a deep pink, and her brow was creased in worry. She scanned the room. "Is it gone?"

No, he suspected the critter was still under the bed and probably suffering from a massive coronary. He didn't want to lie, but neither did he want to risk having her freak out again. "You're safe."

Drew thought about making light of the situation and her reaction, but she was undoubtedly embarrassed by it. And he couldn't help sympathizing.

She pointed to the pile of denim on the floor. "Would you please shake those out, then give them to me?"

"Sure." He picked up the overalls, made an effort to examine them carefully, then gave them a vigorous shake before handing them to her. "Here you go."

It was a shame she was going to hide behind baggy clothes again.

She held the sheet in place with one hand and clutched the overalls with the other. Yet she stood her ground, her cheeks rosy, and gave a little shrug. "In case you hadn't figured it out, I hate mice."

"Apparently so." His grin broadened to a full-on smile. "But just for future reference, it wasn't going to eat you in a single bite."

She mumbled something directed at him, clicked her tongue then returned to the bathroom.

When the bathroom door swung open again, and she walked out wearing those damned overalls, he felt compelled to tease her. Instead, he bit his tongue. But he couldn't wipe the smile off his face.

"I realize you found this funny," she said, "and I admit that I overreacted."

"No," he lied. "Some people have an aversion to things like mice, bugs and snakes." He took a seat on the bed.

"And I'm one of them. But you see, one day, when my twin sister and I were playing, we had a bad experience with rats. So that came into play just now."

"You have a twin?"

She paused a beat, and her eye twitched, just as it

had a few minutes ago, when he'd asked her if she'd ever been to Houston. "Yes, I do."

"Identical?"

"No. People used to think we were, especially since there's a strong family resemblance and we were the same size and had the same coloring. But no, we're fraternal twins."

Had Drew run into her sister before? If so, that could be the reason Lainie seemed familiar.

"Where does your sister live?" he asked.

"I'm…not sure. I haven't seen her since… Well, it's been a while."

He was tempted to ask why, but he suspected they'd had a falling-out of some kind. And he'd had enough drama within his own family to last a lifetime.

"Anyway," Lainie said, "I need to go back to the house. I only have an hour to get dinner on the table."

"You sure you're okay?"

"I'll live. I'm just glad you reminded me that the darned critter wasn't able to eat me in a single bite." She smiled and winked. Then she bit down on her bottom lip. "Hey, do me a favor, please. Don't tell the guys about this."

"My lips are sealed. It'll be our little secret." This time, he winked. "Thanks for helping me get settled."

"And for providing you with a little entertainment? You're welcome. I was just doing my job. Or trying to, anyway." Then she headed for the door.

He nearly added, *And thanks for the lovely vision I'll never get out of my head.*

Lainie had never been so embarrassed in her life. She couldn't believe she'd screamed like a wild woman and stripped down to her panties in front of a virtual stranger—and a handsome one at that.

So much for getting a fresh start in Brighton Valley. If word of this got out, she'd have to move again. Fortunately, Drew had been nice about the whole thing, but he must think she was a nut job, which she probably was. What normal woman would have reacted like that? And all because of a tiny little mouse.

She blew out an exasperated sigh. As much as she'd like to avoid Drew for the rest of her life—or at least, for the duration of his stay—she was going to have to face him again this evening, at the dinner table. And speaking of dinner, she didn't have a clue what she was going to fix. She'd been so focused on getting her column turned in on time that she'd neglected to do any prep work. And now she'd have to regroup and think of something that was quick and easy.

She had ground beef in the fridge. Hamburgers with all the fixings wouldn't be too difficult to pull off. By the time she'd gotten across the yard and near the house, she had a menu planned. Thank goodness for the canned beans in the pantry and the ice cream she'd stored in the freezer.

She'd no more than reached the back porch of the main ranch house when she spotted Sully and Rex, another old-timer, sitting outside, swaying away the afternoon in rocking chairs. They were watching—or rather critiquing—a younger cowboy working with a horse in the corral.

"Damn fool kid," Rex said. "Someone had better fire his ass before he gets himself killed."

"You got that right." Sully slowly shook his head.

"Aw, hell." Rex got to his feet and reached for his

cane. "I'm going to find Nate. This is crazy. That kid shouldn't be left to work on his own."

Rex had no more than taken a single step when he spotted Lainie and tipped his worn cowboy hat at her. "Little lady. If you'll excuse me?"

"Of course," she said.

Rex grumbled something under his breath as he took off in search of the acting foreman.

"So," Sully said. "I see you're finally home after your trip to town."

"Yes, I got back a little while ago. I've been helping Drew get settled in the cabin on the knoll."

Sully glanced at his wristwatch. "Looks like it's about time for dinner."

Yes, and if she didn't get inside quickly, she wouldn't have it on the table by five o'clock. Joy had warned her that the men were in the habit of eating at set times— and not one minute later.

"I know you're probably busy," Sully said, "but I thought about something after we discussed your friend's problem."

For a moment, the only problem Lainie could remember was her own. What normal woman dropped her pants in front of a stranger, and all because of a tiny mouse? But Sully hadn't been privy to that secret. At least, not yet.

"What problem is that?" she asked.

"You know," he said, as he got up from his rocker and followed her into the kitchen. "The friend who wrote you the letter about having her heart broken."

"Oh, yes."

"I thought about something else you can tell her," Sully said.

Too late. The column was already in Mr. Carlton's inbox. But Lainie wasn't about to turn down any sage advice she might be able to use later. "What's that?"

"You can't expect someone else to make you happy. You'll only end up miserable if you do because the time will come when the two of you will part ways, through death or divorce or whatever."

Wasn't that the truth? Time and again since childhood, Lainie had learned that lesson the hard way. She never knew her mother, and her father died before she and her twin entered kindergarten. Three years later, her grandmother followed suit and left them wards of the state. Then Erica was adopted and snatched away. Even while Lainie was in the hospital for her heart surgery, the nurses kept changing, thanks to their varied shifts.

So if there was anything to count on, it was that life was unpredictable. And the only one who could make her happy was herself.

She'd thought her luck might have changed when she met Craig, but she'd never expected him to make her *happy*. She had, however, expected him to be honest with her.

"When my wife died," Sully said, "I missed her so much. For a while, I thought my life was over. I couldn't see a purpose for it after she was gone. But my buddies stepped in and gave me a kick in the backside. They told me to quit feeling sorry for myself and to focus on others."

Lainie opened the commercial-sized refrigerator and pulled out a huge package of ground beef. "What did you do?"

"I volunteered at a local soup kitchen. And it made

all the difference in the world. Tell your friend to find something to do that's bigger than herself. Once she gets off the pity train, she'll be surprised at how good she'll feel."

"More wise advice," Lainie said. And more fodder for a future column.

"You might want to give her some options, like volunteering at the animal shelter or collecting blankets and toiletry items for the homeless."

Actually, that's exactly what Lainie would so. She'd go to the library and do some online research about the needs in the community. Then, when she found an opportunity to make a suggestion like that to someone, she'd have a good-size list of volunteer possibilities to provide as a wrap to the column.

"That's a great idea, Sully. I'll make that suggestion the next time I talk to my friend." She offered him a warm, appreciative smile, dropped the meat on the counter then opened the pantry and pulled out several packages of buns. "Thanks again for the advice."

"Sure. Anytime. Say, you need any help?"

Boy, did she. And on so many levels. But he was talking about dinner—and the need for her to get it on the table by five. "Sure, would you mind firing up the gas grill?"

"I'd be delighted." Sully went outside to the deck.

Before forming the meat into patties, Lainie washed her hands at the sink, then dried them with the dish towel that had been resting on the counter. She couldn't help glancing out the kitchen window at the cabin on the knoll. Her hand lifted, and she fingered the length of the scar that hid under the cotton and denim.

She'd just about reached her wit's end when it came

to dealing with handsome men, especially those who left her feeling guilty or embarrassed or lacking in any way. Fortunately, she'd be moving on again soon. Only this time, when she chose a new job, it might be best to consider one at a convent.

Lainie had just finished wiping down the countertops and putting away the last of the breakfast dishes when the ranch telephone rang. She snatched the receiver from its wall-mounted cradle. The cord, stretched from years of use, dangled to her knees. "Rocking Chair Ranch. This is Lainie."

"Hey, kid."

She was more than a little surprised to hear Mr. Carlton's voice on the other end.

"I knew you could do it," he said, his tone almost jubilant. "That column you sent to me yesterday was great. In fact, it was everything I'd hoped it would be."

Thank goodness. Or rather, in this case, thank *Sully*. Either way, she was relieved to know she'd hit the mark. "Thank you, Mr. Carlton."

"You mentioned the internet service wasn't very good at the ranch, so I hope you received the additional letters I sent. I hadn't gotten your column yet, but I had a good feeling."

"Yes, I did. I had to go into town to find Wi-Fi so I could send it to you. And while I was there, I checked my email and downloaded them onto my laptop." She hadn't looked at them yet. She was waiting until she found both the time and the enthusiasm to tackle the chore. But her boss didn't need to know that. "I'll read them over the weekend."

"Good, but you might want to get started on them

right away. I'll need your next column turned in by Monday at noon."

"So *soon*?" Monday was only a few days away. She leaned against the wall and wrapped the curly phone cord around her index finger. "I thought my deadlines were on Wednesdays."

"Now that we're back on track, I'll need more time to review your column."

"I'm afraid I'm not following you."

"When the last Dear Debbie quit without notice, I had to find a replacement and make adjustments. The column comes out every Friday, so I pushed your deadline back to give you time to write it. But that meant I had to review it quickly. I'll admit that your column isn't a huge priority to me, especially since the readership isn't that big. But the fans we do have are very loyal. And they're vocal."

Lainie didn't doubt that the lovelorn column was at the bottom of the editor's priority list. Not that she knew what was at the top. She had no idea what the Brighton Valley residents expected to see in terms of news and special interest stories. At least, not yet. She'd have a much better idea after she researched her new community and the various organizations needing volunteers the next time she went to town. She'd even take her camera with her. Who knew what photo op she might find? Or what interesting tidbit she might learn. There were sure to be plenty of people or activities going on that she could use for a future article.

Mr. Carlton cleared his throat. "A Monday deadline isn't going to be a problem for you, is it?"

She'd wrapped the phone cord so tightly around her finger that it had turned red, so she loosened it as she attempted to reassure her boss. "No, not at all. I'll get my next column to you with time to spare." Now all she had to do was to reassure herself that she'd come through for him again.

And to pull that off, she'd have to find Sully. Maybe she could bribe him with brownies.

"That's just the kind of response I like in my staff," Mr. Carlton said. "My *full-time* staff."

He didn't have to say any more. If Lainie wanted a bigger and more important position at *The Brighton Valley Gazette*, she'd need to keep her self-doubt at bay.

"You won't be disappointed, Mr. Carlton."

"We'll see about that." He muttered something under his breath—or possibly to someone else. "Listen, Debbie—or rather, Lainie. I have a meeting and need to get ready for it. I'll let you go so you can get started on the next column. I can't wait to see it." Then he hung up without saying goodbye.

Lainie completely freed her finger from the cord, released her death grip on the receiver and returned it to the wall mount. Then she straightened her stance and blew out a ragged sigh.

She had plenty on her to-do list today, like cleaning out the refrigerator and mopping the kitchen floor. She hadn't considered her usual household tasks to be a burden until she thought about those darned letters, just waiting for a clever response.

She'd better read them now, while she ate her own breakfast. That way, she could ponder her answers while she worked.

After retrieving her laptop from her room, where it rested on the pine dresser, next to her prized high-definition camera, she returned to the kitchen. She wanted to be available in case the on-duty nurse or one of the men needed her, so couldn't very well hole up elsewhere.

She toasted a slice of sourdough bread. After smearing it with peanut butter, she poured a cup of coffee and seasoned it with cream and sugar. Then she took a seat at the table and got to work.

Twenty minutes later, she'd chosen a couple of interesting letters. One of them gave her a perfect opportunity to share Sully's advice about getting off the pity train and thinking about someone else for a change. But she was still at a loss when it came to providing any suggestions for the other. Sure, she always had an opinion. But what if she steered someone in the wrong direction? Or what if her words came out dull and uninteresting?

In spite of her best intentions, she couldn't seem to wake up her muse or stir her thoughts. So she went about her chores, racking her brain to come up with something to write.

Darn it. Could she do this again? Heck, she hadn't even done it last time without help.

Once the kitchen was spick-and-span, she sat at the table again, a fresh cup of coffee beside her laptop. She tried to focus on Mr. Carlton's praise, but even that wasn't enough to instill a burst of confidence.

That column you sent to me yesterday was great. It was everything I'd hoped it would be.

Maybe so, but Lainie hadn't done it on her own. She'd been stymied until Sully...

Yep. Sully.

She needed to find the retired cowboy and ask for more of his simple but sage advice. So where was he?

He'd gone outside for a walk after breakfast, but

he could be back now. She closed her laptop, scooted her chair away from the table then got to her feet. She made her way to the sink and looked out the window in search of the man who might be able to help her keep her job at the *Gazette*.

Sully wasn't in the yard, but when her gaze drifted to the cabin on the knoll, she spotted another man. A much younger one who'd shed his fancy duds for worn jeans and a long-sleeved black T-shirt that molded to his muscular form.

Well, what do you know? Drew Madison might *appear* to be a country gentleman with the financial resources to hire others to do physical labor. Yet there he was, tearing apart the old porch as if he wasn't afraid to roll up his sleeves and get the job done himself.

Apparently, he'd gone to the hardware store earlier this morning because a pile of new lumber was stacked off to the side. But it wasn't the tools or the supplies that commanded her interest. It was the man in action.

Rugged and strong.

Masculine and focused.

Heat rushed her face, and her tummy went topsy-turvy. But her visceral reaction only served to send up a host of red flags and set off alarms in her head.

She couldn't trust herself when it came to choosing a man. Neither of the two who'd struck her fancy in the past had turned out to be honest, kind or worthy of her time and affection. Not a single one. So what made her think this guy was any different?

Instead of gawking at Drew, she studied him carefully, trying to spot the flaws he hid behind his Western wear or under his hat.

He was handsome, that was a fact. But handsome

men, especially the last one, had done a real number on her in the past. She turned on the tap water and washed her hands as if that simple act might rid her of a silly attraction to a guy who'd probably broken more hearts than wild horses.

Drew tore a rotted piece of wood from the porch railing, then slung it to the pile he'd made off to the side. It felt good to work with his hands for a change. And he took a sense of pride in the fact that he was, in some small way, helping out the Rocking C Ranch. Better than tackling that blog.

As he swung his hammer to break away the last stretch of porch railing, he got a weird feeling in his core, a second sense that suggested someone was watching him. Instinctively, he turned around.

At first, he didn't see anyone. But then he looked at the house, where a feminine shape stood at the kitchen window.

It had to be Lainie. Who else could it be?

Then she disappeared from sight.

Had he caught her watching him? Or had she merely glanced out the window in passing, a coincidence that he'd turned at just the right time to find her there?

"Whatever," he muttered, gripping the hammer tighter. It was hard to say for sure. Besides, it didn't really matter. He had work to do, and now that he'd built up a sweat, he wanted to finish. He kicked a rotting board out of the way, just as a familiar voice of one of the retirees called out to him.

"Hey, you. College boy. What's going on?"

Drew turned from his work and spotted Rex Mayberry, his late granddad's old friend, limping toward him, using a cane. He wore a tattered hat over his bald head, and a wooden matchstick wiggled in the corner of his mouth. Just the sight of him was enough to draw a smile.

"I'm just trying to pay for my keep." Drew lifted his left arm and wiped the sweat from his brow with a sleeve. "How 'bout you? Feeling okay today?"

"As long as you don't count bad knees, crappy vision and dentures, I'm doing just hunky-dory." With his wry, crotchety sense of humor, Rex was the kind of man who didn't usually say much. But when he did, people gave him their full attention.

At least, Drew always had. He'd been about six years old and living on his grandfather's ranch the first time they'd met. It hadn't taken him long to respect the wisdom behind the man's words. But it wasn't just his comments that had been notable. Rex had been a damn good cowboy, one of the best. So it was tough to see him now, stooped and gray.

Rex let out a chuckle. "I'll bet that rich, candy-ass uncle of yours would be pissed if he saw you now."

Drew smiled. "Yep, you've got that right. J.P. doesn't think much about cowboys, rodeos or ranching. But what he doesn't know won't hurt him."

"I'm sure as hell not gonna tell him. Not after him and me had words after your high school graduation."

Drew hooked his thumbs into his back pockets and frowned. "I wasn't aware of that."

"Yeah, well, I figured your granddad would have wanted me to speak up on his behalf. So I did."

"What'd you say?"

"I told him that you were one of the best horsemen I'd ever seen. And that you were a born rancher. You would've turned the Double M around—if you'd had the chance—and then you would have been able to keep it in the family."

"I might have. If Uncle J.P. would have loaned us the money to pay the back taxes." Drew had only been eleven when his grandfather died, so there hadn't been much he could do to keep the ranch going. His mother had inherited the Double M, but she hadn't been able to make a go of it, especially after her cancer diagnosis. But that had been her secret until her health deteriorated to a certain point.

"I thought it was lousy of J.P. to offer his help, but only if he could call all the shots."

Drew had hoped his great-uncle would loan them the money to pay the back taxes, but J.P. had refused, saying he hadn't reached financial success by squandering his holdings.

Andrew, J.P. had said at the time, *you have a hell of a lot more going for you than being a cowboy. And you're too smart to risk your neck at a foolhardy way of life. So I'll tell you what I'm going to do. I'll pay for your college tuition, which is an investment in you—and in your future.*

"It was probably just as well," Drew said. "My mom had been in remission, but about that time, she got word that the cancer had come back. So J.P. told her to sell the ranch and move to the city with Kara Lee. Mom had access to better medical care there. And selling the ranch provided her with the money to pay for it."

Rex chuffed. "I know it was probably the right thing to do for her, but I'm not so sure about your sister. She had a hard time changing high schools."

Neither of them mentioned the fact that Drew's mom

had died anyway, leaving Kara Lee in Drew's care until she graduated.

"And what about you?" Rex asked. "You gave up your boyhood dreams at the request of your uncle."

"Yes, but not completely. I'm still a cowboy at heart."

And so was the old man leaning on his cane.

"Hold on," Drew said. "I'll bring out a chair for you. That way, you can watch what I'm doing. I'd hate for you to think I'm too book smart for my own good."

"Sure, I'll sit here for a spell. And just for the record, I never had much use for a man who thought he was too good to get his hands dirty or work up a good lather."

"Yes, I know."

"Your grandfather and me, we were cut from the same bolt of cloth. We thought a hard day's work and good deeds never hurt anyone. No, sir."

"I might work indoors most of the time," Drew said, "but I haven't forgotten any of the lessons you guys taught me."

"I'm glad to hear that. I was afraid those college professors would ruin you." Rex lifted his worn felt cowboy hat and raked his gnarled fingers through what was left of his graying hair. "Now get me that chair."

Drew winked at his old friend and mentor before climbing onto the porch. He entered the cabin and returned with one of two chairs from the small dinette table. He placed it in a shady spot.

The old man took a seat and leaned the cane against his knee. "I still think you could have been a champion bronc rider if you'd continued on the circuit."

"Maybe so. But under the circumstances, I don't have any major regrets. I have a good career with Esteban

Enterprises. And someday soon, I'm going to create my own company, Silver Buckle Promotions."

"That's one heck of a name. I like it."

"Yep. I'm putting my education to good use. Besides, I still work in the rodeo world, only now I'm a promoter."

Drew had just turned back to his work when Rex asked, "So what's this I hear about you interviewing us? Are you writing an article for the newspaper?"

"No, I'm going to write a blog."

Rex let out a humph. "I'm not sure what that is, but I hope it'll help keep this ranch afloat."

Drew tore up a piece of the floorboard and tossed it on top of the pile of old wood. "That's just one part of the plan. And you'd better believe I'll give it my all." He wasn't so sure about the blog, but he knew he'd do a good job with the rest of the promotion. The Rocking C provided the old cowboys with an affordable and familiar place to live out their last years. So it was too important not to help them get the financial support they needed.

"That's good to know because I like it here— especially the food. That Joy is one fine cook. I was afraid that her temporary replacement wouldn't be worth a darn, but she's actually doing okay. What's her name? Lonnie? Lindy?"

"Lainie."

Rex nodded. "Yeah, well, she's been holding her own so far."

Drew glanced toward the house. When he didn't spot Lainie standing at the window, a pang of disappointment struck. But he shook it off. He wasn't here for fun and games. He had work to do.

Only problem was, he hadn't planned on meeting Lainie. Nor had he expected to get a glimpse of her wearing a pair of sexy panties. As the memory replayed in his mind, a smile spread across his face.

"She's a pretty one," Rex said.

Drew peeled his gaze away from the empty kitchen window and turned to his old friend. "I'm not sure I'm following you."

"The hell, you say." Rex laughed and pointed his thumb at the house. "Kid, I've always been able to read your face like a book."

That might have been true when Drew was a kid, but he'd learned to mask his expressions over the years. That is, unless he was caught off guard.

To throw Rex off course, he reached for the first excuse he could concoct. "I'm getting hungry and wondered if lunch was ready."

"Don't lie to me. The food won't be on the table 'til noon. And I watched you pack it away at breakfast. You might be working hard, kid, but not enough to want lunch at ten o'clock."

Okay, so he'd been caught. "If you haven't noticed, I've been working my tail off here."

"Yeah, right." Rex chuckled.

Rather than let the conversation continue, Drew turned back to demolish the rest of the porch. He wasn't going to give Rex further reason to connect romantic dots that weren't there.

Only trouble was, Drew couldn't help but wonder if there actually might be a few dots that could use a little connecting.

Chapter 4

Lainie had no sooner whipped up a batch of corn bread to go with the chili simmering on the stove, when Sully entered the house through the mudroom, whistling a spunky tune.

"Hey," she said, as she continued to pour the batter into the large, rectangular pan. "You're just the guy I was looking for. Where've you been?"

"Me?" He furrowed his bushy white brow. "I was out taking a morning walk. Then Nate asked me if I wanted to ride into town with him. What's up?"

"Not much. I talked to my friend and shared your advice with her. She realized you were right about the jerk she'd been dating. But then she told me about another friend of ours with a problem, and we're at odds on what to tell her."

Sully pulled out a chair and took a seat at the table. "So what's troubling that gal?"

"She's been saving her money for nearly a year and has enough to purchase a used car, which she desperately needs. Her old one keeps breaking down, and the repairs have been costly. On the upside, she now has a new, better-paying job. She needs dependable transportation, but her kid brother wants to borrow a thousand dollars to cover his rent and the late fee."

Sully rested his clasped hands on the table and steepled his fingers. "Can she spare the money?"

"Yes, if she doesn't buy the car." Lainie placed the pan into the prewarmed oven and set the timer. "Her brother promised to repay her next month, but to complicate matters, he hasn't always repaid the loans she's given him in the past."

"Sounds like she has every reason to turn him down this time."

"I think so, too, but she's been taking care of him ever since their parents died." Lainie could certainly relate to the woman's love and compassion. If she and her twin hadn't been separated, she'd feel the same sense of responsibility.

"How old is the boy?"

"He's twenty-four now and living on his own. But she's worried about him getting evicted, especially since he can't seem to keep a job."

"Apparently, he hasn't had to. His sister keeps jumping in to save the day."

"She means well," Lainie said.

"Yes, but by bailing him out every time he gets into a jam, she's robbing him of the ability to learn from his mistakes."

Wow. That was an interesting way to look at it. And wise, too.

"Listen," Sully said. "If her no-account brother can't come up with the money to cover his rent this month, how is he going to pay it next month and also be able to repay her as promised?"

"Good point."

"Your friend is allowing her heart to get in the way of her brains. Her brother might have one sob story after another, but it's time for him to grow up. And it's time for his sister to let him."

"You're absolutely right. Thanks." Lainie could work with that sound advice. She'd just have to put her own spin on it.

The back door squeaked open. When she glanced up, she spotted Drew entering the kitchen. His hair was damp and freshly combed, suggesting that he'd recently showered. He'd changed clothes, too.

White button-down shirt. Clean jeans. Shiny cowboy boots.

Their eyes met, and Lainie found it impossible to look away.

He closed the gap between them, and she caught an alluring whiff of masculine soap. Her breath caught, and her voice squeaked out a greeting. "Hey, Drew."

He responded with a "Hey" of his own, his deep voice rumbling through her. She wasn't sure she'd be able to conjure a response until Sully cleared his throat, drawing Lainie's attention away from the handsome man who stood a mere arm's length away.

"If you two will excuse me," Sully said. "I'm going to rest up before the noon meal." Then he shuffled out of the room.

"Something sure smells good," Drew said.

He clearly meant the food, but by the way his gaze

caressed her, she wasn't sure. Nevertheless, she couldn't very well stand here like a ditz. So she gathered her wits and said, "I saw you earlier when I glanced out the window and into the yard. I thought you were only going to fix a couple of steps. I had no idea you were going to replace the porch."

"The whole thing was shot. I wasn't going to nail new lumber to bad."

"That makes sense." But what didn't make sense was the way her pulse was racing. Or the way he was looking at her right now. It seemed as if he could see right into her heart.

She touched her throat to check the top button on her flannel shirt before trailing her fingers along the soft blue fabric that covered her chest. When she reached the waistline of her jeans, she realized what she'd been doing and placed her hands on her hips.

He grinned.

And why wouldn't he? He probably thought she was flirting with him, that she had something romantic on her mind, but she didn't. Well, maybe just a little, but she wouldn't allow her curiosity and sexual awareness to get the better of her.

"No overalls today?" he asked, arching a single brow.

"They're in the laundry. I have two pairs, actually. But I don't always wear them. I like them, though. I got them on sale at the local feed store. Very utilitarian. You know?"

She nearly winced at her response. Could she sound any more ditzy or moonstruck?

He nodded, his gaze again scanning her from the topknot on her head to her shoes, then back again. Her toes curled inside her sneakers, causing her to sway.

Oh, for Pete's sake. She had to put a stop to the girlish-
ness. She was practically swooning.

Back to business. She turned to the counter, picked
up a spoon and started stirring the chili in the pot.

"So when will you finish those repairs?" she asked,
her back to him.

"I tore apart the old porch and hauled off all the bad
wood. I'll start on the new carpentry tomorrow."

"That'll make entering the front door a little awkward. It's a big step."

"Not for me."

No, she supposed it wouldn't be. The man had to be
six feet tall or more. Looking at his handsome face was
hard enough. But when he spoke with a faint Southern
drawl, his voice had a lulling effect on her.

She placed the spoon on a plate, stepped away from
the stove, then brushed her hands on her denim-clad
hips, as if her jeans had somehow gotten dusty.

Oh, my gosh. Stop fidgeting and get it together, Lainie.

She offered him her best attempt at an unaffected
smile and changed the subject yet again. "I hope you
like chili beans and corn bread because that's on the
menu for lunch."

"It sounds good."

Her face heated. She hadn't meant to tell him something he could figure out for himself by looking at the
stove, but the man was too distracting.

"I was going to interview one of the retired cowboys before we eat," he said. "But now that I've caught
a mouthwatering aroma of what's to come, I'd rather
hang out in here. Is there anything I can do to help
you?" He nodded toward the cupboard. "I'd be happy
to set the tables."

"Sure, thanks."

Nate and the young ranch hands usually ate in the kitchen. The retirees were served in the dining room. But he'd know that from being there for several meals, so there was no need to offer further instruction.

Off he went with the plates into the dining room. Moments later he returned for the silverware.

As he moved about the kitchen, close enough to bump into her, close enough for her to catch his musky scent, it was difficult to think, let alone respond to any friendly chatter.

She ought to be thankful for his help, but the only thing that would truly help her right now would be for him to go in search of one of the cowboys, like he'd planned to do.

"I can finish up," she told him. "Why don't you round up someone to interview before lunch?"

And take your sexy smile, hunky self and mesmerizing scent with you.

Drew didn't know why he'd insisted on helping Lainie in the kitchen. As a kid, he'd resented doing what he'd considered women's work. But later, after his mother started chemo and was sick more often than not, he'd taken on meal preparation for their family of three. That included the planning, shopping and cooking. So he'd gained a new respect for cooks—male or female.

But that still didn't explain why he'd stepped up and was now counting out mismatched flatware from the drawer. Lainie was certainly capable of handling things on her own.

The fact that he found her attractive was undoubtedly

a contributing factor. And if anything, the more time he spent with her, the more appealing he found her to be.

She didn't wear makeup, which gave her a whole-some, girl-next-door look, which he found alluring. Hot, even. And her faint floral scent? It was enough to make a man perk up and take notice of her every move.

She rocked those baggy jeans and that oversize T-shirt like an urban model, the kind that didn't give a damn about what other people thought. And she pulled it off right down to her sneakers.

Once again his mind drifted to the mouse encounter, when he'd gotten a peek at her shapely legs and those sexy panties, and he'd begun to see her in a whole new light. An arousing one.

He found the contradiction, the soft femininity of silk and lace hidden behind durable denim, to be in-credibly sensual. It not only spiked his testosterone, it piqued his curiosity. And that, he decided, was what prompted him to offer his help today.

After he finished setting both tables, he returned to the kitchen, pausing just inside the doorway to watch Lainie work. Her back was to him, so she was unaware that he'd stolen the opportunity to study her.

She snatched a potholder from the counter, then opened the oven door, withdrew the corn bread and placed it on one side of the stovetop to cool. Next she checked the chili beans simmering in a pot.

Rather than continue to admire her, Drew said, "I finished setting the table. Is there anything else I can do?"

She turned to face him, her cheeks flushed a deeper shade of pink. She touched her collar, fiddling with the top button. When she caught his eye, her hand dropped to her side.

"You can fill the glasses with ice." She nodded to the countertop, where two large gallon jars held tea. "Most of the men like to have sweet tea with all their meals."

"Consider it done."

As Drew made his way toward the cupboard and near Lainie, she bit down on her bottom lip. "Don't get me wrong. I appreciate this, but I'm not used to having help."

"It's no problem."

She offered him a waifish smile. Something in those expressive brown eyes suggested that she'd been on her own for a while. And that it hadn't been by her own choosing.

He pulled glasses from the cupboard. "You mentioned having a twin—and that you hadn't seen her in a while."

When Lainie didn't immediately respond, he realized that he'd overstepped. He didn't have the right to pry or to ask about the dynamics of her family, but for some reason, his curiosity grew too strong to ignore.

"I take it you and your sister aren't very close," he said, prodding her.

"We used to be." Her voice came out soft, fragile, stirring his sympathy along with his interest.

"Did you have a falling-out?" he asked.

She paused for the longest time, and he just stood there, a glass in hand, waiting while the moment turned awkward.

He was about to apologize for getting too personal when she said, "Her name is Erica, but I called her

Rickie. We haven't seen each other since we were nine and she was adopted."

Wow. Drew hadn't seen that coming.

"Were you adopted, too?" he asked.

"No, I…remained in foster care."

The waning sense of awkwardness rose up again, stronger than ever. Under any other circumstances, he might have turned away, changed the subject. Yet he felt compelled to dig for more information, even though each time she answered one of his questions, it only served to trigger another.

"Have you considered looking for her?" he asked. "I mean, now that you're adults."

"I think about that all the time, but it was a closed adoption, so there's not much I can do."

"Feel free to tell me to mind my own business, but why didn't her parents adopt you, too?"

"It's complicated." She reached for her collar again. A nervous habit, he supposed. "We were both living in foster care at the time. I… Well, I had a few health problems back then and was moved to a home with better access to medical care. While I was gone, a family came along and chose her, but not me."

"I'm sorry." That must have hurt like hell.

"Don't be. I was sad, but I understood why. I've dealt with it."

"Have you?"

"I just said I had."

"I mean, most kids would have felt hurt, left out, rejected. Some might even carry those feelings for years."

"Not me. Don't worry about it."

"I'm sorry if I stirred up any sad memories."

She shrugged. "Like I said, I've dealt with it." Then

she turned her back to him and returned to her work, ending a conversation that had gotten way too personal and revealing for his own good.

Yet for some crazy reason, he was tempted to embrace her, to press her head to his shoulder and tell her he sympathized with her over the rejection and the loss of her sister. But he didn't.

He might be a sucker for innocent, vulnerable women, but he wasn't about to take on another one now. Not when he had his plate full with a pregnant sister on bed rest.

"How about you?" Lainie asked. "Do you have any siblings?"

"Yes, a kid sister." And she was the only family he had left. Well, so far. "She's expecting a baby boy at the end of March."

"That's nice. Uncle Drew, huh?"

He grinned. "That's right."

"I take it you're close."

"Yeah, we're pretty tight." At Kara Lee's wedding, Drew had been the one to give her away. Then he'd stood back, his head held high, a smile on his face.

He'd been glad to know that she'd finally grown up, that she'd have a home and family of her own. That she'd have the happiness she'd always deserved. He'd assumed that Craig was an honorable man. That he'd step up and take care of Kara Lee from that day on, for richer or poorer, in sickness and in health.

But that wasn't to be. And it hadn't been death that parted them, but a parade of lovers. The last straw was the sexy brunette whose video had gone viral.

A woman who hadn't had any more respect for sacred wedding vows than Craig Baxter had.

* * *

While Lainie tidied up the kitchen after the evening meal, Drew and one of the retired cowboys remained at the table, having a cup of decaf.

Drew had set up a small video recorder, a real nice one. The kind that, if Lainie hit the lottery, she'd buy.

"Damn it. I can't get this thing to record."

Lainie had planned to stay in the background, but she couldn't help going to the rescue. "Here. You have it on the wrong mode. That's all." She triggered the right one. "There you go."

The elderly cowboy, Gilbert Henry, laughed. "Guess you're an old soul like me, Drew. Can't figure out that newfangled equipment."

"Something like that."

Lainie scrubbed a counter that didn't need cleaning and listened to Gilbert talk about his time in the Marine Corps during the Korean War, his return to the States and his marriage to Pearl, his high school sweetheart.

"We bought a house in Wexler," Gil said. "We had dreams, me and Pearl. She wanted a big family, and I was prepared to give that little gal anything she wanted. But I guess God or Fate had other plans. We tried to have a baby for nearly ten years. Finally, we adopted two little boys—brothers who'd been orphaned at a young age."

Lainie couldn't help but wish that a couple like Gil and his wife had been around when she and Rickie needed a home.

"Ray was the oldest," Gil said. "And was he a real pistol. Sharp as a tack, but never did like school. Jimmy was the youngest. And quiet. For a while, we never

thought he'd ever say a word. But once he did, he jab-
bered from morning until night."

"Where are they now?" Drew asked.

"When Ray was sixteen, he got caught up with the
wrong crowd and ended up on drugs." Gil clucked his
tongue. "And he got sent to the state pen for a while,
too. Damn near broke Pearl's heart and caused a divorce
when I refused to bail him out. But hell, he was going
to have to serve time anyway and I didn't trust him to
show up in court."

"That must have been very hard on you and your
wife."

"Yep. But in the long run, Ray's incarceration turned
out to be a blessing. Thanks to a prison ministry, he
turned his life around. Believe it or not, he's a preacher
in Louisiana. He doesn't have a big fancy church. He
spends a lot of his time on the street corner, passing out
Bibles and giving sandwiches to the homeless. But he
seems to be happy doing that."

"How about the younger boy?" Drew asked.

"We lost him in Desert Storm."

Lainie stopped scrubbing and looked over her shoulder at the man.

Gil's voice cracked. "I keep his Silver Star on my
nightstand to remember him by."

"I'm sorry to hear that," Drew said.

"Me, too. But you should have seen the letters some
of his buddies sent to us and the articles written in the
paper. I'm damn proud to know I raised a boy who
didn't balk when it came to dying to save the men in
his platoon."

Lainie had already tidied up the kitchen, but rather
than leave the men alone, she began reorganizing the

pantry, which really didn't need it. Joy kept an organized kitchen. She also kept two bottles of wine in there and had told Lainie she was welcome to open either or both. But Lainie wouldn't do that.

She shuffled some of the canned goods, wasting time so she could continue to eavesdrop and hear what Gilbert had to say. But after mentioning Pearl's death two years ago, just days after their sixtieth wedding anniversary, the interview stalled.

"Well," Gil said, as he got up from his seat. "I guess that's pretty much all I have to say."

"Thanks for your candor and your time," Drew told him.

Lainie watched Gil shuffle from the room, her heart heavy with the bittersweet memories he'd shared. She knew each of the retirees at the Rocking C had unique backgrounds, filled with both sad and happy times, but hearing Gil's story reminded her that they weren't forgotten stories.

Drew shut off the video recorder and blew out a ragged breath. "Writing this blog is going to be even more difficult than I thought it'd be."

"Because of Gil's interview?"

"Yes. You were in here and heard his story. My heart goes out to that guy. His life seems pretty tragic, and I'm not sure how to go about writing it."

Lainie closed the pantry door, turned to face Drew and leaned against the kitchen cupboard. "All you have to do is put the right spin on it. You can choose to portray Gil as a tired, grieving old man. Or you can show him as a loving husband and proud father who raised sons who have made this world a better place."

"Good point. The older boy spent time in prison, but he learned from his mistakes."

"And the younger brother made the ultimate sacrifice for his country."

"Yeah. Gil and his wife were good parents, whose sons have sacrificed for others. I'm not sure if I can do them all justice."

"Sure you can. Follow your heart, and you'll do right by them."

He stared at his notes and frowned. "But I don't even know where to begin."

"I could help out. I have a degree in journalism." Shoot. Why had she made an offer like that?

"No kidding?"

She crossed her arms and shifted her weight to one hip. "Don't look so surprised. This job at the ranch is only temporary. And while it's come in handy for the time being, I'm going to work at a newspaper someday."

Actually, she was working for one now, but that was her secret. Besides, writing the Dear Debbie column certainly didn't make her an investigative reporter or a photojournalist.

A grin stretched across Drew's face, lighting his eyes. "I'm impressed. I don't suppose I could hire you to give me some editorial direction for that blog? Would you be up for that?"

Did he mean to pay her for her time? She was going to offer her services for free, but she could sure use the additional income. "You want to hire me?"

"Absolutely. I'm not sure what the going rate is, but I'll gladly pay it."

Lainie tempered her enthusiasm and said, "Sure. I'd be glad to help. Besides, it's for a good cause."

"It certainly is. I'd hate to see this place close."

"Me, too. The men seem happy here, even when they complain about the competency of some of the young ranch hands."

He laughed. "Sully calls them 'whippersnappers.'"

Lainie had heard plenty of comments from all the men. And she'd watched out the kitchen window one day when a couple of them, using a cane and a walker, approached the corral and gave one of the young hands a scolding for doing things wrong. It was a real sight. She'd wished she'd had her camera handy.

"You know," Lainie said, "I also have a minor in photography."

"No wonder you knew how to work my video recorder. Do you have a camera?"

"Yes. And I can take pictures of the ranch and the men to go along with your blog."

"That'd be great. We can show the young cowboys at work, as well as the old guys."

Lainie had a feeling she was going to like collaborating with Drew on the blog project. She might not have the perfect job at the *Gazette* yet, but at least she could get some more experience on her resume.

"I feel like celebrating," he said. "Too bad we don't have any champagne handy."

Toasting with crystal flutes and drinking sparkling wine with a handsome rodeo promoter sounded tempting. And while she knew where Joy's wine was, she wasn't about to lower her guard around a man like him. She'd been attracted to two other men in her life, and both had proven to be lacking in character.

And now here was another. Would the third time be the charm? Or another disaster?

Either way, she'd need to keep her wits about her.

"I have cookies and milk," she said in her best kindergarten teacher's voice.

"Then that'll have to do." Drew tossed her a dazzling smile, his eyes sparkling like fine champagne.

Yes, it would have to. Lainie removed several snickerdoodles from an airtight plastic container in the pantry and placed them on a plate. Then she poured them each a glass of milk.

All the while, Drew watched her. His gaze intensified, as if he knew that she wore white lace lingerie under her clothes, the one feminine luxury she'd refused to give up during the last reinvention of herself.

He reached for a cookie. "I'm looking forward to putting our heads together on the blog."

The thought of their heads touching, their breaths mingling...

Oh, for Pete's sake, Lainie. What were you thinking?

She took a sip of milk in an attempt to shake the inappropriate thought, but when she stole a peek at him and spotted his boyish grin, it didn't work. Images of romantic scenes continued to hound her.

She should have known better than to offer to help him with that stupid blog. With her luck, the assignment would end up being more trouble than it was worth.

So she did her best to shake off his mesmerizing gaze and her heart-stirring reaction to it by stuffing a cookie into her mouth.

Like it or not, she was stuck working closely with the gorgeous cowboy, and she'd just have to keep her growing attraction to him in check. Or she'd have to stuff herself with more milk and cookies.

Chapter 5

Over the next few days, while Lainie washed the dinner dishes, Drew conducted his first interviews in the kitchen.

"Since you offered to help me write that blog, or however many stories we have to tell," he'd told her, "you should hear what the men have to say."

Lainie agreed. And it certainly wasn't a hardship. The retired cowboys' memories and reflections were both touching and entertaining.

But their stories weren't the only thing that held her interest each evening. Drew's voice had a mesmerizing effect on her, and in spite of her efforts to ignore his soft Southern drawl, she found herself increasingly drawn to the rodeo promoter.

She was also touched by the kindness and respect he'd shown the old guys, which made her think he might be different from the men who'd let her down in the past. Clearly, her first impressions of him hadn't been on target.

After placing a meat loaf in the top oven and the russet potatoes in the bottom, she washed her hands at the sink and peered out the window at his cabin, which now had a new front porch.

Drew wasn't anywhere in sight, so she leaned to the right and arched her neck to get a better view of the barn and yard. She still didn't see him, but she spotted Nate working with a fidgety colt in the corral. She'd heard about the acting foreman's skill with horses, but to see him in action was an amazing sight.

She'd already taken a number of shots of the cowboys, old and young alike, and this was a perfect opportunity to get another. She shut off the faucet, dried her hands on a dish towel and hurried to get her camera.

Moments later, she opened the mudroom door and stepped into the yard, her camera lens raised.

"Good job," a familiar, mesmerizing voice called out. "I'm glad to see you're taking advantage of a photo op."

Lainie didn't have to glance over her shoulder to see Drew's approach, but she turned to him anyway.

He looked good today in that black hat cocked just right and that chambray shirt, pressed with a dash of starch—thanks to a laundry service, no doubt. And those jeans? He wore them as if they were a part of him.

As he closed in on her, his scent—something alluring, manly and no doubt expensive—stirred her senses. Her heart rate soared, and her arm wobbled, nearly causing her to drop her camera.

Oh, for Pete's sake. Get it together, girl.

Determined to shake off the effect Drew had on her,

she nodded toward the corral. "The men told me that Nate was the resident horse whisperer, so I thought I'd get a couple pictures of him for the blog."

"Good idea." Drew offered her a heart-strumming smile and followed it up with a playful wink that would tempt the most diligent female employee to play hooky from work. "I'd better not interrupt you."

He had that right. She had a job to do, a photo to take. So she adjusted the lens and checked the light. After catching several shots of Nate, she lowered the camera to her side and focused on Drew. "I missed seeing you this morning. Where'd you run off to?"

"I met a friend for breakfast at Caroline's Diner."

She wondered if his friend was male or female, but decided it would be rude to come right out and ask. However, that didn't mean she couldn't prod him for a little more information.

"From what I saw, it seems that Caroline's is the place where all the locals eat. The food is good, and the desserts are amazing," she said. "Don't you think?"

"That's for sure." He splayed a hand on his flat belly and grinned. "But I'd better not make a habit of filling up on her hotcakes and maple syrup."

Maybe not, but he still hadn't given Lainie a clue about who he'd met, so she pumped a little more. "You and your friend must've had a lot of catching up to do. It's nearly lunchtime."

"Before heading back to the ranch, I stopped by the hardware store to buy more lumber. My cabin isn't the only one with a rickety, worn-out porch."

"You mean you're going to fix each one?"

"I might." He lifted his hat long enough to rake a hand through his hair.

"That's a nice thing for you to do." It was also generous, which was yet another reason to believe he might be a man worth her time and affection.

Lainie lifted her camera to take a picture of him, but he waved her off, blocking his face with his hand.

"Cut that out," he said, his tone playful and light. "That blog isn't about me."

"Okay, cowboy." She lowered her lens, but her gaze lingered on him. She really ought to return to the house, but she couldn't seem to make a move in that direction.

The thump of her heartbeats counted out several seconds until footsteps sounded and she spotted Bradley Jamison approaching.

The young ranch hand cleared his throat. "Excuse me. I hate to interrupt."

It was probably best that he did. Lainie offered him a smile. "What's up?"

"Nate said I could use one of the cabins for a few days. I don't want to cause you any trouble, ma'am, so I'd be happy to clean it up, if it needs it."

Drew answered Brad before Lainie could. "I thought you slept in the bunkhouse. Is someone giving you a hard time in there?"

"Oh, no. The cabin's not for me. It's for my mom. She just got hired to work at the new children's home down the road. Once she's on their payroll, she'll get room and board there, but she doesn't start until Monday, and her lease is up tomorrow. So it would only be a couple of days."

"The new *children's* home?" Lainie asked.

Brad nodded sagely. "It's a place for abused and neglected kids. A man and his wife bought the old Clancy place and opened it up last month."

"I know where that ranch is," Drew said. "It's got a big house, but it's pretty old. I doubt it's up to code."

"It wasn't at first. But last summer, the community church got involved with the project, and so did the Wexler Women's Club. The couple in charge are trying to get a grant of some kind, but in the meantime, they'll have to slowly add kids as they go."

Still stunned by the idea of a children's home down the road, Lainie asked, "How many kids live there?"

"I think about twelve. Most of them are from the city. My mom told me the idea was to move them to a country environment so they could see a new way of life."

"That's an interesting concept," Drew said.

"Yeah." Brad replaced his hat on his head. "My mom was pretty impressed when she went out and saw it for herself. From what I understand, each kid is given certain chores, and they're also assigned a few animals to take care of—like pigs, sheep, goats and rabbits."

Lainie hoped they didn't plan to work the children too hard. She'd had one set of foster parents who'd been awfully strict and expected more out of her than seemed fair.

"What's your mom's job going to be?" Drew asked.

"They hired her as a counselor. After she divorced my stepdad, she went back to school. It took a while because she had to work during the day and take classes at night, but she finally got a degree."

"Good for her." Lainie liked the woman already.

"Yeah, I'm proud of her." Brad kicked the toe of his boot at the ground, stirring the dirt. "She's glad she'll be there before Christmas. A lot of those kids never had a tree or presents before. Their funds are limited, though, so she can't go all out with decorations and stuff, but she doesn't think it'll take much to make them happy."

"Actually," Lainie said, "regular meals and a warm, safe place to sleep helps a lot." Of course, that wouldn't change the reality those kids lived with each day, the memories they carried. "Don't worry, Brad. I'll make sure the cabin is ready for your mom."

Drew placed his hand on Lainie's shoulder, giving it a gentle squeeze. "No, you don't have to do that. I'll do it for you. You never know, a mouse might be lying in wait."

Lainie's cheeks warmed. She was tempted to plant an elbow in his side and shoot him a frown. But in truth, he'd just offered to do her a huge favor.

"Thanks," Brad said. "I really appreciate this. And just so you know, my mom said she'd be happy to help out around here. She'll cook, clean, run errands...whatever. She'll even keep some of those pesky old cowboys out of your hair. She's good with people, even difficult ones."

"I'm looking forward to meeting her," Lainie said. "And I'm sure we'll keep her busy while she's here."

"Well, I'd best get back to work or Nate'll have my hide." Brad tilted the brim of his hat to Lainie, turned and strode toward the barn.

Rather than let the subject of their conversation drift back to that embarrassing mouse encounter, Lainie steered it in another direction. "I hadn't given Christmas much thought, but I really ought to put up some holiday decorations, including a tree."

"I'm going to my sister's house on Christmas Day, but the rest of the time I'll be on the ranch, so I can help you." Drew nodded toward a couple of older men rocking on the porch. "Imagine the memories Christmas must dig up for these guys."

True. More fodder for Drew's blog…and for another human interest column for her to propose to Mr. Carlton. She could see it now: *A Cowboy Christmas*.

As Lainie began making a mental list of the chores to be done, she had a lightbulb moment. "Oh, wow."

"What's wrong?"

"Nothing. I just had an idea. What if we have a joint Christmas party for the children here at the Rocking C?"

"That'd be nice, but it would be a huge undertaking."

"Maybe, but I'm sure Rex, Sully and the others would help. And it would give the men a special purpose, not to mention something to look forward to."

Drew looked out in the distance, his brow creased in concentration. After a couple of beats, he brightened. "You know, a party like that would lend itself to one heck of a blog post."

"You read my mind." A grin slid across Lainie's face, and a tingle of excitement spread through her.

She couldn't remember the last time she'd looked forward to Christmas, but she'd do whatever she could to create a special holiday for those kids. Decorations, a tree, holiday baking…

"We can do this." Lainie clutched Drew's arm in camaraderie, but she nearly jerked away when the body heat radiating through his shirt sent an electrical zing through her.

She tried to blame the spark on the energy emanating from their new joint venture, although she feared it was more than that.

"I'll find out who's in charge of the children's home," Drew said. "And I'll see how they feel about joining us for a Christmas party at the Rocking Chair Ranch."

"And I'll talk to our nursing staff," Lainie said, "although I can't see why they'd object. A party would be good for young and old alike."

"There's only two weeks before Christmas, so we have our work cut out for us. We'd better get busy." Drew gave Lainie's shoulder a nudge with his arm, reminding her of his presence, of his heat. They'd become a team, and by the way he was looking at her, he liked that idea.

She liked it, too.

As Drew turned and walked away, she studied his back, admiring his sexy swagger, his broad shoulders and the perfect fit of his jeans.

A romantic wish tingled through her, warming her cheeks once again. Maybe Santa would be good to her for a change.

And if she was lucky, she just might wake up on Christmas morning and find a cowboy under her tree.

Drew was always up for a challenge, which is why he'd searched every nook and cranny of his cabin to find a cell signal. He was determined to set up a temporary but functional home office, although he wasn't having much luck. About the time he considered giving up and driving to town for Wi-Fi, he picked up a signal near the kitchen area.

As long as he moved the dinette table about three feet from the east wall, he could connect to the internet, which would make it a lot easier to work while he stayed at the ranch for the next two weeks.

Once he set up his laptop and got online, he did some research on the children's home Brad had mentioned earlier this afternoon. It was called Kidville, and from the pictures posted on the main website page, the outside looked like a small town in the Old West.

"Interesting," he said, as he continued to read up on the place that had been founded by Jim and Donna Hoffman, an older couple who had a heart for kids.

The more Drew learned about the Hoffmans and Kidville, the more determined he was to meet with them and see it for himself. With the Wi-Fi service he now had, it didn't take him long to find the number for the administrative office and ask for whoever was in charge.

A couple minutes later, Mr. Hoffman answered. "This is Jim. How can I help you?"

Drew introduced himself and revealed his affiliation with Esteban Enterprises, the rodco and the Rocking Chair Ranch, and his admiration for what the Hoffmans were doing.

"Thanks," Jim said. "For nearly ten years, my wife and I dreamed of creating a place in the country where we could provide a safe, loving environment for abused and neglected city kids. So when we retired from our county jobs, we set our plan in motion. We've had a few hurdles along the way, so Kidville has been nearly two years in the making."

"I'd imagine funding would be one of those problems."

"Yes, that's true. But thanks to the help of the community church, the Wexler Women's Club and the Brighton Valley Rotary, we were able to remodel the house and get it up to code, paint the barn and set up a playground. But until we get more financial backing, we're nearing our capacity."

"I think it would be fairly easy to drum up support

for such a worthy cause." Drew went on to explain his promotional plan for the retired cowboys' home.

"As a nonprofit, I'm afraid we don't have the funds to pay for any advertisements or PR companies," Jim said.

Apparently, Drew hadn't made himself clear. "I didn't expect you to hire me or Esteban Enterprises. To be completely candid, I'm not exactly sure what I can do to help you and Kidville, but just for the record, nothing tugs at my boss's heartstrings more than rodeos, aging cowboys and children."

Drew didn't mention anything about a Christmas party on the Rocking C, but he did suggest a meeting with the Hoffmans. He could propose the idea at that time.

"Why don't you come by Friday afternoon?" Jim suggested. "We'll talk more then, and I can give you a tour of Kidville."

"Sounds like a plan. And if it's okay with you, I'll probably bring my…um, associate. It was her idea to do some joint promotion, and there's no telling what we might come up with if we all put our heads together."

"I'll make sure my wife is available. Would two o'clock work for the two of you?"

"That's perfect. We'll see you then." After the call ended, Drew continued to sit at the dinette table, his cell phone in hand. He had a good feeling about Kidville. And he couldn't wait to share the news with Lainie.

He glanced at the clock on the microwave. It was closing in on five o'clock and would soon be time for dinner. If he'd learned one thing in his week spent on the Rocking C, it was that the meals ran on a strict schedule.

He wouldn't say anything about it at the table. Instead, he'd wait until after everyone ate, when it was quiet in the kitchen.

And when he had Lainie to himself.

Other than several murmurs of appreciation for a tasty meal, the men had eaten quietly, their focus on the meat loaf, buttered green beans and baked potatoes. Even Drew, who sat at the kitchen table with the young ranch hands, hadn't said much, but by the glimmer in his eyes and the grin on his face, he seemed to be pleased about something.

Lainie tamped down her curiosity for now. She'd wait until after dinner to question him.

In the meantime, while the men had ice cream and chocolate chip cookies for dessert, she carried the plates and flatware to the sink, rinsed them off and placed them in the dishwasher. By the time she returned to the table for the empty bowls and spoons, the ranch hands were already filing out the back door, with Drew in the midst of them.

Lainie continued her work, putting away leftovers and wiping down countertops, but she couldn't help wondering what Drew was up to. For the past few evenings, he'd interviewed the retired cowboys in the kitchen, a routine she'd come to look forward to.

She glanced out the kitchen window. The lights were off in his cabin, so he hadn't turned in for the night. She'd just placed the detergent in the dishwasher when the back door swung open and clicked shut. She turned to see Drew striding through the mudroom on his way back inside.

His smile, as dazzling as it'd ever been, lit his eyes, and her pulse rate kicked up a notch.

"Got a minute?" he asked.

"Sure. What's up?"

He pulled out a chair from the table for her. "I thought you might like an update."

She sat down, and he took a seat next to her. "I did a little research, and Kidville, that children's home, appears to be everything Brad said it was and more. So I made an appointment for us to take a tour on Friday at two. Can you slip off for an hour or so?"

"I'd really like to, but I'm not sure. I'm usually busy with the meal prep for dinner at that time."

"I've got you covered. Brad's mother will be here by then, and a few minutes ago, when I mentioned what I had in mind, he called her. She said she'd be happy to cook dinner—or do anything else to help out. She's coming to stay that day anyway, so she's going to arrive a few hours early. You'll have plenty of time to show her around the kitchen."

"You've thought of everything."

"I try to cover all my bases." His wink turned her heart inside out.

They'd not only become teammates, but it seemed as if they were well on the road to being friends.

She liked the thought of that.

"Did you know that Kidville has a small orchard and a good-size vegetable garden?" Drew asked. "They're going to grow most of their produce, and they're raising chickens."

A niggle of concern crept over her, stealing her smile. "I know the kids will have chores, but I hope they won't be expected to do all the work."

"Jim Hoffman and his wife believe children should

be given age-appropriate responsibilities, and I see the reasoning behind that."

"Me, too. I just hope this doesn't turn out to be a farm run by child labor." Lainie's thoughts drifted to the time she'd lived with the Bakers, the memory taking her back to a place and foster family she'd hoped to forget.

"You have a faraway look in your eyes," Drew said, drawing her back to the here and now.

"I'm sorry. My mind wandered for a moment."

"To a bad personal experience?"

Lainie didn't usually talk about her early years—at least, not in detail. But she'd grown close to Drew in the past few days, and if they'd truly become friends, she should be up front with him. "I told you that I grew up in foster care. For the most part it wasn't too bad. If I'd been able to stay with the first family…" Tears filled her eyes, and she blinked them away. So much for the candor of friendship.

"I'm sorry that you had such a crappy childhood," he said.

"It wasn't all bad." She swiped at her lower lashes, stopping the overflow. "Most of the families I lived with were decent. In fact, I actually liked Mama Kate, the first foster mother my sister and I had. She was an older, dark-skinned woman who had an easy laugh and a loving heart as big as her lap. She never turned down a kid needing a placement, so there were a lot of us. Yet she managed to find special time for each of us. My sister and I counted ourselves lucky to live with her."

"Why'd you have to leave?" Drew asked.

"One night, about six months after we moved in, Mama Kate had a stroke and had to give us all up."

"That's too bad. Where did you go next?"

Lainie bit back a quick response. She wasn't sure she wanted to be that up front. She and Rickie had moved to a receiving home, where her heart condition was finally diagnosed. She endured several back-to-back hospitalizations, which was when she and her sister were separated. After her surgery and a long inpatient recuperation period, she learned that Rickie had been adopted. Sadly, they'd never had a chance to say goodbye to each other.

But Lainie wasn't going to share that.

She reached for her collar, fingered the top button then skimmed the next three before dropping her hand to her lap. "Next stop was to the Bakers' house. Talk about all work and no play."

"So that's why you're worried about the children and their chores at Kidville," Drew said.

"The Bakers seemed to think that I was there to cook, clean the house and do the laundry."

"An unpaid servant, huh?"

"Pretty much. At least, as far as my foster mother was concerned." Lainie tilted her hand and flicked her fingers at a crumb she'd neglected to wipe off the table. "Her name was Glenda, which always reminded me of the good witch, only spelled differently. But she wasn't very good—or nice. She once called my fifth grade teacher to complain about the amount of homework I was assigned. She told Mrs. Fleming that I wouldn't be allowed to do any of it, especially the reading, until after my household chores were done. But by then, I was exhausted."

Drew reached across the table and covered her hand with his, warming it. He brushed his thumb across the top of her wrist. She suspected he meant to have a comforting effect, a calming one. But his touch spiked her pulse, arousing her senses instead.

"I'm sorry, Lainie. That must have been very difficult for you."

"It was." Her voice came out a notch above a whisper, and when she met his gaze, she spotted sympathy in his eyes.

She was glad for the connection they'd made, for his understanding, but she didn't want his pity. She had the urge to jerk her hand away from his and to reach for the collar of her blouse. But she couldn't seem to move.

As her heart pounded a strong, steady cadence, an unfamiliar emotion rose up inside, one that stirred her senses and reminded her just how inexperienced she was. Especially when it came to things like openhearted discussions, honest emotion and a friendship drifting toward romance.

She was at a complete loss. Should she pull her hand away from him now?

Or should she leave it in his grip forever?

Drew made the decision for her when he turned her hand over, palm side up, and clasped her fingers in his. He squeezed gently, relaying compassion and reassurance. Yet at the same time, it triggered a blood-swirling feeling she'd rather not ponder or put a name to.

"I don't think you need to worry about the Hoffmans," he said. "I have a good feeling about them. And if we all work together, I think we can boost financial support for both the Rocking Chair Ranch and Kidville."

Lainie withdrew her hand from his, albeit reluctantly. "Are you talking about the Christmas party?"

"Yes, but why stop there? What about an Easter egg

decorating party, pumpkin carving… I could go on and on."

"Wow. That's creative," she said.

"Just doing my job," he said, shrugging off her compliment. Then he brightened. "You know, something tells me this is going to be a successful venture. We should celebrate."

"That's a little premature, don't you think? We haven't even toured the children's home or met the people in charge."

"Okay, then we can toast our new venture." His playful, boyish expression made it difficult to tell him no.

So Lainie returned his smile. "With a glass of milk and cookies?"

"Do you have anything better suited for adults?"

"Coffee?"

He lifted an eyebrow. "How about something stronger than caffeine?"

The wine stash. Lainie hesitated.

Oh, why not. Joy had told her to help herself.

"As a matter of fact," she said, "I do. You have your choice of merlot or chardonnay."

"Either works for me. You pick. I'll find a corkscrew."

Lainie watched Drew head for the kitchen drawer and realized this wasn't going to be a celebration. It was more of a christening, like breaking a bottle of bubbly on the bow of a ship ready to set sail for the very first time.

As she went to the cabinet and selected the merlot, she hoped that if she and Drew were about to launch a romance, it wouldn't end up a disaster of *Titanic* proportions.

Chapter 6

Lainie handed Drew the bottle of merlot, and he pulled the cork, releasing the scent of oak and blackberries.

She'd been right. It was too early to actually celebrate anything, but he'd had another motive to consider tonight a special occasion. He wanted to get to know her better, to spend some time with her, and he hadn't been able to come up with a better reason to stick around in the kitchen this evening.

She removed two wineglasses from the small hutch and set them on the table, allowing him to fill them halfway.

Then he lifted his glass in a toast. "Here's to helping the young and old alike."

"To cowboys and children." She clinked her glass against his, then took a sip.

He did the same, yet it wasn't their team effort to encourage charitable contributions for both ranches that he was thinking about. He actually liked the idea of working closely with Lainie. He liked it a lot.

"Are you looking forward to visiting Kidville?" he asked her. "Or..." He paused, realizing that her time spent in foster care might make a visit to a children's home, even one as unique as that one appeared to be, stir up bad memories. And he didn't want to open a Pandora's Box of emotion.

"I'd like to take that tour," she said softly. "Thanks for including me. Besides, it'll be good for the blog, right?"

"Yes, that's true. At this rate, we'll have enough blog content for months." He studied her face, those big brown eyes, the soft, plump lips. Her high cheekbones, like those of a top model, bore a slight blush.

Once again, it struck him that he'd seen her somewhere before. In his dreams, most likely. But in those nocturnal musings, she hadn't been dressed in baggy denim or blouses buttoned to the throat. She'd worn sexy silk panties, which she kept hidden from sight and only revealed to her lover.

"Have you started the blog yet?" she asked.

Not really. When it came to sitting down in front of his laptop and actually opening up a Word document, he'd been dragging his feet.

"I'm still conducting the interviews," he said. "I plan to talk to the younger men, too. Nate has an interesting story."

"Does he?" Lainie ran the tip of her tongue across her top lip, licking a drop of wine.

Drew sucked in a breath. For a moment, he lost his

train of thought. So he focused on his wineglass. Anything but that mouth, those lips and that tongue.

"I'd heard that Nate got married recently," she said, "but not to the mother of his baby."

Oh, yeah. They'd been talking about Nate.

"You heard right," Drew said. "A few months back, a woman he'd once dated showed up here at the ranch, pregnant and battered by her new husband. She was looking for Nate and claimed the baby was his."

"How tragic." She did that thing with her tongue on her lip again, and he nearly forgot what they were talking about.

Nate and the baby. Right.

"Because of that beating, she went into premature labor," Drew said, "she gave birth to little Jessie, then died from a brain bleed."

Lainie cupped her hands around the stem of her goblet and scrunched her brow. "That poor woman. How sad."

"It sure was. Her husband is now in prison for murder." Drew reached for the bottle and replenished his wine. "More?"

She shook her head and placed her hand over the top of her glass. "What happened next?"

"Nate took custody of the baby and hooked up with Anna, the hospital social worker who'd been assigned to his case." Drew took a sip of wine. He wondered if Lainie liked the merlot. She wasn't drinking much.

She fingered the stem of the glass, her brow slightly furrowed. "Nate fell in love with his social worker?"

"Do you find that odd?"

Lainie smiled. "I can't imagine a handsome young cowboy falling for any of the ones I had as a child."

"Then Nate was lucky. Anna's both pretty and loving. But for a while, he was afraid she'd find him lacking as a father, and that he'd lose custody of the baby as a result. But he was wrong, and now they're married."

"You were right. That's an interesting story. But I have a question. You said the baby's mother 'claimed' Nate was the father. Was he?"

"At first, Nate wasn't sure. He told me that DNA didn't make a man a daddy. And that you don't have to be born into a family to belong to one."

"That's true," Lainie said, brightening. "It's an interesting take—and a good piece of advice. I'll have to keep it in mind."

"Advice? I'm not following you."

She blinked a couple times, then let out a little giggle and shrugged her shoulders. "I'm sorry. I was just thinking out loud."

And probably ruing the fact that she didn't have a family of her own. Drew was about to comment, then realized he'd be wading into a slew of emotion he didn't want to deal with. He had enough of that with Kara Lee, which had been made worse by maternal hormones. So he let it go.

He looked at Lainie's left hand, the one he'd once touched, once held. She wasn't wearing a ring, so he concluded she wasn't involved with someone.

For a man who never mixed business with pleasure, he was tempted to make an exception this time.

"Is there a special man in your life?" he asked.

"No, not anymore. Actually, there really never was. Not one who was special."

Drew sat up straighter, pumped by what sounded like good news. "That's a little surprising."

"What is?" She lifted her glass, studied the burgundy color in the kitchen light, then took a drink. "That I'm not engaged or seeing someone right now? Actually, the few men I thought were decent ended up disappointing me. I can ferret out the heart of a story, but apparently, I'm not very good at judging a man's heart and character."

"Sounds like you're recovering from a painful breakup."

Her shoulder twitched. Not quite a shrug, but a tell just the same. One that told him she'd been hurt in the past and possibly betrayed.

"I was too trusting," she said. "But I'll be a lot more careful in the future."

Drew couldn't say he blamed her. He'd built a few walls of his own, although that didn't mean he hadn't found the time for a casual but intimate relationship every now and then. And when he did, he was pretty selective.

The truth was, he found Lainie to be both attractive and completely acceptable in that regard. Would she feel the same way about him? To be blunt, would she be interested in having a short-term affair while they were both on the Rocking C?

Oh, hell. That was a crazy thought.

Lainie was the type of woman who was probably looking for a husband and kids—just like Kara Lee, who'd been on the prowl for Mr. Right and thought she'd found him in Craig Baxter.

And look how that had turned out. No, Drew didn't have any misperceptions about love and living happily ever after.

So who was he to mess with Lainie's heart?

He threw down the last of his merlot and said, "I'd better turn in for the night. Thanks for talking to me. I'll see you tomorrow."

"I'll be ready."

He returned the cork to the nearly empty bottle and placed it in the fridge. But before turning to go, a thought overtook him. "Do you have anything other than jeans or overalls to wear?"

Her brow furrowed. "Yes, why?"

"I realize we're just going to a ranch, but I told the Hoffmans you were my associate. So I thought you might want to… You know, dress the part?"

She looked down at her jeans and baggy blouse, then rolled her eyes. "Don't worry. I know how to dress professionally."

"I'm sorry. I didn't mean to offend you. In fact, you have understated class and look great no matter what you wear. Forget I said anything."

"You're forgiven." Her smile was pretty convincing. "Would business casual be acceptable?"

"That'd be perfect." He lobbed her an appreciative grin, then headed outside.

By the time he'd shut the back door, his lips had quirked into a full-on smile. Now he had something to look forward to.

And so did his nocturnal musings.

At nine o'clock on Friday morning, Brad's mother, Molly Jamison, arrived at the Rocking C Ranch driving a white Ford Taurus that had seen better days—or make that years. Lainie had been looking forward to meeting her, so she went outside to greet her in the yard.

But when a petite redhead in her midthirties climbed

out of the car and pulled out a suitcase that was nearly as big as she was, Lainie's steps slowed.

Brad had to be close to twenty, so Lainie had imagined his mother to be in her forties or fifties. But she must have been a teenager when she'd given birth.

Not that it mattered. Tamping down her surprise, Lainie crossed the yard, introduced herself and reached out her hand in greeting. "It's nice to meet you. Do you need help with your luggage?"

"I don't have much," Molly said. "Just a single suitcase and an overnight bag."

Before Lainie could offer to show her where she'd be staying, Brad came out of the barn wearing a great big grin on his face. "Hey, Mom. I'm glad you're here. I'll take your stuff and put it in the cabin. I know you're eager to get a tour of the house and meet the men who live here."

"Thanks, honey." Molly blessed her son, who stood a good six inches taller than her, with a warm smile. "I'm also ready to roll up my sleeves and help out."

"Let's start with a tour of the kitchen," Lainie said.

Molly resembled a young, red-haired Dolly Parton, but without the big hair, double Ds and the sparkle. Still, she had a sweet smile and a happy voice. Lainie liked her instantly.

She and Molly also had a lot in common, including the fact that they'd had to pull themselves up by their proverbial bootstraps, a fondness for the elderly and underprivileged children and a willingness to work.

So when it was time to go with Drew to Kidville, Lainie didn't have any qualms about leaving. The men would be in good hands with Molly.

Now, as Drew slid behind the wheel of his black

pickup, which boasted all the bells and whistles, Lainie sat in the passenger seat, checking out the GPS and what appeared to be an upgraded sound system. The impressive, late-model truck had that new-car smell. At least, it did until Drew shut the driver's door, filling the cab with his faint, woodsy scent. "Ready?" He glanced across the console at Lainie, stirring her senses to the point of distraction. "Buckle up."

"You bet." But it wasn't just her body that needed to be secured with a seat belt. When it came to Drew, she feared her heart might be in for a bumpy ride.

She tried to keep her mind on the road ahead—and not on the bigger-than-life cowboy driving. But that was hard to do when he cut another glance her way, his eyes sparking. "You look great, Lainie."

Her cheeks warmed at the compliment.

"It wasn't easy to lay aside my overalls."

"Seriously?" He shot another look across the console, his brow furrowed.

She laughed, made a fist and gently punched his arm. "I'm kidding."

"Seriously," he said, "that's exactly the professional style I had in mind."

"I told you that I knew how to dress." She'd chosen a pair of low heels, black slacks and a tailored white blouse. She'd topped off her outfit with a red plaid scarf, then pulled her hair up into a topknot.

"I'm sorry for doubting you. You look great." He grinned, then winked before returning his gaze to the road ahead. A couple of miles later, he pointed to the right. "There it is. It sure looks a lot different than it did when the Clancys owned it. The perimeter used to be surrounded by rusted-out barbed wire and leaning posts. But not now. The Hoffmans have made a lot of changes to the place. If I hadn't seen pictures on the internet, I wouldn't have recognized it from before."

Lainie noted the solid, six-foot fence made of cinder-block posts and wooden slats. "It looks like they meant to protect the property and keep the children safe."

Drew turned into the driveway, where they stopped in front of a black, wrought iron gate. Using an inter-com/phone system, he called the office. Once he iden-tified himself, the doors swung open, granting them access to the property.

He continued on to a graveled lot and parked be-tween a white minivan and a red sedan. They got out of his truck and headed for an arched entryway made of adobe brick. A wooden sign overhead read: Welcome to Kidville, Texas. Population 134.

"Do you think they have that many children living here?" Lainie asked.

"Brad said there was about a dozen, and Jim gave me the impression they'd just begun taking in kids. I think that's just their way of making Kidville sound like a real town."

She nodded, then continued along the dirt road, pass-ing under the sign. Her steps slowed as she took in the grassy areas, a red schoolhouse, a newspaper office and even a hotel. The only areas without the quaint, Old West look were a volleyball court, a baseball field and a playground that provided a swing set, several differ-ent slides and a colorful climbing structure.

"Kidville's layout is amazing," she said. "No, it's ac-tually mind-boggling."

"Yeah, it's pretty cool." Drew gestured for her to take the wooden sidewalk that led to the hotel.

"I've never seen anything like it." Sure, she'd watched television shows with similar settings, carefully constructed building facades and wooden sidewalks that portrayed Western life in the late 1800s. She'd also experienced living in a children's home for a while, but she'd never imagined seeing the two combined into one.

Drew had to be equally impressed because he took out his cell and began to take a picture.

"No, don't." She reached for his arm to stop him. "I would have brought my camera with me, but I'm sure they have privacy rules in place to protect the children. We should get permission from the Hoffmans first."

"Good point." Drew returned his cell to his pocket. "I hadn't thought about that. I'm glad you did."

"Where are we supposed to go?" she asked.

"Jim told me that the main office is located in the hotel, although he and his wife live in that white, two-story house next to the ball field."

Lainie spotted it right away. "Do you think all the children sleep in the house?"

"It looks big enough for some of them, but I didn't ask him about the number of kids they had or the living arrangements. Brad mentioned that his mom would be staying here, so there could be other staff members supervising children at night in some of the outbuildings."

In spite of the quaint setting, apprehension crawled through Lainie's stomach. Her thoughts drifted back to the day her caseworker had taken her from the hospital to the receiving home, where she was to complete her recovery.

She'd been walking slowly that day, more from fear and loneliness than pain. The woman had sensed her distress and had taken her hand to provide comfort and reassurance.

That lasted only about five minutes. Then Lainie was handed over to an employee who cared more about her need for a cigarette break than Lainie's need to feel safe and secure.

How odd, she thought, that those feelings would creep back again today, as if she were being taken to a new home and to yet another, unfamiliar placement.

She wiped her palms on her slacks. When Drew's arm bumped her shoulder, she was tempted to take his hand in hers for reassurance. And it annoyed her that, at times, the past still seemed to have power over her.

"It sure is quiet," Drew said. "I wonder where all the kids are."

"Probably in school. A lot of children who come from broken, neglectful homes have never lived in an environment that encouraged education. So many of them lag behind in the classroom and struggle with their studies."

"Did you?" he asked.

"Yes, before my dad died. After that, I tended to bury my nose in a book and focus on my homework."

"Instead of boys?"

"Absolutely. Boys were a dead end." And in her experience, so were the grown-up versions for the most part. "My studies helped me forget what was going on around me." She scanned the quiet grounds. "I wonder if the kids are tutored here or if they go to a public school in town."

"Let's find out."

As she and Drew approached the hotel, a balding,

heavyset man in his late fifties opened the door and came outside to welcome them. "I'm Jim Hoffman."

Drew introduced himself and Lainie, and they all shook hands.

"Come inside. My wife wants to go on the tour with us, but she's got some business to take care of first." Jim led the way into the hotel.

Lainie didn't know what she'd been expecting. Something to match the exterior façade, she supposed, but the reception area looked more like a modern living room, with overstuffed sofas and chairs upholstered in faux leather, a southwestern style area rug and potted plants throughout.

A tall, slender redhead in her late fifties sat on one of the sofas, next to a boy with messy, dark hair who appeared to be seven or eight. She was telling him to be patient, that he'd see his little brothers soon.

"But you don't understand." The boy's brown eyes filled with tears. "They don't have nobody but me to take care of them. What if someone doesn't turn the light on for them at night? Abel is scared of the dark. And what if they don't know how to rub Mario's tummy when it hurts?"

"I promise to call their foster parents," the redhead told the worried child. "I'll make sure they know what to do."

The boy swiped at his tear-streaked face. His frown eased a bit, but he didn't appear to be completely convinced that all would be well.

"Donna?" Jim said, "I'd like to introduce you to Drew and Lainie, the people I told you about from the Rocking Chair Ranch."

"It's nice to meet you." She offered them a warm

smile, then turned to the boy and placed her hand on his small, thin shoulder. "This is Andre. Mrs. Tran, his social worker, just brought him this afternoon to stay with us. He's going to join us for the first part of our tour, which will be the schoolhouse, and then we'll introduce him to his new friends and teacher."

The child sniffed, then bit down on his bottom lip.

"Hey, Andre," Drew said. "It's nice to meet you."

The boy studied Drew, scanning him from his hat to his boots. Sizing him up, it seemed. "Are you a cowboy?"

Drew smiled. "Yes, I guess you could say that."

The boy's eyes widened, and his lips parted. "A *real* one?"

"Well, I grew up on a ranch. And I work with the rodeo now."

"Do you have your own horse?" the boy asked.

"I used to."

Andre's shoulders slumped, clearly disappointed. He glanced down at his sneakers, one of which was untied, then looked at Drew. "But you do know about horses, right?"

"I sure do."

The boy looked at the Hoffmans and frowned. "Mrs. Tran told me there were horses here. But that's not true. They don't have any."

"We don't have any *yet*," Donna said. "We're working on it, though."

"We do have plans to buy a couple of good riding horses in the future," Jim interjected. "But in the meantime, we have plenty of other animals, like rabbits and sheep and goats. We even have barn kittens and a couple old dogs who'll lick your face and play ball with you."

"I know," the boy said. "But…" He scrunched his face and blew out a sigh, clearly perplexed about something. Then he looked at Drew. "Can I ask you a question?"

"Sure. Go ahead."

"When people have a bad leg and can't walk too good, can they still ride a horse?"

"I'm sure they can." Drew looked at Donna, who placed her hand on Andre's small shoulder.

"When Andre was four," she explained, "he broke his foot. The bone wasn't set properly, and there wasn't any follow-up treatment. So it left him with a pronounced limp. But fortunately, we have an appointment for him to see an orthopedic surgeon next week, and we're hopeful that they'll be able to correct that for him."

"But in case they don't," Andre said, his big brown eyes seeking out Drew, "do you think I can still learn to ride someday? I want to be a cowboy when I grow up, and you can't be a very good one if you don't have a horse."

"I'll tell you what," Drew said, "if it's okay with the Hoffmans, I'd be happy to give you a riding lesson, even if I have to borrow the horse."

The boy turned to Jim. "Is it okay? Will you let me?"

"I don't see why not. I'll talk to Mr. Madison and see what we can work out. But for now, you'd better go to the schoolhouse and meet your new teacher and the other children."

Donna stood and reached for Andre's hand, helping him up. Then she walked with him to the door.

Lainie followed behind, observing the boy's uneven gait. One of his legs was clearly shorter than the other. Her heart ached for him, and she lifted her hand to finger her chest. She knew how it felt to have her medical care neglected, to face a painful surgery without anyone to offer comfort and reassurance.

Would one of the Hoffmans stay at Andre's bedside, like the loving parents of other hospitalized kids had done? She certainly hoped they would.

When they reached the red schoolhouse, they went inside. The classroom smelled of crayons and white paste, reminding Lainie of days gone by. The teacher was collecting a math worksheet from her six students—seven, now that Andre had arrived.

"This is a combination class," Jim explained while his wife led Andre to the teacher. "They're in first, second or third grade."

The teacher, a blonde in her midthirties, offered the boy a kind smile. "I'm Mrs. Wright, Andre. I heard you were coming, and I'm so glad you're here. You're just in time for recess and an afternoon snack."

After leaving Andre with his new classmates, Donna led the tour outside, letting the door close behind them.

"That poor child has had a real time of it," Donna said. "He's the oldest of three boys, and up until child protective services stepped in to rescue them from an abusive home, he did his best to look out for his younger brothers."

"Where are the other boys?" Lainie asked Donna.

"In a separate foster home. We'd like to bring them here, but we don't have the staff or the resources to take in preschoolers yet."

"That's something else we're working on," Jim said.

Lainie hoped adding younger kids would be a priority over the horses. And that the Hoffmans would be able to take in Andre's brothers soon. It was so unfair, and the injustice of the situation sparked her into action.

"Siblings shouldn't be separated," Lainie said. "I can tell you right now, we'll do whatever we can to help you get more funding—and to provide Andre's brothers a home at Kidville."

Donna pressed her hand to her throat. "I'm overwhelmed—and so glad to hear that."

Lainie glanced at Drew, aware that he might not approve of her making a commitment like that without talking it over with him first. It would be nice to have his blessing, but she'd meant what she said. Kidville was going to be her newest project—and she hadn't even gotten the full tour.

Chapter 7

Drew had been impressed with Jim Hoffman, even before seeing him in person, so he was ready to climb onboard. But he wouldn't have blurted out a half-baked commitment without first discussing it with his "associate."

He might have been annoyed with Lainie for making a unilateral decision for them both, but when she looked at him with those soulful brown eyes, he'd been toast.

Hell, how did a man say no to a woman like her?

Besides, Kidville was a good cause.

"Here's what I have in mind," he said, as he fell into step beside Lainie. "Rocking chairs are associated with young kids, as well as the elderly. So Esteban Enterprises can easily cross-promote Kidville and the ranch at the same time."

"Don't get me wrong," Jim said. "We'd appreciate

your efforts to bring in more financial support, but I worry about splitting the pot. I'd hate to see the Rocking C only get half of what they expected."

"Actually," Drew said, "I think we'll double the pot."

Jim glanced first at his wife, who gave him a cautious nod of agreement, then back to Drew. "Then we're game if you are."

An animated smile erupted on Lainie's face. "We'd like to start by inviting your children to attend a Christmas party at the Rocking C. We'll provide the refreshments, of course. And I'll even coax one of the retired cowboys to play Santa."

That'd be a nice touch, Drew thought. He could even publish a blog post about it afterward.

Lainie continued to lay out her plan. "If it's all right to take pictures of the children, it might make the promotion more personal and touching, which would encourage potential benefactors to be more generous. Christmas and kids should be a heartwarming draw."

"You're probably right." Jim scrubbed his hand over his receding hairline. "But we have a couple of children who should stay out of the limelight, if you know what I mean. So I'd like to look over any pictures you take before they're published or posted."

"Absolutely," Lainie said. "And just so you know, I plan to propose an article for *The Brighton Valley Gazette*. That is, if you don't mind. I'd let you look it and the pictures over before we go to press."

"Well now," Jim said, "this meeting is proving to be very productive."

"I think so, too," Lainie said. "Should we schedule the party on Christmas Eve? That would give us time to decorate the ranch, buy some gifts for the children and locate a Santa Claus suit."

"That would be awesome," Donna said. "Some of our children have never had a real Christmas."

"I know." Lainie's voice was soft and almost fragile. "I spent a few years in foster homes when I was a girl. And some of the kids I grew up with had sad backgrounds."

"I'm sorry to hear that," Donna said.

Lainie shrugged. "It's all in the past. But that's why I want to help your kids now."

Drew was a little surprised she'd been so forthcoming, but then again, the Hoffmans were an easy couple to like and to trust.

"I hope we can get some donations rolling in quickly," Lainie added. "I'd like to see you be able to bring Andre's brothers here as soon as possible."

Donna placed her hand on Lainie's arm. "Believe me, Jim and I want to see that happen, too, but since you're no stranger to foster care, you probably have an idea how long these things can take. It's not just the funding we need, it's licensing and paperwork, too. I'm afraid you'll have to be patient until Jim and I work through the system."

Lainie's cheeks turned a deep shade of pink. "Yes, of course. Sometimes I let my heart and enthusiasm run away with me."

Drew realized she was eager to see Andre's family reunited because, after losing touch with her twin sister, she knew how the poor kid felt. He could certainly understand that. He felt sorry for Andre, too, but for a different reason. He admired the wannabe cowboy's loyalty to his younger brothers and his determination to look out for them.

Family came first. Drew understood that. His mom might have passed away, but he was committed to looking out for his sister—whether she was a preschooler or a grown woman—for the rest of their lives.

"Let's continue the tour." Jim led them toward the barn. "Like I said, we don't have any horses yet, but I'll show you what we do have. We've done a lot of research on animal therapy and have put it to work here. It's a big part of our program."

Donna chimed in. "Each child will have their own animal to look after, which will give them something to love. And it will also teach them responsibility."

Twenty minutes later, after seeing two frisky Australian shepherds, four fluffy kittens, a chicken coop called the Peep-Peep Palace, a mama duck and her ducklings, as well as goats and sheep, the tour ended.

Lainie and Drew thanked the Hoffmans and promised to be in touch soon. Then they climbed into the pickup and headed back to the Rocking C.

They'd barely gone a mile down the road when Drew glanced across the seat and spotted Lainie sporting a grin.

"You sure look happy," he said.

"You're right. Helping the Hoffmans and those children has given me a real purpose."

"You've got good instincts. I'll give you that much."

Her smile deepened. "Thank you."

"However, don't ever pull a stunt like that again."

Her brow furrowed, and she cocked a sideways glance at him. "What are you talking about?"

"In the professional world, we don't offer services

until we've discussed them with the entire team. Lucky for you, I agreed wholeheartedly with your idea and plan to run it past my boss for his approval. But if I'd had any qualms, I would have had to do some fancy backpedaling, and then we'd both look like idiots."

Her once happy expression sobered. "I'm sorry. You're right."

"Don't get me wrong," he said, "I appreciate your enthusiasm, and I'm glad supporting the Hoffmans and Kidville gives you a sense of purpose, but it's not the same for me. Promoting them is my *job*."

"I'm sorry if I overstepped. I shouldn't have used the word *we*."

A pang of guilt, as well as sympathy, lanced his chest. He hadn't meant to scold her, especially since this was more than a job to her. But he couldn't get carried away with soft, tender feelings—especially for Lainie. He had enough to worry about without taking another waif under his wing.

Yet just looking at her now, seated next to him in the truck, her eyes bright and focused on whatever she had on her mind, he wouldn't consider her vulnerable. She looked strong, proud…and lovable.

Whoa. Don't even go there. Drew returned his focus to the road. He'd better watch his step when he was around Lainie. Not to mention his heart.

In spite of being reprimanded by her "business associate" for being unprofessional, Lainie entered the house with her heart nearly bursting and her head abuzz with holiday plans. She'd thought she might be too excited to eat. That is, until she took her first step into the mudroom and the warm aroma of tomatoes, garlic and basil accosted her.

Molly stood at the stove, holding a wooden spoon in one hand and a potholder in the other.

"Something sure smells good," Lainie said. "Thanks for covering for me."

"You're welcome. I love to cook." Molly lowered the flame, then turned away from the pot simmering on the stove. "How'd the tour go?"

"Oh, my gosh." Lainie wasn't sure she could put her thoughts and feelings into words. "Kidville is amazing."

Molly burst into a smile. "That's exactly how I felt after my first visit. I'm so glad I get to work there."

"I can see why." Lainie scanned the kitchen. "Need any help?"

"No, I've got it all under control. But do you mind keeping an eye on the spaghetti sauce for a couple of minutes? I forgot to give Brad a letter that came in yesterday's mail, and he's waiting for it."

"No problem. Take your time."

Molly had no more than shut the back door, when the telephone rang. Lainie answered and was surprised to hear Mr. Carlton's voice on the other end.

"I've gotta tell you," the editor said. "If you continue to turn in quality columns like the one we just published, I might have to hire an answering service to handle all the calls we're receiving from Dear Debbie fans. I told you they're pretty vocal, and this time they weren't complaining. They like the direction the column is going. Of course, we did change the font and the layout."

Seriously? He was taking credit for the positive reader response?

Okay, so the advice she'd given had come from the mouth of a wise old man. But Lainie had written the column herself, using her own words, and she was going to stake a claim on some of that success, if not all of it.

"We also made it easier to find the column—right next to the obituaries." He chuckled. "Kind of apropos, don't you think? Life's a bitch, and then you die."

Lainie went silent. Did she really want to work for this guy?

"Just a little editorial humor, kid. But I'm glad Dear Debbie is finally back on track."

"Thanks. It's nice to know that you and the readers like what I've done. I also want to give you a heads-up about something else. I'm sending you a proposal for an article about a local children's home called Kidville. I took a tour, and it was impressive."

"I've heard about that place. What do you have in mind?"

She told him more—about the unique setting, the administrators and their animal therapy plan. But just enough to whet his appetite.

"Send me that proposal," he said, giving her the green light she'd been hoping for.

When the call ended, she was tempted to hole up in her room and outline her proposal, but she couldn't neglect the Dear Debbie column when she was on a roll. And that meant she'd have to come up with a clever answer to at least one of the latest letters.

Lainie had just checked the spaghetti sauce when Molly returned to the kitchen.

"What else can I do to help?" Lainie asked.

"Actually, not much. The tables are set, and I have everything else under control."

It certainly looked like it. The salad was made and in a bowl on the counter. The garlic bread was wrapped in foil and ready to pop into the oven.

"Are you sure?" Lainie asked.

"Absolutely."

"Then if you don't mind, I'll take off for a while, but I'll be back to help you serve dinner."

"Take your time."

Lainie thanked her, then with her confidence bolstered by Mr. Carlton's phone call, she slipped off to her room to look over the latest Dear Debbie letters.

Only trouble was, five minutes turned to ten, and as the tick-tocks of the windup clock on the bureau grew louder and louder, she feared she was going to be a one-column wonder.

There was, however, one letter that struck an interesting chord. It had been written by a woman who'd dreamed of getting married, creating a home of her own and having babies.

I met a great guy at work and was immediately attracted to him. He's sweet, funny and cute. I couldn't believe someone hadn't snatched him up already, and before long, I fell head over heels for him.

And that's my problem. I just found out that he's a widower with four small children.

If I marry him, I'd have to give up my dream of having a family of my own.

Lainie understood the woman's dream as well as her dilemma, but she sympathized with those poor, motherless kids. Her first impulse was to tell the woman that the two adults involved would have to be fully committed to the children or everyone would be miserable.

I fell head over heels for him…

Did she love the man enough to be his life partner? To join his team and mother those children as her own? It was impossible to know.

Lainie blew out a sigh. Doling out the wrong advice would be devastating.

What would Sully tell the woman? She glanced at the clock on the bureau. There was no time to ask him now. It was almost five o'clock, so she shut down her laptop and left it in her room. Then she went to help Molly serve the meals.

When she entered the kitchen, the young ranch hands had already gathered, and Brad was introducing them to his mom.

But it wasn't Molly or the cowboys who caught Lainie's eye. It was Drew, who stood off to the side, leaning against the doorjamb, his arms crossed in an alluring, masculine pose. When his gaze zeroed in on her, any plans she might have had scattered to the wayside.

"Got a minute?" he asked.

For him? She was tempted to say, "I've got all night." Instead, she nodded and let him lead her out to the front porch.

Once Drew and Lainie stepped outside and out of earshot, she asked, "What's up?"

"I'm not sure if you had a chance to speak to any of the nurses yet, but Chloe Martinez called a few minutes ago. She and her husband Joe own the Rocking C and plan to be home for Christmas. So I mentioned our plan to host a party for the kids."

"What'd she say?"

"Chloe loved the idea. In fact, she'd like to help pull it all together, but she and Joe are just finishing up their graduate programs at the university in Houston, and they can't leave school until the twenty-third."

"So the party's still on." Lainie beamed, her enthusiasm impossible to ignore. "That's awesome. There isn't any reason we can't get started with the planning and prep work."

"I guess not, but there could be a few bumps in the road."

Lainie's smile paled, and her lips parted. "What do you mean?"

"There's no telling what the old guys will think about it. Some of them, like Rex and Gilbert, can get a little crotchety. They might not appreciate having a bunch of children running around."

"Seriously? You think they'd be upset?"

Drew hadn't meant to steal her happiness, but he'd wanted to warn her of the possibility so she wouldn't be disillusioned if things didn't work out the way she wanted them to. He'd had his share of disappointing holidays.

"There's no way to know how they'll react until we tell them," he said. "And the sooner the better."

Lainie nodded, worry etched on her face.

He placed a hand on her shoulder to offer support and comfort. "Come on, let's go."

Then as he guided her into the house, his hand slipped around her in a show of solidarity. At least, that's what he told himself he was doing as they continued to the dining room, where the retired cowboys sat around the table.

"While you're all together," Drew said, "we wanted to share something we have in the works." He glanced at Lainie, who was biting down on her lower lip, which he found arousing. And distracting, so his words stalled for a beat.

Fortunately, Lainie shook off whatever apprehension she'd been having and spoke up for both of them. "Earlier this afternoon, Drew and I visited a home for abused and neglected children that's located a few miles down the road."

"You mean the one at the old Clancy place?" Sully asked.

"Yes, that's it." Lainie went on to sing the praises of the Hoffmans and their innovative home. "So we had this brilliant idea about hosting a Christmas party for those kids here on the Rocking C."

Drew's hand slipped from her shoulder, his fingers trailing along her back until he drew away and moved closer to the table. "What do you say, guys?"

"Christmas is a lot more fun when little tykes are around," Gilbert said. "We'd better get a bigger tree than that scrawny stick we had last year."

Rex agreed. "My Jennilyn used to make a big deal out of decorating the house, baking all kinds of sweets and wrapping gifts. And that reminds me, we ought to have something under that tree for those kids."

"How many are living there?" Gilbert asked. "It might be nice if we took up a collection, then sent someone shopping for us."

At that, Sully chimed in. "I'm pretty good at wrapping. A few years back, I helped the local Four H Club at their gift wrapping booth they had at the Wexler mall."

"I'm glad to hear you're onboard," Lainie told Sully.

"Hey," he said. "I like kids."

"Good," Lainie said, "because you'd make a perfect Santa."

"Ain't that the truth?" Rex howled with laughter. "And Sully won't need any stuffing around his middle, either."

Sully puffed out his chest. "I'd be delighted to be Santa Claus." Then he turned to Rex. "I'd rather have a little meat and muscle on me than look like a bony ol' scarecrow."

Gilbert slapped his hand on the table and let out a hoot. "Now there's an idea. If we host a Halloween party for those kids, we can prop Rex up in the cornfield and let him play the part."

Lainie's excitement lit her pretty face. "You guys are the best, you know that?"

"Ah, shucks," Sully said. "No, we aren't."

"Speak for yourself, Sully," Gilbert said. "I'm thinking I'm pretty dang good."

Drew couldn't help but laugh at the men's humor. When Lainie looked at him, he gave her a wink.

And not just because their Christmas party was a go. If he had his way, promoting Kidville and the Rocking Chair Ranch wasn't the only joint venture they'd start up.

Four days later, Drew shook his head in disbelief. Somehow, he'd let Lainie rope him into making Christmas cookies.

"You do realize it's still more than a week before the party." He draped the red-and-white checkered apron she'd suggested he wear over the back of a chair. He didn't mind assuming kitchen duties. Heck, he'd done most of the cooking and cleaning after his mom got sick. But he'd never dressed the part. "I don't know why we have to bake cookies tonight."

"Because there's so much to do at the last minute." She sprinkled flour on the open breadboard, then handed him a rolling pin. "And this is something we can do ahead of time."

"But the cookies won't taste very good if they aren't fresh."

She didn't seem the least bit concerned. "I plan to freeze them and thaw them the night before the party. Don't worry. I know what I'm doing." Then she reached out, touched his forearm and smiled. "You agreed to help me, remember? You said you'd do anything that needed to be done."

"Yes, but when I made that offer, I was thinking more along the lines of getting the tree and decorating it."

"You can do that, too."

He'd had every intention of doing his part and more. He just hadn't expected to work in the kitchen. Or to be swayed into doing so by the singe of Lainie's touch or the warmth of her smile.

She placed a lump of dough on the floured board. "I appreciate your help. Do you know how to do this?"

"I'll manage." He'd seen his mom make biscuits before. And once, while she'd been on chemo and sicker than a dog, he'd stepped in and taken over for her. They'd purchased the heat-and-serve variety at the grocery store after that.

Lainie unscrewed the lid of a mason jar to use for cutting out circles. "I wish I had some real cookie cutters. Then we could make trees and stars and other Christmas shapes. But this time, plain round ones will have to do." She pointed to the lumpy side of the dough. "Roll it out evenly or the cookies will be lopsided."

Okay, boss." Drew rolled out the dough flat and even, but the edges were cracked. "Am I doing this right?"

Lainie took a moment to look over his work. "That's perfect." She handed him the jar lid. "Make the circles as close together as you can."

He followed her instructions, then placed them on the pan.

"Let's get the first batch in the oven," she said, setting the timer.

He glanced at the large mixing bowl on the counter. They'd hardly made a dent in the dough. "How many of these are we going to make?"

"Dozens and dozens. I love frosted sugar cookies, don't you?" She didn't wait for his answer and went back to work, her holiday excitement impossible to ignore.

It was also easy to appreciate. She had a girlish look to her, not to mention a little flour on her nose. Yet at the same time—maybe it was the yellow gingham apron she wore—he saw a domestic goddess.

Lainie was going to make a good wife and mother. A pretty one. He imagined coming home each night after work and finding her in the kitchen, preparing his meals, and a zing shot through him.

He quickly shook off the thought. Was he nuts? Bumping elbows with her tonight was one thing. But words like *permanent*, *long-term* and *forever* weren't in his vocabulary.

Before long, a sweet cookie aroma filled the room. After Lainie pulled the first pan from the oven and replaced it with the next, she removed powdered sugar and a bottle of vanilla from the pantry. Then she took milk from the fridge and placed it on the counter, next to a cube of butter that was already softening.

From the amount of dough still in the mixing bowl, Drew figured they were going to have a boatload of cookies, yet Lainie measured out only a small amount of powdered sugar.

He studied her as she worked. She still had a dusting of flour on her nose, although she wasn't aware of it. And her sweet smile made him smile, too.

"Aren't you going to frost all of them?" he asked.

"Not the ones we're going to serve at the party. I'll do that the night before."

"I don't understand."

"I'm going to frost a couple of them now. Don't you want to see how the finished product is going to look and taste?"

Actually, Drew loved sweets. "Sure. Why not?" He watched as she whipped up the frosting in a bowl with a handheld mixer, then she added a couple drops of green food coloring and blended it together with a spoon.

"Mama Kate used to make the best cookies," Lainie said.

"Your first foster mom, right?"

Lainie nodded. "She always let me help her since I didn't play outside with the other kids."

Drew could understand why a girl might prefer time in the kitchen, cooking and baking. But by the way Lainie had said it, he got the idea that she rarely went outdoors. "Did you prefer being indoors?"

The spoon she'd been using to mix the frosting

stilled, then she started stirring again. "Back then, I wasn't really able to."

A bad memory? Or maybe it was just a simple, heartfelt reflection of the days she'd lived with Mama Kate and it made her sad.

He told himself it really didn't matter which, but for some reason, it did. "Why not?"

At first, she didn't answer and continued to mix the frosting. A couple of beats later, she said, "I was a little sickly back then."

She'd mentioned something about having health issues, but he hadn't considered them serious. "You mean, from an illness?"

She clicked her tongue and continued stirring. "It was no big deal. It's all in the past."

He was about to quiz her further, but she switched the subject on him as swiftly as a champion stock car driver shifted gears and changed lanes.

"Donna gave me a list with the children's names, ages and sizes," she said. "The men chipped in to buy gifts for them, and I volunteered to do the shopping. Do you want to go with me?"

"Not on a bet."

She laughed at his quick and telling response. But he didn't mind. He liked the sound of her laughter, the lilt of her voice.

"I hate to shop," he said.

"But you dress so well."

"That's different. I go to my favorite men's store sometimes, but not all that often. There's a clerk who works there and knows what I like. So I usually just give her a call and bam. Done. But in general, I'm not into shopping."

"Why?"

He shrugged. "When my mom was sick, that job fell on me. So I've always considered it a chore."

"But one that needs to be done." Lainie dripped more food coloring into the bowl. "You were responsible—and a good son. I'll bet your mom was proud of you."

"She was, but she hated having to rely on me to do everything." Drew could still remember her stretched out on the living room sofa, weak and pale and only a wisp of the woman she'd once been. Tears streaming down her cheek as she apologized for not being strong enough to take care of him and his sister anymore.

"I'm sure she enjoyed being your mom and felt badly when she had to give it up. That's how I'd feel, if I were a mother."

Drew glanced at Lainie, who had a maternal air about her this evening, especially when she wore an apron and baked cookies.

"Do you plan to have kids?" he asked.

"Yes, someday. But for now, I have the children at Kidville."

He was glad she'd taken those kids under her wing. She was clearly eager to make them happy. He suspected she'd do the same with her own someday.

She turned to him with a spoonful of green frosting in her hand. "Here, try a bite."

He opened his mouth and relished the creamy, sweet taste bursting on his tongue.

"What do you think?" she asked.

"It's good." He withdrew a clean spoon from the drawer, dipped it into the small mixing bowl and offered it to her. "Your turn."

"Okay." Her mouth opened and closed around the

spoon, tasting it herself. Then she ran the tip of her tongue over her lips.

His knees went weak, and an almost overwhelming urge rose up inside, pressing him to take her in his arms and kiss her. But he couldn't do that. He shouldn't, anyway, so he tamped down the compulsion the best he could.

Still, he continued to study her.

"Hmm, this is really good." Her voice came out soft. Sweet. Smooth.

He couldn't help himself; he reached out and brushed the flour from the tip of her nose. Their gazes locked. Her pretty brown eyes darkened, and her lips parted.

His heart pumped hard and steady, and his hand stilled. The temptation to kiss her senseless rose up again, stronger than ever. But he wouldn't do that.

He shouldn't, anyway.

Yet as he struggled to do the right thing, the smart thing, desire trumped common sense.

Chapter 8

Drew cupped Lainie's jaw, and his thumb caressed her cheek. Now was the time to release her and apologize for making such an intimate move, such a presumptive one, but the moment dissipated in a heartbeat.

Her lips parted a little wider. Whether it was in anticipation or surprise, he wasn't quite sure. But at this point, he didn't care which it was—as long as she didn't stop him. He set the spoon on the counter.

At least, he tried to. It clattered to the floor, but neither of them looked anywhere but at each other.

He took her in his arms, bent his head and lowered his mouth to hers.

The kiss was hot, yet sweet. And the taste? Sugar and vanilla and everything a man ever craved.

His tongue swept into her mouth. Her breath caught,

but she didn't pull away. Instead, she clung to him as if she might collapse if she didn't.

The kiss intensified, and so did his hunger. He couldn't seem to get enough of her taste, enough of *her*. He might have suggested that she go with him to the privacy of the cabin if he hadn't heard approaching footsteps and someone clearing their throat.

Lainie damn near jumped through the roof as she broke away from Drew's embrace, landing on the tip of the spoon and sending it sliding toward the doorway and ending at Sully's feet.

The jovial old man grinned from ear to ear. With his white hair and beard and wearing a red-and-green plaid shirt, he looked a lot like old St. Nick himself. Just the sight of him put a new spin on the old tune of "I saw Mommy Kissing Santa Claus."

In this case, it was Santa Sully who'd gotten the romantic eyeful.

"Hey, kids." Sully looked around the kitchen. "What's cooking?"

Besides Drew's blood pressure?

"I'm…sorry," Lainie said, lightly touching her lips. Her fingers trailed down to her collar. The top button of her blouse, barely visible under her apron, had come undone, and she fumbled to close it up tight. It was almost as if she was trying to hide behind that blouse, just as she'd hidden the pink, sexy panties under the denim overalls the day of the mouse encounter.

Drew would give just about anything to know why she seemed compelled to cover up. Was she wearing skimpy undies now?

"What are you sorry for?" Sully asked her, as he stooped to pick up the spoon. He set it on the counter, then turned to them with a big ol' grin that sparked a Santa-like glimmer in his eyes. Even his chuckle had a ho-ho-ho quality about it.

"Because I'm supposed to be working." Lainie quickly turned her back to them, reached for a cookie on the cooling rack that sat on the counter and showed it to Sully. "Would you like one? I'd be happy to frost it for you."

"Don't mind if I do," the oldster said. "I came down here looking for a bedtime snack. And a sweet one sounds pretty darn good."

Lainie got right on it, frosting not one but two cookies and handing them both to Sully. She waited while he wolfed one of them down.

"What do you think?" she asked.

"They're great. Best I've had in ages."

"Too bad I didn't have a Christmas tree cookie cutter."

Sully chomped into the second cookie. "You could call these ornaments."

"You're right."

As Lainie and Sully launched into a conversation about baking, the tree decorating and the gifts she planned to purchase and wrap for the kids, Drew retreated to the sink and started washing the bowls.

To him, it was just a bunch of nervous jabber, an attempt to put the kiss behind them and to pretend it hadn't happened. But it *had*.

And if it had the same effect on her that it had on him, it wasn't one either of them was likely to forget.

More than twelve hours had passed since the cookie baking session turned into a romantic moment and ended with an earth-shaking kiss. Yet Drew's memory of Lainie's sweet taste and the feel of her body in his arms hadn't faded a bit.

He'd tried to broach the subject with her after Sully left the kitchen last night, but she hadn't wanted to talk about it. She claimed she wasn't feeling well, that she needed to get some sleep and that she'd finish the baking in the morning.

She had looked a little tired. It was hard to say for sure, but he suspected, in reality, she was both shaken and troubled by the kiss.

He could understand why. He'd been stunned by it, too. But since he hadn't been ready to face any of those *now what* questions, especially when he didn't have an answer, he'd counted himself lucky and had gone back to his cabin.

All during breakfast, Lainie had bustled about the kitchen, but she'd hardly glanced his way. And the only thing she'd said to him was, "Good morning."

Even when Sully came in from the dining room for a second cup of coffee and thanked her for a tasty meal, she'd followed it up with a simple, "You're welcome."

Her cheeks bore a constant flush, though. So he decided the only thing bothering her was that kiss.

It might have been an ornery move on Drew's part, but he'd set up an after-breakfast interview with Sully in the kitchen.

He doubted Lainie'd like having both men return to the scene of the passionate crime, but after Sully went on his way, Drew would broach the subject. And who knew? He might even instigate another kiss.

But things hadn't worked out the way he'd planned. Moments after Sully took a seat at the table and Drew poured them each a cup of coffee, Lainie slipped out of the kitchen and didn't return.

"Something's bothering Lainie," Sully said. "Is she upset because you kissed her last night? Or just about being caught?"

"I'm not sure." Drew took a sip of coffee. "Some women aren't easy to figure out. And Lainie's one of them. But just for the record, I don't have any regrets. It was a great kiss."

"She certainly seemed to be enjoying it," Sully said. "My guess is that she's not sure what to do about it."

Drew wasn't, either. But that didn't mean he wouldn't like to kiss her again. Lainie was proving to be… Well, intriguing, to say the least.

"I really like that little gal," Sully said.

"I do, too." Drew stared at his coffee for a second. "What do you know about her?"

Sully lifted his mug, blew at the steam rising from the top and took a sip. "Not much. She's a sweetheart. Pretty, too. But her friends are a little iffy."

"Seriously? That surprises me."

"Yeah, me, too. But it's probably because she has a big heart. Too big, I suspect."

"What do you mean?"

Sully sat back in his chair. "It's nothing, I guess. It's just that, over the last couple weeks, she's come to me with one question or another. It seems that either one of her girlfriends or someone she knows has a problem, usually due to their own making." Sully slowly shook his head. "I gotta tell you, Lainie really needs to choose some new friends. Some of them don't have the sense the Good Lord gave a goose."

Was that a red flag? Had Sully spotted a flaw in

Lainie that Drew had failed to notice? Or were her questionable friendships merely the sign of a warm, loving heart? Either way, Drew intended to find out.

Sully clucked his tongue. "I guess everyone has a weakness."

"You're right." And Drew figured some of them also harbored a few secrets.

For a while the men didn't say anything.

"Cookies aside," Sully said, "how're the party plans coming along?"

"Everything seems to be on track."

"Say," Sully said, "I was thinking. Why don't we wrap up that Christmas party with a good, old-fashioned hayride and a sing-along? The church my wife and I used to attend would have one each summer to celebrate the children's promotion to their Sunday school classes. And we all had a lot of fun."

"Good idea. The kids would probably like that."

"There's an old wagon in the barn," Sully said. "You should check it out. It's probably an antique by now and hasn't been used in years. So you'd need to clean it up and fill it with straw. They don't have any draft horses on the Rocking C, but you could hitch it up to the John Deere. Might be a good idea to mention it to Nate and see if he agrees."

"Yeah. I'll share the idea with Lainie, too."

That's not all Drew would like to share with her, but for the time being, his romantic plans had hit the skids.

That might not be a bad thing. Maybe he should back off for a while—or at least, take things slow and steady.

Yet that didn't mean he wouldn't dream about her tonight and relive that sweet, arousing kiss all over again.

* * *

Lainie stood in the kitchen, chopping celery, pickles and hard-boiled eggs to mix into the potato salad she was preparing for lunch. But her mind wasn't on her work. It was on that luscious, romantic moment she'd shared with Drew in this very room last night. A tingle raced up her leg to the back of her neck.

As he'd held her in his arms and kissed her senseless, she'd completely lost her head until Sully interrupted them. At that point, she'd finally returned to earth. Yet even now, she wasn't back on solid ground, and she didn't know what to do about it.

One kiss would surely lead to a second, but then what?

Dread picked at her. She wasn't ready for an intimate relationship—and not just because of that horrible debacle at that hotel lounge in Houston, when Craig Baxter's wife caught him and Lainie together and assumed the worst.

Lainie didn't blame Kara Baxter for thinking that her husband had a lover. To be honest, that's the direction the relationship had been heading, but Lainie had been reluctant to become intimate. And for good reason.

She fingered her chest, felt along the cotton fabric that hid the raised ridge. In college, her first real boyfriend and almost-lover had balked at the sight of the long pink scar.

"Why didn't you warn me?" he'd asked.

She'd cried, and he'd apologized, but the whole evening had turned out to be disappointing and they'd broken up. After that, she'd vowed to be more careful with her affections.

Then Craig came along, and she'd decided to give

him a chance. Looking back at the way things had ended between them, she thanked her lucky stars—and her ugly scar—that she hadn't let him convince her to make love.

But tell that to the world. While the cell phone cameras focused on Craig and his pregnant wife, Lainie had rushed to her car in the parking lot, but she hadn't been able to outrun the internet. By nine o'clock the next morning, the scene had gone viral, the comments devastating. You'd think people would consider Craig the villain, but they seemed more focused on how he hovered over his wife, how he cooed to her, caressed her...

And that left Lainie to take all the heat. Even the blogosphere and all the network gossip shows got on the bandwagon, leaving her both hurt and angry.

She took out her frustration on a stalk of celery, chopping it hard and nicking her finger in the process.

"Ouch!" She tossed the paring knife in the sink.

See? That's what happens when you let your emotions get in the way of good sense. You screw up.

She sucked her finger, the metallic taste of blood lingering like a bad memory and an unearned reputation as a temptress and a home wrecker, when all she'd ever wanted was to love and be loved.

Now, here she was, considering another attempt at a relationship.

Was Drew different from Craig? Could she trust him to see past her scar and into her heart? Quite frankly, she wasn't sure, but she was tempted to give him the benefit of the doubt and risk being hurt again.

She glanced down at the flannel and denim she'd pulled out of the closet after her morning shower. She'd kept her curls contained in a topknot, but on a whim, she'd applied a coat of pink lip gloss and a little mascara.

It felt good to tap into her femininity again. Maybe it was time to start dressing the part. She might not have the money to buy expensive clothes, but she'd always been style conscious. And she wasn't going to wear loose tops and baggy pants the rest of her life.

For now, though, she'd focus on preparing lunch.

"Hey, Lainie?"

She turned toward the doorway, where Drew stood, his hair stylishly mussed, and wearing a dazzling smile. Why did he have to be so appealing?

Drew made his way into the kitchen. "Sully had a suggestion for the party. What do you think about wrapping up the festivities with a hayride and a sing-along?"

"I think that's a great idea."

"There's an old wagon behind the barn. We'd have to clean it up, but it should work out perfectly for what we have in mind. Do you want to see it?"

"Absolutely." She turned to the sink, and washed her hands then grabbed a dish towel to dry them. "Let me put the potato salad in the refrigerator."

Minutes later, they'd left the house and walked around the barn, where a large, buckboard style wagon was parked on a thick patch of grass in the back.

"This is it," Drew said.

At first glance, it looked to be about a hundred years old and weather-beaten. It didn't just need a good cleaning, it could use a coat of paint, too.

"It has potential," she said.

"I've already checked out the structure, and it looks all right. One of the wood slats on the side needs to be replaced, but with a little work, it'll do just fine."

"The kids are going to love a hayride, especially Andre. I'll bet he'll be in seventh heaven."

"I was thinking about him," Drew said. "The next time I'm in town, I'm going to buy him a child-size cowboy hat."

Lainie leaned her hip against the wagon's open tailgate and gazed at him. "That'd be really sweet. I'm sure he'd love it."

He shrugged a single shoulder. "I figured he would."

"You know," she said, pressing her palm on the open tailgate and finding it sturdy, "you promised to let him ride a horse. He'll be disappointed if it doesn't work out for some reason."

"I know. That's why I've already talked to Nate about it. He suggested we use a gentle mare named Felicity."

Lainie hopped up on the tailgate and took a seat. "I'd planned to call the Hoffmans later today to talk about the party plans. If it's okay with you, I'll ask them if Andre can come here before the party to ride Felicity."

"Sure, go ahead. I'd be happy to work around their schedule."

"Then if they don't have any objections, I'll set up a day and time that works for everyone."

Drew continued to study her, his gaze sweeping her face. "You're something else, Lainie."

She wasn't entirely sure what he meant, but her chest warmed and her heart fluttered at what was surely a compliment. She crossed her ankles and swayed her legs, a nervous reaction that might seem a little girlish, but there was something very grown up about what she was feeling—and about the way Drew was looking at her.

"There's something else I wanted to bring up while we're out here alone," he added.

Uh-oh. Here it comes. The kiss chat she'd been dreading. Yet for some reason, she wasn't the least bit worried about having it now.

"It was fun last night. I'd like to finish what we started."

Was he talking about the kiss? Or the baking session? Either way, she didn't dare ask.

"After that," he said, "maybe we can roll out the remaining dough and make more cookies."

Heat singed her cheeks, and her heartbeat kicked up to a lively pace. So he'd been referring to the kiss. She was tempted to slip off the tailgate and make a mad dash to the house, but before she could move, Drew closed in on her, blocking her escape route.

"I hadn't meant for that to happen," she said, "but it…just did."

"It was a nice kiss, don't you think?"

That's not how she'd describe it. She'd use words like *sweet, arousing* and *sensual*.

"Just *nice*?" she asked.

"Actually…" His lips quirked into a crooked grin. "On a scale of one to ten? I'd rate it an eleven or twelve."

Now it was her turn to smile. "Something tells me you've had plenty of kisses to compare it to, so I'll take your word for it."

"You haven't?" he asked.

She wasn't about to admit that she lacked any real experience worth counting. "I thought it was pretty good."

"Good enough to try it again someday?"

She ought to tell him no, to set up some boundaries between them, to protect herself from entering another bad relationship, but she couldn't deny the truth.

"Sure," she said. "Maybe someday."

He closed the two-foot gap between them, which seemed to be his way of saying, *Then why not now?*

For the life of her, she couldn't come up with a single objection.

He placed his right hand along her jaw. His fingers slipped under her ear and reached the back of her neck. The pad of his thumb caressed her cheek, scrambling her brain and setting her senses on high alert. All the while, he studied her face as if he could read every single detail about her life, every memory in her heart.

Lainie could've sworn he was going to kiss her again, and she wasn't sure what to do about it—if anything.

Fight? Flight?

Or should she just roll with it?

Preparing to make a move of some kind, she placed her palms on the tailgate and shifted her weight. As she sat back down, one side of the tailgate cracked and her seat gave way. She let out a scream, grabbed Drew and brought him crashing to the ground with her.

Chapter 9

Drew had been blessed with quick reflexes, but when the wood cracked and the bracket broke, he didn't have much time to react.

He tried to catch Lainie, as her fingernails dug into his arm, but she still slid down the slanting tailgate, pulling him to the ground with her.

He rolled to the side, thankful for the thick patch of long grass that softened their landing, and propped himself up on his elbow. He hovered over her, brushed a silky strand of hair from her face and searched her eyes. "Are you okay?"

"I think so." She blinked a couple of times. "Nothing hurts."

"Good." He probably ought to help her up, but he liked being stretched out beside her, gazing at her pretty face, taunted by her soft floral scent. It was an arousing position.

Admittedly, there were better, more romantic places for a proverbial roll in the hay than a patch of grass, next to an old buckboard wagon, but he wasn't about to suggest a change in position, let alone location. Not while he had Lainie in his arms again. He felt compelled to kiss her long and hard.

He really shouldn't. But she was studying him intently, practically inviting him to do it.

When her lips parted, he was toast.

As their lips met and his eyes closed, they returned to that blissful, intimate state they'd reached last night. Their bodies naturally took off from where they'd left off.

Drew rolled her with him to the side, finding a comfortable spot away from the wagon, and continued to kiss her thoroughly. Tongues mated, breaths mingled and hearts pounded out in need.

He stroked her back, his hands bunching up the flannel fabric that separated his fingers from her skin. But a simple article of clothing, no matter how blousy, couldn't hide the soft, feminine body underneath.

He slid his hands along the curve of her spine and down the slope of her hips. As his mouth continued its gentle yet demanding assault, Lainie let out a soft whimper, sending a rush of desire coursing through his veins.

Unable to help himself, he slipped his hand under the hem of her shirt, seeking the woman inside. As he felt along her warm skin and explored the curve of her waist, his testosterone flared. He inched his way up to the edge of her satin bra, soft and sleek, and sought her breast. But the moment he cupped the full mound, she jerked away as if he'd crossed an invisible line.

And hadn't he? Considering the circumstances,

where they were and how they came to be there, she probably thought he was way off base.

She'd seemed more than willing, though. That is, until now.

"I'm sorry," he said. "I guess I got a little carried away."

She sat up, lifted her hand to her collar, fingering the flannel fabric, and slowly shook her head. "No, I'm the one who should be sorry. I didn't mean to overreact. I hope you don't think I was being a tease."

A flush covered her throat, indicating her own arousal. She bit down on her lip, which was still plump from the gentle assault of their kiss. "It's just that…" She scanned the area around them. "This isn't the time or the place."

She had a point, but he made light of it by tossing her a playful grin, hoping to ease her discomfort or embarrassment. "Well, the timing was okay with me. And I admit this probably isn't the place. But no one saw us, so we're the only ones who know what happened."

She got to her feet and, after righting her shirt, she pointed at the wagon. "I think, once that tailgate is fixed, this will work out perfectly for what we have in mind."

He wasn't about to mention what *he'd* had in mind, what he was still thinking, but he followed her lead and rose from the grassy ground.

"Or better yet," she said, "maybe we should ask around the neighboring ranches and see if we can borrow something similar."

Avoiding a person or a subject seemed to be her primary line of defense.

His first thought was to mention it, to take her back to the subject at hand, but it was probably in his best interests to let it go for now. Did he really want to talk about what they'd just done and what it might mean?

He was definitely attracted to her. And the clock was ticking since he'd be leaving the Rocking C after the party.

"I planned to call the Hoffmans later today," Lainie added. "So I'll ask if they have any concerns about the kids having a hayride, although I don't think they will."

She clearly didn't want to address their undeniable attraction, the heated kiss they'd just shared or where it might lead. He should leave it at that, right?

"While I'm on the phone, I should probably lock in a time for the party. How do you feel about two o'clock? Or should we include the children for lunch?" She bit down on her bottom lip again, but this time, when she looked up, her eyes glistened like warm honey. "There's so much I want to do."

"You're really excited about this party, aren't you?"

"More than you know." She ran a hand through her hair, which had gotten mussed with the tumble and the kiss. Her fingers caught on a tangle, and she tugged through it. "But it's not just about this particular party. After Christmas, I'm going to stay in close contact with the Hoffmans and do everything I can to support Kidville. My heart's gone out to those kids, especially Andre."

Drew felt the same way. "I'd like to continue helping them, too. I mean personally and not only through Esteban Enterprises."

"Jim and Donna will be happy to hear that. They're going to need all the support and manpower they can get." Again, she pointed to the buckboard. "And speaking of manpower, who's going to refurbish this wagon and make sure it's safe to carry the kids? And where do we get the straw?"

"I'll take care of it. And I'll rope Sully and Rex into helping me. It'll be good for them to have a job to do and something to look forward to."

Lainie smiled. "That reminds me, I need to get back to the kitchen, or lunch won't be on the table by noon." Then she turned and walked away as if nothing had happened, as if they'd never kissed.

Drew studied her from behind, watching the sway of her denim-clad hips and the way that flannel shirt ruffled in the light afternoon breeze. He felt badly about feeling her up, especially if that's what had unsettled her. But he'd felt compelled to learn what she was hiding underneath her unflattering fabric façade.

And if things worked out the way he hoped they would, one day soon he'd find out.

Lainie hurried toward the house, determined to escape Drew and the powerful yet unsettling feelings he stirred up inside her. But now that she'd kissed him and experienced his heated touch, she doubted her efforts would work.

He'd set her soul on fire, and as he'd caressed her, she'd nearly melted into a puddle on the grass. His touch created an ache deep in her core, and she'd nearly forgotten she had a physical flaw.

But when his hand moved dangerously close to her chest, she'd suddenly realized that he was just one tantalizing stroke away from stumbling upon her scar. And she'd freaked out like a feral cat. How embarrassing was that?

If things progressed between them, if they became

lovers—and if truth be told, she wasn't opposed to that any longer—she'd tell him about the surgery and prepare him for what he was about to see. The last thing she wanted was for him to be repulsed, just as Ryan had been when he'd frozen up and turned a romantic moment ugly.

But then again, Drew seemed to be different from Ryan—and certainly from Craig. Could she risk being completely honest with him?

She was healthy and whole now. Besides, it might not matter to Drew that she bore a hardened ridge and a pale white line that would never go away.

At the possibility that he might accept her completely, an idea sparked and a new game plan arose.

She'd start looking like herself again. First step: wearing lipstick instead of the gloss she'd applied earlier. And she'd choose clothes that were more feminine, more stylish. More flattering. Then, when the subject came up again, and the timing was right, she'd level with him about her surgery.

By the time she opened the back door and entered the house, she felt much better and a lot more confident. And when she spotted Sully seated at the table, she burst into a smile.

"There you are," her old friend said. "I've been looking for you."

Thank goodness he hadn't gone in search of her behind the barn!

"I went with Drew to see the wagon he'd like to use for the hayride," she said. "Is everything okay?"

"Everything's hunky-dory. I just wanted to share some good news."

"What's up?"

Sully leaned back in his seat, clasped his hands and rested them on his rounded belly. "A few years back, I used to be a member of the Brighton Valley Moose Lodge. Every December they'd have a holiday party, and Santa Claus always made a showing. So I called an old friend who's still active with the group and asked if I could borrow their suit after they finish with it."

"What'd he say?"

"They'll loan it to us. And after I told him why we needed it, he offered to have it dry cleaned and promised to deliver it himself." Sully grinned from ear to ear, clearly pleased with his contribution to the party.

"That's great," Lainie said. "Things are coming together nicely. Getting a Santa suit is one thing I can mark off my list, but there's still a lot to do."

"Let me know if there's anything else I can do to help."

"Thanks, I'll keep that in mind." She'd also have to remember to place that phone call to Kidville. She didn't want to make any more plans before talking things over with the Hoffmans first.

After Sully left the kitchen, Lainie glanced at the clock over the stove. She'd better get the chicken in the oven or it wouldn't be ready by noon.

Ten minutes later, using the old-style phone that hung on the kitchen wall, she placed the call to Kidville.

When Donna answered, Lainie launched into their party plans, including the hayride that would wrap up the day. Just as expected, Donna gave her full approval, and they settled on a one o'clock start time.

"There's something else I had on my mind," Lainie said. "We offered Andre a horseback ride, and Drew found the perfect horse for him, a gentle mare named

Felicity. Would it be all right if Andre came to the Rocking C for a lesson within the next few days?"

"That would be awesome. He seems to be adjusting pretty well to being here with us, but he's still very concerned about his little brothers. Maybe visiting the ranch and riding a horse will help him take his mind off his worries, at least for an hour or two."

"Are the younger boys together in the same foster home?" Lainie asked.

"I wish they were. Sadly, there are more children in the county who need a place to live than families willing to take them in. But Mrs. Tran, their social worker, believes siblings should be together whenever possible. So I hope and pray they won't have to be separated too long."

Lainie's heart clenched, and her grip on the telephone receiver tightened. "Are the children adoptable?"

"I expect the youngest boys to be cleared soon. Their father is serving a life sentence without possibility of parole. And from what I understand, he's going to surrender parental rights, which would make Abel and Mario eligible for adoption."

"But what about Andre?" Lainie's grip on the receiver tightened until her knuckles ached.

"I'm not sure. His father ran off years ago, and no one knows where he is. On top of that, the poor kid is facing several surgeries and some extensive rehab, so he's in limbo. At least, legally. Jim and I are doing all we can to make him feel loved and safe."

Lainie had no doubt about that, but still…

"I'd take all three boys in a heartbeat," she said, "if that meant they could stay together. But I'm not prepared to provide them with a permanent home just yet."

"That's sweet of you to even consider it," Donna said.

Lainie wasn't just blowing smoke and offering something she didn't expect to follow through on. It had been a heartfelt offer, and she wanted to make sure Donna realized it.

"I'm serious," Lainie said. "I'd have to do some footwork first. I have a small apartment in town, so I'd need to find a bigger place." Not to mention a better-paying job.

Then again, if Lainie went to work full-time to support a family, she'd need day care for the kids. And that wouldn't allow her to give them all the time and affection they needed—and deserved.

Or would it? A lot of single parents had to work, yet they still found a way to spend quality time with their kids.

"Would the state allow me to adopt as a single woman? Or at least, become a foster mother?"

"I can place a call to Mrs. Tran and ask," Donna said. "Or better yet, I can give you her number."

Lainie sucked in a deep breath, then let out a wobbly sigh. "My position at the Rocking C is only temporary, so I'd need to find a different job first. Maybe it would be best if I called Mrs. Tran after I get settled."

The more she thought about it, the more the idea sounded like a pipe dream that couldn't possibly come true. By the time she was capable of providing those children with a home, Mrs. Tran might have found a better living situation for all of them. Or by then, Kidville would be able to expand and accept younger children.

Hopefully, Andre's little brothers were in loving environments and would have a nice Christmas this year, even if they...

"Say," Lainie said, "could we invite Andre's brothers to the party? We'd include their foster families, too, of course."

"That's a great idea, and I know Andre would be thrilled if they came. I'll call Mrs. Tran and see what she has to say. It might be difficult to coordinate something like that on Christmas Eve since everyone could have different holiday plans. But it might work. In the meantime, when did you want to schedule that riding lesson for Andre?"

"As soon as possible."

"I'm happy to hear that," Donna said. "That little boy has had to face a lot of broken promises in the past."

Lainie could certainly relate to that. The two men she'd once cared about had been big disappointments, too.

But then she'd met Drew. Hopefully, if she were to consider having a relationship with him, it would prove to be a lot more promising than the other two.

Drew stood on the front porch, drinking a cup of coffee and waiting for Jim Hoffman to bring Andre for his riding lesson. The morning air was crisp—not exactly cold, but chilly enough to know winter had crept in on them.

When the screen door creaked open, Lainie stepped outside with a plastic container in her hand. He'd already seen her at breakfast this morning and noted the change in her. She'd ditched the baggy denim for a pair of snug black jeans and a stylish, curve-hugging sweater. She'd even applied lipstick.

But seeing her now, without the full-length apron to cover her up, he realized he was going to have a hell of a time keeping his eyes off her and focused on Andre and his riding lesson.

"What have you got there?" he asked.

"Just a couple of carrots and an apple. I thought Andre could give them to Felicity before or after his ride. But I thought I'd better ask you first." She glanced out to the corral, where Felicity was saddled and tied to a hitching post. "Is that her?"

"She isn't used to getting much special attention, so she'll like having a treat."

"Sounds like she and Andre have something in common," Lainie said.

Drew was getting some special treatment today, too. Not only was Lainie a lovely eyeful, she was wearing a new fragrance, something soft and tropical, which seemed out of place at a ranch. Actually, now that she'd ditched the baggy denim and blousy cotton, she seemed out of place here, too.

He'd found her attractive before, but today, she was beautiful and downright sexy.

From what he'd seen so far, it appeared that she had a good heart, and an unusual thought struck him, one that was a little too domestic for a man who'd made up his mind to remain single the rest of his life.

That decision had been fairly easy to make, when the people who should have loved and supported him as a kid had all failed him one way or another—whether through sickness or desertion.

Okay. So Kara had never let him down, but that was different. She wasn't supposed to look after him. It was the other way around.

"Come on." Drew gave Lainie a gentle nudge with his elbow. "I'll introduce you to Felicity."

They'd just stepped off the porch when a white minivan pulled into the yard.

"Oh, good," Lainie said. "Andre's here."

The moment Jim and the boy climbed out of the vehicle, Andre broke into a happy grin.

"I've never been on a ranch before." His small brown eyes glowed with excitement. "I didn't think today would ever get here."

"That's true," Jim said. "He hardly got a wink of sleep last night, and he's been jabbering nonstop about cowboys and horses ever since we told him about the riding lesson."

"I'm glad we can provide a little fun for him," Drew said.

"So am I." Jim placed his hand on the boy's small shoulder. "I'd love to stay in the yard and watch you guys, but I'm taking a new medication for the next week or so, and I'm supposed to stay out of the direct sunlight."

"Why don't you sit on the porch," Drew said. "I have a feeling several of the retired cowboys will soon join you. They like sitting in those rockers in the shade."

"Great. I'd like to meet them." Jim placed his hand on the pint-size, wannabe cowboy's head. "Have fun, Andre." Then he turned and headed toward the porch.

"This is so cool." Andre scanned the pastures, the corral and the barn. "I wish Abel and Mario could be here to see this."

Drew glanced at Lainie, whose glassy eyes revealed her sympathy. Rather than stir up any sadness—hers or Andre's—he decided to let the boy's comment ride.

But Lainie faced it head-on. "I'll try to set up a visit for your brothers to come to the Rocking C, too."

Why had she offered something she might not be able to pull off? If it didn't work out for any reason, it would only make the poor kid feel worse.

"That'd be awesome." Andre looked up at Lainie as if she held all power, all knowledge... All hope. "Can I come again when they get their lesson?"

"Of course you can. They won't have as much fun without you."

There she went again, committing Drew to something without running it by him first.

Of course, she hadn't actually included him in her plan, but she wasn't going to be living on the ranch much longer. How did she think she'd find time to set up another visit with two separate families?

"Andre," she said, as she stooped to tie the boy's shoes, "tell me about your brothers. I can't wait to meet them."

Aw, man. Why'd she have to go and do that? The poor kid didn't need those sad, painful feelings stirred up. He needed to learn to tamp them down. If Drew had allowed himself to get sucked into the emotions his mom and sister had once faced, he wouldn't have been able to stay strong for them.

"Mario is four," Andre said, "and Abel is six. They have a different dad than me, and I'm glad about that because he's in prison." Andre glanced down at his sneakers, which were now double knotted, then back at Lainie. "I never met my dad, but my mom told me he was a cowboy. And the best one ever. So when I grow up, I wanna be just like him."

Drew's gut twisted at the thought that Andre's deadbeat dad had become a superhero, a mythical cowboy who'd bailed out on his own flesh and blood, just like Drew's old man had done.

"Do you have any idea where your father might be?" Lainie asked.

"No, but he's probably working on a ranch like this one. He's a nice man, and not like Pete. My dad would never hurt a kid or a mom."

At that, Drew's hand fisted, and his heart clenched so hard it almost choked off his air supply.

He wasn't about to stand here and let Lainie resurrect the past, ruining the boy's day—and possibly his future. So he had to put a stop to it here and now.

"Come on," he told Andre. "I've got a hat for you in the barn. Once you're dressed like a real cowboy, I'll introduce you to Felicity, the mare you're going to ride."

"Cool," the boy said, as he limped along with Drew. "I can't wait to ride her."

When he and Andre returned from the barn, Lainie was waiting for them inside the corral and next to the mare.

"You look like a real cowboy." She tapped the top of his new hat. "Now let's see how you look mounted on Felicity."

Apparently she intended to stick around and witness the boy's first ride, which was okay with Drew. He liked having her around—at least, as long as she didn't pry or poke at tender feelings.

As Drew walked toward the gate, Andre limping along beside him, Lainie lifted the plastic container. "I brought this so you could give Felicity a treat before you ride her. I have an apple and two carrots. Which do you want to give her?"

Andre looked at Drew. "Which one would she like best?"

"Let's give it all to her." Drew reached into his pocket, pulled out a Swiss Army knife his sister had given him last Christmas and cut the apple into chunks.

"Is it bad for her to eat big pieces?" Andre asked.

"No, but she'll gobble it up so fast she won't get a chance to taste it. Let's make her work for it." He handed a chunk of apple to Andre, then showed him how to keep his hand open flat while he offered it to her.

Just like the cowboy he wanted to be, Andre took to feeding a horse quickly. All the while, he beamed and giggled.

Felicity seemed to take a real liking to him, too.

"Let's get you in that saddle," Drew said, "so we can start your riding lesson."

Minutes later, as Drew adjusted the stirrups, he glanced up and caught the happy smile on Andre's face. His chest filled with warmth, just knowing he'd had a part in putting it there.

The lesson began, and Andre was a natural. Before long, Drew was able to step back and let the horse and boy move about the corral.

As he leaned against one of the posts, Lainie stood next to him, only the white wooden railing separating them.

"Look at him," Drew said. "He's having the time of his life."

"You're good at this," Lainie said.

At what? Surely she didn't mean he was good with kids. His expertise was horses, although he had to admit to having a soft spot for a disabled kid who wanted to grow up to be a cowboy. But he thanked her just the same.

Then he looked over his shoulder, caught her profile, the thick dark lashes, lengthened by mascara. The turned-up nose. The fresh application of dark pink lipstick.

"You look pretty today," he said.

"Thank you."

"What's the big occasion?"

She shrugged a single shoulder. "I just wanted to look nice for Andre's big ride."

"Then it worked."

Her smile reached her eyes, sparking a glow that made the color look amber.

"Those black jeans are a lot more flattering than overalls," he said, wondering what style panties she wore today. Were they pink and lacy like before? Or maybe satin like the soft bra he'd touched the other day?

He didn't ask, and she didn't comment further. Instead, he checked on Andre, who had a steady grip on the reins. The kid was a quick study, which was good since Drew couldn't keep his mind or his eyes off Lainie.

Maybe it was her scent, which reminded him of a big, frozen piña colada, complete with a slice of fresh pineapple.

She was pretty damned tempting—sweet and intoxicating. What he wouldn't give to get her alone. To see if she tasted as good as she smelled.

He really didn't know that much about her, though. But since he didn't make long-term commitments, did that even matter?

The next time he had a moment alone with her, he just might suggest they have an affair while they were both here.

That reminded him, time was slipping away.

"Are you still planning to edit my blog posts?" he asked.

"Sure. Have you started it yet?"

"I wrote about one of the cowboys, but it's still in draft form and needs work. I thought that you might want to look it over and tell me what you think. It'd be nice to know if I'm heading in the right direction."

"I'd be happy to." She offered him another smile, and he was again struck by her beauty. And by the appeal of a romantic distraction until Christmas.

"I've got some things to do in the kitchen," she said. "So this isn't a good time to see what you've pulled together. What about after dinner tonight?"

Bedtime? He liked the sound of that.

"Perfect," he said. "I'll have my laptop all set up. Once you think the first blog post is ready to go, I'll schedule it and start work on the second one."

"I'm looking forward to it," she said.

So was he. Hopefully, she'd be agreeable to lovemaking. Only trouble was, they'd both be moving on and going their own ways soon. So he'd better suggest it tonight.

Chapter 10

Lainie could hardly wait to finish her evening chores, slip away from the house and head to the cabin where Drew was staying. And she suspected that he felt that same eagerness.

Several times during dinner she'd caught him gazing at her so intensely that it seemed as if he was looking beyond her outward appearance and into her very heart and soul. It had been a little unraveling, but in a good way.

He didn't know about the scar yet, but she planned to tell him about it tonight.

She ought to be nervous about that, but she wasn't. She'd come to realize Drew was special. A flood of warmth had filled her chest when she saw him with Andre today, when she'd observed the kindness he'd shown, the sensitivity. She'd nearly melted when she'd watched him slow his steps so the limping boy could keep up with him.

And that's when she'd lowered her guard and finally faced what she was really feeling for him.

They would work on his blog tonight, but they'd also have a heart-to-heart talk. No more secrets. No surprises.

Besides, Lainie's congenital heart defect had been corrected years ago. And that scar was her badge of courage, as one of the nurses in the pediatric intensive care unit had told her.

She'd have to tap into that bravery while she waited for his reaction to her revelation like a timid little girl being wheeled into the operating room to face the unknown. Would he accept or reject her?

Shame on him if he didn't, yet her heart swelled with hope. She'd come to care deeply for Drew. She might even love him. At least, that's what she'd imagined love might feel like. And if he gave her any reason to believe he felt the same way, she'd come out and tell him to his face.

Once Lainie had washed the dishes and put them away, she blew out a ragged sigh, then glanced at the clock on the wall, ticking out the minutes until she could see him again. It was nearing showtime. So she returned to her bedroom to freshen up—and pull out all the stops.

As she stood in front of the bathroom mirror, she ran a brush through her hair and let the curls tumble down her shoulders the way they used to. She'd gotten tired of hiding her looks, her identity.

Heck, she might even tell him about that fiasco with

Craig. That way, in case he ever heard about it, he'd know the truth.

After reapplying her lipstick and mascara, she used a little blush, although she probably wouldn't need it. Excitement and nervous anticipation were sure to paint her cheeks a warm, rosy hue.

Before leaving for Drew's cabin, she took one last look in the mirror. She wanted to put her best foot forward before knocking on his door tonight.

Pleased by the familiar image looking back at her, she said, "This is it."

Now was the time to let Drew know who she really was. And to find out if he would accept the real Lainie.

After eating dinner in the kitchen with the ranch hands, Drew returned to his cabin to get ready for Lainie. He was excited about her visit—and not just because he wanted her help on writing up his interviews.

Something told him that tonight was going to be special, and that he should be prepared for anything. So he'd taken a shower, slipped into a clean pair of worn jeans and put on a Texas A & M polo shirt. Once an Aggie, always an Aggie. Right?

His hair was still damp when he sat down at the dinette table, his makeshift home office, and booted up his laptop. He may as well set the scene so Lainie would think that work was the only thing he had on his mind, but his hormones had already caused his thoughts to stray in a sexual direction.

He wished he could offer her a glass of wine or a cold bottle of beer. All he had to drink was coffee or soda pop, which would have to do. But an adult beverage would be a lot more conducive to romance.

Then again, so was a sugar cookie.

And a broken tailgate.

He'd just logged on to the internet when an online call from his sister came through. The last time they'd talked, Kara had insisted that she was doing well. Hopefully, that was still the case.

"Hey," he said, once they connected. "What's up?"

"Not much. Just the same old, same old. But I'm hanging in there."

He could see her stretched out on her bed, where several big, fluffy pillows propped up her head. She appeared to be a little pale, but maybe it was just the lighting.

"When's your next doctor visit?" he asked.

"I see her on Monday. Since I've made it another week, she might let me start moving around again."

"I don't blame you for wanting to get out of bed. You've been housebound for so long."

"Yeah, I know. Who'd think going to an obstetrical visit would be something to celebrate?"

He laughed. "Not me. How's that woman I hired to help you working out?"

"She's great. She sits with me during the day and keeps me company. We're watching entire seasons of *Downton Abbey*."

Drew'd pass on that. "And how's her cooking?"

"The best mac and cheese this side of the Mississippi."

"Don't get fat."

She patted her tummy. "Ha, ha." Then her expression turned a little more serious. "How's life on the Rocking Chair Ranch?"

"Not bad. A couple of the retired cowboys are a real

hoot. And all of them are pretty cool, with interesting pasts."

"Have you started writing the blog?"

"Yeah, but it's still just a draft. I've asked a woman who lives here to edit them for me."

Kara readjusted herself in bed. "Who is she?"

"Her name is Lainie. She's filling in temporarily for the ranch cook. She's a nice woman, and she's talked me into helping her plan a Christmas party."

"Hmm." A slow smile stretched across Kara's lips, providing a little color to her face. "Do I sense a little romance in the air?"

A zing hit his stomach. "No, but I have to admit, the thought has crossed my mind." Drew glanced at the clock on the microwave. Maybe he ought to end his call before Lainie arrived. His sister was more than a little nosy and could be pushy at times.

Then again, he could always introduce them. What would it hurt?

He was still pondering a decision when a knock sounded at the door. He didn't have to open it to know who'd arrived.

Aw, what the heck. Why not?

"Hang on, Kara. She's here now."

"Ooh. You mean I get to meet her? That's cool. You usually keep the women you date at a distance."

"Just from you." He scooted his chair back and got to his feet. "And just so you know, we're not dating. Not yet, anyway."

He heard Kara laugh in the background as he answered the door and let Lainie inside.

Damn, she looked good tonight. She was dressed to kill in a pair of sleek black slacks and a white blouse.

And that hair? A man could get lost in soft, flowing curls like that. She'd freshened her lipstick, too. Red this time.

Clearly, Drew wasn't the only one who had romance on the mind, and it took every ounce of self-control not to welcome her with a heartfelt, hormone-driven kiss.

"Are you going to invite me in?" she asked.

"Sorry. Of course." His tongue tripped over the words, and he stepped aside.

Again, he regretted that he didn't have anything to offer her stronger than root beer or an after-the-lovin' midnight snack.

As they crossed the small living area to the laptop, he said, "You're just in time to meet my sister."

Lainie scanned the interior of the tiny cabin, which was obviously empty, and her brow creased.

"She's not actually *here*. She's online— I'm talking to her now." He led her to the laptop, where his sister waited on the screen. A smile tugged at his lips. Kara had been right. He'd always kept his relationships private and hadn't introduced her to any of his lovers in the past. But Lainie was different. Maybe he did have a domestic side he'd kept hidden.

"Kara," he said, waiting to witness their first interaction. "This is Lainie."

Drew wasn't sure what he'd expected, but certainly not his sister's strangled gasp.

He shot a glance at Lainie, who'd slapped her hand to her throat and recoiled as if she'd just spotted another mouse in the cabin. No, worse than that.

"What in the hell is *she* doing with you?" Kara asked.

Drew didn't understand. He glanced first at his startled sister on the screen, then at Lainie, her eyes wide, the color fading from her face.

"I'm sorry," Lainie said. "I had no idea…"

"About what?" Drew was at a loss. What was happening?

He looked back at the screen to see Kara sitting up in bed, no longer resting her head on a pile of pillows, her finger raised and shaking. "Oh, my God, Drew. I don't believe it. You're dating the woman who broke up my marriage."

"Lainie? No way." He'd seen the brunette in question—or rather, her image when that bar scene video had gone viral. Her hair was the same color, and her curls bounced along her shoulders when she strode away from the restaurant confrontation in a huff.

But now that he thought about it, their faces *were* similar. Especially with Lainie's red lipstick.

"I have no idea what's going on," Drew told his sister. "But I'll get to the bottom of this. And when I do, I'll call you back."

Drew disconnected the call, turned to Lainie and folded his arms across his chest. "I don't understand. Who are you? And what's my sister talking about?"

"I can explain," Lainie said. "I did date Craig, but not very long. And just so you know, I haven't seen him since that awful day at the hotel."

Dammit. "You're Elena?"

"Yes, but I can explain."

No wonder she'd seemed familiar to him. And now he was looking at the woman who'd slept with Craig, destroyed his and Kara Lee's marriage and nearly caused his sister to lose her baby. Apparently, he'd been wrong about Lainie or Elena or whatever her name really was.

"Go ahead." His eyes narrowed. "I'm listening."

"I had no idea Craig was married," she said. "I didn't even know who he was—I don't follow the rodeo circuit. He lied to me and led me on."

Drew's stomach twisted into a knot. Craig was an ass, that's for sure. But the whole idea sickened him. Damn. He'd almost gotten involved with a woman his ex-brother-in-law had slept with.

And worse, just seeing Lainie at the cabin with Drew was going to kill his sister. Hell, it was bothering the crap out of him just to think about it.

"Don't look at me like that," Lainie said. "There's no way I would have gone out with Craig if I'd known he was married."

"I can't buy that. How could a journalist be so naïve? That is, if you actually *are* a journalist."

"Now that—" she stabbed her finger at him "—is insulting."

"You can't be a very good one if you didn't figure out Craig was married. He's not a hermit. And practically everyone on the circuit knows Kara."

She sucked in a breath. "I screwed up. Okay? I'm human."

And one who was sexier than he'd ever seen her before. Just look at her all dolled up. Had she planned to come on to him tonight? And if so, for what purpose?

He raked his hand through his damp hair, stymied. Perplexed. Pissed.

"Apparently, you believe the worst about me," Lainie said.

He didn't want to. But maybe it was easier that way, to get angry and cut his losses before she inflicted even more pain on his family. Besides, he couldn't very well choose between Lainie and Kara. And he damn sure couldn't sleep with his ex-brother-in-law's lover.

"Believe it or not," Lainie said, "your sister wasn't the only victim in all of this."

Maybe so, but the only victim who really mattered right now was Kara.

"You should leave," Drew said.

"No. Talk to me."

How could he? "You've put me in an awkward position." And an impossible one, it seemed. "Tell me something. Did you know Craig was my brother-in-law?"

"No, of course not. Do you think I'm scheming you or something?"

"Either that, or again, you're a lousy journalist. If you had even an ounce of investigative chops, you would have found out about my family."

Her expression went from angry to hurt, and she threw up her hands. "I give up. It isn't worth it." Then she turned on her heel and headed for the cabin door. Before reaching for the knob, she paused and turned back to him. "I hope your anger at me won't stop you from helping Andre and the other children at Kidville."

"I wouldn't do that," he said. "I intend to follow through on my commitment to get financial support for those kids."

"That's a relief. And for the record, I plan to make that Christmas party special—with or without your help. Those kids have had too many disappointments in life."

She gave him only a beat to answer, but a flurry of emotion balled up in his throat, making it hard to speak, even if he could have found the words to say.

Then she let herself out, the door clicking shut behind her, severing what little connection they'd once had.

Drew flopped onto his bed and scrubbed his hands over his face. He should be relieved that she was gone, but an ache settled deep in his chest. Now what? He'd always been a fixer, but he didn't have a clue how to clean up this mess.

A hodgepodge of emotion swirled around his heart like a Texas twister. Regret that his sister had been hurt. Disappointment that Lainie wasn't the woman he'd thought she was. And worse yet, fear that she actually was that woman and that he couldn't pursue her now. Not after she'd slept with Craig and had been involved in his sister's divorce.

But he wouldn't try to sort through his tangled up feelings when he had a phone call to make and a sister to calm. The last thing he needed right now was for Kara to go into premature labor again.

Tears streamed down Lainie's cheeks as she marched across the yard and away from the cabin, but she was too crushed and disappointed to swipe them away. She'd been let down yet again by a man she'd once cared about. Only this time, it was different—worse. She'd allowed herself to become way too invested in Drew, when she should have known better than to take that risk.

On top of that, she was angry as hell. He'd not only considered her a floozy and a liar, which was bad enough, but he'd accused her of being a lousy journalist, the one thing she had pride in.

Sure, she should have done a background check on Craig. And on Kara. Heck, she should have done one on Drew, too. But was she supposed to dig into the lives of everyone she met?

"Ooh!" She had to walk off some of the built-up steam before entering the house. She circled the outside of the empty corral, trying to shake off her grief and come to grips with her emotions.

Drew had assumed the worst about her and wouldn't let her explain. Gosh, you'd think he'd at least listen to her side of the story. After all they'd done together— the long talks, the visit to Kidville, the Christmas plans they'd made…

And what about the amazing kisses they'd shared?

Darn it. She'd actually begun to care about him, to believe he was different, that he was worth her affection. Given time, she might have fallen in love with him.

But who was she kidding? Her feelings for him bordered on love already, if she hadn't actually taken a hard tumble into a romantic abyss.

Her heart ached, but as she circled the corral a second time, hurt gave way to anger. She wanted to lash out at someone. Anyone.

It was almost funny, though. In the past, she might have gone undercover or run away, like she'd done after that horrible confrontation with Craig's wife—or rather, Drew's sister—at the Houston hotel restaurant.

But Lainie wasn't about to slip into old habits. She might have had a lousy childhood and faced some difficult hurdles, but she'd come a long way since then. That, in itself, demanded that she hold her head high from now on.

She was Elena "Lainie" Montoya, up-and-coming journalist. She was also "Dear Debbie" to Mr. Carlton.

And from this day forward, she didn't give a rip who knew her true identity or what she stood for.

And she'd no longer struggle with her outward appearance, either. She liked what she saw in the mirror and would embrace it, whether she chose to wear denim or silk, overalls or stilettos.

Lainie had a *lot* going for her. She was a recent college graduate with a bright, shiny future ahead of her. Someday she'd be an investigative reporter who would change the world, one story at a time.

Tired of circling the corral, she headed toward the barn. She paused near the buckboard, which was barely visible in the darkened yard. Her heart clenched as she looked at the grassy ground, where she'd been so swayed by Drew's kiss that she'd nearly convinced herself that he was the guy she'd been waiting for all of her life. And that they could have something special together, but she'd better forget that crazy idea.

One day soon, she'd have it all—a successful career, a family of her own *and* a loving husband. She just hadn't met him yet.

Feeling much better and back in control of her thoughts and emotions, she turned toward the house, but she wouldn't go inside just yet. She wanted more time to suck in the cold ranch air, to remain in the shadows and form a game plan from this night forward.

She'd hardly taken a single breath when the mudroom door swung open, and Sully walked out.

"There you are," Sully said. "I wondered where you ran off to."

Lainie continued to stand outside the ring of the porch light, where Sully couldn't detect any lingering moisture on her face.

"I just wanted a little fresh air and exercise," she said. "Did you need to talk to me?"

"Only to tell you I'm going to Tennessee, but I plan to be back for the Christmas party."

"Seriously?" Panic at the unexpected announcement laced her voice. "Why?"

"My brother's in the hospital."

"I'm so sorry to hear that. What's wrong?"

"His ticker is giving him grief, but the doctors say he's going to be okay. He wants to move to the Rocking Chair Ranch as soon as he's discharged, but his family isn't onboard. I plan to talk to them on his behalf, and then I'll bring him back with me."

"How long will you be gone?"

"A few days. You gonna miss me, sweetie?"

"Of course I will." And on many levels. Lainie certainly understood why Sully had to go, but her next column was due before he could possibly return. "When are you leaving?"

"First thing in the morning. And way before breakfast, so I thought I'd better tell you goodbye now."

How in the world was she going to be able to offer advice to the lovelorn without the wise old man's help?

Worse yet, who was she going to confide in about her own heartache and disappointment?

"You look worried," Sully said.

"Just about the party," she lied. "The kids will be disappointed if Santa isn't here."

"Don't worry, Lainie. I'll be back at least three days before the party. You can count on me."

Apparently, Sully was the only man she could count on, so she eased into the light emanating from the porch, swiping her eyes with the back of her hand and forcing a carefree grin.

As she continued forward to offer Sully a goodbye hug, he squinted and crunched his craggy brow. "Don't you look pretty tonight. But are you crying?"

"No, I had something in my eye."

"That better be all it is, because if one of those cowboys around here has hurt your feelings or toyed with your heart, he'll hear from me."

"Just a piece of straw or an eyelash. But it's out now." She embraced her sweet old friend, breathing in the faint scent of laundry soap on his green flannel shirt and catching a whiff of chocolate. "Did you get into the leftover brownies for another bedtime snack?"

"Don't tell the nurses," he said. "They think I'm getting fat."

If Lainie's heart hadn't been so heavy, she might have laughed. Instead she smiled. "I won't say a word about you raiding the kitchen to appease your sweet tooth. At least, not until after the party. I wouldn't want the kids to see a skinny Santa."

"No worries about that." Sully chuckled. "And just so you know, I've been practicing. How's this? *Ho, ho, ho! Merry Christmas.*"

At that, Lainie did laugh. "It's perfect." Then she followed him into the house.

"I'd better turn in," he said. "It'll be time for me to head for the airport before you know it."

And it would be time for Lainie to turn in that blasted column before she knew it, too.

Once inside her bedroom, she was tempted to crawl into bed and forget about her deadline until tomorrow.

But the sooner she took a look at the latest batch of letters, the better off she'd be.

Interestingly enough, and right off the bat, she spotted a problem she could respond to.

Dear Debbie,

I'm so upset with my sister (I'll call her Connie) that I can hardly see straight. We had a crappy childhood and grew up in a dysfunctional home. Since we only had each other, we've always been very close. But recently, Connie started dating this guy (I'll call him Mike). I told Connie I didn't like him, but she didn't care. Now she spends every waking hour with him and doesn't have time to go to lunch or a movie with me. We don't even talk on the phone anymore.

Last night, Connie came home with an engagement ring. She announced that she was going to marry him in a couple of months and asked me to be her bridesmaid. I told her that was way too soon. She needs to get to know Mike better. I mean, he's still in college and works as a barista at a local coffee place. So it's not like she's marrying a guy who can support her the minute they say "I do."

We argued, and things got ugly. I refused to attend her wedding, so she told me she'd ask Mike's sister to stand up with her. How's that for loyalty?

I'm tempted to disown her—or whatever it is siblings do when they don't want to be related anymore. But I'm not quite ready to do that. At least, not yet.

*So here's my question, Dear Debbie: How do
I talk her out of marrying a guy she's only known
for three months? That's not enough time for her
to find out if he's going to turn out to be a mean
drunk like our father was. I'm only trying to protect her, but Connie doesn't see it that way. How
do I convince her she's wrong?*

Brokenhearted Sister

An answer came to Lainie right away, so she cranked
up her laptop and got to work. The words flowed easily, and her advice was heartfelt and sound.

Apparently, she'd learned a lot from talking to Sully
in the past, from listening to the way he reasoned things
out.

For the first time, she'd responded to the writer as
Elena Montoya, sharing things she'd never told anyone.
She knew a thing or two about being hurt, about having
people betray her. And, sadly, about betraying people
herself, even if it had been completely unintentional.

But it felt good be authentic. To give advice from
her heart. She just wished she'd been authentic with
Drew, too.

Or course, it was too late for that. And maybe that
was just as well. It was one thing sharing her heart and
soul to a stranger and under the guise of Dear Debbie,
and it was another to reopen old wounds and lay herself
open and vulnerable to a man who'd broken her heart.

After shutting down her laptop, she walked over to
the bedroom window and peered out into the night.

She didn't expect to see Drew's cabin in the dark, but with the inside lights blazing, she spotted it right away.

Was he still awake? Was he working on the blog?

Or was he, like Lainie, mulling over what they might have had and lost?

Chapter 11

It was nearing midnight, but Drew wasn't ready for bed or even close to falling asleep. Just a couple of hours ago, he'd called Kara and told her to think about the baby. He'd reminded her that her tiny son needed a peaceful environment in which he could grow, and that's all it had taken to convince her to calm her down.

On the other hand, Drew was still wound up tighter than a guitar string ready to snap. He couldn't get over the revelation that Lainie had been Craig's lover.

Now, as he paced the floor of the small cabin like a caged mountain lion, he wished he could relax. He probably ought to use his time wisely by working on his blog, but the only thing he could focus on was Lainie.

Who was the woman who'd nearly stolen his heart? Angel or vixen?

He wished he knew. His gut told him she wasn't the

type to intentionally date a married man. He'd always been a good judge of character. Shouldn't he trust his instinct when it came to Lainie?

Then again, she had a deceptive side, a major flaw he'd failed to see. Even Sully had pointed it out.

I guess everyone has a weakness, the old man had said.

It seems that one of her girlfriends or someone she knows has a problem, usually due to their own making. Then he'd added, *Lainie really needs to choose some new friends. Some of them don't have the sense the Good Lord gave a goose.*

Drew hadn't met any of her friends, and after what Sully had told him about them, he hadn't wanted to.

Still, if she had some loser friends, was that a bad sign? Or was it the result of having a naïve and loving heart?

She was good with the old cowboys—and with kids like Andre. Didn't that prove she was kind and thoughtful? But then again, was that just an act?

There'd been other incidents and comments made that might've offered him a clue. Like the day she'd touched his forearm and dazzled him with a pretty smile. *You'll help me, won't you? You said you'd do anything that needed to be done.* She'd practically batted her eyelashes, working her wiles on him.

He'd failed to pick up on the possibility that she might've been playing him. Instead, when she'd zapped his nerve endings with her touch and gazed at him sweetly, he'd been captivated and completely swayed.

Sure, helping her plan a Christmas party for the children wasn't a bad thing. But that wasn't the point.

Hadn't she just blurted out the idea, committing him to help before asking him first?

Then there was that sexually charged embrace near the barn earlier today. She'd been kissing him back like there was no tomorrow, when all of a sudden she'd torn her mouth from his and pushed him away as if he'd been a real horn dog. Yet just a heartbeat before, she'd made it pretty clear that she wouldn't mind if he'd taken her right there, in the soft grass and under cover of an old buckboard.

I didn't mean to overreact, she'd said. *Or to be a tease.*

He'd accepted her response at face value, but now he couldn't help wondering if she'd known exactly what she'd been doing.

Had she played on Craig's attraction to her in that same way?

Drew didn't want to believe so, but he supposed it was possible. Hadn't Lainie taken to wearing makeup recently? Was that an attempt to draw Drew deeper under her spell?

There lay the crux of his problem. He couldn't figure her out.

Even if she was as goodhearted as he'd once thought she was and Craig had duped her, like he had so many other people, Drew would still have to give her up for good. How could he date her knowing how his sister felt about her? Besides, no matter what the circumstances had been, she'd also slept with Craig.

Wasn't it easier—and safer—to believe the worst?

Drew blew out a ragged breath. More than two hours had passed since their online showdown, and he still wasn't anywhere near a decision or a judgment. He stopped pacing and glanced at the bed. He really ought to turn in for the night, but his thoughts kept tumbling and rumbling through his brain, making it impossible to rest.

Damn. He'd probably be up until dawn, stewing about Elena.

And ruing the fact that he'd never kiss "Lainie" again.

Much to Lainie's surprise, Drew hadn't avoided her. He showed up in the kitchen for breakfast the next day. But then again, he had to be hungry, and there weren't many other mealtime options in this neck of the woods.

She couldn't help noticing that he didn't look nearly as handsome as he had before. His hair was mussed as if he'd raked his hand through it a hundred times, and dark circles under his eyes suggested he hadn't slept a wink.

Was he worried about his sister? Had she gone into premature labor?

Lainie certainly hoped not. She didn't want Kara to lose her baby or to suffer any more than she already had.

Still, Drew looked worn. Tired. Uneasy.

She'd like to think his haggard appearance had to do with guilt for being so mean to her last night, but his tight-lipped scowl told another story. Clearly, he hadn't softened toward her at all.

Only yesterday, he'd smiled as she bustled about, checking on the older men in the dining room, as well as the young hands who ate in the kitchen. He'd seemed to take pleasure in her movements. But today, as she served the men, replenishing their cups with fresh coffee and putting warm biscuits, butter and honey on the table, he didn't seem to notice her at all.

No, things had clearly changed between them—and

permanently, it seemed. His frosty silence was pretty convincing.

As she continued to work, she did her best to ignore both him and his grumpy expression. But it wasn't easy.

She'd considered looking for a replacement to cover for her until Joy returned from her honeymoon and took over the kitchen duties. But Lainie couldn't leave before the party. The invitation had already gone out to Kidville, and there was no way she'd do anything to disappoint Andre or the other children. So she was determined to soldier on and see it through, at least until Christmas.

Besides, pouring herself into the party plans, baking cookies and creating inexpensive, homemade decorations would keep her busy and, hopefully, ease her heartache.

"These buttermilk biscuits sure are good, ma'am," Brad said.

Lainie thanked him. "Would you like another? I have more warming in the oven."

"No, ma'am. I've already had three and filled my belly to the brim. If I don't quit now, I won't be able to move, let alone work."

As the men began to push away from the table, she placed her hand on Drew's shoulder to stop him. "Can we talk a minute?"

His corded muscle tensed, and his eyes narrowed, creasing his brow. In some ways, his suspicion and distrust hurt her more than if he'd said, "There's nothing to talk about," and stomped off with the others.

"It won't take but a minute," she said.

He neither agreed nor objected, but he remained in his seat while the ranch hands filed out of the kitchen, into the mudroom and then out the door.

Once they were alone, she pulled out the chair next to him and asked, "How's your sister?"

Apparently he hadn't seen that question coming because the furrow in his brow deepened. "She's all right, I guess. It didn't help her to flip out after seeing you with me in the cabin."

Ouch. Yet in spite of the painful barb, she wasn't going to cower or apologize for something that had been all Craig's fault and none of her own doing.

"I'm glad to hear she's okay," she said.

His only response was a slight nod.

"I meant what I told you last night. I had no idea Craig was married. If I had, I would've run for the hills. Granted, I should have done a background check of some kind, an internet search of his name, but I didn't. It won't happen again, though. I'll be more careful and skeptical from now on. And just for the record, I regret not checking up on you, too. I really should have, but I guess there's no need to anymore."

His eye twitched, but he didn't comment. If she were one to resort to violence, she might have shaken him until his teeth rattled. Instead, she pushed away from the table, standing tall, head high, her tears in check. "Someday, you're going to want someone's understanding and forgiveness, and I hope you get it."

"Maybe I won't deserve it."

She took a deep breath, wondering why she was wasting her time on him. Misplaced hope and a romantic delusion, she supposed, but her feelings and disappointment weren't the only things to consider. She had the Hoffmans and the children to think about.

"Do you still plan to support Kidville?" she asked.

"I told you I would."

"Yes, but I thought you might have changed your mind during the night. Of course, it's clear you haven't changed your opinion about me."

When he didn't respond, not even with a telltale blink of the eye, she bit down on her bottom lip, struggling with what to say next. They obviously didn't have a romantic future together, but they still had to cross paths.

"I realize there isn't a snow cone's chance in hell of us becoming friends," she said, opting not to use the word *couple*.

"And just so you know, I didn't ask you to stick around after breakfast so I could convince you otherwise. But we have a party to get through. Can we strike some kind of a cordial truce until I leave the ranch?"

"Sure, we can do that."

She let out the breath she'd been holding, relieved that they might be able to put things behind them. Yet, for some reason, it was important for him to know that she had a loving heart and good intentions.

"I'm going to adopt Andre and his brothers," she said. "Or if that doesn't come together for some reason, I'm going to take them in as foster children."

His response was sharp and immediate. "Are you kidding? How are you going to do that? You can barely support yourself and don't have a home. Why would you subject kids to an uncertain life?"

Lainie wasn't sure what hurt worse—his sharp tone or his lack of compassion. She never should have shared her innermost hope with a man who clearly didn't trust her or care about her feelings.

Sure, Drew had a point. She couldn't very well bring three young children into her life until she found a full-time job and a bigger place to live than a studio apartment. But she wasn't going to be bullied, hurt or taken advantage of any longer, especially by the likes of Craig or Drew.

Instead of fingering her scar and retreating, as she'd been prone to do in the past, she rose up to him and lifted her finger, jabbing his chest. "You're a self-centered jerk. You might not think so, but you're not any better than Craig Baxter. First you hurt my feelings, then you insult me."

As Drew gaped at her, his surly expression morphed into one of surprise.

"Cat got your tongue?" she asked, her own ire rising at a deafening speed.

"There's really not much to say."

"You're right."

She'd never wanted to clobber anyone so badly in her life, other than her drunken father. But he'd died in a barroom brawl when she and Rickie were seven, so she hadn't had to rise to the occasion. Besides, she'd never resort to violence, even if Drew made it oh so tempting.

"To make it easier for both of us," she said, "I'm going to try and find a temporary cook to cover for me until Joy returns. Either way, I'll stay out of your way until after the party. Then, by hook or crook, I'm going to create a home for Andre and his brothers. And you mark my words, I'll pull that off, or I'll die trying."

Then she turned on her heel and marched off, her head held high, but her heart and soul aching.

Drew stood alone in the kitchen, stunned by Lainie's anger and spunk.

Okay, so maybe he'd been an ass and deserved a good

tongue-lashing after his gut reaction to her announcement that she intended to adopt not one, but three kids.

Her family plan was probably heartfelt, but so was Drew's response. He hadn't meant to come across so harsh, but she wasn't the only one thinking about the kids.

To this day he remembered going to bed hungry as an adolescent, his belly empty and growling. After his mom got sick and could no longer work, money was tight and food was scarce, especially at the end of the month when her disability check ran out. So Drew often took less than his share at mealtimes to make sure his mother was able to keep up her strength and his sister had enough to eat.

Andre and his siblings might be separated, but at least they had warm beds and full stomachs at night.

Lainie couldn't blame him for connecting the dots to her living situation. She'd made it clear that she needed to find another job and another place to live. It didn't take a rocket scientist to realize she lacked the resources to provide for herself, let alone a family. What had she been thinking?

He supposed she'd been thinking with her heart. And that being the case, he had to admit that he and Kara might be wrong about her. Needless to say, he'd have to apologize to her, but he had some things to sort through before he chased after her.

The old-style ranch telephone, which hung on the kitchen wall, rang a couple of times. The nurses had their own phone back in the office, so it wasn't a call for them. Still, Drew doubted it was for him and waited for the answering machine to kick on.

When it did, a man's voice filled the room. "Lainie!

It's Stan Carlton at *The Brighton Valley Gazette*. I've got good news, girl. I love that story proposal and want you to get started on it right away. And what's more, the Dear Debbie readership has grown impressively since you took it over. You're doing a great job. I can't wait to hear what the readers have to say when your next column comes out on Friday. Give me a call back at your convenience and we can talk about a raise in pay."

What the hell? Just about the time he thought he'd have to apologize for being a jerk, he hears this?

Lainie had lied to him. She'd told him that she hoped to land a job with *The Gazette*, but she already had one.

To top it off, she'd proposed an article, and it had been accepted. Did she have something underhanded in the works? Something that might exploit the old cowboys on the Rocking Chair Ranch or the children living at Kidville?

Dammit. Rather than offering up an apology, he was going to confront her with her lie.

Lainie tossed her freshly washed bedsheets into the dryer, albeit with a little more force than necessary. There was no point in taking out her anger, frustration and pain on the damp cotton percale, but it did help her work off some steam.

"There you are," Drew said from the doorway, his voice terse and not the least bit remorseful.

She glanced over her shoulder. "What do you want? Did you have more cruel barbs to sling at me, more false accusations to make?"

He leaned his shoulder against the doorjamb and crossed his arms. "Just one. You lied to me."

At that, she slammed the dryer door shut, turned to

face him and slapped her hands on her hips. "How do you figure?"

"Stan Carlton from *The Gazette* called and left a message for you."

"What'd he say?"

"That your proposal was accepted, the Dear Debbie column is going great and that he's giving you a raise."

Finally. Some good news for a change. For a moment, she was so stunned—and pleased—that she forgot Drew had called her a liar. Well, more or less.

"You told me that you wanted to get a job at *The Gazette*," he said, "but apparently you already have one."

"Actually, it was a part-time position as the lovelorn columnist, and it didn't pay squat."

"You?" he said. "What do you know about love, let alone offering advice to people?"

"Not much, but thanks to Sully, I'm learning to problem solve."

Drew pushed away from the doorjamb and straightened. "What's that mean?"

"It's really none of your business. And you probably won't believe me anyway. But I needed to get my foot in the door at the paper, so I took the Dear Debbie position. Since I was at a loss on how to respond, I ran a few problems by Sully, who has more kindness, common sense and understanding of people in his little toe than you have in your big ol' cowboy body."

"You mean you don't have a bunch of troubled friends?" he asked.

She scrunched her face. "I have plenty of friends— smart ones. Nice ones from good families. But we all went different directions after college, and I'm new in

Brighton Valley. I haven't made any local ones yet. Except for the men who live here."

"What about the article you proposed? What's that all about?"

What was this, the third degree? She wanted to tell him to take a very long walk off a short pier, one that stretched over shark-infested waters. But lashing out wasn't going to help much. She needed vindication.

"I proposed a big Sunday spread about the rodeo, the ranch and the children's home in hopes of gaining financial support."

His expression softened. Apparently, he'd begun to realize his assumptions and accusations might have been wrong. "I owe you an apology."

"Yes, you do. But right now, I'm not so sure I want to accept it." She turned around, set the dryer on high and pushed the start button.

When she turned around, he was still standing in the doorway, blocking her exit.

"Excuse me," she said. "I have work to do."

He stepped aside to let her out, and she marched off to find something to do. There was no point in arguing with a man who would never accept her for who she was.

Drew might not have faith in her, but she had faith in herself. Whether he believed it or not, she was going to help Andre reunite with his brothers. And somehow, in the process, she'd finally have a family of her own.

Chapter 12

Over the next couple days, Drew kept to himself, but by Friday, his niggle of guilt grew to a steady throb in the chest. He'd been wrong about Lainie, but he had no idea what to do about it.

He could tell her he was sorry, and she might accept his apology. But what about Kara? She wasn't apt to be as understanding or forgiving. And if not, that would really complicate his life.

Before breakfast, Drew climbed into his pickup and drove several miles down the road to the mom-and-pop market, where some of the locals hung out to while away the time and shoot the breeze. Once he'd parked in front, he entered the store.

A tall, wiry clerk sitting behind the register looked up from the crossword puzzle he'd been working and smiled. "Howdy. Just let me know if I can help."

Drew sniffed the warm air. "Is your coffee fresh?"

"Sure is." The clerk got to his feet. "I just made a new pot. Can I get you a cup?"

"Yes, large. Black and to-go."

"You got it. Want a donut to go with that?"

Why not? He hadn't eaten breakfast. "Chocolate, if you have it."

As the clerk took a disposable, heat-resistant cup from the stack and filled it, Drew asked, "Do you carry *The Brighton Valley Gazette*?"

"You bet." The clerk pointed a long arm to the left of the register. "It's a dollar."

Drew retrieved the newspaper from the rack and returned to the register for his order. He paid with a twenty, pocketed his change and returned to his truck.

Instead of going back to the ranch, he settled in the cab, opened the small-town paper and searched for the Dear Debbie column.

There it was. Right next to the obituaries.

He took a sip of coffee, which hit the spot, then read the first of two letters. It was written by a woman who'd been taken in by a lying boyfriend. But it was Lainie's response that drew his interest.

> *I know exactly how you feel. It's painful to learn that a man you thought was Mr. Right lied to you—or even worse, that he doesn't trust you. And if that's the case, he's not the hero you thought he was.*

Lainie must be referring to Craig's deceit, but Drew had hurt her, too. He was the one who hadn't believed her. So he wasn't feeling very heroic right now.

He continued to read the next letter. The writer was a woman who'd gotten angry with her family and, on principle alone, refused several of her sister's attempts to make amends. Just as he'd done moments before, Drew focused on Lainie's response, which was especially personal—and telling.

My own family was far from perfect. After my mom died, my sister and I were raised by an alcoholic father who couldn't keep a job. Needless to say, life was far from easy.

Not long after my seventh birthday, my dad died in a bar fight, and my sister and I were placed in foster care. I'd been suffering from several medical problems that had never been addressed, one of which was life-threatening and required surgery, so the state stepped in and split us up. We ended up in different homes, and she was adopted. I haven't seen her since.

Forgive me for not feeling very sympathetic to your anger or your plight. I lost the only family I had, and you're willing to throw away yours. Please reconsider. Love and forgiveness are powerful gifts. But even more so to the person who offers them freely.

A pang of sympathy balled up in Drew's chest. He grieved for the child Lainie had been, yet he admired the woman she'd become. How could he have forgotten the kindness she showed the retired cowboys or the compassion she had for Andre and his brothers?

He didn't deserve a woman like her, but he wanted her in his life—if it wasn't too late. Yet he didn't move.

He continued to sit in his pickup, staring at the newspaper in his hand without reading another word.

With each beat of his heart, he realized it wasn't just admiration he felt for Lainie. He loved her. Somehow, he had to make things right with her. And between her and Kara, too.

So he started the engine and headed back to the ranch. When he arrived, he spotted an unfamiliar car parked in the yard and Lainie walking out onto the front porch, her curls softly tumbling along her shoulders. She wore a somber expression and carried both a suitcase and a purse.

Panic rose up from his gut, and he crossed the yard to meet her. "Where are you going?"

"Back to town."

"What about the Rocking Chair Ranch? The men need you." Drew needed her. "What about your job?"

She didn't even blink. "I found a woman to cover for me until Joy gets home. I'll be back for the party."

Drew had no idea how to bridge the rift he'd created between them, but he had to give it his best shot. "Before you go, I want to apologize."

She studied him for a moment, then gave a slight shrug. "Okay. You're forgiven."

So she said. But Drew couldn't read an ounce of sincerity in her expression or in her tone. And he really didn't blame her.

"Can we talk privately?" he asked. "It's important."

She continued to stand there, gripping the handle of her bag and clutching her purse. For a moment, he thought she was going to refuse. Not that he wouldn't deserve it if she did.

He reached for her suitcase without actually taking it from her. "Please?"

She sucked in a deep breath, then slowly blew it out and handed him her bag. "All right. But just for a minute."

He scanned the yard, spotting several ranch hands coming out of the barn and a couple of the old cowboys rocking on the porch. "Let's go to my cabin. I'd rather not have an audience."

She fell into step beside him as they crossed the yard to the cabin. Minutes later, he opened the front door ahead of her and waited for her to enter. Then he joined her in the small living area and set down her bag near the sofa.

"I've been a jerk. I assumed the worst about you, and in that sense, I didn't treat you any better than Craig did." When she didn't object, he continued. "I've seen you with the elderly men, watched as you served them meals and laughed at their jokes. And I've seen you with Andre. You've got a good heart, and only a blind fool would've missed that."

Her expression softened a tad, and she ran her hand through her glossy curls. "I told you that I forgave you."

"Yes, but you really didn't mean it then. Do you now?"

The corner of her lips quirked, revealing the hint of a smile. "Yes, I suppose I do. But it was more than just your distrust and lack of faith in me that hurt. You questioned my competency as a journalist, and..." She clamped her mouth shut as if having second thoughts about going into any more detail than that.

"Again," he said, "I'm sorry. There's so much about you that I admire. I'd really like to start over."

Her brows knit together. "In what way?"

"It would be great if we could roll back the time to when you offered me that sugar cookie. Or when the wagon's tailgate broke."

She didn't seem to see any humor in that suggestion.

"Let's just start at an hour before that call with my sister the other night."

"When we were in the kitchen?" she asked.

"Yes. If we were to start again there, I'd take you outside on the porch with me. Then I'd ask about your early years. And I would've really listened. I would have admitted that it broke my heart to think of you losing touch with your twin."

A tear spilled down Lainie's cheek, and she swiped it away with the back of her hand and sniffled. "Rickie was my only sister, my only family."

The reason he'd wanted to backpedal was to introduce her to Kara in another way, a better one.

"I have a sister, too," he said, "and she's my only family. She's pregnant and going through a divorce."

Lainie blinked back her tears. "I didn't realize Craig was…"

Drew placed his index finger on her lips to halt her explanation. "I believe you, Lainie. And I should have from day one."

"It's weird," she said, her voice as soft as a whisper. "People think I went after him, but it's the other way around. I'd been reluctant to date him at all. Looking back on it now, I realize that I'd always craved having someone to love, and he picked up on that need and used it to his advantage."

"Craig's a womanizer," Drew said. "And apparently, he's pretty damn good at it."

Lainie shrugged. "I'd only met him two weeks before—at a coffee shop next to the office where I'd worked at a temp job after graduation. He picked up the tab, and we chatted awhile. I don't normally talk to strangers, but when he told me he was nursing a broken heart and grieving a failed marriage, I felt sorry for him.

"When he asked me out the next day, I agreed to meet him for lunch at a nearby deli. He asked about my sun sign, which should have been my first clue that he was a player. But I went along with it and mentioned that my birthday was coming up. He surprised me by having a gift delivered to the office—a red dress and an invitation to meet him at Sterling Towers for a birthday dinner. I'm sure you know the rest."

"Pretty much."

"It rankles me now, but I went. But I wouldn't have if I'd known what was going to unfold."

"Kara found you together," Drew supplied.

Lainie nodded. "She'd been crying, and she stormed to our booth and asked Craig what in the hell was going on. He told her, 'Nothing,' and called her 'sweetie' and insisted I was 'nobody.'"

"I'd like to punch his lights out," Drew said.

Lainie smiled. "For a moment, I thought your sister was going to do just that. Instead, she snatched the margarita I'd been drinking and splashed the rest of it in my face. I don't know what stung worse, the icy cold on my skin, the humiliation or hearing Craig call me a 'nobody.'"

Drew's heart ached for Lainie. And for a lot of reasons—Craig's deceit, Kara's blame, the rumors that claimed Lainie was a villainess.

"Several diners held up their cell phones," Lainie

said, "recording the ugly scene. And before I knew it, I became the night's social media entertainment."

"I'll explain all of this to my sister," Drew said. "She'll get over it. Eventually."

"That's okay," Lainie said. "I doubt that she and I will ever see each other again."

As a tear spilled over and trailed down her cheek, Drew brushed his thumb under her eye, wiping it away. Then he cupped her face with both hands and gazed at her. "Sure, you'll see her. That is, if you'll give me a chance to prove myself and go out with me."

Drew was asking her out on a date?

Lainie hadn't seen that coming. "Seriously?"

"You bet I am. My sister will get over blaming you, especially if I vouch for you."

This conversation wasn't at all what she'd expected. As she pondered his words and let them settle over her, she kept quiet.

Drew's thumb made a slow circle on her cheek, singeing her skin. "I've never met anyone like you, Lainie. I never expected to. And now that I have, I've rethought the future I'd laid out for myself."

To include her? She wasn't about to make a leap like that. "I don't know what to say."

"Tell me you'll let me show you that I'm a much better man than Craig."

"You've already proven that a hundred times over."

Drew brushed his lips against hers in a whisper-soft kiss that stole her breath away.

She was tempted to lean into him, to wrap her arms around him and let him take the lead, but she rallied.

"First, before you say anything else, there's something I need to tell you."

His hands slipped from her jaw to her shoulders, but he didn't remove his touch, didn't remove his heated gaze. He didn't even blink. "Fire away."

He trusted her to lay everything on the line?

She sucked in a fortifying breath, then slowly let it out. "When I was a kid, I used to get tired doing the simplest things. But no one ever cared enough to worry about me or take me to the doctor. If they had, my congenital heart defect would have been diagnosed and corrected sooner. As it was, I didn't have surgery until I was eight."

"And that's when you lost touch with your sister."

She nodded. "It was a lonely, scary time. But don't get me wrong. I'm thankful that the state stepped in because then a skilled pediatric surgeon made me healthy. Things were better after that, but I was still very much alone and would have given anything for someone to love. At least, someone special."

"Has there ever been anyone special?"

"My college roommates, but we all went our separate ways. And there was one guy—for a little while. But he wasn't the man I thought he was."

"You mean Craig?"

"No, Craig was my second mistake. Right after I started college, I met a guy named Ryan and thought he might be 'the one,' but he wasn't. I can see that now. He kept pressuring me to have sex, but I wasn't ready. Then one night, I decided to give in, just to please him. But things never even got that far. It turned out badly, and we broke up."

"You don't have to talk about it—if you don't want to."

"I need to." It was the lead-in to what she had to tell him. "After I removed my blouse, Ryan froze up. You see, I have a long, ugly scar that runs along my sternum from my open heart surgery, and he was turned off by it."

"Oh, Lainie." Drew pulled her into his arms, holding her in a way she'd never been held.

She leaned into him, savoring his clean, woodland scent, his warm, comforting arms. "You're an amazing woman—beautiful, sweet, warmhearted. I don't want *you* to freeze up on me, but I'm falling in love with you. And there's nothing more I'd like than to take you to bed and show you just how much. But I'm a patient man. I'm willing to wait until you're ready."

Drew loved her? Could that be true?

She gently pushed against his chest, freeing herself from his embrace. "You haven't seen that scar yet."

"I don't need to." He pulled her back into his arms and kissed her long and deep. His tongue swept through her mouth, seeking and mating with hers until her knees nearly gave out.

She wanted to cling to him for the rest of her life, but she stopped the kiss before it was too late and took a step back. For once, she needed to let her head rule over her heart.

"Just so there aren't any surprises..." She unbuttoned her blouse, slipped it off her shoulders and dropped it onto the sofa. Then she unhooked her yellow satin bra and pushed the straps off her shoulders.

As she tossed it aside and stood before him, baring her flaw, his breath hitched. But not in revulsion. His expression was heated, fully aroused with desire.

"Aw, Lainie. You're beautiful."

Her hand lifted to her collarbone, a habit she couldn't seem to break, but he stopped her.

"Don't." He gently fingered the faded ridge, then bent his head and kissed the length of it. The warmth of his breath soothed her like a balm, healing the very heart of her.

He caressed the curve of her waist and along the slope of her hips, cherishing her with his touch, telling her without words that she mattered to him. Yet he was providing her with more than comfort, he was stirring her hormones and arousing her senses.

Her nipples hardened, and an ache settled deep in her core. When she thought she might die from pure sexual need, he pulled his lips from hers and rested his head against hers.

"I want to make love with you," he said. "But I won't press you until you're sure about me. About us."

She could hardly believe this was happening. "I'd like that, too. And to be honest, I'm ready now."

"You have no idea how glad I am to hear that. But are you sure?"

"It scares me to say this, but I love you, Drew. More than I ever dreamed possible."

He took her hand and led her across the small living area to the bedroom. "Is this your first time?"

She nodded. "I'm sure you're probably used to women with more experience—"

He squeezed her hand. "That's nothing to be sorry for. You're giving me a gift. And it's the best one I've ever had."

He removed his shirt and pants, while she kicked off her shoes and peeled off her slacks. Then he drew her into his arms again and kissed her, caressing her and taunting her with his skilled touch.

Lainie took the time to explore his body, too. Her fingers skimmed his muscular chest, the broad width of his back.

Drew trailed kisses along her throat and down to her chest. Then he took a nipple in his mouth, suckling it, lavishing one breast then the other. She moaned, unable to stand much more of the amazing foreplay.

Before she melted to a puddle on the floor, Drew lifted her in his arms and placed her on top of the bed. He joined her, and they continued to kiss, to taste and stroke each other until Drew pulled back and braced himself up on his elbow. "This might hurt the first time."

"I know. And it's all right." She'd been waiting for Drew—and for this—all of her life.

He entered her slowly at first, letting her get used to the feel of him, the feel of them, until he broke through. It stung, and her breath caught as she gave up her virginity, but her body soon responded to his, taking and giving. Loving and being loved.

As they reached a peak, she cried out, arched her back and let go. An amazing, earth-shattering climax set off an overwhelming burst of love and a sense of absolute completion.

When it was over, they lay still, basking in a sweet afterglow.

Moments later, Drew rolled to the side without letting her go. "It'll be better next time."

"I thought it was pretty amazing now."

He brushed a loose strand of hair from her brow, then traced her scar with his finger, gently and almost reverently. "Don't ever hide this again. Not from me or from anyone. It's a part of the miracle of *you*. Without that surgery, you might not have been here to meet me, to love me."

"You're right. I'm still trying to wrap my mind around it."

"Me, too," he said. "I never expected this to happen, but I can't imagine my life without you in it. I want to marry you—but only when you're ready."

Her heart soared. Christmas had come early this year. For the first time ever, Lainie had a real future stretched out before her and the promise of the family she'd never thought she'd have.

Only it wasn't that simple.

"I might have a deal breaker," she said.

"What's that?"

"I want to apply to be a foster parent so I can take Andre and his brothers. I don't like the idea of them being separated. I realize the state might find me lacking. But I'm determined to do whatever it takes to get those kids into the same home—either mine or in another where someone will love and care for them."

Drew slowly shook his head. She waited for his objection, but instead, one side of his mouth quirked in a crooked grin. "I have to admit that getting a wife and family in one fell swoop was never on my radar, but a lot's changed since I met you."

"You mean you're up to being a foster dad?"

"I am if we're in this thing together. Hell, maybe we can help find more foster families or adoptive parents in the area."

Her breath caught and excitement built as the wheels

began to churn in her mind. "We can create a blog, high-lighting kids who need forever homes."

Drew laughed. "Maybe we've found a higher calling than rodeos and advice columns."

"That's true. But my biggest and highest calling is you. I love you, Drew." Then she kissed him, sealing those words the only way she knew how.

The Christmas party had been a huge success, and everyone seemed to have had a great time.

Joe and Chloe Martinez, the ranch owners, arrived earlier that morning and had been pleased at how Lainie had pulled things together in such a short period of time.

"I had a lot of help," she'd told them.

Drew had purchased the tree, as well as the ornaments. And the retired cowboys had all pitched in to help him with the decorating.

Molly, Brad's mother, had slipped away from Kidville several different evenings to help Lainie with the baking. They'd also wrapped all the presents and placed them under the tree.

Sully had returned a few days ago with his brother Homer, a happy-go-lucky fellow who seemed to fit right in with the other retired cowboys. As soon as Homer unpacked his things, he'd jumped right in to party mode, offering his help whenever needed. So Lainie had gladly put him to work.

While Homer made himself useful by decorating the tree, wrapping gifts and frosting sugar cookies, Sully practiced his ho-ho-ho to perfection. The wise old man was a natural Santa as he chatted with the children and passed out candy canes.

Lainie couldn't believe how well the party turned out. Or how many great photo ops she'd had that day.

There'd been a few disappointments, though. Andre's brothers had yet to arrive. And Kara, who'd been invited, hadn't been able to come because she was still taking it easy. But she'd invited Drew and Lainie to her house to spend Christmas Day. Somehow, Drew had convinced Kara to give Lainie a chance. Lainie hoped they'd be able to get past the whole Craig fiasco, and Drew insisted they would.

Dark clouds had gathered all morning, and the rain began just before noon, so they'd canceled the hayride and rescheduled it for a warmer, drier day.

Now, as the party was coming to an end, the children sat amidst torn wrapping paper and open boxes, admiring their gifts and munching on cookies. Lainie was glad she'd been able to offer them a few hours of fun.

"Congratulations," Drew said. "Things didn't go exactly as planned, but from the looks on those little faces, the party's been a huge success."

"Thanks, but I couldn't have done it without your help."

When he slipped his arms around her, she leaned into him and rested her head on his shoulder.

"I have a present for you," Drew said.

"You didn't have to do that." Just having him in her life, sharing his bed and loving him was gift enough for her.

"I've been working on it for a week, and..." He glanced out the window and grinned. "Looks like it just arrived."

Lainie wasn't sure what he was talking about, but moments later a knock sounded at the door. Jim Hoffman, who'd been standing nearby, opened it for a petite woman and two small boys.

It had to be the social worker, along with Andre's brothers. But why would Drew say he'd been working on getting them here all week? She'd been the one to invite them. "Come on in," Jim said. "I'm glad you finally made it, Mrs. Tran." Then he called out, "Andre. Look who's here."

The boy, who'd been reading his new cowboy book, broke into a happy smile and shrieked, "Mario! Abel!" He scrambled to his feet and hurried to the door, his limp hardly noticeable.

The boys greeted each other with hugs and kisses.

"That's *my* present?" she asked Drew. "Looks like it's Andre's."

"It's the paperwork in Mrs. Tran's folder that's your gift," he said.

Bewildered, Lainie cocked her head and looked at the man she loved. "I don't understand."

"Congratulations, foster mommy. It's a boy. Actually, it's three of them."

Lainie's jaw dropped. "Are you kidding? They're going to let me take them? I... Well, my little studio apartment is going to be cramped, but I'll make it work. Somehow."

"No need." Drew reached into his back pocket and pulled out a folded sheet of paper. "I just signed a lease for a three-bedroom house in Wexler. It'll have to do for now."

"You did that for me?"

"I did it for *us*. Kids need a daddy, too. Don't you think?"

"Drew Madison, you're amazing. Have I told you lately that I love you to the moon and stars?"

"Just this morning, but I'd like to hear it again." He tossed her a dazzling smile.

"I plan to tell you every single morning and night for the rest of our lives."

"I have one last gift for you," Drew said.

"What more can you give me? My gosh, look at them. Their reunion is heartwarming. And so is their excitement." She pointed to the tree, where the three adorable brothers gazed up at the twinkling lights in wide-eyed wonder. "This has been the best Christmas ever."

"It's just the first of many— and it's not over yet." Drew reached into his shirt pocket, withdrew a business card and handed it to her.

DISCREET SERVICES
Damon Wolfe, Owner

She studied it carefully. "What's this?"

"The guy I hired to find Rickie."

"But it was a closed adoption."

"Damon is the best of the best. He told me to leave it to him. If Erica "Rickie" Montoya can be found, he'll find her."

She looked at him, her eyes glistening with tears. "I can't believe this. Drew, this is the very best gift anyone could ever give me."

He held her in his arms and kissed her again. "That's nothing compared to the gift you are to me. Come on, honey. Let's ask the Hoffmans to take a picture of us and the boys so we can have more than a memory of our first Christmas together."

"Good idea."

Lainie had always found the holidays to be depressing. But not any longer. She couldn't wait to create more of her very own family memories from this day forward.

And next Christmas couldn't come too soon.

* * * * *

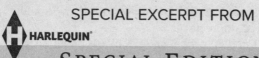
"Amanda, I didn't mean to upset you. I don't ever want to do anything that scares you."

She sucked in a deep, ragged breath, looking so terribly lost and sad. Her eyelids fluttered open. She stared straight ahead, talking to his chest.

"You don't understand, Blake. There are days when… when everything scares me." Her voice was barely above a whisper. His heart jumped. He thought of that first day, when she ended up unconscious in his arms.

Everything scares me.

She'd kicked her shoes off earlier, and in her bare feet the top of her head barely reached his shoulders. He put his fingers under her chin and gently tipped her head back.

He wanted to kiss this woman.

Wait. What?

No. That would be wild. He couldn't kiss her. Shouldn't. But how could he not?

Her hair tumbled off her shoulders and down her back in golden curls. Before he knew it, his free hand was slowly twisting into those curls. She didn't pull away. Didn't look away. He lowered his head until his face was just above hers. He felt her breath on his skin. She smelled like citrus and spice and blueberries and red wine. Her lips parted and she stared at him with her enormous eyes.

"I swear I don't want to scare you, Amanda. But… may I kiss you?" His voice was a raw whisper. "Please let me kiss you."

His words came out as a plea. He'd never begged for anything before in his life. But here he was, begging this sweet woman for a kiss. Ready to drop to his knees if that was what it took. He heard his father's voice in his head, mocking his weakness. That was when he started to straighten, started to come to his senses. Then he heard her whispered answer.

"Yes."

Was there any sweeter word in the world? Adrenaline surged through his body, and his hand tightened in her hair. His eyes opened to meet those two oceans of blue. Dangerous blue. Deep enough to drown in.

She was frightened, but she was trusting him. And that realization scared him to death.

Don't miss It Started at Christmas… *by Jo McNally, available December 2019 wherever Harlequin® Special Edition books and ebooks are sold.*

Harlequin.com

Looking for more satisfying love stories
with community and family at their core?

Check out **Harlequin® Special Edition**
and **Love Inspired®** books!

 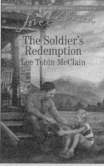

New books available every month!

CONNECT WITH US AT:

Facebook.com/groups/HarlequinConnection

 Facebook.com/HarlequinBooks

 Twitter.com/HarlequinBooks

 Instagram.com/HarlequinBooks

 Pinterest.com/HarlequinBooks

ReaderService.com

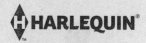

ROMANCE WHEN
YOU NEED IT

HFGENRE2018

Don't miss *Stealing Kisses in the Snow*,
the heart-tugging romance in

JO McNALLY's

Rendezvous Falls series centered around
a matchmaking book club in
Rendezvous Falls, New York.

As Christmas draws ever closer, so do Piper and
Logan. Could these two opposites discover that all
they want this Christmas is each other?

Order your copy today!

www.HQNBooks.com

PHJMSKIS1119

"Are the *kinder* okay?"

"Yes, they'll be fine." Uncomfortable with his small intrusion into her family, she said, "Kevin had a bad dream and woke us up."

"Because of the rain?"

She wanted to say that was silly but, glad she could be honest with Michael, she said, "It's possible."

"Rebuilding a structure is easy. Rebuilding one's sense of security isn't."

"That sounds like the voice of experience."

"My parents died when I was young, and both my twin brother and I had to learn not to expect something horrible was going to happen without warning."

"I'm sorry. I should have asked more about you and the other volunteers. I've been wrapped up in my own tragedy."

"At times like this, nobody expects you to be thinking of anything but getting a roof over your *kinder*'s heads."

He didn't reach out to touch her, but she was aware of every inch of him so close to her. His quiet strength had awed her from the beginning. As she'd come to know him better, his fundamental decency had impressed her more. He was a man she believed she could trust.

She shoved that thought aside. Trusting any man would be the worst thing she could do after seeing what Mamm had endured during her marriage and then struggling to help her sister escape her abusive husband.

"I'm glad you understand why I must focus on rebuilding a life for the children." The simple statement left no room for misinterpretation. "The flood will always be a part of us, but I want to help them learn how to live with their memories."

"I can't imagine what it was like."

"I can't forget what it was like."

Normally she would have been bothered by someone having sympathy for her, but if pitying her kept Michael from looking at her with his brown puppy-dog eyes that urged her to trust him, she'd accept it. She couldn't trust any man, because she wouldn't let the children spend their lives witnessing what she had.

Don't miss
An Amish Christmas Promise *by Jo Ann Brown,*
available December 2019 wherever
Love Inspired® *books and ebooks are sold.*

LoveInspired.com

Love Harlequin romance?

DISCOVER.

Be the first to find out about promotions, news and exclusive content!

Facebook.com/HarlequinBooks

Twitter.com/HarlequinBooks

Instagram.com/HarlequinBooks

Pinterest.com/HarlequinBooks

ReaderService.com

EXPLORE.

Sign up for the Harlequin e-newsletter and download a free book from any series at **TryHarlequin.com.**

CONNECT.

Join our Harlequin community to share your thoughts and connect with other romance readers!
Facebook.com/groups/HarlequinConnection

HARLEQUIN®

**ROMANCE WHEN
YOU NEED IT**

HSOCIAL2018